VORACIOUS CHILDREN

VORACIOUS CHILDREN

Who Eats Whom in Children's Literature

Carolyn Daniel

Routledge
Taylor & Francis Group
New York   London

Published in 2006 by
Routledge
Taylor & Francis Group
270 Madison Avenue
New York, NY 10016

Published in Great Britain by
Routledge
Taylor & Francis Group
2 Park Square
Milton Park, Abingdon
Oxon OX14 4RN

© 2006 by Taylor & Francis Group, LLC
Routledge is an imprint of Taylor & Francis Group

Printed in the United States of America on acid-free paper
10 9 8 7 6 5 4 3 2 1

International Standard Book Number-10: 0-415-97642-1 (Hardcover)
International Standard Book Number-13: 978-0-415-97642-8 (Hardcover)
Library of Congress Card Number 2005030507

Library of Congress Cataloging-in-Publication Data

Daniel, Carolyn.
   Voracious children : who eats whom in children's literature / Carolyn Daniel.
      p. cm. -- (Children's literature and culture ; v. 39)
   Includes bibliographical references and index.
   ISBN 0-415-97642-1 (acid-free paper)
   1. Children's literature-History and criticism. 2. Food in literature. I. Title. II. Series: Children's literature and culture ; 39.

PN1009.5.F66D36 2005
809'.933559--dc22
                                                                     2005030507

informa
Taylor & Francis Group
is the Academic Division of Informa plc.

Visit the Taylor & Francis Web site at
http://www.taylorandfrancis.com

and the Routledge Web site at
http://www.routledge-ny.com

CONTENTS

SERIES EDITOR'S FOREWORD

Dedicated to furthering original research in children's literature and culture, the Children's Literature and Culture series includes monographs on individual authors and illustrators, historical examinations of different periods, literary analyses of genres, and comparative studies on literature and the mass media. The series is international in scope and is intended to encourage innovative research in children's literature with a focus on interdisciplinary methodology.

Children's literature and culture are understood in the broadest sense of the term *children* to encompass the period of childhood up through adolescence. Owing to the fact that the notion of childhood has changed so much since the origination of children's literature, this Routledge series is particularly concerned with transformations in children's culture and how they have affected the representation and socialization of children. While the emphasis of the series is on children's literature, all types of studies that deal with children's radio, film, television, and art are included in an endeavor to grasp the aesthetics and values of children's culture. Not only have there been momentous changes in children's culture in the last fifty years, but there have been radical shifts in the scholarship that deals with these changes. In this regard, the goal of the Children's Literature and Culture series is to enhance research in this field and, at the same time, point to new directions that bring together the best scholarly work throughout the world.

Jack Zipes

ACKNOWLEDGMENTS

Special thanks to Heather Scutter for her kind, thoughtful, and generous attention; to Nina Philadelphoff-Puren for her guidance; and to Monash University for the Postgraduate Publication Award.

A version of chapter 6 has been published in *Papers: Explorations into Children's Literature* 13, no. 3(2003): 5–21.

INTRODUCTION

EATING MIGHT SEEM ORDINARY, everyday, even obvious. But, while it can be a relentlessly mundane activity, merely a way of supplying the body with energy, it can also be one of the most sublime of all bodily experiences. Food is a hot topic. But while the celebrity chef's conjuring up of rare gastronomical delights is regarded by contemporary Western culture as a source of endless fascination and accolade, the often thankless responsibility for the thrice-daily preparation and supply of family meals is nothing short of tyrannous.

Because, in the West, we are relatively wealthy, most of us don't have to worry about where our next meal is coming from. Nevertheless the subject of food and eating is full of contradictions and a major cause of social anxiety. In our culture food is, paradoxically, compulsively consumed and obsessively consuming. We are compelled to consume it, as a biological necessity, but eating it properly has become a collective obsession. Above all, food is never just something to eat: even when it is mundane and everyday it carries meaning. Food events are always significant, in reality as well as in fiction. They reveal the fundamental preoccupations, ideas, and beliefs of society.

Children's literature is a largely underutilized source of historically relevant information about the intimate details of everyday life. It offers the researcher a snapshot of prevailing culture. Reading fictional food events provides us with knowledge about the social and family relationships, manners and morals of a given period. When adults write about and for children, as is almost exclusively the case in stories published for children, they also disclose cultural concepts of childhood and attitudes

1

toward the child. Food fantasies are a traditional ingredient in children's stories: ideologically children are supposed to be especially appreciative of food. The British classics in particular are a rich source of fictional feasting: copious quantities of rich, sweet and, by contemporary standards, fat-laden foods are frequently served to children who seem to have huge appetites. What, one might ask, is the meaning of all this gluttony?

The White Witch in C. S. Lewis's *The Lion, the Witch and the Wardrobe* poses the same question. She is an aggressive, powerful, and fetishized figure in Lewis's narrative who, according to Lucy, "is a perfectly terrible person" and whom all the good Narnians "simply hate."[1] The Witch has "made a magic so that it is always winter in Narnia" and "she can turn people into stone and do all kinds of horrible things" (*Lion,* 42). This Medusa-like Witch seduces and poisons Lucy's brother Edmund with addictive Turkish delight and, once intoxicated, he agrees to betray his brother and sisters to her.

Edmund is traveling on the Witch's sled when they come upon a "merry party" of woodland creatures partaking of a feast. The food on the table "smelled lovely" and includes a plum pudding decorated with holly (*Lion,* 106). Although this meal is described very simply, sufficient detail is included to allow Lewis's readers to recognize that this is a special Christmas celebration and that the food is sweet, rich, and attractive. At this particular point, the story is related from Edmund's point of view and he is rather hungry for his breakfast. The lovely Christmas feast the narrative implies is likely to seduce and stimulate the appetites not only of the protagonist but also of the story's readers. Food descriptions in fiction, like menus in restaurants and television cookery programs, produce visceral pleasure, a pleasure which notably involves both intellect and material body working in synaesthetic communion. Lynne Vallone describes the food metaphor as "speaking" synaesthetically within literature—meaning that we "taste the words with our eyes."[2]

At the Witch's approach the "gaiety went out of" the faces of the merry party; they stopped eating and "the baby squirrels squeaked with terror" (*Lion,* 105).

> "What is the meaning of this?" asked the Witch Queen. Nobody answered.
> "Speak, vermin!" she said again. "Or do you want my dwarf to find you a tongue with his whip? What is the meaning of all this gluttony, this waste, this self-indulgence?" (105–106)

According to the Witch these "vermin" are indulging themselves inappropriately and eating more than is proper, given their lowly status. Notably, they are out of (her) control. Conversely, by implication, because they are eating gluttonously and lack control they are categorized as vermin, that is, as disease-ridden scavengers. Lewis's narrative reflects Puritanical discourses that link lack of appetitive control with immorality and it echoes the axiom "you are what you eat." Those who eat excessively or inappropriately, Lewis's discourse (and Western culture) implies, are vermin or "spies and traitors" as the Witch subsequently refers to them (107). This reflects the notion that gluttonous or inappropriate consumption connotes a lack of subjectivity. To be a proper (human) subject one must eat in a controlled manner, according to cultural rules. Eating, and specifically the cultural imperative to eat correctly, is a significant means by which society controls individual identity.

When the Witch finds out that the feast is a gift from Father Christmas (and thus that Aslan is on the move and her own magic is weakening), she roars with anger and bites her lips "so that a drop of blood appeared on her white cheek" (*Lion*, 106). Her bloodied mouth plays on cultural fears of bloody incorporation. It is a motif that is central to the horror movie and evokes notions of the *vagina dentata*.[3] The Witch punishes the merry party by turning them and the plum pudding to stone (*Lion*, 106–107). She is thus cast as the antithesis of the "natural" fecund, nurturing female; her unremitting evil is confirmed and her subsequent defeat justified and inevitable. The reader accordingly understands that Aslan, although still a mysterious figure, is good and that the Witch is irredeemably wicked.

The food event can thus be seen to be a valuable literary device with many layers of meaning. Through the stimulation of their appetites, Lewis is able to rehearse his narrative intention to attentive readers. The feast enables him to develop and strengthen his major theme and to reiterate the relative positions of the characters in relation to it. He also, arguably, encourages his readers to thoroughly despise the Witch by firstly evoking a lovely meal and then having her turn it to stone. While Lewis's narrative has the Witch condemn gluttony it may also be seen to didactically condemn readers' appetites—appetites stimulated by the literary feast itself.

The White Witch's question, "What is the meaning of all this gluttony?" proves to be a useful starting point for an exploration into the role of food and the meanings it carries in children's literature. Food in literature is always symbolic, since "characters in literature do not eat to live because they are not alive."[4] While both the characters and the food they eat may be fictional, literary meals have a powerful "mimetic effect" (Vallone, 47), which reinforces the "obviousnesses"[5] of cultural ideologies. The symbolism of food in children's literature in particular is a significant area for study because children's fiction is a category of literature written by one powerful group, not for equals, but for another less knowledgeable, less socially enabled and thus subordinated and vulnerable group. Children's books are, as Peter Hunt points out,

> overtly important educationally and commercially—with consequences across the culture, from language to politics: most adults, and almost certainly the vast majority in positions of power and influence, read children's books as children, and it is inconceivable that the ideologies permeating those books had no influence on their development.[6]

The feasting fantasy in children's literature is a particularly good vehicle for carrying culture's socializing messages: it acts to seduce readers; through mimesis it "naturalizes" the lesson being taught; and, through the visceral pleasures (sometimes even jouissance) it produces, it "sweetens" the discourse and encourages unreflexive acceptance of the moral thus delivered. Hence, while ostensibly pandering to hedonism, a feasting fantasy frequently acts didactically. Jacqueline Rose describes children's fiction itself as "something of a soliciting, a chase, or even a seduction."[7] It is "impossible" she argues, because it hangs upon the "impossible relation between adult and child," a relation which is inevitably unequal and coercive. For Rose, children's fiction

> sets up a world in which the adult comes first (author, maker, giver) and the child comes after (reader, product, receiver)...children's fiction builds an image of the child inside the book, it does so in order to secure the child who is outside the book... [it] sets up the child as an outsider to its own process, and then aims, unashamedly, to take the child *in*. (Rose, 1–2, emphasis in original)

The feasting fantasy strengthens this effect, stimulating and fulfilling the readers' sensuous and emotional desires and, vicariously, their appetites. As the child inside the book enjoys the feast, the child outside the book is firmly secured and subjected to the text's inherent ideologies. In this respect the food trope has tremendous persuasive power.

One of the most fundamental cultural messages that children have to learn concerns how to eat correctly, that is, to put it simply, what to eat and what not to eat or who eats whom. As I have already shown, we must eat according to culturally defined rules in order to achieve proper (human) subjectivity. In other words it is vital, for the sake of individual and social order, that every human subject literally embodies culture.

"WITHOUT FOOD EVERYTHING IS LESS THAN NOTHING"

This is Bunyip Bluegum's claim in Norman Lindsay's *The Magic Pudding*.[8] His comment is literally true in as much as we cannot survive without food. It is also true in the sense that a well-provisioned picnic basket adds much to the success of an adventure. As well as being nutritional and producing pleasure, however, food has enormous cultural significance. I have argued that we must eat correctly in order to be "human" and that it is vital for children to learn what they can and cannot eat according to prevailing cultural rules. All cultures are highly selective in their definitions of food and non-food and their definitions do not necessarily relate to nutritional value. In "Negation" Freud surmised that, expressed in the language of the "oral, instinctual impulses," the decision to eat or not to eat—that is to take something inside oneself or to keep it outside—was the basis for all future decisions.[9] The inside/outside, edible/inedible dualism is fundamentally significant in terms of the structure of Western philosophical thought whereby everything inside/edible is aligned with the self and is defined as good while everything outside/inedible is aligned with the other and defined as bad.[10]

Structuralism produces conflict in philosophical thought, however, so that in Western culture inside/self is associated with mind/reason, and is pitted against outside/other, body/passion. Phallocentric logic extends these definitions so that male is opposed to female; mind/reason/culture is aligned with the male and body/passion/nature is conversely assigned to the female. This pattern of thought not only sets up male and female as oppositional, which leads to cultural misogyny, but can also produce individual feelings of disembodiment and result in denial of the body's material needs. This pathological thought process can be manifested through eating disorders such as anorexia. As Susan Bordo argues, prioritizing the mind over the body and its needs alienates the anorexic from the hunger the body feels. In this case the anorexic's starvation is motivated by the dream of being "without a body," the desire to achieve "absolute purity," and transcendence of the flesh.[11] In Western culture, representations of the female body disregard its flesh-and-blood realities and concentrate on a body image that symbolizes femininity. Femininity is signified by thinness, which in turn connotes properly controlled desire and morality. As the female body is constructed by structuralist phallocentric discourses as an object so, conversely, the subject is ideally male and bodiless.[12]

On the one hand, because my work involves thinking about the eating body it necessarily highlights structural oppositions but, on the other, it also reveals their arbitrariness. Thus, for example, while self/human and other/monster may be defined by "good" and "bad" eating respectively (so that the ultimate "bad" eater, the cannibal, is defined as the antithesis of humanity), judgments about what constitutes good or bad food for Westerners (such as, say, the flesh of a pig as opposed to the flesh of a dog) can be seen to be entirely subjective. While the inside and outside of the body are defined dichotomously, the realities of the eating body mean that food passes from the outside to the inside and subsequently to the outside again, distorting notions of what is properly inside/self and outside/other. When we eat food (an object) it literally becomes part of us (a subject). The processes of ingestion, digestion, and excretion force us to acknowledge that our bodies are not finite cohesive structures but permeable corporeal organisms constantly in flux with the outside. By revealing the arbitrariness of the dualisms food/non-food, inside/outside, the illogic of phallocentric ideologies is also revealed. I draw attention to the cause, effect, and arbitrary construction of phallocentric discourses, where relevant, in the chapters that follow.

Elizabeth Grosz argues that an understanding of "embodied subjectivity" or "psychical corporeality" would avoid the impasse posed by dichotomous accounts that divide the subject into mutually exclusive categories of mind and body.[13] Working, ultimately, toward the same purpose, Elspeth Probyn argues that thinking about the eating body will allow us to "rethink the ethics of bodies."[14] As she points out, eating is *real* and studying the body that eats provides a way of highlighting culture's structures and the way individuals interact with them and within them. Unlike representations of the sexed body, the practices of the eating body are, she claims, "not divorced from their representations or those of the body that analyses them." Studying the eating body, she believes, is a way of "returning cultural theory to a consideration of the real" (Probyn, 19). In this book I highlight cultural discourses that divide the subject into mutually exclusive categories of mind and body; I consider the reader's embodied subjectivity in terms of intellectual and physical reactions to tantalizing descriptions of food as well as the cultural repercussions of the circumstances relating to the feast; and, I examine psychological explanations for Western culture's collective reticence with regard to the physical realities of corporeal existence. It is my contention, for example, that the pleasures or thrills produced by the literary feasting fantasy are pleasures of embodied subjectivity—visceral pleasures produced by intellectual activity—and that this is why so many commentators describe food as the sex of children's literature.[15] By examining edible/inedible, inside/outside, subject/object dualisms (among others) in food narratives written for children, and the psychological bases for their existence, this book works toward making misogynist discourses more transparent.

THE MAGIC THAT MADE HUSH VISIBLE

Mem Fox's *Possum Magic* is a quest narrative, following an ancient tradition in which a hero strives for something of value such as treasure or a beautiful woman. In this storybook the quest is for personal identity, a universal, internalized, and significantly contemporary goal. Grandma Poss makes Hush invisible to keep her safe from snakes. Hush has lots of adventures but there comes a time when she wants to be visible again. Most pertinently Hush wants "to know what [she] looks like."[16] In Julie Vivas's illustration Grandma Poss leans over a pool of water with a fuzzy outline of Hush beside her. But Hush has no reflection in the mirrored surface of the pool. Because she cannot see herself she has no sense of identity, no sense of self. Because she is invisible she lacks subjectivity and, therefore, agency.

But Grandma Poss has trouble finding the magic to make Hush visible again and, although Hush tells her she doesn't mind, "in her heart of hearts she did" (*Possum Magic,* 17). Eventually Grandma remembers that, "it's something to do with food. People food—not possum food" (18). And she and Hush set off around Australia to find the food that will make Hush visible.

> They ate Anzac biscuits in Adelaide,
> mornay and minties in Melbourne,
> steak and salad in Sydney
> and pumpkin scones in Brisbane.
> …in the far north of Australia,
> …they found a vegemite sandwich (21–22)

Hush's tail appears. "Later, on a beach in Perth, they ate a piece of pavlova" and "Hush's legs appeared. So did her body" (24). Next, in Hobart "they saw a lamington on a plate." After nibbling the lamington Hush is finally visible "from head to tail" (26). "From that time onwards" once a year, on Hush's birthday, Grandma Poss and Hush "ate a vegemite sandwich, a piece of pavlova and a half a lamington, just to make sure that Hush stayed visible forever" (28). The foods that Grandma Poss and Hush eat are seen to be quintessentially Australian and their journey is a search for national and cultural identity as well as visibility or subjectivity. Fox's narrative suggests that an individual's sense of self does not arise spontaneously but is derived by literally consuming culture. By eating these significantly Australian foods, Hush becomes visible and can be recognized as having a legitimate place within Australian society; she thus eats her way into culture. This reflects and supports the notion that *we are what we eat* and that food narratives teach children how to be proper human subjects.

Applying a postcolonial reading to this storybook, which was published in the early 1980s, it is pertinent to point out, however, that the national and cultural identity Fox writes about is limited: geographically to the coastal regions of Australia and gastronomically to exclude indigenous foods and flavors.

In Fox's narrative food is the magic that makes Hush visible. It constructs her as a subject and thus may be said to stand in, metonymically, for culture itself. For Michel Foucault culture is the magic that makes individuals visible. Following Nietzsche, Foucault argues that cultural discourses of truth, power, and knowledge distinguish between normal and deviant behavior, thus determining individuals' actions and constructing them as subjects. For Foucault power does not "crush" individuals; it does not need to because

> [it is] one of the prime effects of power that certain bodies, certain gestures, certain discourses, certain desires, come to be identified and constituted as individuals... The individual is an effect of power, and at the same time, or precisely to the extent to which it is that effect, it is the element of its articulation. The individual which power has constituted is at the same time its vehicle.[17]

In Fox's story the consumption of certain foods constitutes Hush as an individual. The various foods might be said to carry certain discourses or stories about what it means to be Australian, including lifestyle, attitudes, desires, and even power relations (who gets the biggest slice?). As Hush consumes these foods, she also consumes Australian-ness and is constituted as an Australian. As a visibly legitimate Australian subject Hush embodies culture or as Foucault puts it, she is an "effect of power." Simultaneously she is also "the element of its articulation." Hence by her annually repeated consumption of proper Australian food/culture she confirms, for all those (child readers) now able to see her, just what it means to be Australian.

Having eaten into Australian culture, Hush is visibly an individual. Grandma Poss is additionally visibly designated as specifically female by the apron she wears (notably she is the only character in the book who is clothed). Judith Butler argues that the body is "always already a cultural sign" and is "never free of an imaginary construction" as either male or female.[18] To Foucault's argument that there is no position outside power/knowledge,[19] Butler adds there is no classification outside of the culturally assigned binary opposites male and female. For Butler embodying culture means acquiring the necessary skills, "bodily gestures, movements, and styles of various kinds," to "constitute the illusion of an abiding gendered self" (179). Butler argues that the body is a "politically regulated cultural construct," "a signifying practice within a cultural field of gender hierarchy and compulsory heterosexuality" (177). Gender is an "act" which is both "intentional" and "performative." It is "a strategy of survival within compulsory systems" performed through a "stylized repetition of acts" under "duress" (177–79). For Butler then, gender is performed rather than possessed. Its performance must be reiterated repeatedly in order that the illusion appear natural. Each and every successful performance reiterates the systems of power relations that produce the illusions in the first place. Even something as simple as Grandma Poss's apron reinforces the systems of power relations that produce the illusion of femininity. The apron is a symbol of domesticity, a stereotypical accoutrement of the maternal figure in children's fiction. Grandma Poss's apron is metonymic of culture; it defines her and serves to reiterate the definition of proper femininity.

CUT-AN'-COME-AGAIN PUDDIN'

Probably the ultimate food fantasy is the mythic cornucopia, the symbol of plenty. The fairy tale "The Magic Porridge Pot" is one example; Lindsay's *The Magic Pudding* is another. This "Puddin'" is "a Christmas steak and apple-dumpling Puddin'" (*Magic Pudding*, 21), "for if you wanted a change of food from the Puddin', all you had to do was to whistle twice and turn the basin round" (36). Notably this is a pudding with a capital "P"; it is a very cantankerous talking pudding, called Albert. He has discernible facial features in the illustrations and long spindly arms and legs. He is "always anxious to be eaten" (21) and sings out:

> "Eat away, chew away, munch and bolt and guzzle,
> Never leave the table till you're full up to the muzzle" ...
> A peculiar thing about the Puddin' was that, though they had all had a great many slices off him, there was no sign of the place whence the slices had been cut.
> "That's where the Magic comes in," explained Bill [to Bunyip Bluegum].
> "The more you eats the more you gets. Cut-an'-come-again is his name, an' cut, an' come again, is his nature. Me an' Sam has been

eatin' away at this Puddin' for years, and there's not a mark on him." (22–23)

In the first place, it should be noted, underlying the narrative, which involves the pudding owners' quest to keep their prize from being stolen by envious "professional" pudding thieves, are discourses about Australia as a land of plenty in need of protection from plundering colonialists.

Second, to my mind, Lindsay's narrative can be read as disturbing cultural notions of what is properly edible. Jacques Lacan refers to the system of meanings and identities from which subjectivity is derived, as the symbolic order. Notably this is a patriarchal structure defined by language. Individuals locate themselves within the field of language in order to take up a place in the human world.[20] Albert (the Puddin') is framed within the narrative as a sentient being with opinions, feelings, and desires. His ability to talk makes him part of the symbolic order; he thus acquires subject status. In structuralist terms, the consumption of one subject by another is akin to cannibalism. Certainly, in E. B. White's *Charlotte's Web*, for example, the narrative discourse condemns the adult humans for their desire to eat Wilbur the pig; his ability to talk means that he must not be eaten.[21] However, while Wilbur is an animal with, White's narrative implies, the right to live, Albert is a pudding and puddings are clearly categorized as food. Moreover, Albert wants to be eaten and encourages his owners to "guzzle" as much as they can.

In terms of this and other stories about never-ending sources of food, the fantasy is, I believe, linked to the subconscious nostalgic desire to return to the mother's breast and to recreate the primal relationship. Many commentators agree that such desire pervades contemporary life.[22] The sensuous satisfaction and physical and psychological pleasures derived from breast-feeding create a fundamentally important and lasting attachment to the mother/breast and to sweet, rich foods. In Western culture such foods symbolize love, comfort, and safety and are coded to create a familiar atmosphere, a "homely" maternal environment suggestive of the primal relationship. It is my contention that sweet foods often metaphorically stand in for the idealized maternal aesthetic in fictional texts. Similarly, sweet foods can be used to seduce storybook protagonists with promises of "heaven," which equate to a return to the primal relationship.

One of the delights of Lindsay's story is the comradeship shared by the pudding-owners. Bluegum Bunyip, Sam Sawnoff, and Bill Barnacle form the "Noble Society of Puddin' owners" (*Magic Pudding*, 44). Their companionable sharing of food echoes that described in many British classics. Wendy Katz refers to the food in Kenneth Grahame's *The Wind in the Willows*, for example, as a sign of "coziness, plenty and cheer" and claims that sharing food reinforces a sense of camaraderie—"good fellowship and good food being synonymous" (Katz, 194; see also Nikolajeva 2000, 129 and Hunt 1996, 11). Hunt suggests that food is "central to the fantasy world of nostalgia"[23] in the British classics and I would suggest that this is also so in *The Magic Pudding*. Additionally, and again particularly relevant to Lindsay's story, Hunt argues that the British classics have attained their status not only because of the nostalgia they evoke, but also because of their rurality, their male dominance (and their sense of "mateship" perhaps for the Australian classic in question), their insistence on play and fantasizing about how things used to be, and their satisfying sense of closure (Hunt, 8).

Food in seemingly never-ending quantities is a regular feature in classic British stories for children and this trend is echoed in many early Australian stories, which were often produced for the British market. It is fascinating to consider just why food was such an important part of the adventure stories of the period. It is my belief that deprivation shapes desire and that the appeals of food narratives are historically relevant and various, being sensuous as well as appetitive. I attribute the prevalence of literary food in the early British classics to the austerity of the traditional nursery upbringing, a child-rearing regime much influenced by Puritanical discourses, which recommended an extremely bland and restricted diet for children. Later on, war-time rationing restricted readers' diets and sharpened their appetites for fictional feasting.

FOODBUNGLING TRICKS

Bunyip Bluegum is the newest member of the Puddin' owners' club and, as such, he must be taught its rules. Instead of "the ordinary breakfast rules, such as scowling while eating, and saying the porridge is as stiff as glue and the eggs are as tough as leather…songs, roars of laughter and boisterous jests are the order of the day." Sam demonstrates by doing a "rapid back-flap and landing with a thump on Bill's head. As Bill was unprepared for this act of boisterous humor, his face was pushed into the Puddin' with great violence, and the gravy was splashed in his eye" (*Magic Pudding*, 48).

"What d'yer mean, playin' such bungfoodlin' tricks on a man at breakfast?" roared Bill.

"What d'yer mean," shouted the Puddin', "playing such foodbungling tricks on a Puddin' being breakfasted at?"

"Breakfast humor, Bill, merely breakfast humor," said Sam, hastily.

"Humor's humor," shouted Bill, "but puddin' in the whiskers is no joke."

"Whiskers in the Puddin' is worse than puddin' in the whiskers" shouted the Puddin', standing up in his basin. (50–51)

This is a carnivalesque episode in the tradition described by Mikhail Bakhtin.[24] Food narratives in children's stories are often "grounded in playfulness"[25] and transgressive of adult food rules, not just in terms of "foodbungling tricks" but also timing, sequence, quantity, and quality. Additionally, the carnivalesque allows a significant space for what Bakhtin refers to as the "material bodily principle"—the human body and its concerns with eating, defecation, and sexuality (Bakhtin, 18). Julia Kristeva theorizes subjectivity as an ongoing process, which requires individuals to maintain a "clean and proper" (that is, a hygienic and socially sanctioned) embodiment of culture. To achieve this the subject has to consign all the improper, uncontrollable, unclean aspects of the corporeal body to the unconscious. But, Kristeva argues, the reality of material existence can never be successfully repressed; instead it "hovers at the borders of our existence, threatening the apparently settled unity of the subject with disruption and possible dissolution."[26] The subject's recognition of the impossibility of excluding this reality provokes the sensation Kristeva refers to as abjection. Abjection is thus a refusal of the impure and defiling aspects of embodied existence, a response to its constant flux with the outside though cyclical incorporation, absorption, and elimination (cited by Grosz 1989, 72).

In terms of abjection, the Puddin' is correct: finding whiskers or hairs in your food is more disgusting than having food in your whiskers. It's even more disgusting if the hair isn't one of yours and worse still if it's one of the dog's. Even disgust is a learned response, however, and culturally specific.[27]

The concept of the child, from adult culture's point of view, is difficult to pin down. On the one hand a child is innocent, pure, and possesses innate wisdom. On the other hand, a child is, at the same time, wild, voracious, primitive, and in need of instruction: the tenets of Romanticism and Puritanism persist and coexist. The way adults write about children, for children, tends to uphold the notion that, while adults are regarded as civilized, controlled, sophisticated, and properly human, children lack these qualities. As far as adult culture is concerned, children must internalize very precise rules about how to maintain a "clean and proper" body, what to relegate to abjection, and how to perform properly in social situations. Children must also learn all sorts of rules about food and eating. Most important—they must know *who eats whom*. Food events in children's literature are clearly intended to teach children how to be human.

1

YOU ARE WHAT YOU EAT

Food and Cultural Identity

Tell me what you eat and I will tell you who you are.
— Jean Anthelme Brillat-Savarin, *The Physiology of Taste*[1]

"Maybe it's always pepper that makes people hot-tempered," [Alice] went on, very much pleased at having found out a new kind of rule, "and vinegar that makes them sour—and camomile that makes them bitter—and—and barley-sugar and such things that make children sweet-tempered. I only wish people knew *that*: then they wouldn't be so stingy about it."
— Lewis Carroll, *Alice's Adventures in Wonderland*
emphasis in original[2]

Mankind's place in the food chain—is this the unspeakable knowledge, the ultimate taboo, that generates the art of the grotesque?—or all art, culture, civilization?
— Joyce Carol Oates, "Afterward: Reflections on the Grotesque"[3]

WHEN BRILLAT-SAVARIN claimed that he could identify someone from the food she or he consumed he was linking the axiom "you are what you eat" to national stereotypes. He was able to do this because food preferences tend to be culturally specific. Using the same premise Peter Farb and George Armelagos claim that the French subtlety of thought and manners is said to be related to the subtlety of their cuisine, the reserve of the British to their unimaginative diet, German stolidness to the quantities of heavy food they consume, and the unreliability of the Italians to the large amounts of wine they drink.[4]

This presumably ironic set of assertions clearly suggests that certain qualities in the foods traditionally consumed by each ethnic group are manifested in their national character. In other words different foods *produce* different people. This implies that food can influence or transform peoples' personalities and behaviors, an idea reflected in the "new kind of rule" Alice discovered.

It is not surprising that different societies from various geographic locations developed different rules about what is and is not good to eat. What is perhaps rather more surprising is the realization that, in comparison with some other cultures, the range of traditional Western cultural food choices is relatively narrow, especially with regard to sources of protein. Cultural food preferences are often based on specific rules with religious derivations. In Western Christian-derived cultures, for example, food rules are historically based on religious practices. In *Leviticus* animals that are *not* readily classifiable as birds that fly, fish that have fins and gills, or animals that walk on all fours, chew the cud, and have cloven hooves are considered to be abominations and are prohibited or taboo. Snakes, for instance, which slither on the ground or in water are not regarded as pure and are therefore not edible.[5] Individual and social morality is upheld only by avoiding meats that break these taboos.

Paul Rozin argues that the avoidance of the flesh of certain animals has to do with the common structural theme that "humans are not animals" and must be emphatically distinguished from them. Humans must especially avoid eating animals that are too "animal-like," fast-moving predators being more animal-like than slow-moving herbivores.[6] Rozin's argument contains two strands of reasoning: first, as the Bible suggests, humans should avoid eating predators—this is because, as I've indicated, what we eat is commonly thought of as being able to change or transform us. From this perspective, it is not unreasonable to think that the flesh of a predatory animal might impart qualities that would make the eater a threat to the rest of society. Eating taboo food then becomes a deviant and immoral act, one that renders the eater impure and dangerous. The second strand of Rozin's argument involves the structural concept that humans must clearly distinguish between themselves and slow-moving herbivorous animals because, although we repress it, we recognize that our flesh is, like theirs, meat that could be consumed. It is only by maintaining an emphatically clear distinction between ourselves as eating subjects in contrast to certain animals as objects to be eaten, that we retain our position at the top of the food chain and avoid becoming part of it. This is why Joyce Carol Oates refers to the precariousness of "mankind's" position as "the unspeakable knowledge."

Human subjectivity is achieved through a psychological process that involves learning to comply with the rules of the social order. These include food rules and strict regulations relating to what Julia Kristeva refers to as the "clean and proper" body.[7] Obviously the definition of a clean and proper body, according to social niceties, is closely linked to food rules. Food rules relate, not only to what is and isn't edible, but also concern who eats what, according to age and gender; when to eat; how to eat (good manners); and, significantly, how much to eat, again according to age and gender. Similarly, the imperative to provide, prepare, and cook food is culturally determined and assigned, even in contemporary society, generally according to gender.

Mealtimes, in children's storybooks and in real life experience, are powerful socializing events. Cultural food rules and attitudes toward food and the eating body are transmitted via the subtexts of children's fiction and of their everyday lives.

ALIMENTARY RACISM

Despite a growing level of homogenization of food choices due to globalization, different cultures tend to eat different foods. Indeed, Sidney Mintz argues that during infancy we are taught how to be *human* by learning to like the foods our culture deems proper human food.[8] Other cultures' food choices can be considered revolting and evoke disgust, especially where meat is concerned. In Western Anglo-Saxon, Christian-derived culture, for example, the meat of sheep, cattle, pigs, and chickens is considered suitable for consumption, whereas in Jewish culture the flesh of a pig is thought to be unclean and Hindus will not eat beef. To Westerners the thought of eating dog meat, which is consumed as a matter of course, or as a delicacy, in some parts of the world, produces shudders of disgust. Revulsion results because on the one hand eating dog meat is deemed to be immoral according to Christian religious prohibitions, and on the other hand the eater is seen to be somehow changed by what they have consumed, to have become less than human. There is, however, a third reason why dog meat is particularly revolting and this is related to the paradoxical way animals are treated in the Western world. While animals are obviously not considered to be the same as humans in Western culture, some animals are accorded a sort of interim status akin to human. When a dog is kept as a family pet, with a given name, it assumes a certain level of subjectivity. As such, dog flesh, like human flesh, cannot be coded as meat to be eaten. Westerners tend to be disgusted by the thought of eating dog meat and this revulsion is extended to those peoples whose cultural food rules authorize its consumption. In Western eyes these people are perceived of as not only immoral and less than human, but also monstrous and to be feared.

In Anthony Horowitz's *Stormbreaker*, fourteen-year-old Alex Rider, who has been engaged by MI6 as a spy, meets multi-millionaire Herod Sayle, who plans to donate and install Stormbreaker computers, manufactured by Sayle Enterprises, into every secondary school in Britain. At the outset Sayle's philanthropy is suspect and Alex is sent undercover to find out the truth. Sayle is portrayed as a decidedly eccentric and cruel, but initially ambiguous character until he and Alex sit down to a meal together. The narrative subtext around food choices reveals Sayle's immorality and criminal intent to the reader. He and Alex are served "some sort of stew" that turns out to contain goat meat (Sayle's Egyptian mother's recipe).[9] Sayle suggests that they also have dinner together the following evening when one of his grandmother's recipes will be served. "More goat?" Alex asks. "Dog," Sayle replies. Alex comments acerbically, "You obviously had a family that loved animals," to which Sayle counters, "Only the edible ones" (*Stormbreaker*, 125). Within traditional British culture goat meat tends to be avoided, but dog meat is definitely not considered to be suitable human food. In contrast, Egyptian culture apparently considers both animals to be edible. Sayle's consumption of these meats firmly establishes his place outside British culture; he and his culture are othered and their food choices orientalized.[10] Within the subtext of the coding of food Sayle's subject-position is clearly that of the exoticized other. Furthermore, however, he is coded as immoral, less than human and therefore monstrous and a threat to the social order. Sayle's intentions can from the beginning of this narrative be read, through the food he consumes, as irrevocably evil, which indeed they turn out to be. While monstrous eating reveals the villain in Horowitz's narrative, traditional British cultural food rules have also been legitimized and the social structure upheld by the author's repetition of an alimentary racist discourse, which insists that eating outside British culture necessarily produces an evil character.

In contrast, in the second book of Phillip Pullman's *His Dark Materials* trilogy, *The Subtle Knife,* we find out, through the subtext, that despite the fact that Will has murdered a man,[11] his integrity is unquestionable because he adheres to fundamental (British) food rules and thus remains within culture. When he and Lyra (who are from different worlds) first encounter each other in an abandoned city of a world unfamiliar to them both, they are hungry. Will finds the makings of a chicken casserole in the little café where they have taken shelter. But the food "hadn't been cooked, and in the heat [was] smelling bad. He swept [it] all into the dustbin" (*Subtle Knife,* 22). Not only does Will know the difference between good food and bad food, but he also proceeds to cook a meal for Lyra who is less able to fend for herself because in her world servants do the cooking (24). Significantly, Will cooks her an omelet. In Western culture and in terms of the coding of food, eggs in particular are coded as wholesome, natural, and eminently suitable food for children. After they've eaten Will asks Lyra to wash up. "I cooked," he said, "so you can wash the dishes." Lyra is "incredulous." "'Wash the dishes?' she scoffed. 'There's millions of clean ones lying about! Anyway, I'm not a servant. I'm not going to wash them'" (27). But Will insists that he will not help her on her quest unless she follows the rules:

> Listen. I don't know how long we can stay in this place. We've got to eat, so we'll eat what's here, but we'll tidy up afterwards and keep the place clean, because we ought to. You wash these dishes. We've got to treat this place *right*. (27–28, emphasis in original)

Will insists on doing the right thing, he knows what *ought* to be done to comply with cultural food rules: he chooses the good food; he knows how to prepare it properly, and he is aware of the need for order and hygiene in the kitchen (thus avoiding the possibility of contamination/pollution which can result in bad food). Will's knowledge of food rules, his ability and willingness to nurture both Lyra and, earlier in the story, his sick mother, plus his insistence upon the fairness of sharing tasks, indicate to the reader that he will be a suitable and reliable companion for Lyra. Significantly, that night, while Will sleeps, Lyra consults her alethiometer (a rare hand-held machine which supplies truthful answers to questions asked by those who are skilled in reading its complex patterning) about Will: "*What is he? A friend or an enemy?*" It answers: "*He is a murderer.*" (italics in original)

> When she saw the answer, she relaxed at once. He could find food, and show her how to reach Oxford, and those were powers that were useful, but he might still have been untrustworthy or cowardly. A murderer was a worthy companion. She felt as safe with him as she'd done with Iorek Byrnison the armoured bear. (29)

In the context of Pullman's novel, Lyra is from a different culture and world to Will, who is apparently from our own. Where we may have had qualms about accepting a murderer as a friend and companion, Pullman keeps realism at bay by having Lyra regard Will's status as a murderer as a particularly positive quality. However, primed by our awareness of the significance of food rules, we are reassured that Lyra's decision to accept Will is the right one.

Elspeth Probyn refers to Westerners' unquestioning derision of the food choices of other cultures as "alimentary racism."[12] J. K. Rowling promotes an alimentary racist discourse in *Harry Potter and the Goblet of Fire*. Ron Weasley views food that is not British with suspicion:

> "What's *that*?" said Ron, pointing at a large dish of some sort of shellfish stew that stood beside a large steak-and-kidney pudding.
>
> "Bouillabaisse," said Hermione.
>
> "Bless you," said Ron.
>
> "It's *French*," said Hermione. "I had it on holiday, summer before last, it's very nice."
>
> "I'll take your word for it," said Ron, helping himself to black pudding.[13]

Ron's closed-mindedness is crushing. He dismisses the bouillabaisse as other along with those who eat it, including Hermione. Her experience is dismissed within the subtext as it is within the larger context of the *Harry Potter* series as I have argued elsewhere.[14] Humor is evoked (mainly for adult readers) by the irony of Ron's unsophisticated dismissal of bouillabaisse in favor of "black pudding," a sausage made with pig's blood. Within Rowling's narrative even the name of the French dish is constructed as the sign of a disease.

In contrast to Rowling's story where the food of the other is explicitly rejected, C. S. Lewis's description of the rich and exotic Calormene food in *The Horse and His Boy*, part of the *Chronicles of Narnia*, makes pleasurable and tantalizing reading.[15] However, Lewis manages to other and exoticize the dark-skinned Calormenes through his narrator's attitude toward their food. Vallone describes the dinner Shasta is offered as "of a vaguely Middle Eastern cast" except perhaps for the fruit fools:[16]

> It was a fine meal after the Calormene fashion. I don't know whether you would have liked it or not, but Shasta did. There were lobsters, and salad, and snipe stuffed with almonds and truffles, and a complicated dish made of chicken-livers and rice and raisins and nuts, and there were cool melons and gooseberry fools and mulberry fools, and every kind of nice thing that can be made with ice. (*Horse and His Boy*, 64)

The items listed are familiar, although the "complicated" combination of sweet and savory in the stuffing and the rice dish would perhaps have been unusual to a British child reader in the later 1950s. Importantly the realities of rationing, following World War II, would, more than likely, have made the sweet richness of the Calormene feast a very pleasurable reading experience indeed. As Vallone suggests, the food Shasta eats is only "vaguely" Middle Eastern, and, in my opinion, may not in itself produce an othering effect. Otherness is signaled by the narrator's qualification "It was a fine meal *after the Calormene fashion*" followed by the interjection "I don't know whether you would have liked it or not." This has the effect of a backhanded compliment, producing ambiguity and implying criticism. The use of this ploy when presenting a new food to children at the family dinner table, for example, would be sure to result in rejection. While Shasta is perhaps glamorized and exoticized by his enjoyment of the Calormene feast, disgust is not evoked because the foods he eats are not taboo. The narrator's coercive interjection, however, signals that the reader's sympathetic identification with Shasta is somewhat subversive. Confirmation of a reading position that is against the grain, however, may in turn produce additional pleasure for the child reader.

In what might be referred to as a straightforward instance of alimentary speciesism, adapting Probyn's phrase, Wilbur the pig, in E. B. White's *Charlotte's Web* is absolutely horrified when he discovers that Charlotte, the spider, eats insects.[17] White intends that the reader share Wilbur's revulsion as Charlotte explains that insects are

> "Delicious. Of course, I don't really eat them. I drink them—drink their blood. I love blood," said Charlotte, and her pleasant, thin voice grew even thinner and more pleasant.
> "Don't say that!" groaned Wilbur. "Please don't say things like that!" (*Charlotte's Web*, 42)

Charlotte is clearly framed as vampire-like by her habit of drinking blood. As such she is aligned, through archetypal images of horror, with monstrosity and abjection. Wilbur is "sad because his new friend was so bloodthirsty" and condemns her particular method of eating for a living as "cruel" (43). He learns to be more tolerant, however, when she explains a spider's place within the food chain. "[D]o you realise," Charlotte asks him, "that if I didn't catch bugs and eat them, bugs would increase and multiply and get so numerous that they'd destroy the earth, wipe out everything?" (43–44). And she logically compares her lifestyle with his:

You have your meals brought to you in a pail. Nobody feeds me. I have to get my own living. I live by my wits. I have to be sharp and clever, lest I go hungry. I have to think things out, catch what I can, take what comes. (*Charlotte's Web*, 43, emphasis in original)

Charlotte eats what humans (and Wilbur) consider to be non-foods; she eats badly. But, while we wouldn't want to share her diet, we can approve of its use-value. In human terms, traditional culturally specific food choices, which revolt Western palates, are similarly shaped by necessity, a fact that is often overlooked in the West where there is a surfeit of nutritious food available.

The subtext around food reveals information about the morality and ethics of certain characters in stories for children. This information directly, and sometimes coercively, influences child readers' formation of sympathetic identification with the characters in the story and can be seen to promote racist, imperialist and speciesist discourses. Above all, good food is seen to denote human self and bad food to signal monstrous other-ness in these narratives although the basis for the dualisms can usually be seen to be cultural and arbitrary.

SHUDDERS OF DISGUST

Food is perhaps the substance most frequently encountered that has the power to provoke a shudder of disgust. Indeed, Margaret Visser argues that disgust "is perhaps most primevally a reaction to dangerous or otherwise revolting food."[18] According to William Miller words such as disgust and revolt "convey a strong sense of aversion to something perceived as dangerous because of its powers to contaminate, infect or pollute by proximity, contact, or ingestion."[19] Inherent in Miller's definition is the notion of something that physically invades and endangers the material body. Contemporary healthy eating discourses are underpinned by social anxiety about the vulnerability and permeability of the body to contaminants, and pollutants (which now include saturated fat).

In *Powers of Horror* Kristeva discusses the way in which proper human subjectivity and sociality are achieved only by excluding the improper, the unclean and the disorderly. She argues that recognition that the body's boundaries are permeable results in abjection, because with this recognition comes a reminder of the subject's relation to death, corporeality, animality, and materiality, conditions that consciousness and reason find intolerable (cited in Grosz 1989, 73). "Food loathing," Kristeva confirms, "is perhaps the most elementary and most archaic form of abjection" (Kristeva, 2). Kristeva's premise converges with Oates's when the former suggests that being reminded of the body's physical and semantic proximity to meat produces disgust, horror, and abjection. Moral and ethical questions about eating meat are inevitably raised and, as Oates argues, the uncomfortable image of the food chain shifts into focus.

Social, cultural, and psychological factors coalesce, reinforcing specific food taboos. The thought of committing a transgression, or of an act of transgression perpetrated by an/other, produces disgust that can be physically manifested in the form of shudders, facial grimaces, retching, and vomiting. Even more extreme reactions can result from a perceived act of transgression. While in Western culture, as I've already suggested, eggs are a most acceptable food, Visser relays the story of a nineteenth-century German explorer in Africa who "was murdered because he horrified his hosts by eating unspeakable eggs." But, she adds, in Pakistan, southeast Asia, the Pacific Islands, and parts of Africa, "eggs are often thought to be delicacies—provided that the inside has turned visibly and palpably into a chicken foetus."[20]

Alice encounters some difficulties relating to eggs in Lewis Carroll's *Alice's Adventures in Wonderland*. Alice is transformed by nibbling a magic mushroom, and finds herself with "an immense length of neck" (*Alice*, 47) in a wood, being attacked by an angry pigeon who fears its eggs are about to be devoured. It accuses Alice of being a serpent rather than a little girl:

> "You're a serpent; and there's no use denying it. I suppose you'll be telling me next that you never tasted an egg!"
>
> "I *have* tasted eggs, certainly," said Alice, who was a very truthful child; "but little girls eat eggs quite as much as serpents do, you know."
>
> "I don't believe it," said the Pigeon; "but if they do, why then they're a kind of serpent, that's all I can say."
>
> This was such a new idea to Alice, that she was quite silent for a minute or two, which gave the Pigeon the opportunity of adding, "You're looking for eggs, I know *that* well enough; and what does it matter to me whether you're a little girl or a serpent?"
>
> "It matters a good deal to me," said Alice hastily; "but I'm not looking for eggs, as it happens; and if I was, I shouldn't want yours: I don't like them raw." (*Alice*, 48, emphasis in original)

Alice has been socialized into a culture where eggs are an acceptable food, indeed a food considered particularly appropriate for children. From the Pigeon's point of view, however, eggs are not food: they are potential fetuses. Importantly, the Pigeon articulates the position of the animal-as-object in the eater/eaten transaction, bringing into question the humanity of humankind.

Alice does however confirm that "little girls eat eggs" and she, and they, are thus classified as "a kind of serpent."[21] While Alice, being "a very truthful child," cannot deny that she has eaten what in the Pigeon's eyes is non-food, she can exonerate herself in terms of human culture by declaring that she doesn't like *raw* eggs. The oppositions raw and cooked are aligned with primitive nature and civilized culture respectively in human thinking as structuralist Claude Lévi-Strauss has maintained.[22] By rejecting a liking for "raw" eggs Alice also rejects her implicit alignment with primitive nature, a position commonly accepted as applicable to children and women in Victorian society.[23]

While the morality of eating eggs is open to question, the ingestion of polluted food is always to be avoided. Pullman's Will adheres to this rule when he disposes of the improperly stored chicken that had gone bad. Leftovers in particular require careful classification. The thought of eating someone else's leftovers, for example, is distasteful, unless perhaps we are physically and emotionally very close to that person. Once partially eaten, what was an appetizing meal ten minutes ago becomes potentially polluting and dangerous. Conversely, to deliberately spoil or pollute previously wholesome food can evoke disgust.[24] In human culture, therefore, leftover partially eaten food scraps are generally classified as non-food. *Charlotte's Web* contains a range of eaters, two of whom eat leftovers. However, because of the way these particular leftovers are classified, the eaters are characterized very differently.

Templeton, the rat, is a self-confessed "glutton" (*Charlotte's Web*, 32) who loves leftovers. He is lured to the fair (where his services in fetching and carrying "words" for Charlotte to weave into her web are required) by the promise of rich pickings. The old sheep temptingly describes the fair as "a rat's paradise:"

> Everybody spills food at a fair ... you will find old discarded lunch boxes containing the foul remains of peanut butter sandwiches, hard-boiled eggs, cracker crumbs, bits of doughnuts, and particles of cheese ... a veritable treasure of popcorn fragments, frozen custard dribblings, candied apples abandoned by tired children, sugar fluff crystals, salted almonds, popsicles, partially gnawed ice cream cones, and the wooden sticks of lollypops. Everywhere is loot for a rat ... why, a fair has enough disgusting left-over food to satisfy a whole army of rats. (119–120)

Here there are repeated inferences of impurity, suggestions of dirt and pollution, of excess, and even of abject body fluids. In particular the image of "candied apples abandoned by tired children" suggests something half-eaten, excessively handled, with the grubby residue of a satiated child adhering to its sticky surface.

After a night of feasting on leftovers at the fairground Templeton is "swollen to twice his normal size. His stomach was as big round as a jelly jar." He reports that he

> "must have eaten the remains of thirty lunches. Never have I seen such leavings, and everything well-ripened and seasoned with the passage of time and the heat of the day. Oh, it was rich, my friends, rich!"
> "You ought to be ashamed of yourself," said Charlotte in disgust. (142)

Templeton is disgusting on a number of levels. First and foremost he is a scavenger and he eats foods that are polluted by having been discarded. Significantly these "leavings" frequently bear the marks of those who have already partially eaten them, which means they are, in terms of human eating habits, contaminated. (Consider again how we must, in general, be fairly intimate with another person to contemplate sharing an apple, for example, where bites leave evidence of teeth marks.[25]) Added to this, the things Templeton eats are "well-ripened and seasoned with the passage of time and the heat of the day," a recipe for gastro-enteritis for human eaters. Furthermore, and most significantly, Templeton lacks self-control, he grossly over-eats and becomes obese.

Visser links the disgust reaction to questions of morality:

> Human beings have always found it easy to believe that wicked-ness might have physical consequences, and conversely that visible and tangible things "out of place" can reflect something evil being done, or a past evil lying hidden and unrequited.

She cites as an example:

> Odysseus's men killed the forbidden cattle of the Sun, and the meat, cut up and skewered as shish-kebabs, wriggled and mooed at them, as a sign of the anger of Zeus. (Visser 1993, 300)

Using Visser's argument it is easy to see that Templeton's "out of place" habit of gorging on polluted non-foods may be interpreted as a manifestation of his underlying moral corruption and evil nature. There are frequent textual references within *Charlotte's Web* to the rat's inherent nastiness. He spends his time "eating, gnawing, spying, and hiding" (32); he is stealthy, crafty, and cunning (33). He can be bribed into helping others (and therefore has his uses and is tolerated) but he is ultimately motivated only by greed, not by any sense of altruism, not even when it is pointed out to him that Wilbur's life is at stake (90) or when Charlotte's egg sac needs retrieving (159–61). He has "no morals, no conscience, no scruples, no consideration, no decency, no milk of rodent kindness, no compunctions, no higher feeling, no friendliness, no anything" (48). He is incorrigible. As Charlotte says, "A rat is a rat" (49).

It seems improbable that readers would regard Templeton as a likeable character[26] whereas Wilbur the pig, condemned to be slaughtered and consumed by humans, appears to be very worthy of the reader's sympathy. But, it could be argued, the description of the leftovers Wilbur eats does not differ significantly from the list of food available to Templeton at the fair. Wilbur's slop bucket contains:

> Skim milk, crusts, middlings, bits of doughnuts, wheat cakes with drops of maple syrup sticking to them, potato skins, left-over custard pudding with raisins, and bits of Shredded Wheat…warm water, apple parings, meat gravy, carrot scrapings, meat scraps, stale hominy, and the wrapper off a package of cheese…left-over sandwich from Lurvy's lunchbox, prune skins, a morsel of this, a bit of that, fried potatoes, marmalade drippings, a little more of this, a little more of that, a piece of baked apple, [and] a scrap of upside-down cake. (*Charlotte's Web,* 29–30)

Both animals eat leftovers, food that humans would not eat, but semiotic coding results in markedly different attitudes being evoked in the implied reader. While the rat eats leftovers that are discarded as non-foods and are thus considered to be potentially contaminating, the leftovers fed to Wilbur have been reclassified as pig slops. While they are therefore still not suitable for human consumption, Wilbur is not polluted nor degraded in the reader's eyes by consuming them. Also, and pertinently, Wilbur shows self-restraint and indeed refuses food when he's lonely and feeling unloved (31) while Templeton, given the chance, gorges himself into a stupor. This assertion is borne out by the opposition in the framing of these characters. Templeton is basically selfish and immoral while Wilbur, following Charlotte's example, learns to be selfless, nurturing, and even maternal.[27] Thus Wilbur's subjectivity is uncompromised whereas Templeton is relegated to the position of other by his foul eating habits.

White's story confirms and reiterates an important food rule: careful attention to the classification of food must be paid in order to avoid physical and moral contamination. Transgressive eating evokes disgust, revulsion and horror and, while spoiled/bad food can literally poison, when food that is perceived to be disgusting is eaten, the eater's credibility as a subject and their morality is damaged. Perceptions of food/non-food and notions of pollution/contamination are, again, often culturally specific and arbitrary.

WHOLESOME FOOD, WHOLESOME CHILDREN

One of the main ideas in this first chapter is that certain foods impart certain qualities to the eater, that is, you are (or you become) what you eat. Some effects are implicit, such as Templeton's repulsive scavenging, which produces, perpetuates, and results from his moral degradation in human eyes. Some foods evoke explicit transformations such as those experienced by Alice during her visit to Wonderland. One of the most important structural features of Carroll's narrative is the way Alice's body grows and shrinks following her consumption of various magic foods.

Food as a metaphor for human behavior has long been part of commonsense lore. In *Julius Caesar* Cassius says to Brutus: "Upon what meat doth this our Caesar feed/That he is grown so great?" (Act 1, Scene 2). From the perspective of modern concerns about health we may wonder whether Caesar has been eating too many hamburgers. In context, however, Cassius is referring to meat as the source of Caesar's power. That food is transformative was used to advantage by Edmund Kean, a nineteenth-century Shakespearean actor, who is reported to have eaten "mutton before going on stage in the part of a lover, beef when he was to play a murderer, and pork for the role of a tyrant" (Farb and Armelagos, 3).

Following the notion that eating badly can have detrimental effects on the eater, the idea that eating healthy, natural food can produce natural, proper children seems logical. This is part of the rationale behind the story of *The Secret Garden* by Frances Hodgson Burnett.[28] Both Mary and Colin are initially rather unpleasant and unnatural children. The story starts with a description of Mary as "the most disagreeable-looking child ever seen...She had a little thin face and a little thin body, thin light hair and a sour expression...she had been born in India and had always been ill in one way or another." Mary's mother "had not wanted a little girl at all" and she was looked after, and kept quiet, by the "dark...native servants." She grew into "as tyrannical and selfish a little pig as ever lived" (*Secret Garden,* 1). The mother of Mary's cousin Colin died when he was born, and he too is a sickly child. He is bedridden and believes that he not only has a hunched back but also that he is about to die. He is very spoiled and prone to intense hysterical tantrums.

Mary and Colin are unnatural in terms of a cultural discourse that views children and childhood as inherently natural and echoes the Romantic notion of childhood as a pure and innocent state. According to this discourse the natural child is uncorrupted, asexual and possesses vitality, spirituality and "energizing animal spirits."[29] Notably this discourse is linked in *The Secret Garden* to imperialism, with proper, natural childhood being aligned with a British upbringing. Mary's early childhood in India is set up as dystopian, the cause of her sickly physical state, her irrational emotional state, and her unnaturalness. As a consequence, Britain and everything British is seen to be utopian. In India Mary is unwanted, enclosed, and overheated: it is "frightfully hot" (2). She is surrounded by disease of plague proportions and, notably, darkness: "She never remembered seeing familiarly anything but the dark faces of her Ayah and the other native servants" (1). Later Mary, although supposedly referring to clothing, tells Martha, the servant girl: "I hate black things" (24).

On the morning when a cholera outbreak upsets her normal routine so that her Ayah cannot attend to her, Mary throws "herself into a passion and beat and kicked" the replacement servant. Following this outburst, Mary is left alone for a while and attempts to make a garden, sticking "big scarlet hibiscus blossoms into little heaps of earth." But unlike the British secret garden with its properly modest British flowers and good British soil which later provides therapeutic comfort, this disproportionate and florid Indian garden provides no consolation and she grows "more and more angry," "muttering to herself," "grinding her teeth" and repeatedly describing her Ayah as "Pig! Pig! Daughter of Pigs!" "To call a native a pig" we are informed, "is the worst insult of all" (2).[30] Mary speaks powerfully and assertively, ostensibly assuming an adult role. From the perspective of the cultural expectations of natural childhood, however, her speech and demeanor are primitive, aggressive, and inappropriate. Significantly, therefore, this episode sets Mary up as an illegitimately speaking subject.

Following the death of her parents from cholera, Mary goes to live at Misselthwaite Manor in Yorkshire, England with her uncle, Colin's father. As a father and an uncle he is inadequate and often absent. Mary's cure begins when she is sent out into the grounds of the Manor and begins to exercise; walking and running along the garden paths "stirring her slow blood and making herself stronger...the big breaths of rough fresh air blown over the heather filled her lungs with something which was good for her whole thin body" (36), and made her hungry. "It's th' air of th' moor that's givin' thee stomach for tha' victuals," Martha the servant girl tells her (37). The fresh air enters Mary's body and "something" changes her. As I have suggested, the body is permeable and various substances can transgress its boundaries. Whereas airborne viruses pose a threat to the body's health, fresh, clean air is seen to rejuvenate. Later Mary encourages Colin to "draw in long breaths" of the soft, fresh, scent-laden air coming in through the open bedroom window and tells him, "That's what Dickon [Martha's brother] does when he's lying on the moor. He says he feels it in his veins and it makes him strong and he feels as if he could live for ever and ever. Breathe it and breathe it" Colin draws in long, deep breaths until "he felt that something quite new and delightful was happening to him" (160). With the encouragement of Mary and Dickon, Colin leaves his bed and ventures out into the garden.

Both Colin and Mary regain their health and strength by taking part in natural child-like activities; their bodies and minds are exercised enabling them to break out of their earlier isolation. This has led to some readers seeing the influences of Christian Science in *The Secret Garden*, particularly in Burnett's speculations about the interrelationship of the mind and body in improving health.[31] As they start to become real children, Mary and Colin become ravenous. They rely on Dickon's mother to provide them with simple but wholesome British fare of which they eat their fill (and for which they pay her with some of their "shillings" [208]), and try to eat frugally of the meals provided by the staff at the Manor in an attempt to keep the doctor from revealing the truth about Colin's improved health to his father. Colin dreams of informing his father himself when he is completely cured. The children consume "good, new milk," "a crusty cottage loaf" and "some buns wi' currants in 'em" provided by Mrs. Sowerby (204), and "home-made bread and fresh butter, snow-white eggs, raspberry jam and clotted cream," and "slices of sizzling ham" at the Manor (206–7). They roast eggs and potatoes in a "sort of tiny oven" built by Dickon, which "with salt and fresh butter in them were fit for a woodland king—besides being deliciously satisfying" (208) and they stuff themselves "full to the brim" with "oat-cakes and buns and heather honey" (210).[32] The discourse produced by the coding of these foods harks back to the notion of naturalness. These foods are wholesome, unadulterated, derived from local produce, they are homemade, evoke the comforting maternal, and most significantly they are, above all, considered to be natural.[33] It is only these simple natural foods that can assuage the children's ravenous hunger, a hunger that is physical and emotional. Friendship, fresh air, physical activity, and natural food coalesce to produce what the children refer to as "Magic"[34] and it is a belief in this "white as snow" magic, as Mary calls it (191), as well as a desire to impress his father, that fuels Colin's determination to walk again.

These children, originally stunted and thin, must consume, according to cultural expectations of childhood, appropriate quantities of natural food in order to be transformed into natural children. In *The Secret Garden* the organic growth of the springtime garden is paired with the natural growth of the bodies of the children. While the garden needs weeding and planting with seeds, the children need fresh air, natural food, and exercise; the garden becomes beautiful and floriferous; the children become proper children who are healthy in body and spirit. The food they eat thus becomes "a method of redemption" (Avery 1994, 158), the fresh air both an agent of and a catalyst for their transformation.

It is significant, I think, that it is only when they become acceptable in terms of cultural expectations of childhood that their father/uncle returns. Maggie Kilgour argues:

> If cultures are defined by what they eat, they are also stereotyped by how they speak, as "barbarian" referred originally to those who could not speak Greek. Food is the matter that goes in the mouth, words the more refined substance that afterward comes out: the two are differentiated and yet somehow analogous.[35]

We also have cultural expectations, aligned with discourses of natural childhood, of the way *children* should speak and behave, how they should act out the roles adults assign to them within the social structure. As I argued earlier, Mary's behavior on the day of the cholera outbreak in India revealed her capacity for primitive aggression. Her speech was framed as illegitimately and inappropriately powerful, her assumed subjectivity noncredible. At the outset Colin is similarly prone to violent hysterical tantrums and he screams and cries until Mary feels "sick and shivering" (*Secret Garden,* 141). What emanates from the mouths of both children, before their cure, therefore, is primitive, often destructive and decidedly *not* part of their culturally assigned roles as proper children. However, by the end of the story their speech and demeanor become more appropriate to natural childhood, they even play with language, adopting the Yorkshire dialect. Their speech is no longer powerfully aggressive, commanding, and adult-like as it had been previously and the children therefore become culturally acceptable. Wholesome food goes into their mouths and language appropriate to their given roles "comes out."

In terms of psychoanalytic theory, proper male sexual identity relies on the need to turn from the mother to the father who represents separation.[36] Thus Colin must pass through the oral phase, the stage of maternal influence, metaphorically represented, in *The Secret Garden,* by the food consumed, before identifying with and being identified by his father. Importantly his father is a guardian of the law of the father: the law of the father is Lacan's expression for language as the medium through which all human beings are placed in culture, a medium represented, and imposed upon them, by the figure of the father in the family.[37] Upon discovering Colin's transformation from a pale, sickly bedridden invalid into a proper child who can walk "as strongly and steadily as any boy in Yorkshire," his father says, "Take me into the garden, my boy… [a]nd *tell* me all about it" (*Secret Garden,* 242, 240, emphasis added). Thus his father asks Colin to speak. In doing so, he also invites him into the symbolic order where he becomes a credible and legitimately speaking subject. *The Secret Garden* perpetuates and strengthens the notion that food is transformative and that the consumption of wholesome food and fresh air *produces* wholesome children.

MEETING THE MEAT

Talking animal characters in children's literature problematize the Western cultural food rules I have so far discussed. They often evoke a sympathetic identification with the reader, and break down the opposition between animal/human, object/subject, and eaten/eater. An important determinant of subjectivity, as I've shown, is the capacity for language. When we *name* our pets we give them perhaps an interim status, somewhere between object and subject. But when we give fictional animals language, we accord them full subjectivity. Consider Blinky Bill, Dorothy Wall's naughty koala "bear" character, Beatrix Potter's Peter Rabbit and Wilbur the pig in *Charlotte's Web*, all of whom talk and express thoughts, opinions and feelings and who are likely to evoke sympathetic identification in child readers. Because talking animals are subjects, their flesh, like human flesh, is neither morally nor ethically edible. Children's stories that feature talking animals tend to uphold Peter Singer's argument for a vegetarian diet. In *Animal Liberation* Singer argues that the capacity of animals to experience pleasure and suffering implies that they have their own interests that should not be violated. Therefore, he believes, they should not be beyond the realms of moral and ethical consideration. He argues that to inflict suffering on animals, including killing them for food, is a form of "speciesism" that parallels racism and sexism within human relationships. These utilitarian principles, he claims, demand the adoption of a vegetarian diet.[38] Children's literature, such as *Charlotte's Web* for example, legitimizes Singer's argument by endorsing the notion that animals have their own interests and the capacity for feeling pleasure and suffering. For the child reader, the real-life duplicity of adult culture's attitude toward animals is revealed by such stories.

Throughout *Charlotte's Web* there are references to the adult human characters' blind assumptions about the pig as meat/object and their culpable desire to fatten him up. The child reader is part of the conspiracy, uncomfortably recognizing the naivety of Wilbur's early misinterpretation of Mr. Zuckerman's comment to Lurvy, "he'll make a good pig," as "words of praise" (*Charlotte's Web*, 28). During the poignant scene when the old sheep tells Wilbur that he's being fattened up to be made into "smoked bacon and ham" and that "[a]lmost all young pigs get murdered by the farmer" (52), the reader not only sympathizes with Wilbur but must inevitably experience feelings of shared responsibility and guilt. The reader's position outside the text is thus a discomfiting one. The reader recognizes Wilbur's subjectivity and identifies with him, but is also aware that the adult characters' treatment of the pig as food/object reflects society's generalized conception of animals. The reader is able therefore to see Wilbur both as object-to-be-eaten and as subject-not-to-be-eaten. There are further moments in the text when the dual connotations of the words used to describe the pig evoke guilty amusement. Charlotte calls a meeting of the barnyard animals. She explains that she needs "a new slogan" to weave into her web so that she can continue to fool the Zuckermans into thinking, "Wilbur is an unusual pig, and therefore... [they] won't want to kill him and eat him." One of the lambs suggests "Pig Supreme" but Charlotte rejects it. "No good," she says, "It sounds like a rich dessert" (87). She decides instead on the goose's suggestion "Terrific." When yet another word is required Templeton is commissioned to fetch one from the dump.

> "How's this?' he asked, showing [an] ad. to Charlotte. 'It says CRUNCHY. 'Crunchy' would be a good word to write in your web."
> "Just the wrong idea," replied Charlotte. "Couldn't be worse. We don't want Zuckerman to think Wilbur is crunchy. He might start thinking about crisp, crunchy bacon and tasty ham. That would put ideas into his head. We must advertise Wilbur's noble qualities, not his tastiness." (96, emphasis in original)

Charlotte attempts to change Wilbur's status from object to "noble" subject using language. From the perspective of animal culture the human appetite for meat is monstrous; in terms of human culture, the animals' capacity for language in this narrative gives them subjectivity and thus makes them worthy, as Singer argues, of moral and ethical consideration. Within the narrative, however, while the animals can understand human language, the only human who can hear the animals talk is the little girl, Fern.[39] She is seen to be the most kind-hearted of the humans. She initially takes on the role of nursing mother with Wilbur as "her infant" (10), then, sitting on a milking stool every afternoon after school, she becomes a passive viewer of life in the barn (51–56). But, "as time went on" and Fern approaches puberty, she visits the barn less often: "She was growing up, and was careful to avoid childish things, like sitting on a milk stool near a pig pen" (174).

It is interesting to note how committed the adult humans in the narrative are to ignoring the subjectivity of the barnyard animals. Despite marveling over the words/language Charlotte inscribes upon her web, these are attributed to a "miracle" (84), not to their author. Despite Wilbur being named and described in words that define his subjectivity, the farmers still look upon him objectively in terms of "extra good ham and bacon" (122). The human capacity for language results in subjectivity, but because, although blatantly obvious, the animals' capacity for language is denied, their subjectivity is refused. It is only after Wilbur is awarded a special prize at the fair, which turns out to be "the greatest moment in Mr. Zuckerman's life. [Because i]t is deeply satisfying to win a prize in front of a lot of people" (153–54), that the farmer relents and decides not to slaughter him. Adult duplicity is revealed in this narrative, just as with Horowitz's evil Herod Sayle. Adults don't really *care* for animals: animals are just meat to them. In the context of *Charlotte's Web*, where animals are more humane than humans, where they care about and nurture each other, tell stories, sing lullabies, and read and write words; where the moral, compassionate ones at least, eat within a logic and culture acceptable to the reader, the human adult protagonists' blindness to the pig's humanitarian subjectivity, and their carnivorous appetites, verge on cannibalism.

No doubt some children who've read *Charlotte's Web* decide not to eat meat, at least not for a while. Certainly many young adults experiment with vegetarianism although not all remain committed to the ideal. White's text questions the morality of meat eating and reveals the duplicity of adults' utilitarian attitudes toward animals but it does not explicitly advocate vegetarianism. There is no alternative to the adults' duplicitous position within the narrative. The lesson children are likely to learn from this story is that eating animals isn't ethical, but the majority of people do it anyway. As part of Western Christian-derived culture, most children have no choice but to accept this duplicitous position as their own and learn to do what the rest of us generally do, which involves psychologically and semantically creating distance between the image of the pig and the pork on our plates.

The levels of horror experienced by the children and Puddleglum in C. S. Lewis's *The Silver Chair*, when they are staying at the house of the giants in Narnia and discover that they have been eating a talking stag, illustrate the reason why we like to maintain as much distance as possible between the notion of ourselves as human and animals as an entirely separate, oppositional category:

This discovery didn't have exactly the same effect on all of them. Jill, who was new to that world, was sorry for the poor stag and thought it rotten of the giants to have killed him. Scrubb, who had been in that world before and had at least one Talking beast as his dear friend, felt horrified; as you might feel about a murder. But Puddleglum, who was Narnian born, was sick and faint, and felt as you would feel if you found you had eaten a baby.[40]

The closer the source of our meat comes to being ourselves the more horrific the idea of eating it is. As far as Puddleglum is concerned he has broken the ultimate taboo, cannibalism, hence his extreme reaction.

Charles Lutwidge Dodgson (Lewis Carroll) was apparently a fastidious and austere eater and an early member of the anti-vivisectionist league.[41] He succinctly and humorously captures the whole monstrous business of having to eat to live when Alice attends a dinner-party with the Red and White Queens in *Through the Looking Glass*. She is most anxious about having to carve the joint: "You look a little shy: let me introduce you to that leg of mutton," said the Red Queen. "Alice – Mutton: Mutton – Alice." But, when Alice takes up the knife and fork, the Red Queen reprimands her: "It isn't etiquette to cut anyone you've been introduced to" (*Alice*, 234).[42] Having been introduced, of course, which involves an exchange of *names*, the leg of mutton has been awarded subject status and Alice cannot consume it. In Tenniel's 1871 illustration, the leg of mutton has a smugly smiling face and is performing a most genteel bow. When the plum pudding arrives at the table, Alice, having learnt her lesson, is most anxious *not* to be introduced this time, "or we shall get no dinner at all" (235). But the Queen goes ahead anyway. When Alice, who is very hungry by this time, does serve up some pudding, the Pudding indignantly protests: "What impertinence!...I wonder how you'd like it, if I were to cut a slice of *you*, you creature" (235, emphasis in original).[43] Despite the topsy-turvy nature of this world, the logic of Western cultural food rules is maintained. Alice is demoted to the status of creature/object because she attempted to eat a talking subject.

The arbitrary distinction between the eaters and the eaten is revealed when instead of the White Queen, "there was a leg of mutton sitting in the chair" and the Queen herself disappears into a tureen of soup. "There was not a moment to be lost. Already several of the guests were lying down in the dishes, and the soup-ladle was walking up the table towards Alice's chair" (237). This nightmarish scenario brings into question the logic of our cultural beliefs. We are all "creatures" just like the animals we slaughter for food and to "cut a slice" of a creature is, as the Pudding points out, just as much of an injustice as it would be if someone were to cut a slice of us. Audible to the human audience or not, the creatures in

White's, Lewis's, and Carroll's narratives all protest their desire and right to live. But what of an animal who apparently wants to be eaten?

The diners at *The Restaurant at the End of the Universe* "meet the meat" on the menu, just as Alice did.[44] But, the moral dilemmas surrounding the eating of meat have supposedly been solved in this version of the future by breeding an animal that "actually wanted to be eaten and was capable of saying so clearly and distinctly" (*Restaurant*, 93).

> A large dairy animal approached Zaphod Beeblebrox's table, a large fat meaty quadruped of the bovine type with large watery eyes, small horns and what might almost have been an ingratiating smile on its lips.
>
> "Good evening," it lowed and sat back heavily on its haunches, "I am the main Dish of the Day. May I interest you in parts of my body? ...
>
> "Something off the shoulder perhaps?" suggested the animal, "braised in a white wine sauce? ... or the rump is very good ... I've been exercising it and eating plenty of grain, so there's a lot of good meat there ... "
>
> "That's absolutely horrible," exclaimed Arthur [a human from Earth's past], "the most revolting thing I've ever heard ... [I] don't want to eat an animal that's standing there inviting me to ... it's heartless."
>
> "Better than eating an animal that doesn't want to be eaten," said Zaphod.
>
> "That's not the point," Arthur protested. Then he thought about it for a moment. "Alright," he said, "maybe it is the point ... I think I'll just have a green salad ... " (92–93)

Zaphod, however, orders steak (rare) and the animal goes off to shoot itself, but not before giving Arthur a friendly wink and reassuring him: "Don't worry, sir ... I'll be very humane" (94). As I suggested in relation to Wilbur the pig's sensibilities, some animals can be seen to be more humane than humans, hence the irony of this animal's last words. The absolute horror and revulsion Arthur feels is related to the fact that speaking subjects, whether they profess a desire to be eaten or not, cannot be consumed. If Arthur did so it would be an act of cannibalism, one subject devouring another. Like Singer, Arthur has no choice but to retreat to a vegetarian diet. Within the context of children's literature, eating the flesh of a talking animal definitely transgresses cultural food rules. Outside the narrative, traditional food rules generally override concerns about the ethics of meat eating although psychological and social anxieties are perhaps revealed in the tendency for Westerners to be reluctant to eat the flesh of a wider range of animals and their disgusted reactions to those who do.

BLURRING BOUNDARIES

While a hint of transgression can appeal to the palate,[45] food rules are not meant to be broken. They are, however, often transgressed in metaphor and fiction. One significant peculiarity of Western culture relates to the way we actively encourage our children to sympathetically identify with animals. One of the ways we do this is by creating narratives with talking animal heroes. Another way is by giving our children *pet* names that include lamb, kitten, and possum. To express our feelings of love we also often refer to children in terms of gastronomic metaphors such as pudding, sweetie, sugar-pie, honey-bun, sausage, pickle, pumpkin, and even lamb chop. This means that, as well as being culturally linked with animals through discourses of the natural child, children are semantically and emotionally linked to animals and other items of food. Just how metaphorical are we being when we refer to our children in culinary terms? Sometimes tiny infants can seem to be so scrumptious that, as my sister recently said about her new granddaughter, "you just want to kiss and nibble on babies... I can't help myself... it's almost like you want to eat them up!"[46]

The conflation between food (especially sweet food) and love is well known. As Rosalind Coward suggests, there is "something about loving [that] reminds us of food, not potatoes or lemons, but mainly sweet things—ripe fruits, cakes and puddings."[47] She explains that endearments based on sweet food items in particular make reference to a period when sugar was a valued luxury item only available to the wealthiest groups. Such endearments carry associations of great value, high price, and luxury. Similar connotations relate to endearments such as treasure, precious, jewel, and pearl (Coward, 90).

Despite cultural taboos against cannibalism adults often play games with children in which we pretend that we are going to eat them.[48] These games typically involve blowing raspberries on the baby's tummy, kissing, nibbling and sucking their toes and fingers, growling and playing giants or monsters, as in "the monster's going to eat you up!" (see also Warner 2000, 139–46). Adults understand the food rules and the way they can be bent but not broken. But children, unfamiliar with the way metaphors work, must find adults' behavior very troubling. Talking about her aunt, one of the baby twins in P. L. Travers' *Mary Poppins* shows how disturbing adults' duplicity can be:

> She liked my trick, too, said Barbara complacently. I took off both
> my socks and she said I was so sweet she would like to eat me.
> Isn't it funny—when *I* say I'd like to eat something I really mean it.
> Biscuits and Rusks and the knobs of beds and so on. Grown-ups

never mean what they say, it seems to me. She couldn't have *really* wanted to eat me, could she?[49]

When, as Marina Warner points out, living requires eating and eating requires the death of another living thing, it is difficult to avoid questioning how is it that I am exempt. How can I avoid eating badly/wrongly and becoming what I eat? And, most importantly, how can I avoid being eaten? Acts of literal and metaphorical consumption abound in myth, legend, fairy story, in literature for both adults and children and in popular culture, and the imagery of eating pervades our language (Warner 2000, 138).

Thinking about the realities of having and being a corporeal body that needs to eat in order to live forces recognition of the body's absence of secure and finite boundaries between its inside and the outside. This undoubtedly causes psychological and social anxieties because it also blurs structural dualisms which rely upon the clear delineation between inside and outside, self and other, subject and object, human and animal, reason and passion, mind and body, order and chaos, and, ultimately, male and female, adult and child. That the process of eating should be subject to strict social rules is entirely logical: it is not at all surprising that a clear-cut definition of ourselves as civilized humans should depend, among other things, upon what and how we eat. Children's literature may well be used to question adult culture but ultimately, like Fern, the little girl who takes care of Wilbur when he's a piglet, children must grow up, put away childish things, and fall in with the majority, assuming boundaries even where these are blatantly arbitrary and create misogyny.

The Good Little Girl

It's funny how often they say to me, "Jane?
Have you been a *good* girl?
Have you been a *good* girl?"
And when they have said it, they say it again,
"Have you been a *good* girl?
Have you been a *good* girl?"

I go to a party, I go out to tea,
I go to an aunt for a week at the sea,
I come back from school or from playing a game;
Wherever I come from, it's always the same:
"Well?
Have you been a *good* girl, Jane?"

It's always the end of the loveliest day:
"Have you been a *good* girl?
Have you been a *good* girl?"
I went to the Zoo, and they waited to say:
"Have you been a *good* girl?
Have you been a *good* girl?"

Well, what did they think that I went there to do?
And why should I want to be bad at the Zoo?
And should I be likely to say if I had?
So that's why it's funny of Mummy and Dad,
This asking and asking, in case I was bad,
"Well?
Have you been a *good* girl, Jane?"

— A. A. Milne, *Now We Are Six*[1]

2

"HAVE YOU BEEN A *GOOD* GIRL?"

Manners and Mores at Teatime

Everything's got a moral, if only you can find it.

—Lewis Carroll, *Alice's Adventures in Wonderland*[2]

The practice of using meals as a measure of the child's adjustment to the social order, the child's observance of social requirements, is especially pronounced in English children's literature. The extent to which tea-time in particular is used to dramatize states of harmony or disharmony is remarkable to a North American reader.

—Wendy Katz, "Some Uses of Food in Children's Literature"[3]

FROM ITS BEGINNING children's literature has disciplined children; we commonly expect tales told to children to contain a moral or a lesson, even if it is not blatantly obvious. Fairy tales, such as those written by Charles Perrault toward the end of the seventeenth century, were appropriated from oral folklore. They were aimed at an educated upper-class audience that also included children. Perrault transformed the stories he heard, deliberately producing, in his collections of tales, a sort of literary discourse that reflected prevalent social values, manners and mores.[4]

As Norbert Elias has shown, there were profound changes in standards of social intercourse, etiquette, and dress in Europe during the sixteenth, seventeenth, and eighteenth centuries.[5] This dynamic evolution, recorded in numerous books on manners in which standards were expressly codified, is referred to by Elias as the civilizing process. A short treatise called "On Civility of Children" by Erasmus of Rotterdam, for example, was widely influential and introduced as a text book for English schoolboys in 1534. It warns against a range of "barbarous" habits such as failing to use a cloth to blow one's nose, dipping one's fingers into the broth (like a peasant), and even double-dipping (Elias 1939, 53–57). The same views were expressed to the peasantry via cheap pamphlets known as "Blue Books." New rules, which emphasized hierarchical social and familial relationships, cultivated feelings of disgust and shame in relation to what had previously been perceived of as "natural" body functions and corporeality.

Special attention was paid to childhood as a newly recognized "separate phase of growth ... [and] the crucial base for the future development of the individual character" (Zipes 1991, 21).

> Childhood became identified as a state of "natural innocence" and potentially corruptible by the end of the seventeenth century and the civilizing of children—social indoctrination through anxiety provoking effects and positive reinforcement—operated on all levels in manners, speech, sex, literature and play. (23)

A gap or discrepancy grew between the notion of adulthood as a civilized, rational, and controlled state, in contrast to childhood, which came to be seen as a primitive state governed by voracious appetites in need of discipline.

From the first commercially produced book specifically for children, Newbery's *A Little Pretty Pocket-Book* (1744), children's literature has reflected adult views about children's behavior. Early stories condemned idleness and denounced disobedience while promoting acculturation and compliance to adult manners and mores. The vast majority of tales written for children, from Newbery's time on, have "played a powerful role in constructing the ideal child as a docile child."[6]

In *Good Girls Make Good Wives: Guidance for Girls in Victorian Fiction* Judith Rowbotham shows that the use of children's fiction as a means of social regulation was clearly recognized by middle-class adults during the Victorian period when it was presumed that strict control over their reading matter would help to ensure that impressionable young minds (especially those of girls) received "only the correct and highest of impressions."[7] This especially applied, Rowbotham argues, to impressions about the "traditional" view of women, so that fiction for girls confirmed that women "were naturally formed to occupy the more passive, private sphere of the household and home where their inborn emotional talents would serve them best" (6). The didactic fiction produced for Victorian girls was thus "fuelled by the wish to control as far as possible, if not stifle, independent feminine desires" (12). In their fiction, good girls always had controlled and modest desires; they were compliant and submissive to those with authority over them.

The notion of the creation and maintenance, through discourse, of girls' desire to be good is intrinsic to Lynne Vallone's thesis in *Disciplines of Virtue*, which examines "girls' culture" in the eighteenth and nineteenth centuries. She shows how the behavior of young women and girls was constantly and repressively under scrutiny. The "successful" girl had to internalize implicit and explicit ideological messages communicated by her family, her community, her social class, and through books. She was socialized by prevailing discourses to believe that she could achieve happiness and virtue through self-control. This involved changing her girlish nature, which was characterized by desire, hunger, anger, ignorance, and aggression. Her goal was "beautiful womanly conduct."[8] For middle-class Victorian women, "beautiful womanly conduct" included being spiritual, nonsexual, and self-disciplined.[9] The ideal woman was represented as a creature of disinterested love and nurture and the moral center of both the home and society. To conform to this ideal, women and girls had to downplay every aspect of their physicality, including desire and appetite. Self-restraint was an integral part of the Victorian female's life: "she was expected to control her behavior, her speech, and her appetite as signs of her dominion over her desires." Anna Krugovoy Silver shows that there are significant differences between representations of girls' eating and boys' eating in Victorian children's literature, revealing that male and female hunger had different implications in Victorian culture. Most significantly, she argues, criticism of girls' appetite focuses on hunger as a sign of sexual desire, more frequently than does criticism of boys' appetite (56).

Fictional food is often used to discipline fictional children and literary meals (especially, in the British classics, teatime) are frequently used to carry both implicit and explicit socializing messages to readers. The gendered skewing of behavioral expectations is on the one hand a reflection of the social valorization of stereotypical masculinity (itself a cultural construct) and on the other, a reflection of cultural anxieties associated with the perceived biological and social roles of women, and a need to control the appetites and desires of the girl child. While the openly didactic fiction of the Victorian era has given way to a generally more therapeutic style, much contemporary fiction still reinforces traditional stereotypical gender roles. Good girls must be very, very good or else they are horrid,[10] whereas boys behaving badly are seen to be merely displaying masculine traits.

"SHORT COMMONS AND HARD FARE"

We know that narrative texts, including books, movies, and even advertising, have enormous influence upon the lives of contemporary children. Various theories, ranging from anthropological, sociological, and psychological to literary disciplines, confirm that children's minds and bodies are shaped by adult concerns. We also know that food and eating are not just of biological importance but are intrinsically linked to the social. Fictional food events and the depiction of mannerly or coarse behavior are instrumental in teaching proper socially acceptable behaviors including those relating to gender.

Margaret Visser has written extensively on table manners and their origins. Table manners are as old as human society itself and are vital to its existence. Indeed, she believes that eating rituals

> [gave] rise to many basic human characteristics, such as kinship systems (who belongs with whom; which people eat together), language (for discussing food past, present, and future, for planning the acquisition of food, and deciding how to divide it out while preventing fights), technology (how to kill, cut, keep, and carry), and morality (what is a just slice?)[11]

Visser also points out that a display of extremely bad manners can cause others to experience us as "threatening, unpredictable, or disgusting" and she adds, "we know that we cannot commune unless 'respect' (which entails social distance and physical propriety) is maintained" (298). Manners and mores are intrinsic to all levels of society and the maintenance of a cultural status quo. Instilling them into a child's consciousness forms a vital part of her or his upbringing. Children are "brought up:" the verb is passive, as Visser notes, "the bringing is done to the child—and the implication is that the road travelled leads to a higher level" (40). Interestingly, Visser maintains that the "universal purpose of good behavior is to demonstrate how *un*like beasts we mannerly people are." After all, it is well known that dreadful behavior is equated with lack of "breeding" (63, emphasis in original). So, proper mannerly behavior, just like proper eating, as I argued in the previous chapter, helps to maintain the opposition between humans and animals, and fends off the image of the food chain. However, as Lyman points out, learning how to behave properly, particularly at the table, is not always a bowl of cherries:

> We are told to eat nicely and not make a mess; or to eat so we will grow big and strong; or not to eat foods that will rot our teeth or make us obese. If we won't eat the cold mashed squash set before us, it is implied that we must somehow bear the guilt for the

starving millions of the world. When parents pretend the food is really delicious, they begin to establish the child's realization that they are not always truthful.[12]

These sorts of rules are commonplace though they vary according to culture and class and have certainly changed over time as Elias has shown. Some of the prohibitions and exhortations listed in Whalley's book of rules for children's behavior, first published in 1701, include:

Rule 1. Come not to the Table unwash'd or not comb'd.
Rule 2. Sit not down till thou art bidden by thy Parents or Superiors.
Rule 6. Find not fault with any thing that is given thee.
Rule 9. Speak not at the Table; if thy Superiors be discoursing, meddle not with the matter.
Rule 21. Lean not thy Elbow on the Table, or on the back of thy chair. (cited by Smith, 7)

As Vallone shows, a comparison of the rules and regulations surrounding food-related activities is particularly fruitful for tracing changing notions of childhood throughout history (Vallone 1995, 47). Eighteenth-century mores demanded that children be subjected not only to strict formalities regarding how they behaved at the dinner table, but also what they were allowed to eat and even the fiction they consumed. Eighteenth-century rationalist Maria Edgeworth believed that fantasy was bad for children. Edgeworth, whose *The Parent's Assistant* was first published in 1796, believed that children's minds had limited storage capacity and that stories of giants and fairies took up space that could be put to better use. While a child might prefer the *taste* of the fantastic, it was their instructor's duty to control the child's palate. "Why should we vitiate their taste, and spoil their appetite, by suffering them to feed upon sweetmeats?" she asks.[13] Indeed, in the Georgian era, fairy tales were considered to be in "*poor taste*" (Vallone 1995, 48, emphasis in original). It is interesting to note the confluence of good taste and morality implied in this discourse, which relates not only to notions of class (see Elias 1978 and Bourdieu 1977) but also to the ideas about the eating body (eating good food connotes subjectivity) discussed in the previous chapter.

Edgeworth's beliefs reflect the childrearing discourses of her era, which were possibly derived from the Puritan concepts contained in John Locke's *Some Thoughts Concerning Education* (1693). Locke's treatise, which laid down principles for child rearing, appears to have had considerable influence in Britain. He recommended that children should "be brought to deny their appetites: and their minds, as well as bodies, be made vigorous, by the custom of having their inclinations in subjection and their bodies exercised with hardships."[14] Locke's writings emphasized the notion that, as the bearers of original sin, children's primitive, untamed appetites were innate and that their underlying sexual energies had to be rigidly controlled, until such time as they had learned self-control. Robert Crawford shows that bodily control mechanisms, particularly self-control, encompassing the qualities of self-discipline, self-restraint, and will-power, have since become fundamental concepts in the Western system of values. Historically such concepts were part of religious asceticism; they underpin philosophical systems and have become components of the work ethic (Weber 1930), and of the "civilizing process" (Elias 1978).[15] It is significant that in the eighteenth century appetitive control thus became an issue of *morality* and that parents were deemed to be responsible for ensuring the moral integrity of their children through applying rigid controls over their appetite and behavior, including their *taste* in reading material, as Edgeworth suggested.

Locke's recommendations also included that children should be fed what were considered to be foods appropriate to their nonadult status: nothing too rich or likely to excite them. He suggested a largely farinaceous (starchy) diet, low-fat and low-salt. Meat was to be served only once a day, with no sugar or high seasoning, with milk or water to drink and perhaps a little fruit. In the eighteenth century, nature was equated with purity, and culture was seen to be essentially corrupting. Thus, the more elaborate and luxurious a food the more it was opposed to nature and seen as corrupting and unsuitable for children. Children's food became the vehicle for their control and subjugation.[16] In some instances the regimen under which children were reared was extreme. In her *Life of Charlotte Bronte* (1857), Mrs. Gaskell reports that the "half-starved" Bronte girls were lectured, when they pleaded for more to eat, on the sin of caring for carnal things and of pampering greedy appetites. This reflected the widely held view that "short commons and hard fare were good discipline for rebellious youth."[17] The behavior of eighteenth-century children was closely monitored, and they were refused food and fiction considered to be bad for them in terms of being too rich for the physical body, or in poor taste in terms of being too fantastic for the rational mind, for fear that excitement leading to immorality and irrationality would result from their consumption.

THE DEATH OF FEMALE DESIRE

This harsh (by today's standards) routine is reflected in Edgeworth's tale "The Birthday Present" in which Rosamond questions her mother about her forthcoming birthday celebrations. Rosamond reveals that she would

dearly love to have "a great meal," "new playthings," and everyone "drinking her health" on her birthday. But her mother deliberately misunder-
stands the little girl in order to reveal her foolishness. She asks Rosamond
whether more can be eaten on a birthday than any other day. Whether
new playthings are better than old. And what logic lies behind the need
for different treatment on a birthday than on any other day. Although
Rosamond is sure that there must be an answer to these questions, since
she so much desires to make her birthday a special occasion, she cannot
think of one. By the end of the story birthday festivities have been denounced as an excuse for a spoiled child's tantrums and falsehoods, and
Rosamond has learned that if she is good everyday she will earn everyday
love, respect, and meals, and that these are worth far more than the momentary self-admiration, excessive sentiment, and treats that result from
the celebration of a birthday.[18] The moral to this story is clearly that little
girls must have modest desires. Thus, according to Georgian concepts of
the child, and in particular the girl-child, greed is to be condemned and
desire must be sublimated.

Christina Rossetti also features a birthday party in her three-part
story "Speaking Likenesses" (1874). Her work communicates rationalist
moral principles similar to Edgeworth's, and she also explicitly condemns
her female protagonists' sensual appetites. As Silver remarks, Rossetti
emphatically praises the renunciation of inappropriate food (and thus
sexual desire), denouncing gluttony by associating it with selfishness and
sexuality (159). "Speaking Likenesses" is a story that consists of three
loosely related tales narrated by a pedantic aunt to her nieces. In the first
tale, eight-year-old Flora's birthday party turns out to be a disaster. She
and her guests behave badly and she is, by Victorian standards, a poor
and ungenerous host. The children quarrel over sugar-plums—who has
eaten more and who picked out only the big ones—and find fault with
every dish presented for dinner. They grumble, whine, whimper, and
wrangle, tossing "the apple of discord to and fro as if it had been a pretty
plaything."[19] They quarrel all afternoon until Flora finally takes off down
a yew-lined lane to get away from her guests. What follows is a dream
sequence in which Flora enters an enchanted apartment where a birthday
feast is taking place. Flora is finally offered some strawberries and cream,
but the birthday "Queen," who is "ugly" with a red face and a scowl, refuses to let her eat any because "it's my birthday, and everything is mine"
("Speaking Likenesses," 333). The Queen's birthday guests are the speaking
likenesses of the tripartite story's title. They are allegories of the various
bad behaviors exhibited by the children at Flora's birthday party. There
is a boy bristling "with prickly quills," another whose body is "facetted at
very sharp angles," a third "hung round with hooks like fishhooks." One

girl "exuded a sticky fluid" and another "was slimy and slipped through the hands" (335).[20] Vallone suggests these likenesses represent "pinching, unctuousness, unpleasantness, and unwanted touching" (48).

Flora tastes not a morsel while the Queen and the birthday guests eat "quite greedily," gulping

> cold turkey, lobster salad, stewed mushrooms, raspberry tart, cream cheese, a bumper of champagne, a meringue, a strawberry ice, sugared pine apple, some greengages... Several of the boys seemed to think nothing of a whole turkey at a time: and the Queen consumed with her own mouth and of sweets alone one quart of strawberry ice, three pine apples, two melons, a score of meringues, and about four dozen sticks of angelica, as Flora counted. ("Speaking Likenesses," 339)

The monstrosity of these children is confirmed by what Silver refers to as their "supernatural" consumption of food (159) while Flora's characterization as the good girl is confirmed by her determination to "not take so much as a fork" ("Speaking Likenesses," 339), recalling the Victorian cultural ideal whereby "small appetites are symbolic of virtue, self-control and femininity" (Silver, 161). The feast itself is, however, attractive, and arguably has subversive potential. Flora (and the reader) must watch the Likenesses gobbling tantalizingly exotic food. The food described is appetizing and appealing, so no disgust is evoked, except perhaps for adults by excess.[21] There is therefore pleasure, albeit second-hand, for the (child) viewer within and outside the narrative. This pleasure is soured or subverted, particularly for the female spectator, however, by the didacticism implicit in the text. The lessons/morals being taught differ according to gender. On the one hand, while the boys are framed as monstrous, they "think nothing" of consuming a whole turkey. Thus, it seems, their monstrosity is negated or dismissed and they are given license and autonomy to act greedily because they are boys. On the other hand, the "Queen" of the nightmare birthday party is intrinsically condemned through the subtext which emphasizes her voracious orality and greed through the archetypal image conjured up by the significant phrase "consumed with her own mouth" and the listing and counting of the fruits and ices she eats. Even, I would argue, the *volume* of the portions she consumes (a "quart [over a litre] of strawberry ice, three pine apples, two melons, a score of meringues, and about four dozen sticks of angelica") emphasizes the size of the mouth with which she consumes and the extent of her insatiable appetite. The mouth of the girl or woman is a site of cultural anxiety, being linked, through universal mythological images and psychology, to the mysterious and fearful generative capacity of the female, the *vagina dentata* and fears of castration, as much classic art and contemporary horror films continue to show.[22] Even the *fruit* that Flora/the Queen consumes is arguably significant. It is, after all, Eve, the original fruit-eater, who is blamed for the entrance of sin and death into the world.[23] This feasting fantasy is framed as tantalizing and seductive but is inevitably corrupting. Flora's and the reader's desire for the food is deliberately created and then guilt is induced by the textual condemnation of Flora. This narrative thus functions "unashamedly, to take the child reader *in*"[24] using food as a tool of seduction. Desire is created, within the text and in the reader, but it is then condemned and constructed as sinful.

Flora awakes from her dream and has learned her lesson, as the narrator-aunt confirms:

> And I think if she lives to be nine years old and give another birthday party, she is likely on that occasion to be even less like the birthday Queen of her troubled dream than was the Flora of eight years old: who, with dear friends and playmates and pretty presents, yet scarcely knew how to bear a few trifling disappointments, or how to be obliging and good-humoured under slight annoyances. ("Speaking Likenesses," 342)

The lesson Flora learns is that gluttony is a sin and that the female appetite (including sexual desire, as Silver points out) must be firmly controlled. Rossetti makes it clear that Flora has not dreamed of any fantastic wonderland (as Alice does) but only of a reflection of the world she knows. As Auerbach and Knoepflmacher argue, "Flora dreams inescapability. Her dream vision is an uncompromising indoctrination."[25] There is neither hope nor pleasure in her dream, nor much in the lives of those to whom, within the narrative structure, the tale is being told. Not only does the tale of Flora contain dire warnings of the punishments likely to be endured by noncompliant little girls, the subtextual relationship between the embittered aunt/narrator and the group of girls to whom she tells the story is relevant. Initially the aunt literally bribes the girls into helping her with her sewing, proclaiming, "no help no story" ("Speaking Likenesses," 343). She bullies them into silence, deals sarcastically with their interjections, and refuses them any level of control over the direction or content of the tales she tells. This reflects the acculturation Victorian little girls must endure in order to overcome their "girlish" natures and become socially acceptable women.

The second tale (which is something of a nonstory) in "Speaking Likenesses" involves Edith, who has been promised a "gipsy feast" by her mother (343). The feast is to be substantial, including "sandwiches and tarts," "Cold fowls, and a syllabub, and champagne, and tea and coffee, and potato-rolls, and lunns, and tongue" (344). Somewhat precociously and perhaps in order to hasten the feast, Edith offers to take the kettle and decides to light the fire. Unable to light it, and with the kettle in any case empty, Edith's situation is "neither pleasant nor dignified" and she begins to cry (346). She is framed as willful, self-centered, and ineffective and the anticipated feast never takes place. Importantly, Edith's tale reiterates the lesson Flora (and the reader) has already rehearsed. It creates desire in its promise of a substantial feast, which is then frustrated.

Being good and the curbing of desire form the moral behind the third of Rossetti's trio of tales, which is a story along the lines of "Little Red Riding Hood:" Maggie makes a journey through the woods to return a basket of goodies to its rightful owner. Despite being lonely, cold, hungry, and tired she resists a whole series of temptations. The first is presented by a boisterous group of children (who are apparently "those monstrous children over again" from the first tale ["Speaking Likenesses," 354]) who invite her to play. The second temptation arrives in the form of a boy with no eyes whose "face exhibited only one feature, and that was a wide mouth…full of teeth and tusks" (355–56). He clearly plays the Wolf to Maggie's Red Riding Hood and is a speaking likeness of her own hunger (Auerbach and Knoepflmacher 1992, 355, n6). He begs for food from her basket but she must refuse him. In effect, she is not only responsible for her own desire/appetite but also for his. The third temptation manifests as a "kindly" "glowing gipsy fire" before which "some dozen persons" who represent figures of death, sat "toasting themselves…all yawning in nightcaps or dropping asleep." Maggie makes "desperate" efforts to resist and, despite being "Chilled to the bone, famished, cross, and almost fit to cry with disappointment" ("Speaking Likenesses," 358), she completes her task and returns home where she is greeted by "a loving welcoming hug" and a supper of tea and buttered toast in front of the parlor fire (360). While Flora is punished for her lack of self-control and Edith is denied her feast because she is willful and precocious, only Maggie is rewarded because she proves herself to be a good girl, with modest desires and a controlled appetite.

Rossetti's tripartite story reinforces the imperative that little girls' desires must be denied. The reason why little girls' desires were particularly targeted was that, as Rowbotham shows, there was an inherent contradiction in the Victorian view of women: while they were the upholders of moral standards for society, they could, if not properly guarded and protected from the contaminations of the public sphere by men, become the frailer sex morally as well as physically. Women were considered to be potentially both angels and prostitutes, and thus little girls had to be rigorously trained to resist temptations (Rowbotham 1989, 6). Didactic Victorian fictions, such as Rossetti's, deliver the uncompromising message that salvation or virtuousness would be achieved only through the death of desire: while Flora dreams of the savagery of growing up and Edith becomes a frustrated "nonheroine of a nonstory," effectively mocking narrative expectations and subtextually denying desire, only Maggie achieves something like a happy ending "by killing all her needs" (Auerbach and Knoepflmacher 1992, 322). Additionally, within the subtextual narrative, the five little nieces listening to their aunt's tales must bend their wills to hers. Thus, on a number of levels Rossetti's "Speaking Likenesses" serves to reveal the unrelenting mean-spiritedness of the adult world's expectations of girls' behavior and the lack of hope and absence of pleasure that the world holds for them. As Gillian Avery confirms, Victorian values, reflected in literature for children, tended to regard the girl child as someone who "has to be beaten out on the anvil of a stern and repressive regime to shape her for her new station in life"[26] that new station being adulthood and beautiful womanly conduct. In terms of Judith Butler's notion of gender as a strategy performed under duress,[27] it can be seen that Victorian girls and women were under considerable physical and moral pressure to perform an acceptable feminine role which restricted their desire and denied them power within society.

ALICE'S "CURIOUS DREAM"

While I have grouped Edgeworth's and Rossetti's fictions together because of their inherent and explicit didactic discourse, it is interesting to note that Rossetti actually wrote "Speaking Likenesses" after, and in response to, Lewis Carroll's much more child-centered *Alice's Adventures in Wonderland* (1865). The emphasis in Rossetti's and Carroll's respective works is very different. Whereas Carroll wanted to keep his dream child a little girl forever, Rossetti's girls are forced to accede to adult responsibilities and seem to have no carefree childhood at all.

Auerbach and Knoepflmacher argue that many Victorian women writers, like Rossetti, who wrote parodies of *Alice,* recognized in his sentimental fantasies Carroll's need "to detain, refrain, and contain the growing girl." Carroll's needs were thus "totally inimical to [these women's] own yearning[s] for autonomy and authority" (Auerbach and Knoepflmacher 1992, 6). Carolyn Sigler concludes that "Speaking Likenesses" is an aggressive critique that deliberately satirizes not only *Alice,* but also the didactic conventions of Victorian fairy tales and domestic fiction, together with the gender conventions that inform them.[28] In this respect narratives such as Rossetti's can be read as darkly subversive and the underlying message they contain seen perhaps to be not aimed at the children their tales are ostensibly addressed to, but at restrictive Victorian society itself.

Carroll's fantasy appears to reject the didacticism, the moralism, and the piety prevalent in many other Victorian stories for children. And, as the dining table is undoubtedly in reality "a constraining and controlling device, a place where children eat under the surveillance of adults" (Visser, 54), it is not surprising that Carroll's project led him to introduce the scenario of high-tea into *Alice's Adventures in Wonderland*. The Mad Hatter's Tea Party, a parody of the formal British meal, has become one of the most famous of all literary meals. It is also a microcosm of Wonderland as a whole in that the problems Alice encounters at the table are largely to do with differences in opinion over manners, mores, and language. While in Wonderland, Alice and the reader are constantly reminded of the normal *good* behavior of real life by being presented with its nonsensical opposite.

As Alice approaches the tea table, the narrative describes how the March Hare and the Hatter are resting their elbows on the sleeping Dormouse and using it as a cushion which, as Alice observes, must be "very uncomfortable for the Dormouse" (*Alice*, 60). Elbows are notoriously problematic at mealtimes as Whalley's Rule 21 (above) confirms, and Carroll was no doubt aware. But Alice is also given license to behave in ways contrary to Victorian social niceties and to ignore the subsequent condemnation: although warned off by cries of "No room! No room!" Alice indignantly declares, "There's plenty of room!" and sits down "in a large arm-chair," thus assertively making a space for herself. She ignores what polite society (Whalley's Rule 2) and the March Hare tell her about this breach in etiquette.[29] In this encounter, and throughout Carroll's narrative, power relations constantly change or shift. Alice often acts and speaks assertively, contradicting and subverting Victorian ideologies about the girl child's social position.

When the March Hare offers Alice some wine, she looks around the table and sees nothing but tea. "I don't see any wine," she remarked. "There isn't any," said the March Hare. "Then it wasn't very civil of you to offer it," said Alice angrily" (*Alice*, 60). The Hatter and the March Hare are to all intents and purposes, grown-ups and it would clearly not be polite for Alice, as a child, to answer an adult back in this way in reality. She asserts her subjectivity, behaving as if she is their equal, which is certainly not how the majority of Victorian adults regarded children. There is evidently some slippage between the categories of adult and child in Carroll's fantasy as well as between those of animal and human. The "adults" at the tea party similarly behave badly (although both seem to be aware of proper social etiquette[30]) and again the power-relations shift in favor of Alice as she takes on the role of teacher/parent reproaching them for their transgressions. The Hatter's first words to Alice are "Your hair wants cutting" and she reprimands him: "You should learn not to make personal remarks…it's very rude" (60). Although she seems to manage the "mad" partygoers fairly well, Alice doesn't particularly enjoy herself and is disturbed by their totally unconventional conduct. Altogether, she decides, it was "the stupidest tea-party I ever was at in all my life!…I'll never go *there* again!" (68, emphasis in original). Although Carroll wrote Alice's story 140 years ago and cultural mores about social etiquette and table manners have changed, the conduct of the Hatter and the March Hare is still considered to be bizarre, because both Alice and the reader know that they consistently break the rules which govern how one is *supposed* to behave at a tea party. Moreover, as she only gets bread and butter to eat and the company is disagreeable, Alice decides to leave.

The reader is reminded throughout her adventures that Alice is a sensible little girl who knows how one ought to behave. She is typical of all children in that she "always took a great interest in questions of eating and drinking" and in her considerable knowledge of food rules, such as that a diet of treacle will make little girls ill (*Alice,* 65)[31] and that drinking unidentified liquids out of bottles labeled "Drink Me" is not a good idea:

> wise little Alice was not going to do *that* in a hurry. "No, I'll look first," she said, "and see whether it's marked '*poison*' or not"; for she had read several nice little histories about children who had got burnt, and eaten up by wild beasts and other unpleasant things, all because they *would* not remember the simple rules their friends had taught them: such as, that a red-hot poker will burn you if you hold it too long; and that if you cut your finger *very* deeply with a knife, it usually bleeds; and she had never forgotten that, if you drink much from a bottle marked 'poison', it is almost certain to disagree with you, sooner or later. (13–14, emphases in original)

Although Wonderland is an upside-down world and Carroll is trying to be anti-didactic, deriding the moralizing texts ("nice little histories") generally produced by their so-called "friends" for Victorian children,[32] he signals that in life there are some rules that simply *must* be followed. Alice's reward for her sensible behavior in adhering to these "simple rules" (and the reader's vicarious reward) is to find that the bottle contains a delicious drink.

> [As the] bottle was *not* marked 'poison'... Alice ventured to taste it, and... [finding] it very nice, (it had, in fact, a sort of mixed flavour of cherry-tart, custard, pine-apple, roast turkey, toffy, and hot buttered toast,) she very soon finished it off. (14)

Alice assumes quite literally that, as the bottle is *not* marked poison, it must be safe. Her thinking and actions thus contrast with much of what occurs and is said to her in Wonderland, which cannot be taken literally or at face value. Although she has had to learn to adapt to the conditions and characters she meets in Wonderland, Alice's behavior reflects not only her awareness and knowledge of the real world, but also that she is very much aware that she is in an unreal fantasy land. From the reader's point of view, Carroll makes it clear that while Alice is in Wonderland Victorian hegemonies may be attacked and even broken down, but this does not affect the way the real world works. This is made explicit at the end of the story when Alice has grown to her "full" *real* size and proclaims, to the characters in the courtroom, in exasperation: "You're nothing but a pack of cards!" (109) thus signaling their *un*-reality. The whole pack of cards rises up into the air and flies around her only to become dead leaves fluttering down from the trees upon her face as she wakes from her dream and finds herself "lying on the bank, with her head in the lap of her sister" (109–10).

The unreality of Wonderland is reiterated by her sister's daydream about Alice's "curious dream" (110). Although in comparison to Wonderland reality is "dull," it is the *real* sounds of the sheep bells' tinkling, the "clamour of the busy farm-yard," and the "lowing of the cattle in the distance" that have induced the "dream of Wonderland" (111). Thus, Carroll deconstructs the fantasy he has created and impresses upon the reader the impossibility of both Wonderland and the dream of subverting Victorian ideologies.

Because it allows the reader time out from the established social order, Carroll's story may be classified as carnivalesque. John Stephens (following Mikhail Bakhtin) has shown that carnivalesque texts offer characters a temporary liberation from adult controls but "incorporate a safe return to social normality."[33] The transitory nature of the freedom Alice has enjoyed and its cessation are confirmed by her interaction with her older sister. Despite Alice's assertive behavior in the dream, the *real* Alice is still a good little Victorian girl: compliant and submissive to those with authority over her. When Alice wakes she must straight away do as she's told and "run in to [her] tea" as her sister instructs: "it's getting late" (*Alice,* 110).

Alice learns to adapt to the idiosyncrasies of Wonderland, changing physically and behaviorally in order to fit in. Initially Alice tends to apply the rules of Victorian social etiquette to the situations she encounters in Wonderland—she displays politeness, good manners, obedience, a socially acceptable range of worldly knowledge about the arts and the sciences, modesty, and reserve. But when these attributes fail her she has to learn new strategies, which include being more independent, resourceful, daring, adventurous, and even assertive (Honig, 77). It is perhaps significant that Alice's changes in size are initially often unexpected, uncontrolled, frightening, and inappropriate. But she learns quickly and soon becomes better equipped to deal with the social situations and characters she encounters. Alice's acquisition of the social skills necessary to negotiate her way through the rest of Wonderland is signaled by her ability to also control her physical size. With the caterpillar's help,[34] she acquires two pieces of mushroom and by "very carefully" nibbling "first at one [piece] and then at the other" she succeeds in bringing herself to her "usual" height (*Alice*, 48–49). Thereafter, (apart from when she returns to her normal "real" height and to reality at the end of the story) Alice is able to control her height by judicious mushroom nibbling. Control over her size was one of the original goals Alice had set herself as she wandered through the wood: "The first thing I've got to do . . . is to grow to my right size again; and the second thing is to find my way into that lovely garden. I think that will be the best plan" (37). Carroll signals, through explicit control of her physical presence, Alice's implicit acquisition of the relevant social presence needed to negotiate Wonderland. Significantly, Alice is rewarded for having acquired these new skills and displaying them so decisively at the Mad Hatter's Tea Party by finding "once more" the long hall with the little glass table. Using the gold key she is able at last to let herself into "the beautiful garden, among the bright flower-beds and the cool fountains" (68). Thus, Alice's stronger social presence, her assertiveness, and power are rewarded and celebrated in Carroll's narrative.

Honig argues that Alice emerges "unscathed" from her dream of Wonderland and is "transformed into a self-confident, opinionated, and forthright person" (Honig, 83), but I do not entirely agree that Alice's experiences change her so completely. It seems to me that, like Jane in A. A. Milne's poem "The Good Little Girl," Alice is good at reflecting what adults want to see. She performs in accordance with adult expectations by carefully maintaining the impression that she is a proper, polite, and controlled child. But, this is just a facade; Alice shows that she is not necessarily a perfect Victorian girl (from an adult's perspective) when she has the audacity to follow the white rabbit down the hole in the first place. Although she adheres to certain social niceties in Wonderland, she quickly adapts to her circumstances and is not always as well mannered and subservient as Victorian etiquette would demand. Alice's task, in Carroll's story, is to learn how to perform her role appropriately in a range of social situations. As Butler argues, the body is a signifier of social practice. Alice's various metamorphoses signify the learning process she goes through and her eventual acquisition of the skills necessary to cope with prevailing social situations. Significantly a variety of food items act as catalysts in this process. What Alice has learned to do in Wonderland is to perform according to her audience. She is a good girl when she has to be but she has learned to transform herself and to express assertion when it is appropriate. Alice knows what is good for her in more ways than one.

Although Alice is licensed in Carroll's narrative to indulge her desires and to try various food items, it is interesting to realize that the only "real" foods she eats are a cake decorated with currants that spell out the words "EAT ME" (15)[35] and some tea and bread and butter at the Mad Tea Party. While the liquid Alice drinks from the bottle *not* marked poison is recognizably a fantasy substance, the bread and butter she (apparently) eats at the Mad Tea Party is part of the subtext and something of a narrative diversion: "Alice did not quite know what to say to this [the Hatter has just scolded her for making personal remarks]: so she helped herself to some tea and bread-and-butter, and then turned to the Dormouse..." (65–66). This food is *real* and, importantly, is recognizably an appropriate food for a child to eat at teatime within Victorian child-rearing practices. Although Alice eats a "real" cake as well, which would have been a treat in terms of the nursery diet, she doesn't actually consume anything during her fantastic adventures that might have been considered immoral or harmful and she is therefore relatively abstemious (in relation to later fantasy narratives) and *not* changed nor harmed irrevocably by what she eats. Her morality and innocence are explicitly preserved. While Carroll has created a fantasy world where Alice can enjoy a semblance of fantasy flavors, he has no wish to make her appear to be anything other than innocent. By maintaining the opposition between fantastic and real foods, Carroll portrays Alice, wandering through the gardens of Wonderland, as the epitome of the romantic pastoral child and a symbol of uncorrupted innocence. Alice is, above all, seen to be a good girl. The efficacy of the nursery diet and its power to confer moral status are also upheld.[36]

It is also significant that the muddled and amusing way events occur or things are said in Alice's dream world are only so because they oppose known rules. As such, even though Wonderland becomes "curiouser and curiouser" (16), it merely serves to reinforce social rules about *proper* etiquette and manners. Thus, as I have already suggested, the *Alice* stories interrogate but ultimately affirm the social order. As Stephens confirms, "by breaching boundaries [carnivalesque narratives] explore where they properly lie" (Stephens 1992, 135). Carroll's story is an enjoyable fantasy and must have been a welcome break from the openly didactic oppressiveness of Victorian children's usual reading fare, but ultimately, because of the narrative's subtextual adherence to social manners and mores, it still contains implicit messages advocating and reinforcing compliance to the social order. Indeed, Carroll's containment of Alice, and his desire to produce a portrait of eternal innocence, was in itself oppressive. However, Juliet Dusinberre claims that Carroll's "pioneering" picture of Alice was probably the first book produced for children in which readers could enjoy a story in which a child is set free from parental authority.[37] In this respect it almost certainly provided a degree of therapeutic value for its readers.

CONTEMPORARY TEATIME TALES

So far I have revealed that Edgeworth's and Rossetti's explicitly didactic texts drive home the message that girls' desires and behaviors should be modest and controlled. Ultimately, Carroll's narrative, while ostensibly very different, does not belie this message. Furthermore, I have suggested that implicit in Rossetti's description of the foods the "Likenesses" devour at the birthday feast, is the notion that boys' gluttony/excessive desire is implicitly condoned while girls' greed is denoted sinful and must be carefully controlled. The differential treatment of girls' and boys' naughtiness is not confined to Georgian/Victorian literature.

Beatrix Potter's Peter Rabbit, for example, is "very naughty."[38] He is explicitly warned by his mother against going into Mr. McGregor's garden: "your Father had an accident there; he was put in a pie by Mrs. McGregor" (*Peter Rabbit*, 11), but Peter disobeys her and squeezes under the gate (12). In the vegetable garden he eats "some lettuces and some French beans; and then he ate some radishes. And then, feeling rather sick, he went to look for some parsley" (13–14). Mr. McGregor chases Peter who loses both his shoes and his "quite new" blue jacket with brass buttons in his efforts to escape (15–16). He eventually outruns Mr. McGregor and returns home to his mother who is "busy cooking." She wonders "what he had done with his clothes. It was the second little jacket and pair of shoes that Peter had lost in a fortnight!" (20). Mrs. Rabbit sends Peter to bed and doses him with camomile tea while his siblings, Flopsy, Mopsy, and Cottontail, "had bread and milk and blackberries for supper" (20). While camomile tea can be rather bitter and Peter misses out on the supper, which his (always compliant) sisters enjoy, his punishment hardly fits his crime (losing two pairs of shoes and two jackets, disobeying his mother, and nearly getting killed!). As Perry Nodelman points out, naughty Peter is being stereotypically male: noncompliant, incorrigible, heroic, and tenacious.[39] Peter Rabbit's actions and the ineffectual punishment he receives reinforce and legitimize the stereotype.

In contrast, and like Edith in Rossetti's "Speaking Likenesses," Connie, in Enid Blyton's *Faraway Tree Stories*, is punished for her precocity. She visits the Land of Treats with the other children and they come across an ice-cream man who is handing out free ice-creams:

> They were enormous, and you could have any flavor you liked.
>
> "You've only got to say 'Chocolate!' or 'Lemon!' or 'Pineapple!' and the man just dips his hand in and brings you out the right kind," said Moon-Face, happily.
>
> "He *can't* have got every flavor there," said Connie. "I shall ask for something he won't have and see what happens."
>
> So when her turn came she said solemnly, "I want a sardine ice-cream, please."
>
> And hey presto! The ice-cream man just as solemnly handed her out a large ice-cream, which was quite plainly made of sardines because the others could see a tail or two sticking out of it!
>
> "Ha, ha, Connie! Serves you right!" said Jo.
>
> Connie looked at the ice-cream and wrinkled her nose. She handed it to the ice-cream man, and said, "I won't have this. I'll have a strawberry ice, please."
>
> "Have to eat that one first, Miss," said the ice-cream man. So Connie had to go without...[40]

Connie is a smart-aleck. She is noncompliant; she flouts implied conventions and dares to doubt adult claims to omnipotence. Again, similar to the stories about Flora and Edith, the narrative promises delicious food and then frustrates desire. The food text is, once again, shown to be an ideal vehicle for socializing messages.

In Dorothy Wall's story, *The Complete Adventures of Blinky Bill*, the "naughty [koala] bear" creates havoc in Mrs. Smifkins' farmhouse kitchen. He finds a dishful of eggs and delights in smashing them all; he drinks all the milk and is about to make a start on some cakes under a wire cover when he catches "sight of a tiny mouse peeping out of his hole." Blinky and "Mr. Mouse" team up and search the kitchen for cheese. In the process Blinky spreads sticky "paw marks and blobs" everywhere. Eventually they find some cheese and Blinky encourages the mouse to hurry up and grab it. However, Mr. Mouse is caught in a trap and killed. "Well [Blinky mutters to himself], if that's cheese I don't want any." Having had a fright he determines to get out of the Smifkins' kitchen, but in his haste he knocks over Mrs. Smifkins' "very best fruit dish." "Poof!" he said as he took a hurried glance at the broken dish. "Serves her right for killing Mr. Mouse."[41] Within the text Blinky Bill is positioned as a naughty boy but his misdemeanors are not commented upon. Indeed, it is Mrs. Smifkins who is seen to deserve punishment. This is a regular pattern throughout the Blinky Bill stories. Blinky's mother despairs because he is so naughty but is proud of his spirit and typically forgets to punish his escapades because she is "so pleased to see him safely home." Although he fears being spanked, he is instead hugged and petted (*Blinky Bill*, 44). Indeed, following one of his first naughty adventures, he feels he qualifies as a "man of the world" (41). Furthermore, Blinky thinks his friend Snubby, "must be a girl" as he's too afraid to go adventuring (50) and Blinky's mother tells Snubby's mother that she'll "never make a man of Snubby" (90). The link between behaving badly and masculinity in Wall's narrative is clear.

Lucy is a good girl in C. S. Lewis's *The Lion, the Witch and the Wardrobe*. When she finds her way into Narnia she meets Mr. Tumnus, the Faun, who invites her to tea.[42]

> "Well, it's very kind of you," said Lucy. "But I shan't be able to stay long...."
>
> Lucy thought she had never been in a nicer place.... And really it was a wonderful tea. There was a nice brown egg, lightly boiled, for each of them, and then sardines on toast, and then buttered toast, and then toast with honey, and then a sugar-topped cake.[43]

Lucy is exceedingly polite and the foods she eats with the Faun are, while obviously a treat, very suitable for a child within the context of the nursery diet. For example, it is noteworthy that she doesn't eat both honey and butter on the same piece of bread.[44] She eats buttered toast, then toast with honey, not toast with butter *and* honey. Also, although the cake she eats is sugar-topped, it is eaten at the end of the meal as dessert. Within (adult) Western cultural practices, as Mary Douglas's work on the major British food categories has shown, food is generally split up into meals and drinks. Meals are internally ranked by courses and externally structured by a temporal order; daily into breakfast, lunch, dinner, etc.; weekly culminating traditionally in Sunday dinner, and annually by a sequence of ceremonial meals.[45] Thus the meal Lucy consumes complies with adult food rules. She eats and behaves correctly and is thus connoted as a good, and moral, little girl.

Edmund, on the other hand, who also goes to Narnia alone and is given food by the first person he meets, is a truly wicked and corrupt boy.

His subsequent evil deeds are foreshadowed when he receives from the White Witch and consumes "several pounds of the best Turkish delight." The Turkish delight is not part of a meal and is therefore not classified as "real" food according to adult food rules.[46] It definitely transgresses notions about suitable foods for children in terms of quality and quantity. Edmund soon finds that "the more he ate the more he wanted to eat" (*Lion,* 37). Indeed, he is so overcome by the sweetness of the Turkish delight and the Witch's spell that he forgets his manners and speaks with his mouth full. Edmund becomes addicted to the sensuous pleasure of the sweet and sticky food and there are clear implications of immorality in his actions. He breaks accepted food rules, displays bad manners, and gives in to his sensuous desires. Edmund's corruption is visible to the Beaver who recognizes that he has "joined [the White Witch's] side:" "the moment I set eyes on that brother of yours," Mr. Beaver explains, "I said to myself 'Treacherous.' He had the look of one who has been with the Witch and eaten her food. You can always tell them if you've lived long in Narnia; something about their eyes" (80).[47] Lucy's goodness and trustworthiness and Edmund's lack of moral fiber and capacity for wickedness are signaled by their consumption of food. Indeed, "food becomes the principal difference between Edmund and Lucy."[48] It is important to note, however, that, unlike the behavior of Blinky Bill, Peter Rabbit, and the bad boy, Likenesses in Rossetti's story, Edmund's behavior is never condoned in Lewis's narrative. He is framed as truly wicked rather than just a naughty boy. Nevertheless, while he subsequently suffers for his treacherousness when he is "terribly wounded" in battle (162), he is ultimately forgiven and ironically rewarded by subsequently being given the title "King Edmund the *Just*" (67, my emphasis).

Max, in Maurice Sendak's *Where the Wild Things Are*, is a naughty little boy and he is sent to his room for his bad behavior. However, he too is ultimately forgiven because, when he returns from his adventure, his supper, which "smelled good," is waiting for him and, significantly, it is "still hot."[49] Nodelman argues that the meals provided by adults to children at the end of children's stories confirm "the benefits for children of an adult authority" (Nodelman 1999, 73). Max's return signifies his acceptance of his mother's authority, it is true, but, concomitantly, if his mother had made him go without supper, or if his supper had been cold and congealed, not only would the effect of reparation have been missing, Max's mother would also have been connoted as a bad mother. That is, his mother has to forgive him unconditionally if she is to be seen as good. It may thus be said that the same (patriarchal) cultural discourses that produce the good mother also forgive and excuse Max's bad behavior.

It is interesting to mix and match the preceding narratives and wonder whether the impetus of the storyline would be different if the gender of the protagonists were changed. How would Max have fared in an encounter with Blyton's ice-cream man? Would he have had to go without? The valorization of the transgressions of a naughty "girl" koala, who behaved like Blinky Bill, for example, is unimaginable. If Peter Rabbit had been Peta, or if Edmund had gone to tea with Mr. Tumnus, these narratives just wouldn't have the same effect or connotations. The gender bias present in these stories continues in more recent novels.

Maria Tatar argues that contemporary authors tend toward providing therapeutic pleasures rather than didacticism. They aim to produce catharsis and to help turn readers into "well-adjusted" individuals[50] Louis Sachar's *There's a Boy in the Girls' Bathroom* provides a typical example. Bradley Chalkers sits at the back of his fifth-grade classroom and has no friends. "He was an island."[51] All the other children hate him and he hates them. He is an outcast because he lacks social skills and he behaves badly; he is everything Visser claims prevents communality. He threatens to spit on the new kid (*Boy*, 5) and to beat up girls (49), he is an inveterate liar, and he won't do his school- or home-work. In terms of fifth-grade social niceties Bradley is threatening, unpredictable, and disgusting. As he reveals to the school counselor, his problem is that everyone thinks he is a monster. And "how does a monster stop being a monster?" "I mean, if everyone sees only a monster, and they keep treating him like a monster, how does he stop being a monster?"(90).

Bradley "got kicked out of the last [birthday party he] went to" for sitting on the birthday cake (184). The carnivalesque image of a boy of around seven years old sitting on an elaborately decorated, candle-bedecked cake is amusing but has significant sociocultural resonances and the idea of Bradley's bottom coming into contact with the cake evokes disgust. The birthday cake is an important part of the birthday ritual in Western culture. The candles celebrate the child's survival for another year and mark the transformation to a new age. The cake is also, arguably, a marker of wealth (if shop-bought), or of the skill (and worth) of the person who made it, if homemade. To destroy such a significant icon is an incredible blunder and implicitly reflects Bradley's complete social ineptitude.

Sachar's is an uncomplicated and amusing story with the characters simply drawn. Bradley's counselor teaches him social skills, he makes a friend, he's invited to another party and successfully negotiates all the relevant rituals involved with present buying and giving, party games, and the birthday tea. He is no longer an island.[52] It is interesting to note, however, that although Bradley is initially ostracized by his peers, he is neither punished nor condemned by adults for his blatant and deliberate antisocial conduct. His mother insists, despite his determined failure at school and his threatening and rude behavior, that, "Deep down, he really is a good boy" (*Boy*, 19).

Elizabeth Parsons shows in her revealing analysis of Emily Rodda's *Bob the Builder and the Elves* how the subtext of this particular narrative blatantly corroborates traditional gender stereotypes and upholds the patriarchal hierarchy. The elves, who invade Bob's house, are feminized by their love of housework, interest in cleanliness, and their provision of food. Parsons explains that while "housework is traditionally coded as feminine, ... in the elves' case this sense is heightened by their penchant for floral details, like a vase of flowers on the table and rose petals strewn in the bath," so that they are in fact coded as "ultra-feminine" and antithetical to Bob.[53] The elves make lunches for Bob (whose masculinity is a hyped-up version of the Aussie-male stereotype) that involve fairy bread and fairy cakes. (These foods are normally associated with children's birthday parties and they not only infantilize Bob, but also bring his heterosexuality into question as Parsons shows.) In this story the elves are given the role that is usually associated with parents, most often with mothers. Notably Bob is most concerned about what his mates think; his masculinity is at stake and he'll "never live it down."[54] Bob's new neighbor, Lily Sweet, is aligned with the elves and thus with maternity, by her involvement in housework and, Parsons suggests, her interest in the elves' babies.

Bob's hypermasculinity is intended to be comic but can be read instead as valorizing the "unfortunate stereotype" of inarticulate Australian men (Parsons, 34), including a tendency toward violence in order to express anger. Bob is frustrated because he can't find a way (not even in a book that's been recommended to him) to get the elves out of his house and he resorts to violence.

> "What! You mean I read that book in a tent for the whole rotten afternoon for nothing?" he shouted. "You mean whoever wrote that book's a ratbag? A crook?" he clenched his fists, and looked around in rage. "Where's he hang out? I'll soon show him what's what. That low, miserable..." (*Bob*, 52)

Both the narrator and his future wife, Lily, explain away Bob's violent outburst using soothing maternal language, giving rise to what Parsons believes is "the promotion of a suspiciously patriarchal representation of wifely duties" and approbation of his violence (34).[55] Furthermore, Parsons finally argues, "That a wife's role is so intricately connected to nurturing, housework and tiptoeing around a potentially violent male involves the promotion of seriously regressive information about gender relationships within marriage" (35).

Just like Rossetti's narrative, Sachar's and Rodda's stories are basically blind to male misconduct. Indeed, they contain the expectation that "boys will be boys." The skewed positioning of girls/women in relation to boys/men in matters of food, manners, and behavior is by no means confined to fictional narratives written for children and is a reflection of the real world, as Valerie Walkerdine has shown in her studies of gender in the education system. She argues that cultural, educational, and familial child-rearing practices disavow boys' physical and verbal violence. Implying that some mothers overnurture, she asserts that "the modern form of mothering covers over, and indeed supports, a fantasy of certainty, of the independent male child who is in omnipotent control over a calculable universe, who has the power to explore and explain." In the classrooms in which she conducted her research, she heard "again and again…female teachers downplay and ignore the reported violence of boys," and believes this to be symptomatic of cultural attitudes that view boys as "independent, brilliant, proper thinkers." Although the boys are admittedly naughty, this is

> understood as a positive attribute, one at the very least to be al-
> lowed and probably positively fostered as the basis of independent
> thinking. On the other hand, girls are, by and large, described as
> lacking the qualities boys possess. They are no trouble, but then
> their lack of naughtiness is also a lack of spark, fire, brilliance.[56]

There is then a sociocultural leniency toward the bad behavior of boys. Boys are, after all, made of slugs and snails and puppy-dogs' tails,[57] and they are culturally expected to be naughty, to get dirty, to wriggle and not be able to sit still, to make rude noises, to fight and swear. And for this they are judged to be "just being a boy" or "a real boy," one who will grow into a *real* man. Concomitantly girls must be good. And, in order to become good girls they must be carefully controlled and constantly monitored (as A. A. Milne's poem intimates).

Texts such as Rodda's promote a patriarchal gendered hierarchy through an implicit affirmation of traditional gender roles. Parsons points to the class and intellectual inequalities between Bob and Lily and wonders why "charming and intelligent Lily would settle for an aggressive and inarticulate life partner who seems to have so little to offer her?" She suggests that the text implies that Lily needs a man so that she can get married and have children to sing lullabies to, like the elves she finds so endearing (35). Conversely, of course, the text also carries the message that girls must not only be intelligent and hold down a decent job (Lily is a librarian), they must also be "sweet" (Lily's last name is Sweet) domesticated, maternal, nurturing, and conciliatory in order to attract the interest of a man.[58] On top of this they must also be conniving. (It is the elves who introduce Bob to Lily. She actively recruits their help having brought them with her when she moved in next door.) The narrative also reinforces traditional stereotypes of masculinity and femininity, implicitly normalizing the notion that men are untidy and inept at housework, and that women will tidy up after them and feed them; that men are barely articulate, nearly illiterate and hate reading, and that motherly females will solve problems for them; that men naturally react violently when they are angry, that there will be no repercussions when they do so, and that women will react to such behavior with sympathy and conciliatory behavior. And, more than this, from the male perspective, the text implies that intelligent women are willing to accept such behavior from men in order to achieve what is shown to be their life's goal: marriage and looking after men and children.

As I have argued, although the messages or morals are not as blatantly obvious in Carroll's story of Alice and in the examples of twentieth-century texts I have used as they are in Edgeworth's or Rossetti's, they all reiterate stereotypes and hegemonies and thus they affect the way child readers learn to constitute their gendered identities in the real world. Fictional food events most usually occur within the subtext of a narrative and, because these are encoded with messages about gendered social roles and have a powerful mimetic effect, they produce explicit discourses pertaining to social and cultural ideologies. Their power is reinforced by the habitual naturalness or obviousness of food events that renders their inherent ideological messages invisible. Moreover, fictional food offers pleasure to the reader and can thus be seen as a sweetener for the bitter pill of socialization. Collectively, the stories featured in this chapter produce a discourse which confirms that behaving badly is a marker of masculinity but girls who are naughty must be punished. The question they implicitly pose to the girl reader is: have you been a *good* girl?

3

SWEET DREAMS AND FOOD FETISHES

[Rat appeared] staggering under a fat, wicker luncheon-basket.

"Shove that under your feet," he observed to the Mole, as he passed it down the boat... "What's inside it?" asked the Mole, wriggling with curiosity.

"There's cold chicken inside it," replied the Rat briefly; "coldtonguecoldhamcoldbeefpickledgherkinsaladfrenchrolls-cresssandwidgespottedmeatgingerbeerlemonadesodawater—"

"O stop, stop," cried the Mole in ecstasies: "This is too much!"

"Do you really think so?" inquired the Rat seriously. "It's only what I always take on these little excursions; and the other animals are always telling me that I'm a mean beast and cut it *very* fine!"

—Kenneth Grahame, *The Wind in the Willows*[1]

"You can keep a cold off by feeding it," explained [Billy] Bunter. "It's the safest way. Send me up something—nothing much. I don't want to spoil my lunch. A cold chicken will do, and some beef. A few vegetables, some poached eggs, and a pie or two—nothing much!"

— Frank Richards, "The Artful Dodger"[2]

"What's that? [said Gandalf] Tea! No thank you! A little red wine, I think, for me."

"And for me," said Thorin.

"And raspberry jam and apple-tart," said Bifur.

"And mince pies and cheese," said Bombur.

"And more cakes—and ale—and coffee, if you don't mind," called the other dwarves through the door.

"Put on a few eggs, there's a good fellow!" Gandalf called after him, as the hobbit stumped off to the pantries. "And just bring out the cold chicken and pickles!"

"Seems to know as much about the inside of my larders as I do myself!" thought Mr. Baggins, who was feeling positively flummoxed...

—J. R. R. Tolkein, *The Hobbit*[3]

A great ham sat ready to be carved. A big tongue garnished round with bright green parsley sat by its side. An enormous salad with hard-boiled eggs sprinkled generously all over it was in the middle of the table. Two cold roast chickens were on the table too with little curly bits of cold bacon set around. The children's eyes nearly fell out of their heads. What a feast! And the scones and cakes! The jams and the pure yellow honey! The jugs of creamy milk!

—Enid Blyton, *The Mountain of Adventure*[4]

[Harry] had never seen so many things he liked to eat on one table: roast beef, roast chicken, pork chops and lamb chops, sausages, bacon and steak, boiled potatoes, roast potatoes, chips, Yorkshire pudding, peas, carrots, gravy, ketchup and for some strange reason, mint humbugs... [And for dessert] blocks of ice cream in every flavour you could think of, apple pies, treacle tarts, chocolate éclairs, and jam doughnuts, trifle, strawberries, jelly, rice pudding.

— J. K. Rowling, *Harry Potter and the Philosopher's Stone*[5]

FOOD FANTASIES are a traditional ingredient in classic British children's literature. These stories often include sensuous, mouth-watering descriptions of the foods the characters eat; sweet and rich foods are frequently included in vast quantities as well as foods that contemporary discourses on health condemn as fat-laden. While mealtimes play an important role in fiction in terms of creating verisimilitude and fictional feasting undoubtedly functions to give the reader a vicarious experience of gluttony, lavish descriptions of food, in the context of British classic fiction for children, also have important social, cultural, and psychological functions.

Food is a regular component of fairy tales that have medieval oral antecedents. Famine was a frequent and devastating feature of life in Europe in the Middle Ages and deprivation inevitably shapes fantasies and desires.[6] The magic world of fairy tales often promised rich, sweet, and plentiful food. While "Hansel and Gretel" is usually the best remembered fantasy food fairy story I want to start by looking at a very short story which the Brothers Grimm called "The Sweet Porridge," but which is known as "The Magic Porridge Pot" in contemporary versions. In "The Sweet Porridge" a "poor but pious girl" meets a woman in the woods who gives her a magic porridge pot. The pot provides the little girl and her widowed mother with an endless supply of "good, sweet millet porridge" and it "put an end to their poverty and hunger."[7] Drummond and Wilbraham cite William Harrison's *A Description of England* (1577), showing that during times when the main crops failed and famine ensued, which was not an infrequent occurrence, "the poor man" was forced to live on "horsse corne, beanes, peason, otes, tares, & lintels."[8] During the period 1437 to 1439, for example, "when there was a succession of wet summers and harvests were ruined, the peasantry was reduced to eating such herbs and roots as they could gather from the hedgerows, and thousands died" (Drummond and Wilbraham, 88). The scenario in "The Sweet Porridge" reflects similarly desperate circumstances; the girl's mother is a widow, so the earning capacity of the husband/father figure has been lost and the girl is presumably searching for something edible in the woods. It is not hard to understand how such persistent hunger and hopeless conditions could lead to a fantasy such as a magic porridge pot. It is not so much what is eaten that is at issue when you are starving but that there should be sufficient of whatever there is to eat. Good, sweet porridge, and plenty of it, could fulfill that desire. "The Sweet Porridge" is thus a story that relies upon habitual and chronic hunger as a driving force.

"Hansel and Gretel" is a more complex story and, although it too features starving children, appears to reflect a significantly different food fantasy. The woodcutter's family is poor and they "did not have much food around the house, and when a great famine devastated the entire country, [the woodcutter] could no longer provide enough for his family's daily meals" (*Grimm Tales*, 58). At the suggestion of their stepmother, Hansel and Gretel are abandoned in the woods. The hungry children come across a house made, in the Grimm version, of "bread" with "cake for a roof and pure sugar for windows" (61).[9] Cane sugar was a very costly commodity and had been imported from India or Arabia since the eleventh century. It was used for making marzipan and other sweetmeats (Drummond and Wilbraham , 37–38). Sugar would only have been available to rich nobles and not to woodcutters and their families. The house made of sweet food represents something exotic, very rich, and beyond the reach of the peasantry. When your diet is poor and monotonous, a story featuring plentiful, appetizing food is bound to have appeal, but I believe this fantasy goes beyond the desire to alleviate hunger: it also represents economic desire.

The exoticism and richness of the sugary food in the fantasy represent not only the riches of the nobility but also their ability to avoid the hunger and drudgery of the peasants' daily life. The Grimm version ends with the children filling apron and pockets with the pearls and jewels they have found in the witch's house and taking them home to their father. "[I]n the meantime" their stepmother has died and so "Now all their troubles were over, and they lived together in utmost joy" (*Grimm Tales*, 64). Their future is secured by the wealth with which, like the nobility, they can now live in relative ease and luxury. Unlike the magic porridge pot that merely alleviated hunger, the jewels provide the woodcutter's family with riches and instant freedom from their menial existence.[10]

A HARSH REGIME

During the eighteenth and nineteenth centuries the children who had access to books, and for whom the stories were written, were largely from wealthy middle- and upper-class families. According to Flora Thompson's autobiographical *Lark Rise to Candleford* children of the rural laboring classes in late nineteenth-century England relied for reading material on cheap chapbooks, which were passed from family to family, or books that came to them by "chance." School library books were all of the "goody-goody, Sunday-school prize type."[11] Julia Briggs and Dennis Butts confirm that while middle-class children were able to choose their own books and had a wide selection of "adventure, school, nonsense, fantasy and fairy tales available" to choose from, the children of the poor, "bare-foot and under-nourished,"[12] grew up in urban or rural slums without access to literature.

Furthermore, during the period stretching from the late eighteenth century through to the beginning of World War II young children from wealthy British families almost certainly rarely ate with their parents and other adults (apart from servants) and their diet was generally austere, bland, and monotonous by today's standards. Middle- and upper-class children spent their childhoods almost entirely within the self-contained space of a nursery over which a nanny or nurse presided until such time as boys were sent to boarding school. (Girls were generally tutored at home by a governess.) The nursery was often situated at the top or in far-flung and remote parts of the house and it was frequently a spartan area, furnished with items not needed elsewhere.[13] Children might only have seen their parents, most likely their mother, for perhaps one hour a day. Jonathan Gathorne-Hardy quotes Jane Austen's niece, speaking about her aunt's childhood:[14]

Children were kept in the nursery, out of the way not only of visitors, but of their parents; they were trusted to hired attendants, they were allowed a great deal of exercise, were kept on plain food, forced to give way to the comfort of others, accustomed to be overlooked, slightly regarded, [and] considered of trifling importance. (Gathorne-Hardy, 61)

In the previous chapter I showed how John Locke's recommendations, which relied on Puritan concepts, had influenced eighteenth-century child-rearing methods, and how rich food was thought to morally corrupt children. Locke's insistence on plain fare for children is reflected in the ideas of Dr. William Cadogan who wrote an influential essay published in 1748, on the nursing and management of children. Cadogan's essay was originally sent to the governors of a foundling hospital, which was pioneering new attitudes in child-care. In it he complained about the children's food: "There are many faults in the quality of their food: it is not simple enough, their papps, panados, gruels are generally enriched with sugar, spice and sometimes a drop of wine; neither of which they ought ever to taste."[15]

Approximately one hundred years after Cadogan, Dr. Pye Henry Chavasse produced an authoritarian book of questions and answers about child-rearing which went through fourteen editions from 1839 to 1885. His recommendations were directed at "mothers of every station" in contrast to earlier books that had implicitly been aimed at the upper classes (Mars, 154).

To the question, "Have you any objection to pork for a change?" Dr. Chavasse insists: "I have the greatest objection to it. It is a rich, gross, and therefore unwholesome food for the delicate stomachs of children." When asked about sweets and cakes, Chavasse reaches an apoplectic climax: "I consider them so much slow poison. Such things cloy and weaken the stomach and thereby take away the appetite and thus debilitate the frame. If the child is never allowed to eat such things, he will consider dry bread a luxury." (Mars, 155)

"Tasty" food was thus strictly relegated to adults (159). In order to limit children's consumption in this way it was necessary to feed them separately and they were thus confined to meals taken in the nursery which typically consisted of boiled meat or steamed fish, cabbage, and milk-based puddings like rice and tapioca. (Murcott 1997, 48 n16). Mars shows that the physical separation of children from adults was also related to the Victorian perception of them as inherently sinful. They were generally confined to the nursery until they were changed from their natural state to a civilized one that rendered them fit for adult culture and company. Thus, children's tendency toward "untamed behavior" had to be eradicated before they could be allowed to eat with the adults in the dining room (Mars, 156).

Ethel Turner's *Seven Little Australians* (1894) reflects this attitude. The Woolcot children are accustomed to eating their meals in the nursery, although the narrator is at pains to point out that nursery tea is "more of an English institution than an Australian one."[16] In Australia generally, the narrator explains, a feeling of "*bon camaraderie*" exists "between parents and young folks...So even in the most wealthy families it seldom happens that the parents dine in solemn state alone" as, it is intimated, is unfortunately the case in Britain. But in this particular Australian family, given "a very particular, and rather irritable [and English] father, and seven children with excellent lungs and tireless tongues, what could you do but give them separate rooms to take their meals in?" (*Seven Little Australians,* 11). Thus, as Mars intimates, the children's "untamed behavior" is given as the reason for their relegation to the nursery, even in egalitarian Australia.

The children's tea usually consists of "great thick slices of bread and butter" and very weak tea (16). Pip complains angrily that meanwhile in the dining room his father and stepmother are "having roast fowl, three vegetables, and four kinds of pudding...it isn't fair!" Although the children had eaten boiled mutton, carrots, and rice pudding for their one o'clock dinner Pip still wants to know "Why shouldn't we have roast fowl and custard and things?"(16). "We're only children [sister Judy explains "in a good little tone"]...let us be thankful for this nice thick bread and abundance of melting butter" (17). But no, Pip is tormented by the smell of the chicken and he knows "they'd got a lot on the table" because he has "peeped in the door." Pip takes his plate and sets off downstairs only to return with "quite a large portion" of chicken on his plate. Nell follows her brother's example. At the dining table she meets Colonel Bryant, her parents' dinner guest: "Well, my little maid, won't you shake hands with me? What is your name?" he asks. Nell introduces herself and offers her left hand, "since her right was occupied with the plate." This provokes her father to comment, "What a little barbarian you are, Nell!" (17). Following her request for chicken her father "almost savagely" severs a leg from the joint and puts it on her plate (18). "Now run away," he tells her, "I don't know what has possessed you two to-night." But Nell pleads her sister Meg's case "with a beautiful look of distress that quite touched Colonel Bryant" and also receives a wing "hacked off...in ominous silence." Her return to the nursery is "hailed with uproarious applause" (19). By the time six-year-old Bunty, who is "fat and very lazy" (13), tries his luck, however, his father has entirely lost his patience and the boy is sent away without any (19). The children's desire to share the adults' food is met with disapproval and intimations of barbarism and possession from their father.

Nineteenth-century dining practices were so strongly hierarchical, Mars maintains, that upper-class British children were effectively removed from an interactive family life and spent very little time with either of their parents. Indeed, *Mrs Beeton's Book of Household Management* (1861) stated that "the mother is too much occupied to do more than pay a daily visit" to the nursery (cited in Mars, 156). This concurs with the following excerpt written by George Bernard Shaw, who was born in 1856:

> I hated the servants and liked my mother because on one or two rare and delightful occasions when she buttered bread for me, she buttered it thickly instead of merely wiping a knife on it. Her almost complete neglect of me had the advantage that I could idolise her to the utmost pitch of my imagination...It was a privilege to be taken for a walk or a visit with her, or on an excursion. (quoted by Gathorne-Hardy, 78)

The parallel distances the mother maintained from child-rearing and food preparation, confined to daily visits to the nursery and daily instruction of the cook, reflected, according to Mars, the fact that food in its uncooked state, and children, are closer to nature than befitted the delicate sensibilities of the ideal of Victorian feminine gentility (Mars, 157).[17] Thus, in the case of upper-class Victorian culture, proper femininity is, paradoxically, inherently maternal but not physically associated with proximity to children. In wealthy households the separation of children and adults could be maintained by employing nursemaids and a nanny, housemaids, and cook but the nursery system was by no means confined to the gentry. Gathorne-Hardy shows that from 1850 onward it was quite common for a "genteel tradesman" to engage a nurse and, by the end of the nineteenth century "you were barely considered middle class if you didn't have at least a nursemaid for the children" (Gathorne-Hardy, 67). Thompson's recollections of late nineteenth-century rural working-class society concur: "Everybody who was anything...kept a maid in those days—stud grooms' wives, village schoolmasters' wives, and, of course, inn-keepers' and shopkeepers' wives. Even the wives of carpenters and masons paid a girl sixpence to clean the knives and boots and take out the children on Saturday" (*Lark Rise,* 165). This is evident in P. L. Travers' *Mary Poppins.* The Banks family is not particularly wealthy. They live in the smallest house in Cherry Tree Lane, a house which is rather dilapidated and in need of a coat of paint. Mr. Banks, who works, of course, at a bank, had told Mrs. Banks that she could either have a nice, clean, comfortable house *or* four children. Nevertheless the family employs a cook, a maid, a gardener/handyman, and a nanny.[18]

While children were restricted to a plain and simple diet, some foods were considered *only* suitable for children and were deemed inappropriate for adults, particularly men. In *Seven Little Australians,* Nell prepares a tray for her father who is working in his study. On the tray are a glass of milk and a plate of mulberries. Nell's father has not had a glass of milk since he "was Pip's age [fourteen] . . . [and] would as soon drink the water the maids wash up in" (26). Despite Turner's narrator's ironic insistence on the existence of feelings of *bon camaraderie* between parents and children, there are clearly very distinct boundaries separating them. Thus, during the period, historically specific cultural concepts of the adult and the child, and of "proper" masculinity and femininity, were reflected in and reproduced by the coding of the foods considered to be appropriate for them.

In addition to the simplicity of their diet, nursery children were taught that food was not to be wasted nor taken excessively, and eating between meals was strictly frowned upon. Greed, according to Molly Keane's memoir, was "a depravity to be commented on and corrected whenever evident." Born in 1904, she reports being left with "a deep-rooted sense that the enjoyment of food was unattractive, something to conceal."[19] The moral implications of greed are also emphasized by Gwen Raverat (1885–1957) who, although obviously from a wealthy family, remembers that she was only allowed porridge for breakfast with salt, not sugar. Twice a week she was also allowed:

> one piece of toast, spread with that dangerous luxury, Jam. But, of course, not butter too. Butter and Jam on the same bit of bread would have been an unheard-of-indulgence—a disgraceful orgy . . . There was only bread-and-butter and milk for tea, as Jam might have weakened our moral fibre . . . sugar was thought to be unwholesome; and fruit, though a pleasant treat, rather dangerous.[20]

The idea that eating butter and jam on the same piece of bread could be considered indulgent and "a disgraceful orgy" is extremely oppressive by today's standards. There is a clear indication in these examples of the notion that the foods children ate should be restricted, not so much perhaps for their physical health but more importantly, because of matters of morality. These examples show that the notion of immorality is linked particularly to certain rich, sweet food items. It is important to realize, however, that these attitudes toward children and food were not universal.

"PRICELESS" AMERICAN CHILDREN

Questions of childhood diet and health were dealt with differently according to historic cultural beliefs and prevalent medical models. Peter Stearns has completed an interesting analysis of cultural attitudes towards children's weight during the period of the late nineteenth and continuing through to the twentieth century. His description of the American model, compared to my outline of the British approach, shows that there were significant differences in professional and lay attitudes toward children's weight in the United States and Britain. In general, it appears that American methods of child rearing were far more lenient than the British regulatory approach.

Stearns shows that while American ladies' journals began to promote slenderness and weight control for adults (especially women) in the 1890s, it was not considered necessary for children to be so regulated. In fact, medical advice put pressure upon parents to ensure that children were not *underweight*. "Special recipes to build up underweight children, particularly boys, dotted the pages of the new Parents' Magazine, including praise for snacks between meals and the consumption of fatty foods."[21] The evolution of an American middle class during the nineteenth century shaped notions of the family and home as a refuge from the outside world, and promoted a belief in childhood innocence. Religious mores shifted and the idea of original sin and the need for harsh discipline were downplayed in favor of more indulgent parental styles. There was an intensification of what one social historian has termed the "pricelessness" of children (Zelizer, cited by Stearns, 24), which was signaled by granting allowances, lavish birthday celebrations, and treats such as candy bars, ice cream, and "Eskimo pies." American cultural trends in the valuation of children emphasized growing latitude and indulgence and these were deeply embedded in family ideology. Concomitantly, the moral considerations surrounding control of appetite as a sign of virtue in adults were seen not to apply to children who were taken to be inherently innocent (Stearns, 24).[22]

Gillian Avery shows that, in direct contrast to the nursery diet of British children, American children were allowed fruit, salads, oysters, "johnny cakes, toast swimming in butter; fish, flesh and game at breakfast; jellies and ices at night; tea and coffee."[23] On a visit to North America, Anthony Trollope (1862) compared American children eating fish or beef-steak and pickles for breakfast to the breakfasts of bread and milk he had eaten in the nursery under the supervision of a nursemaid when he was the same age (Avery, 158). Of significance, in light of current concerns, is Stearns' conclusion that the high rate of contemporary American childhood obesity results directly from historical cultural attitudes toward their diet (26).

DEPRIVATION SHAPES DESIRE

Avery's study of American children and their books confirms that fictional content reflected a distinct difference between American and British cultural attitudes towards children. She describes nineteenth-century fictional American children as growing up in a "liberated atmosphere," which was reflected in their "robust and confident" characters (Avery, 155). While fictional English children seemed always to be "under the watchful and anxious eyes of parents," American characters were off enjoying adventures (157). In reality, English children did play and enjoy fantasy escapades, but they were closeted and protected from the harsher realities of life. American children, on the other hand, were rather more likely to have been exposed to practical, down-to-earth aspects of life. Avery maintains that an American childhood was more "purposeful and practical" than that of many upper-class English children (157).

It appears that the content of the English family story, and especially girls' books, held little appeal for American child readers because the action was "inevitably severely constrained." Victorian values of "disinterested and honourable conduct and truth-telling" (Avery, 155), such as those displayed in the work of Christina Rossetti discussed in the previous chapter perhaps, thus tended to stifle the narratives in nineteenth-century English fiction. Avery maintains that

> English family stories reflected the rigours, moral and physical, then thought appropriate for the nursery and schoolroom.... they seem oppressive now in the lofty demands that they make on the child, and the reader notices the degree of moral responsibility expected even of the youngest. (156)

In addition, Avery argues that "for [British] children brought up austerely on a diet in which boiled mutton, potatoes, rice pudding and bread and milk played the most prominent part it was entrancing to read about what their American contemporaries apparently took as a matter of course" (158). Avery infers that British children would have been especially appreciative of fictional food, more so, perhaps, than their American counterparts. I believe that deprivation shaped British readers' desires, increasing their vicarious pleasure and the intensity of their emotional satisfaction. Similarly, I suggest, British writers of children's stories, who had experienced a nursery upbringing, would in all likelihood sympathize with their readers' thwarted appetites, and understand and share their particular appreciation of fantasy food. The sympathetic identification of authors with readers, coupled with their commitment to providing reading pleasure unqualified by didactic moralizing, resulted in the tendency for them to include elaborate food descriptions in their work. The tradition of lavish food fantasies in classic British children's literature is therefore directly attributable to the strictly hierarchical structure of Victorian society, which virtually banished children from middle- and upper-class families to the rigors of the nursery and condemned them to a meager diet of simple, bland food. This is not to say that American children's stories did not feature food: they often did. But, I would argue, it is not described with quite the relish evident in the British classics.

CRAVING FOR SWEETS

The nursery regime continued in Britain up to World War II when a "general levelling of diet" occurred and put an end to what had been a "hallowed English tradition" (Avery, 157–58). But dietary limitations enforced by the family gave way to government-imposed restrictions. Post-war rationing in Britain continued to affect the general population through to the mid-1950s and frugal family feeding habits learned during periods of rationing undoubtedly had repercussions through the 1960s and even the 1970s. During the period of rationing following World War I, for example, a shortage of fats and sugars in the diet of the general population apparently produced cravings in many people, particularly children. In fact, Drummond and Wilbraham argue, the desire for sweets became almost an obsession not only with children, but with many adults as well (438).

Children (and presumably adults) who craved sweets would no doubt have particularly appreciated episodes such as Blinky Bill's escapades in Mrs. Smifkin's farmhouse kitchen: [24]

> There were dozens of jars of jam and preserves [including] plum, apricot, orange, peach, loganberry, pineapple, and melon ... Breaking the paper top with his claws he dipped his paw in and scooped up the lovely red jam. He tasted it, licked his lips and decided to try the next bottle.... Every pot of jam was sampled, and that naughty bear's paws and face were covered ... All his pretty fur on his chest and tummy dripped jam. (*Blinky Bill*, 127)

Here the reader can vicariously enjoy the transgressive pleasure of the exotic and very sweet, fruity flavors, sensations that were restricted for British children. The koala "bear" actually gets to try "*every* pot of jam," an indulgence probably appreciated by children who had been taught that greed was "a depravity" as Molly Keane had been. Also, and importantly, Blinky Bill dips his paws into the jars and licks the jam off, eventually getting so covered that he drips jam, a clear transgression of adult rules about good manners. The vicarious tactile pleasures involved have sensual as well as obviously transgressive appeal. It should be noted that as well as delicious sweet and sticky jam fantasies, Wall's readers were being fed ideological notions about rural Australia as a land of plenty. This idealization of the natural, the rural, and homemaking mirrors similar ideals contained in Enid Blyton's fiction as I will show later.

Evidence of excessive eating which directly opposes the strictures of both the nursery regime and wartime frugality can also be seen in Frank Richards' portraits of Billy Bunter (from 1908) and his sister Bessie (from 1919), who were so preoccupied with eating that his books were reputedly banned in some libraries.[25] Tolkein's characterization of Bilbo Baggins (1937) also lays great emphasis on the hobbit's penchant for food and Edmund's wish for Turkish delight in Lewis's *The Lion, the Witch and the Wardrobe* (1950) is very extravagant for an evacuee. Even Lucy's tea with Mr. Tumnus, where they eat an egg *each* is excessive given that during the period of rationing, eggs were limited to one a week (Barker, 9).

Enid Blyton (1897–1968) is probably the children's author most people first think of when the topic of fictional food fantasies is mentioned. Blyton, who is still one of the most popular of children's authors, as is evidenced by the continuing presence of large numbers of her books in chain-store book departments, is worthy of further scrutiny. Born during the Edwardian era into a middle-class family, her books are permeated with the Edwardian principles so universal before World War I: honor, a good clean fight, and a sense of fair play (Barker, 4). Her upbringing, Barker argues, influenced her descriptions of fictional meals. Apparently the Edwardians were "notorious gluttons" who frequently partook of meals with multiple courses and who indulged in rich foods even at breakfast (Barker, 4). Kenneth Clarke wrote of them: "How they ate! Local oysters and liver pate, steak and kidney pudding, cold turkey and ham, treacle tart, double Cottenham cheese and always, to fill in corners (as was often said with satisfaction), a slice of plum cake" (cited by Barker, 5). It is important to note here that Barker and Clarke are referring to adult eating habits; children, as I have argued, tended to eat very differently.

Blyton's fictional feasts directly reflect the (adult) Edwardian extravagant cholesterol-laden diet. Psychologist Michael Woods argues that the food in Blyton's books is

> more reminiscent of an orgy in an Edwardian emporium than a modern child's idea of a good "blow-out." Enid Blyton writes of

tongues, ham, pies, lemonade and ginger-beer. This is not just food, it is archetypal feasting, the author's longing for the palmy days of her own childhood. (cited by Barker, 5)

However, I don't believe that Blyton's childhood was as palmy as Woods presumes, nor that her upbringing influenced her descriptions of fictional meals in quite the way that Barker suggests. Given her middle-class upbringing and the cultural context in which she was socialized, I would argue that it is very unlikely that as a child, she regularly enjoyed foods such as she describes in her books. As well as this Blyton's emotional relationship with her "aggressive and domineering" mother[26] seems to have been highly unsatisfactory. She also suffered a huge psychological blow around age twelve when her father, with whom she was very close, left the family home. I don't believe that Blyton's food fantasies mirror the feasting and abundance she actually enjoyed as a child, but rather that they perhaps reflect a childhood desire for such food and, importantly, a longing for the maternal love and emotional satisfaction that the food fantasies also represent.

Barker shows that Blyton's most prolific period of writing took place during the war era when food rationing meant that the majority of people in England were eating less than they had throughout the whole of the twentieth century. Following the outbreak of WWII, food rationing began in January 1940 and continued until 1954. The average weekly rations consisted of one shilling and sixpence worth of meat,[27] eight ounces (220 grams) of sugar, four ounces of butter or fat, one egg, one ounce of cheese, with jam and honey also heavily rationed (Barker, 9). Fresh vegetables were in short supply, unless grown in the home vegetable garden.

> While the Famous Five were consuming fat red radishes, their readers were being fed banana sandwiches made with parsnips and banana essence or carrot tart glazed with lemon jelly to make a pudding, and while the Secret Seven breakfasted off well-buttered home-baked bread with chunky marmalade, their devotees never even saw fruit like oranges and bananas and had to make do with the infamous Woolton Pie, a combination of carrots, parsnips, turnips, and potatoes, covered with white sauce and pastry. (Barker, 10)

Barker points out that Blyton can hardly be portraying the period realistically. However, I don't believe that she was pursuing realism. I think that the original appeal of Blyton's food fantasies was intensified by the reader's knowledge that their own family teatime was never likely to be as scrumptious as the feast Blyton served for them. And, for contemporary readers, the appeal lies in the huge quantities and the exoticism of the homemade foods in her narratives which, because of healthy-eating discourses and the lack of time generally available in contemporary households to produce such meals, are usually denied them. From this perspective it can be seen that a large proportion of the readers' enjoyment is vicarious, a form of voyeurism, a chance to experience gluttony second-hand.

Nicholas Tucker, too, believes lavish descriptions of food formed an integral part of the appeal of children's fiction during times of general austerity. But he admits that he is unclear about "how popular such descriptions are with children today, at a time when there is plenty of attractive food around and fewer adult-imposed restrictions on what children are allowed to eat."[28] Tucker assumes that the appeal of fictional food is limited to its ability to provide vicarious gluttony. However, I believe that the appeals of literary feasting are far more complex and relate to cultural mores, social issues, and psychological factors. Food fantasies provide no physical satiation of appetite—indeed they probably increase hunger—but they can, I believe, provide intense emotional satisfaction in a number of ways. I shall concentrate on Blyton's stories because they are so rich in material about food and because of their ongoing popularity and therefore relevance

"JUST THE VERY THINGS I LONGED FOR"

Blyton describes her feasts with sensuous simplicity: for breakfast the "inn-woman" brings the Famous Five "a large tray. On it was a steaming tureen of porridge, a bowl of golden syrup, a jug of very thick cream, and a dish of bacon and eggs, all piled high on crisp brown toast. Little mushrooms were on the same dish... 'Toast, marmalade and butter to come, and the coffee and hot milk,' said the woman... 'And if you want any more bacon and eggs, just ring the bell.'"[29] For high tea they enjoy "'Pork pie—home-made, of course... And what's this—golly, it's a cheese! How enormous! Smell it, Julian—it's enough to make you start eating straightaway! And more of that home-made bread!' There are new-laid boiled eggs to begin with... and an apple-pie and cream to end with."[30] The children are always described as excited by and appreciative of the food offered. "'It's like magic!' said Anne staring. 'Just the very things I longed for!'" (*Five on a Hike*, 69). They're always hungry when they sit down and seem able to put away huge quantities of food. Readers experience Blyton's feasts vicariously: not only can they appreciate the sight of the food laid out on the table but they also smell and taste the cheese, the bread, and the baked ham.

Vallone describes the food metaphor as "speaking" synesthetically within literature—meaning that we "taste the words with our eyes."[31] I suggest that, just as it is possible to recreate an image from memory in the mind's eye (and some people are able to do this far more effectively than others) some people can re-experience, from memory, certain tastes, smells, or tactile sensations.[32] We know that smells and tastes can be powerful memory triggers, why not the written word triggering the re-experience/memory of smells and tastes? Maurice Merleau-Ponty suggests this relationship between the senses when he claims that the senses "communicate" with each other and are "transposable, within certain limits, on to each other's domains."[33] The body is a "synergic system, all the functions of which are exercised and linked together in the general action of being in the world" (Merleau-Ponty, quoted by Grosz, 99). Emmanuel Levinas, too, argues for a "kinesthetic intertranslation" between one perceptual system and another. Thus "the visual resonates with the sayable; the light is capable of eliciting a tactile, textured response; hearing can be visualised" (in Grosz, 100). The facility to re-experience from memory, or to imagine tastes and smells, I suggest, is also a large part of the appeal of watching television cookery programs, looking at images in food magazines, and contemplating the complex dishes described in restaurant menus. It is also, I suspect, one of the reasons why some people are more creative cooks than others.

Thus, I suggest, not only can readers of Blyton's fantasy feasts take voyeuristic pleasure from descriptions of middle-class Julian, Dick, Anne, and George indulging themselves on plentiful, rich, fatty, salty, and sugary foods, foods that, when the stories were first published in the late 1940s and 1950s would have been generally unavailable to readers, they may also, to a certain extent, be able to share their meal.[34]

In addition, Blyton's descriptions of laden tables provide readers with a range of emotional experiences. First, anticipatory tension builds because of the known reality of regular mealtimes and the reader's existing knowledge of Blyton's habit of describing gargantuan meals. This tension is released through the reader's enjoyment of the lavish descriptions of food that always seem to be written in an excited, almost breathless, staccato manner with plenty of exclamation marks. This emotional release results in a sense of satisfaction. The experience of release was or is presumably stronger, as I have argued, for readers whose real-life eating experiences involve rigidly enforced control mechanisms, whether resulting from adult, government, or even self-imposed restrictions.

Blyton's feasts not only feature abundant quantities and a variety of rich foods but they nearly always contain "home-made" and "home-grown" items. As a student teacher Blyton received Froebel training which encourages the themes of housekeeping, cooking, farming, and gardening as means of expression for young children. This is shown by the child-centered approach in her books and the frequent use she makes of little homilies on nature (Barker, 6). In *Five Go on a Hike Together* the children obtain their lunch from a "plump old lady" who, although she's "busy today and [hasn't] got time for cooking," provides them with home-made meat pie, ham and tongue, hard-boiled eggs, and salad. "There's no vegetables though," she apologizes, "You'll have to make do with pickled cabbage and my own pickled onions and beetroot in vinegar." She'll "open a bottle or two of our own raspberries and you can have them with cream [for dessert] if you like. And there's the cream cheese I made yesterday too" (88–89). Barker argues that Blyton frequently promoted her vision of utopia in her stories. Her ideal was "one in which the earth-mother or a substitute earth-mother provides food (preferably home-grown) for her cubs. The various mothers, cooks, and farmers' wives (always female personages, it should be noted) are regarded by their creator with benevolence" (Barker, 7). Blyton has George (a girl) reiterate this notion: "My mother does all those things [bottling and pickling] [and] I'm going to [too] when I'm grown-up. It must be so wonderful to offer home-made things by the score when people come to a meal" (*Five on a Hike*, 89). The women in Blyton's narratives are frequently plump, cheerful, and generous to a fault. They always seem to find the labor-intensive provision of huge quantities of food utterly fulfilling.

MATERNAL COMFORT

The mother figure in many of these stories is idealized and has archetypal sensuous appeal related, as Freud theorized, to early experiences of breast-feeding.[35] The type of food provided by the cheerful motherly figure is significant because it is often rich, sweet, and creamy and, in this respect, I believe has a direct fascination for children whose mothers were, or are, literally or emotionally absent. Bernard-Shaw's emphasis on the thickly buttered bread his mother prepared for him on rare and, obviously in his eyes, very special occasions, is telling in this respect.

Margaret and Michael Rustin have suggested that the provider of sweet foods in a children's story can stand in for an absent and longed-for mother. Referring to Lewis's *The Lion, the Witch and the Wardrobe*, they argue that Edmund is seduced by the White Witch in "the age-old fashion" with delicious sweet and sticky Turkish delight, which gives him "sensuous pleasure" and to which he becomes addicted.[36] Edmund receives and "shovels down" "*several pounds* of the best Turkish Delight.

Each piece was sweet and light to the very centre and Edmund had never tasted anything more delicious"[37] Significantly, the Rustins argue that,

> The alliance made between Edmund and the Queen rests on her astute recognition of his weak spot—the part of himself that is feeling hungry for his mother's love and care can be drawn into a relationship with her based [partly] on his longing...for comfort at an infantile level, which the food represents (this is reminiscent of so much of the consumption of sweet stuff by children)...Edmund is already feeling poisoned by his own emotions and seeks relief from persecution and terror through moral oblivion achieved by abandonment to infantile sensuality. (Rustin and Rustin, 45–46)

Freud argues that breast-feeding leads to a lifelong association between the mother figure and the sensuous nature of food and eating (Freud, 288). Kim Chernin concurs, and emphasizes the role of the mother-as-food in providing comfort to her infant: the infant cries and mother's presence comforts. The sucking, sipping, and nibbling sensations that constitute breast (and, for that matter, bottle) feeding, and the warm, sweet, milky food she provides, produce a life-long association of such foods and sensations, and the mother herself, with comfort. When we are stressed or lonely, then, we yearn for the mother to appease our anxieties in the way she always did.[38] Sweet, creamy foods are always in some way related to maternal comfort, and children's (and arguably adults') desire to consume "sweet stuff" is thus part of a longing for the physicality and sensuousness of the maternal relationship. This, I believe, is an integral part of the appeal of the sweet, rich foods so frequently featured in classic feasting fantasies. For contemporary children, who perhaps feel that they have missed out on the ideal childhood portrayed in so many arcadian texts, these narrative elements coalesce to produce strong feelings of nostalgia.

PREPUBESCENT *JOUISSANCE*

While I have argued that food narratives are appealing because they provide sensuous delight, it is interesting to speculate about the reader's capacity for epicurean pleasure. Additionally, it is fascinating to consider just what the act of reading food narratives does to readers. Stephanie Theobald has written anecdotally about the sensuous appeal of classic feasting narratives. She relates that, prior to her discovery of the sexually explicit popular fiction written by Jacqueline Susann, she enjoyed reading Enid Blyton. "Until the age of 11," she confesses, "it was Enid Blyton's *Famous Five* picnics that turned me on. All that business about Ann laying out the ham and the fresh-baked bread and the lashings of ginger beer used to trigger some weird prepubescent jouissance."[39]

Jouissance, as Roland Barthes uses it in *The Pleasure of the Text*, expresses the ultimate pleasure experienced through reading. His use of the word has been translated as ecstasy, bliss, or rapture. Jouissance is a profoundly intense readerly response to a narrative, it is "unspeakable," in the sense of being impossible to explain and is only discovered "between the lines" of a narrative.[40] Additionally, Barthes argues that language has the ability to wound or seduce the reader (38). It seems to me that jouissance is a particularly individual and unpredictable response to a text and that it is heavily reliant upon the reader's extra-textual knowledge, desires, and sympathies. I believe that for the text to affect a reader as intimately as Barthes suggests is possible, there must be some further connection between the narrative and the reader's desires and experiences, such as perhaps, in the case of sweet and creamy food descriptions, the prolonged absence of a mother-figure, or an extremely lonely, deprived, or austere early childhood.

Julia Kristeva links jouissance (which she finds in moments of symbolic transgression such as "madness, holiness and poetry") with the semiotic, a pre-oedipal mother-child relationship/space that precedes subjectivity and the symbolic order.[41] As such any emotional nourishment, or jouissance, a reader receives from the consumption of a food text may be described as transgressive in as much as it involves a desire to return to the maternal aesthetic, a space which, in terms of psychological development, should have long since been abandoned.

Theobald qualifies her use of the word jouissance by describing it as "weird" and "prepubescent." Do her qualifications reduce the strength of her experience or dilute it in some way? Is nostalgia casting a rosy glow over her memories of childhood? Certainly her use of the word jouissance is knowing, powerful, and significant. I think that, given the right circumstances, reading a lavish and sensuous description of a feast may provide intense emotional satisfaction and that the quality of the readers' response may be strengthened by their desire for the quantity, quality, richness, and exoticism of the foods described, or supplemented by their desire for a longed-for and idealized maternal figure. I am quite sure that these responses may not just be dismissed as greed. Greed cannot be satisfied by textual food. Indeed, textual food is likely to intensify pangs of hunger, to increase desire. But textual food can afford emotional nourishment, intense pleasure, and sometimes even jouissance.

Barthes (in the same treatise) writes about his own experience of reading about food and considers whether the appeal of literary feasting can be put down to pure greed:

In an old text I have just read (an episode of ecclesiastical life cited by Stendhal) occurs a naming of foods: milk, buttered bread, cream cheese, preserves, Maltese oranges, sugared strawberries. Is this another pleasure of pure representation (experienced therefore solely by the greedy reader)? But I have no fondness for milk or so many sweets, and I do not project much of myself in to the detail of these dishes. Something else occurs, doubtless having to do with another meaning of the word "representation." ... The novelist, by citing, naming, *noticing* food (by treating it as notable), imposes on the reader the final state of matter, what cannot be transcended, withdrawn ... [the novelist thus] speaks "reality" (what is seen but not demonstrated); the [naming of foods in the] novel ... adds to the intelligible of the "real" the hallucinatory tail of "reality": astonishment that in 1791 one could eat "a salad of oranges and rum," as one does in restaurants today: the onset of historical intelligibility and the persistence of the thing (orange, rum) in *being there.* (45–46, italics in original)

Here I think Barthes is referring to the fundamental down-to-earth authenticity of the food on the plate and to the shared reality of being/having a material (eating) body. He emphasizes the real-ness of its corporeality and the pleasures to be had from acceding to the desires of embodied subjectivity. In other words, Barthes acknowledges that the food narrative forms a very strong and meaningful connection between his daily personal *bodily* experiences and desires and the narrative, thus creating verisimilitude and, as he says, a powerful notion of "*being there.*" He concurs that the naming of foods goes beyond mere greed and from it he receives pleasure. Later, in *The Pleasure of the Text* he raises the question of the enjoyment he and others experience in "the representation of the 'daily life' of an epoch," the "curiosity" felt about "petty details: schedules, habits, meals, lodging, clothing, etc." Now he argues that for him such details go beyond "the hallucinatory relish of 'reality.'" He asks whether other readers "receive bliss [jouissance] from a singular theater: not one of grandeur but one of mediocrity?" (53). He argues that literary "meals" (as well as other everyday representations of daily reality) can lead to jouissance. Their absence from a text, he intimates, can lead to disappointment (53–54). It is clear, however, that it is not necessarily food fantasies that produce jouissance for Barthes but the "theater" of "reality." In this respect Barthes seems to be referring to what Raymond Williams calls "a structure of feeling;" Barthes' "singular theater" being similar to what Williams refers to as a representation of "the culture of [the] period," one which contains details familiar to the reader and makes "communication possible" across time, for example, between writer and reader.[42] Undoubtedly, a sense of communion between text and reader, such as Barthes describes, which also appeals to and fulfills the desires of embodied subjectivity, can produce profound satisfaction.

While the reported reading experiences of both Barthes and Theobald are revealing, consideration of the child's reading experience is necessarily largely speculative. According to John Stephens, the child reader also produces meaning from the text based on what she or he understands from the words on the page, which is processed and evaluated according to the child's existing knowledge and "style." The meaning of a text is not therefore determinate but is best characterized as "a dialectic between textual discourse (including its construction of an implied reader and a range of potential subject positions) and a reader's disposition, familiarity with story conventions, and experiential knowledge."[43]

I would like to speculate further about what a food narrative might do to a child reader given the special circumstances of deprivation I have described and the text's inherent therapeutic value. Hugh Crago refers to "absorbed" or "ludic reading," which is virtually a trance-like state where readers willingly become oblivious to the world around them.[44] Although this is by no means a universal phenomenon and "many" readers do not read in this deeply absorbed manner (Crago, 169), it is worth investigating. It appears that, for readers with the ability to become so absorbed in a book, aesthetic quality has little to do with their enjoyment. Instead, as Schlager found, children's preferences had more to do with matching the books' themes to their own particular developmental stage and inner world. Successful "merging" of reader and book is apparently far more likely when there is a partly or wholly metaphorical correspondence between the content of the text and the reader's experience than when it was literal (cited by Crago, 169). Crago explains that

> human addiction to "story" is an aspect of our symbol-making nature: our very language is strongly metaphorical and our dreaming almost always uses the language of symbol and analogy. When we read a story that is obviously very similar in its characters and events to our own life experience, we may read it with enjoyment and appreciation, consciously appreciating the parallels... [However,] For a print text to "plug into" the [normal consciousness] and temporarily replace it as an ongoing source of images, feelings and self-talk, exquisitely fine unconscious matching must occur, so that the reader "recognizes" something of high personal significance, while simultaneously failing to pin down its precise meaning. (169)

Crago is convinced that such "matching" is akin to falling in love. He argues that, when we fall in love or when we become deeply absorbed in a narrative, "an instinctive, largely unconscious recognition of similarity occurs, while consciously, the individuals concerned are aware only of a powerful emotional 'pull' and a sense of 'rightness' or 'fitness' in being with the other person (or text)" (169). Texts that have this effect are likely to be read again and again and "brooded over in memory." They become "potent influences over the reader's future self concept and life path" (170).

It is worth considering Crago's notion of "exquisitely fine unconscious matching" in terms of my construction of the image of a child reader, deprived of craved-for emotional comfort and/or sweet food, who encounters a description of a delicious feast of rich, sweet foods provided by a motherly figure in a story book. It is my contention that, given these circumstances, the food text can exert a very "powerful emotional 'pull'" as Crago suggests, so that the reader feels a "rightness" or "fitness" or, perhaps, a sense of *belonging* with regard to the text. Thus, the food text is, to my mind, capable of doing something exceptionally intense, pleasurable, and profound to the reader, which may also have therapeutic consequences. At the same time, however, the reader's creative input into the experience should be acknowledged. Reading is, after all, an active and productive pastime in this regard. Thus, I might suggest, the text and the reader act synergistically to produce a cathartic emotional outcome.

FOOD FETISHES

In her anecdotal account, Theobald describes fictional food as a focus of childhood sexual desire; it "turned [her] on." No doubt there are those who would object to the linking of children with sexuality at any level, but Theobald is not alone in describing the response to food in children's books in such terms. Keith Barker, for example, cites Dahl's descriptions of the chocolate factory as "border[ing] on the orgasmic" (4) and Perry Nodelman, among many other literary critics, including Wendy Katz,[45] understands food to function partly as a substitute for sex in children's fiction: "The sensuous delight of these descriptions of food [in a range of classic texts] reveals that in children's fiction, eating seems to occupy the place that sex does in adult fiction."[46] Maria Nikolajeva repeatedly shows that "meals in myths and fairy tales are circumlocutions of sexual intercourse."[47] It is not just literary theorists who make the connection between food and sex.

Theobald's account suggests that for her food was/is a sexual cue or fetish. Here I refer to the notion of a fetish as an object that generates or triggers sexual/sensuous desire.[48] Certainly the connection between food and sex is complicated, involving an intertwining of two drives or appetites that, as Sarah Sceats argues, are not easy to disentangle or identify as distinct. She points out that the link between food and sex is "constantly reinforced in Western culture, from images insinuating the fellatio of chocolate bars, sausages and asparagus to the almost routine comparison of breasts with fruits or the attribution of aphrodisiac qualities to oysters and other genitally suggestive foodstuffs."[49] Furthermore, Sceats (echoing Freud) suggests that children are particularly adept at transposing sexual and alimentary pleasures because of their "polymorphous sexuality" and because the "mental dams" preventing adults from doing so have not yet slipped into place (28).

Some writers have been reluctant to mention children and sex in the same sentence. In his essay "On Three Ways of Writing for Children," Lewis relates the reactions of a father to the scene in *The Lion, the Witch and the Wardrobe* where Lucy takes tea with Mr. Tumnus: "Ah, [the father comments] I see how you got to that. If you want to please grown-up readers you give them sex, so you thought to yourself, 'That won't do for children, what shall I give them instead? I know! The little blighters like plenty of good eating.'"[50] But, unfortunately Lewis rejected the idea that food was a substitute for sex in his stories. In doing so, Nikolajeva believes Lewis was being either naive, insincere, or both. He failed to acknowledge the parallels between food and sexuality, despite the fact that he was aware of the symbolic and ritual significance of food. Nikolajeva suggests that he couldn't admit to the notion because, as he was writing for children, "he had to observe the proprieties" (Nikolajeva, 129). I would like to suggest that the very fact that Lewis included the anecdote in his essay is significant even if prevalent cultural mores prevented him from explicitly admitting the connection between food and childhood sexuality. Clearly food in children's stories does function to titillate appetite/desire, to allow voyeuristic and sensuous pleasure and to provide intense emotional satisfaction in ways that parallel the functions of sexual activity in stories for adults.[51]

TRANSGRESSIVE CONSUMPTION

The sensuous appeal of textual food is not limited to children, of course, as myriad cookbooks, magazines, and television programs show. A major component of the appeal of food in narratives for children, in the eroticized images of foods in food magazines and in advertising, and in erotic novels for adults, such as Linda Jaivan's *Eat Me*,[52] is that they transgress cultural mores. It is significant that the foods most frequently used as sexual metaphors in advertising and, arguably, most drooled over in "gastroporn" imagery, are sweet, creamy, fattening foods, such as ice cream and chocolate. These foods contravene, in mouth-wateringly sweet and fattening detail, the dietary control mechanisms imposed on contemporary individuals by Western culture. As well as concern for physical health, Western culture's prohibition on sweet food reveals a continuing preoccupation with immorality. Such foods are described as "wicked," "sinful," and "naughty but nice." Desire for sweet, rich, creamy foods also threatens individual subjectivity and the (patriarchal) social order because of the associated desire for the pre-oedipal maternal aesthetic.

Relatively expensive ice cream and chocolate products are marketed primarily to adult women, while cheaper sweets are popularly considered to appeal to children, which is why literary feasting fantasies so often feature them in enormous quantities. J. K. Rowling's Harry Potter buys vast numbers of sweets on his first train trip to Hogwarts, including chocolate frogs that hop around (in the movie version of *Philosopher's Stone*).[53] And, in Blyton's *Faraway Tree Stories* the children frequently eat huge amounts of sweets. In the "Land of Goodies" the children find a house reminiscent of Hansel and Gretel's gingerbread house, with walls made of sugar, chimneys of chocolate, a marzipan door, and gingerbread windowsills. Currant buns, biscuits, and boiled sweets grow on trees, as do plates full of green jelly. The children discover a barley-sugar fence and are each given a cake with their name on it in pink sugar letters. "Into shop after shop went the children and the others, *tasting everything they could see*. They had tomato soup, poached eggs, ginger buns, chocolate fingers, ice-creams, and goodness knows what else."[54] The volume of sweets and foods eaten by the children in these narratives is clearly fantastic, but appealing because it caters to greed.

Allison James argues that children's sweets in particular are a form of resistance to adult culture and involve a rejection of its rituals and symbols. Because adult culture generally considers children's sweets to be "rubbishy," "despised," "diseased and inedible," James contends, children give them "great prestige" and consider them to be particularly desirable.[55] Further, children's sweets belong to the "public, social world of children" and the consumption of different sweets by adults and children reflects the "inherent contradiction between their separate worlds" (James, 301).

Children's sweets, like the "nursery food" in *Seven Little Australians* mentioned earlier, are culturally considered to be unsuitable fare for adults as Professor Dumbledore finds out in *Harry Potter and the Philosopher's Stone*. Visiting the hospital wing at Hogwarts after Harry's battle with the evil Lord Voldermort, Dumbledore finds that Harry's friends have left him "what looked like half the sweet shop" as "tokens" (*Philosopher's*

Stone, 214). Dumbledore decides to recall his youth by sampling one of Bertie Bott's Every Flavour Beans. He had been, he explains, "unfortunate enough in [his] youth to come across a vomit-flavoured one" but thinks that he might "be safe with a nice toffee" (217). He pops a golden-brown bean into his mouth only to choke and to be forced to confess (rather poignantly in the movie version) to having tasted earwax (218). In terms of taste, children's and adult's worlds are indeed seen to be very different and contradictory, as James suggests. Specific categories of sweets, food, and fiction are classified by adult culture as suitable for children's unsophisticated tastes but as distinctly unappetizing to adults.[56] Children's subject positions are thus created for them in terms that are often explicitly antithetical to adult culture.

Fictional children are often shown not only to eat the wrong foods (too much sweet stuff) at the wrong time (between meals, or midnight feasts) but also to eat foods in the wrong sequence. Tucker comments that the picnics Blyton's characters frequently enjoy are often "hurriedly put-together dishes...with sausages, fried eggs, honey and jam eaten all at once. Such a meal may be nauseating to adult tastes, but just the sort of thing a smaller child might like."[57] These conglomerations of foods are a form of resistance to adult culture, as James has shown in relation to children's sweets. They are appealing to children because they flout the rules and specifically because adults find them so "nauseating." Feasts such as Tucker describes thus appear to question the subject positions created for children within established adult order in a way that can be labeled carnivalesque (Stephens 1992, 120–21).

Stephens has shown that carnivalesque texts may be divided into three types: first, "those that offer the characters 'time out' from the habitual constraints of society but incorporate a safe return to social normality" (Maurice Sendak's *Where the Wild Things Are* [1963] is a good example); second, those that strive "through gentle mockery to dismantle socially received ideas and replace them with their opposite" (for example *Fungus the Bogeyman* [1977] by Raymond Briggs); and, third, those which are "endemically subversive of such things as social authority, received paradigms of behaviour and morality, and [of] major literary genres associated with children's literature" (Stephens 1992, 121; Stephens cites *Out of the Oven* [1986] by Jan Mark). Texts that transgress adult food rules generally fall into either the first or third of these "types." Those stories that fall into the first category and contain episodes of excessive sweet eating or midnight feasts, for example, offer a "time out" experience which is separate from the habitual constraints of social and familial eating but does not undermine social normality. In Blyton's stories the children's transgressive eating always takes place during one of their adventures.

They subsequently return safely home and, significantly, when at home they are compliant to the expectations of adult society. The children's transgressive eating thus contributes to the escapist discourse underlying the narrative. Tucker suggests, in his analysis of Blyton's stories, that the "orgy of eating" that occurs at some stage in most of her work is "one more pleasant fantasy to add to the effortless adventures of this idealized group of children" (Tucker, 111).

Interestingly, both James and Tucker infer that children's sweet/eating habits are disgusting and implicitly align them with the abject. Abjection and disgust are visceral reactions which, Julia Kristeva argues, result from psychological taboos relating to body functions, to the maternal body specifically, and thus the semiotic.[58] Patrick Fuery links the semiotic with Bakhtin's concept of the carnivalesque; both disrupt the social order/symbolic[59] and contain elements that are irrational, improper and unclean. While carnival is socially sanctioned and controlled, however, the abject is taboo and should be repressed.[60] The semiotic and abject oppose (patriarchal) social order and thus proper notions of subjectivity (Grosz 1989, 78). So, while children may indulge in the "despised" sweets and unregulated eating habits described in their fictions such practices must be confined to childhood and are clearly dangerous for adults.

4

THE LAND OF MILK AND HONEY

Representing the Mother

The mother...is the core and very heart [of the family]...A mother
is one who gives her own body to be eaten. She first nourishes the
child in her womb and then gives it her milk.

—Elias Canetti, *Crowds and Power*[1]

Breast milk and honey are the only two natural foods, made only
to be eaten. They're not anything else...[just] food and food
alone...When you're a baby, you live in the land of milk and
honey.

— Thomas Fox Averill, *Secrets of the Tsil Cafe*[2]

Concerning that stage of my childhood, scented, warm, and soft to
the touch, I have only a spatial memory. No time at all. Fragrance
of honey, roundness of forms, silk and velvet under my fingers,
on my cheeks. Mummy.

— Julia Kristeva, "Stabat Mater"[3]

IMAGINE A LAND WHERE HUNGER and anxiety are unknown, where there
is only constant warmth, comfort, satiety, and satisfaction. There is no
self and other, no inside and outside, and no desire because nothing is
lacking. This is a place of total fulfillment.

The primal experience precedes perception, but arguably has indelible
and profound effects upon an individual's formation of identity. According

to Christopher Bollas aesthetic experience originates with the body of the mother. He argues that "the aesthetic 'moment' predates consciousness and cognition... [it comes] before thought/word/language."[4] This "moment" articulates the experience of "deep rapport" with the mother, when self and other, subject and object "rendezvous."[5] During this earliest period of life the mother's "idiom of care" largely determines the formation of the child's notion of self, which is developed and transformed by the environment. The aesthetic moment Bollas claims, is "the first human aesthetic" the child experiences and it prefigures and foreshadows all future aesthetics including the propensity for literary metaphor and image. In later life this experience can be evoked through "an existential memory" resulting in feelings that are "familiar, uncanny, sacred, reverential, and outside cognitive coherence" (Bollas, 41–44). Bollas is not alone in emphasizing the significance of the primal bond between mother and infant. Social attachment theorists like John Bowlby and Mary Ainsworth emphasize the "emotional" nature of the link with the mother's body (cited by Natov, 63). Winifred Gallagher quotes Thomas Insel, who claims "the mother... forms an environmental unit with her infant"[6] and Myron Hofer who further argues that the primal bond between mother and baby results in so close a relationship that, "For a baby, the environment *is* the mother" (Gallagher, 120 emphasis in original).

Jessica Benjamin uses object-relations theory to emphasize the significance of the mother-child dyad, arguing that it rivals the oedipal triangle in psychological importance; recognition from the m/other, she explains, "makes meaningful the feelings, intentions, and actions of the self."[7] Benjamin underlines the paradoxical mixture of otherness and togetherness experienced by both the mother and the child in the relationship (15) and the reciprocal nature of their need for each other (24).

The mother-child dyad, encompassing the environment/space of "deep rapport" referred to by Bollas is alluded to in the title to this chapter: "The Land of Milk and Honey." Roni Natov points out that the use of metaphor to describe the primal bond between the bodies of the infant and the mother is significant. She refers to Mark Johnson who claims that all thought begins with and includes the body (Natov, 63). The primal experience also involves absolute fulfillment. This unique and sublime state exists in contrast to what follows. For the infant hunger, cold, and loneliness are new sensations; they act to signal and define the infant's previous experience. Once the lack of warmth, food, and comfort is realized, desire for their restoration presumably follows. The subconscious yearning for the restoration of the primal state is arguably present in all subsequent desire. Natov concurs, claiming that "desire for the mother is at the heart of much of the literature of childhood, particularly in books for young children." Picture books especially, she asserts, "evoke the body of the mother and early states of desire" (65). Sarah Sceats goes further, claiming that such desire permeates contemporary life: "The modern world manifests an overwhelming human yearning for wholeness, oneness or integrity, a yearning apparent in oral appetites, sexual desire, religious fervour, physical hunger, 'back to the womb' impulses, [and] death wishes."[8] Janice Doane and Devon Hodges agree, claiming, "Ultimately, the work of symbol formation, art and culture themselves, can be attributed to our attempts to make reparation, to regenerate the mother."[9] Nancy Chodorow, too, places an implicit emphasis on the universality of the desire to recreate the primal relationship, asserting that, "people come out of it with the memory of a unique intimacy which they want to recreate."[10] It is my belief that food, especially sweet, rich food, often metaphorically represents the body of the mother in popular culture and that the desire for such food includes a subconscious yearning for the restoration of the primal relationship with her.[11]

MOTHER'S MILK

Freud emphasized the importance of the initial feeding relationship in his early work. He argued that during the "oral stage," sensations are generated which exceed satiation and satisfaction. The experience of suckling, he claimed, can be intensely pleasurable; initially hunger is quelled but later the rhythmical pleasure of suckling itself is sought.

> No-one who has seen a baby sinking back satiated from the breast and falling asleep with flushed cheeks and a blissful smile can escape the reflection that this picture persists as a prototype of the expression of sexual satisfaction in later life. The need for repeating the sexual satisfaction now becomes detached from the need for taking nourishment.[12]

Freud's much-quoted proposition that sexual satisfaction is derived from early feeding coincides with what Sceats refers to as a "commonsense" view (25); it does seem natural to assume that a baby receives tremendous sensual satisfaction from the early feeding relationship. Rosalind Coward, too, affirms that, "there's a meshing of nourishment and sensual gratification between mother and child."[13] The baby receives physical pleasure on a number of levels: the satiation of hunger, sensual satisfaction, as well as comforting sensations relating to the fragrance, warmth, and soft roundness of the mother's body, as Kristeva recalls in the epigraph above, even if bottle fed. The early feeding relationship, as the source of an infant's first profound pleasures, has resonances throughout an individual's life and has important cultural significance. The physical and psychological satisfaction derived from feeding creates a fundamentally important and lasting attachment to the mother and to sweet, rich, foods.[14] The breast is a metonym for the mother's body and a metaphor for the milk it produces.[15] As her milk is consumed so is she, and whenever "comfort" foods are craved for, so is the primal mother-child relationship.

Desire for the mother figure is clearly present in Michael Ende's *The Neverending Story*, which contains an extraordinary evocation of the whole environment and experience of the primal state. Bastian's mother dies when he is a small boy leaving him withdrawn and lonely. His father is emotionally distant, immersed in his work and is, in Bastian's dream, "shut up in a transparent but impenetrable block of ice."[16] Bastian becomes engrossed in a magic book; as the hero of the story Bastian saves the world of Fantastica, but some of his more selfish actions result in unfortunate events that leave him dissatisfied, lonely, and alienated. Toward the end of the story, when he is searching for a way to return to his own world, Bastian follows a winding path through a rose garden to the "House of Change." It is the

> funniest house he had ever seen. Under a tall, pointed roof that looked rather like a stocking cap, the house itself suggested a giant pumpkin. The walls were covered with large protuberances, one might almost have said bellies, that gave the house a comfortably inviting look. There were a few windows and a front door, but they seemed crooked, as though a clumsy child had cut them out. (*Neverending*, 338)

This house with its comforting and inviting fat belly-like shape is the home of Dame Eyola. Bastian is "irresistibly drawn" to the sound of her singing (339). She is "as round and red-cheeked and healthy-looking as an apple. Bastian was almost overpowered by a desire to run to her with outstretched arms and cry: 'Mama, Mama!'" (339). Dame Eyola has "the same sweet smile and the same trustworthy look as [Bastian's] mother." "As he stood looking at her, he was overcome by a feeling that he had not known for a long time. He could not remember when and where; he knew only that he had sometimes felt that way when he was little" (340).

Dame Eyola's body produces fruits, flowers, and leaves. When Bastian has eaten all the fruit in the fruit bowl "she plucked fruit from her hat and dress until the bowl was full again" (342). She explains to Bastian: "It all grows out of me. Just as your hair grows out of you. That should show you how glad I am that you've finally come. That's why I'm flowering and bearing fruit. If I were sad I'd wither. But come now, don't forget to eat" (343).

Bastian was embarrassed. "I don't know," he said. "Is it all right to eat something that comes out of somebody?"

"Why not?" asked Dame Eyola. "Babies drink milk that comes out of their mothers. There's nothing better."

"That's true," said Bastian with a slight blush. "But only when they're very little."

"In that case," said Dame Eyola, beaming, "you'll just have to get to be very little again, my dear boy."

Bastian took another fruit and bit into it. Dame Eyola was delighted and bloomed more than ever. (343)

The narrative makes it absolutely explicit that Dame Eyola produces food on demand from her body just as a breast-feeding mother does. Furthermore, she experiences great pleasure from feeding him. Bastian derives sensuous satisfaction from eating her food, just as Freud describes. The fruit is better than anything he has ever tasted before. "He sigh[ed] with well-being...each new fruit gave him a more rapturous sensation than the last" (341). Bastian falls into a delicious dream-like state where he is "irresistibly lulled by her sweet voice" (345).

> He had slipped into a sweet half-sleep in which he heard her words as a kind of chant. He heard her stand up and cross the room and bend over him. She stroked his hair and kissed him on the forehead. Then he felt her pick him up and carry him out in her arms. He buried his head in her bosom like a baby. Deeper and deeper he sank into the warm sleepy darkness. (345)

The House of Change is a womb-like space; Dame Eyola is a fruiting/lactating mother figure whose food and comforting presence take Bastian back to the primal relationship where he literally becomes a baby again. He even sleeps in a crib, albeit "a very large crib, or rather it was as large as a crib must look to a baby" (346). Bastian spends the summer with Dame Eyola, but gradually his cravings for her food and nurturing lessen and he realizes that he is ready to leave her and return to the real world. Significantly, he is now able to give love to his still grieving father. Dame Eyola is an obvious mother figure of the pre-oedipal/oral stage. Bastian moves on to the oedipal stage when he is ready to approach and relate to his father.

Bastian's fruit eating is reminiscent of a passage in C. S. Lewis's *The Last Battle*, the final book in his Narnia series. Although there is no maternal figure present in this part of Lewis's narrative, the hedonistic pleasure the food affords and the carefree environment in which it is eaten are symbolic of the deep rapport of the primal experience Bollas refers to. After the last battle the children reach a paradisaical "country where everything is allowed,"[17] where the grass is green and the sky is "deep blue" and where the wind of an early summer "blew gently on their faces." "Not far away from them rose a grove of fruit trees, thickly leaved, but under every leaf there peeped out the gold or faint yellow or purple or glowing red of fruits such as no one has seen in our world."

> What was the fruit like? Unfortunately no one can describe a taste. All I can say is that, compared with those fruits, the freshest grapefruit you've ever eaten was dull, and the juiciest orange was dry, and the most melting pear was hard and woody, and the sweetest wild strawberry was sour. And there were no seeds or stones, and no wasps. If you had once eaten that fruit, all the nicest things in this world would taste like medicines after it. (*Last Battle*, 129–30)

The fruit Lewis describes is otherworldly; it is the perfect food, a sort of fruity ambrosia. Although not as explicit as Ende's narrative, Lewis's writing evokes a hedonistic scenario redolent of the primal relationship. David Holbrook suggests that, in terms of the context of Lewis's Narnia series, his protagonists are "in Heaven," but that in psychoanalytic terms they have "reached the True Breast."[18]

The comforting image of an idealized maternal figure and environment are produced in Nina Bawden's *Carrie's War*. Carrie and her little brother Nick are evacuated to Wales during World War II. They are billeted with a rather strange couple whose house is cold and austere. But they derive much comfort from visiting Hepzibah whose kitchen is "A warm, safe, lighted place... Coming into it was like coming home on a bitter cold day to a bright, leaping fire. It was like the smell of bacon when you were hungry; loving arms when you were lonely; safety when you were scared." Thus, the kitchen is a maternalized space, a place where warmth, the promise of food, bodily contact, and security conflate to produce feelings of comfort. When the children first meet Hepzibah she is "smiling. She was tall with shining hair the colour of copper. She wore a white apron, the sleeves of her dress were rolled up, showing big, fair, freckled arms, and there was flour on her hands."[19] She has "a rather broad face, pale as cream, and dotted with freckles. Carrie thought she looked beautiful: so warm and friendly and kind" (*Carrie's War*, 52). The feelings of homely, maternal comfort evoked by the descriptions of the kitchen and of Hepzibah herself are embellished and reinforced by sensuous descriptions of food. Carrie is shown the dairy where "there were speckly eggs in trays on the shelf, slabs of pale, oozy butter, and a big bowl of milk with a skin of cream on the top. [She] felt hollow with hunger" (48). Carrie's hunger is partially satisfied when she and Nick are invited to tea.

The cloth on the table was so stiffly starched that it stuck out at the corners. There was a huge plate of mince pies, golden brown and dusted with sugar, a tall jug of milk, a pink ham, and slices of bread thickly spread with the lovely, pale, sweaty butter Carrie had seen in the dairy. (51)

After tea Nick, who is ten, two years younger than Carrie, goes to sit on Hepzibah's lap:

He put his head on her shoulder and she turned and picked him up and sat him on her broad lap, her arms tight about him. She rocked him gently and he nestled close and put his thumb in his mouth…Carrie looked at Nick on Hepzibah's lap and felt jealous. (54)

Hepzibah rocks Nick and he nestles in and suckles like a baby. She embodies the love and comfort of the primal relationship evoked by the conflation of place, food, and warmth.

Tom, the water baby in Charles Kingsley's Victorian fantasy, meets a "pretty lady" who is a mother figure called Mrs. Doasyouwouldbedoneby.

[S]he has the sweetest, kindest, tenderest, funniest, merriest face [anyone] ever saw…[and] Tom saw that…she was the most nice, soft, fat, smooth, pussy, cuddly, delicious creature who ever nursed a baby;…when the children saw her, they naturally all caught hold of her, and clung round her neck, and caught hold of her hands; and then they all put their thumbs in their mouths, and began cuddling and purring like so many kittens.[20]

Tom receives special attention from her and revels in it:

[S]he took Tom in her arms, and laid him in the softest place of all, and kissed him, and patted him, and talked to him, tenderly and low, such things as he had never heard before in his life; and Tom looked up into her eyes, and loved her, and loved, till he fell asleep from pure love. (*Water Babies,* 119)

Significantly, Mrs. Doasyouwouldbedoneby's sister and alter-ego, Mrs. Bedonebyasyoudid, has provided Tom and the other water babies with "all sorts of nice sea-things [to eat]—sea-cakes, sea-apples, sea-oranges, sea-bullseyes, sea-toffee; and to the very best of all she gave sea-ices, made out of sea-cows' cream, which never melt under water" (112). These are very special rich, sweet foods, which, again, conflate with the bodily contact, comfort, and love provided by the mother figure to produce the idealized maternal aesthetic.

Dickon's mother in Frances Hodgson Burnett's *The Secret Garden* provides Mary and Colin with simple but wholesome traditionally British fare including fresh milk, homemade crusty bread, currant buns, oat cakes, and heather honey.[21] As I suggested earlier, the foods the children eat in this narrative represent the oral phase, the stage of maternal influence. Colin's recovery, which results from a coalescence of the influence of the natural foods he eats, together with fresh air, physical activity, and the emotional support of his new friends, leads to his progression to the oedipal stage where, like Bastian, he is able to break through his father's grief and relate to him.

Even though what is on his plate is never specifically mentioned in the story, a loving maternal relationship is evoked in Maurice Sendak's picture storybook *Where the Wild Things Are* because when Max's adventure is over and he returns to his room his meal is waiting for him and it is significantly, still hot.[22]

It is interesting that these examples feature male protagonists receiving maternal comfort. Although Carrie is also hungry for motherly love and would have liked to sit on Hepzibah's lap, she does not do so because she is trying to be a mother-replacement for her little brother. She therefore denies herself this pleasure. An example of a girl receiving maternal comfort is to be found in Philip Pullman's *Northern Lights*, but the episode is not described as giving quite the same degree of pleasure as is described in most of the previous examples. Ma Costa's canal boat gives Lyra physical shelter but she provides emotional sustenance by folding "her great arms around Lyra and press[ing] her to her breast." The warmed milk she prepares for Lyra, who is tired and has been badly frightened, is synonymous with maternal comfort and safety. "A minute or two later [Lyra] was sound asleep."[23] In the morning the hot breakfast Ma prepares for Lyra of a "couple of rashers of bacon" and an egg (*Northern Lights,* 107) is coded, in terms of the narrative, as nutritious and sustaining and thus it acts to reiterate the good mother paradigm. In this example, the good mother image is maintained, but the episode is not described as hedonistically pleasurable for the female hero. It is interesting to speculate about the significance of the gender of those receiving comfort in these examples. I can only suppose that perhaps girls are not seen to be as hungry for maternal comfort as boys either because they have not had to separate from their mothers so entirely or because they are considered to be able one day, as mothers themselves, to re-experience the mother-child primal relationship. Or is it because, as Freud argued, girls' desires should be directed toward the male/father and we are culturally uncomfortable with the notion of a (grown) girl receiving comfort at the maternal breast? It is certainly difficult to imagine Ende's narrative written about a girl instead of a boy.

These examples have the protagonists receiving emotional nourishment (in varying degrees) as well as gastronomic pleasure from the food provided by maternal figures. The food symbolizes love, comfort, and safety and is coded to create a familiar atmosphere, a "homely" maternal environment suggestive of the primal relationship. If, for example, Max's meal had been stone cold and congealed when he returned, the effect of reparation and healing evoked by his return to the mother in the narrative as it stands, would have been entirely absent. The desire to return to or to restore the rapport and fulfillment of the primal relationship is clearly present in representations of food linked to the maternal aesthetic in many stories for children. The narrative emphasis on the protagonists' desire for sweet comfort foods also indicates the oral stage, the pre-oedipal phase of maternal influence.

PARADIGMS OF MOTHERHOOD

Given the initial constancy of the primal relationship and the intense pleasures of feeding, the sudden realization that the breast/mother is absent/unavailable must be profoundly shocking for the infant. The feelings of loss and helplessness that result have significant psychological repercussions. Chodorow asserts that, during this period of "infantile dependence," most psychological activity is a reaction to the child's feelings of helplessness. The child cannot get along without its mother because she acts as "external ego, provides holding and nourishment, and is in fact not experienced by the infant as a separate person at all." Chodorow suggests that the child will "employ techniques which attempt to prevent or deny its mother's departure or separateness" (Chodorow, 59). Melanie Klein devised a theory concerning the "techniques" employed by an infant to counter the feelings of helplessness and frustration felt during its mother's absence. The child, she claimed, is only concerned with gratification or its lack:

> Thus, the breast of the mother which gives gratification or denies it becomes, in the mind of the child, imbued with the characteristics of good and evil. Now, what one might call the "good" breasts become the prototype of what is felt throughout life to be good and beneficent, while the 'bad' breasts stand for everything evil and persecuting.[24]

As I have suggested, the breast metonymically stands in for the body of the mother. Klein's theory can be extrapolated to produce a semantic link between notions of the good mother and food/love/comfort and between the bad mother and lack of food/love/comfort. This supports my assertion that representations of food, especially sweet, rich foods, evoke the presence/body of the mother and both produce feelings of comfort/love.

Klein goes on to suggest that the breasts become the target of destructive fantasies that are "of a definitely cannibalistic nature... In his imagination the child attacks [the mother's breast], robbing it of everything it contains and eating it up." These fantasies are then projected onto the mother producing a dread of being eaten (Klein, 291). As Maria Tatar and others have pointed out, Klein's analysis posits breast-feeding as a cultural universal but her argument conceivably still holds true for babies who are bottle-fed. The infant's aggression, in this case, is targeted upon the nurturer's body and then is turned into a characteristic of the nurturer.[25] Chodorow tones down Klein's claims somewhat by asserting:

> Orality and the oral attitude of incorporation (the fantasy of taking in the mother or her breast) as a primary infantile mode, for instance, is not an inevitable extrapolation from nursing. It is one defensive technique for retaining primary identification (a sense of oneness) when this is being eroded—when the mother is beginning to be experienced as a separate person... Separateness during this early period threatens not only anxiety at possible loss, but the infant's very sense of existence. (Chodorow, 59–60)

In other words, the infant may struggle to maintain or restore the "oneness" of the primal bond by imagining or fantasizing about the incorporation/consumption of the mother, so that, in effect, two can become one again. At the same time, conflict is produced by the periodic and routine absence of the breast, which signals and reiterates that the mother is an/other person. The resentment that the child experiences when the breast/mother is absent is understandable. That this resentment should turn to anger and ephemeral feelings of hatred and aggression is also understandable. The mother thus becomes the object of the child's love when she is present and of momentary hatred when she is absent. Notably, this psychological struggle takes place in the context of and is produced largely by the child's *feeding* relationship with the mother and results in ambivalence. Psychological ambivalence toward the mother figure is reflected in popular culture.

E. Ann Kaplan claims that there are three main paradigms of motherhood represented in popular culture. The first, the "all sacrificing 'angel in the house'" is the idealized mother figure I have already featured. The second is her opposite and the embodiment of what Klein referred to as the "bad" breast, the mother who is "evil, possessive... destructive [and] all-devouring."[26] The bad mother, an archetypal figure linked to what Barbara Creed refers to as the "monstrous feminine," and to the *vagina dentata*,[27] is the subject of the next chapter. The third paradigm of motherhood is the smothering mother, one who is "over-indulgent, satisfying her own needs" (Kaplan, 48).

SMOTHERING MOTHERS

The woman who exclusively devotes herself to mothering runs the risk of smothering her child and losing her own identity. She becomes the mother who seeks all fulfillment through her child, who is often implicated in cases of literary childhood obesity through overindulgent feeding, and who metaphorically embodies the engulfing qualities of the abject. Elizabeth Grosz, referring to the work of Luce Irigaray, explains how the mother

> with no access to social value in her own right…becomes the mother who has only food (that is, love) to give the child. Unable to give the child language, law and exchange—the phallus—she has only nurturance, and its most tangible manifestations—eating, defecating—through which she may gain social recognition and value. She risks choking or smothering the child with an excess that fills it to the point of freezing, or leaves it starving for more.[28]

Grosz continues: "This is not an effect of nature nor is it a social necessity but it is the result of women's submersion in maternity and thus her eclipse as woman" (122). Sceats, referring to the work of Stephanie Demetrakopoulos, suggests that some women, because of their perceived lack of legitimate social and political power, manipulate their lactation powers by overfeeding their children, or infantilizing their husbands "by replicating childhood experiences of indulgent feeding (love) by their mothers" (21).[29]

Both Roald Dahl and J. K. Rowling caricature the overfeeding smothering mother and link her with the obese child. In Dahl's *Charlie and the Chocolate Factory*, nine-year-old Augustus Gloop is overfed; he is

> so enormously fat he looked as though he had been blown up with a powerful pump. Great flabby folds of fat bulged out from every part of his body, and his face was like a monstrous ball of dough with two small greedy currant eyes peering out.[30]

Dudley Dursley, cousin to Harry Potter in Rowling's series, is also morbidly obese. He is "so fat his bottom drooped over either side of the kitchen chair,"[31] he is lazy— "he hated exercise;"[32] stupid—it looks like "hard work" when he's thinking; baby-like—his mother calls him "sweetums," "popkin" (*Philosopher*, 21) and "Dinky Duddydums" (22);

and animal-like—he's "pink and porky" (*Chamber*, 9) and "a pig in a wig" (*Philosopher*, 21). Dudley's mother overfeeds and infantilizes him and, notably, in relation to Sceats's claim about some women infantilizing their husbands, "Dudley looked a lot like [his father, Harry's] Uncle Vernon" (*Philosopher*, 21). I suggest that in terms of the context of Rowling's narrative Dudley's mother's overindulgence of her son serves to emphasize the lack of love and care Harry receives, helping to ensure the reader's sympathetic identification with the hero. Dudley's mother's smothering love is implicitly represented by the excessive number of extravagant material goods bestowed upon him on his birthday (she implicitly controls the quantity he receives by promising him more), explicitly symbolized by the much larger portions and superior quality of food she feeds him in comparison to Harry and semantically emphasized by the "baby talk" she uses when she addresses him. In subtextual terms, both Rowling's and Dahl's narratives condemn the fat child and set them up as comic figures deserving of ridicule and physical punishment.[33]

Augustus is depicted by illustrator Quentin Blake, standing with his equally enormous mother. Dahl's narrative implies that she is to blame for his obesity because she makes no effort to curb his appetite, and overindulges his desire for chocolate. When Augustus finds one of Willy Wonka's Golden Tickets hidden in a chocolate bar wrapper she tells the newspapers that:

> He eats *so many* bars of chocolate a day that it was almost *impossible* for him *not* to find one. Eating is his hobby, you know. That's *all* he's interested in … And what I always say is, he wouldn't go on eating like he does unless he *needed* nourishment, would he? It's all *vitamins*, anyway. (*Charlie*, 36–37, emphases in original)

Mrs. Gloop is cast as a disgusting and abject creature: her last name conjures up the "gloop" sound made when spooning out jelly/jello and Charlie's Grandma Josephine dismisses her as a "revolting woman" (37). By mirroring his obesity and through her misguided overfeeding, she is seen to be directly to blame for Augustus's repulsive fatness. Because Mrs. Gloop's explanation of her son's aberrant desire in terms of *need* is irrational, and because Augustus is so obviously fixated on oral satisfaction and is therefore, stuck in the oral phase, Mrs. Gloop is implicitly framed as reluctant to allow Augustus to separate from her. She is therefore, like Petunia Dursley, a smothering mother.

In psychoanalytic terms the child's quest for proper subjectivity, an identity separate from its mother, relies upon, according to Kristeva, its recognition of and ability to delineate between self and other, between the maternal body and its own body. Part of this process involves defining its own bodily boundaries—the inside and the outside and the clean and proper aspects of the self. This occurs around the time the child is being toilet-trained and involves not only defining certain biological functions of the body as improper, unclean, abject, and disgusting, but also constituting a proper social body so that sociocultural expectations are met.[34] Developing a sense of abjection with regard to the body's corporeality—its need to incorporate and consume food and to expel waste—means regarding with disgust and horror objects and fluids that are incorporated and expelled such as certain foods, feces, urine, spit, vomit, etc. In its need to separate from the mother, who is already associated by her reproductive capacities with corporeality, the child associates her body with the abject, the reviled, the repugnant, all that is horrifying and disgusting. The maternal body thus becomes a source of fear. The child is simultaneously drawn to the mother as the source of oneness, deep rapport, satiation, and sensual satisfaction and repelled by her because of abjection, and because subjectivity can only be developed by metaphorically pushing her away. Kristeva recognizes this paradox and emphasizes that the abject "simultaneously beseeches and pulverises the subject."[35]

Elizabeth Grosz, referring to the work of Jean-Paul Sartre, Mary Douglas, and Kristeva, explains the way in which the "clinging viscosity" of body fluids is culturally linked to abjection and specifically with "the horror of femininity [and] the voraciousness and indeterminacy of the *vagina dentata*." Body fluids, she explains, graphically confirm that the body is permeable, and, therefore, that it is vulnerable to infiltration and pollution. While the autonomous, clean and proper body represents order and epitomizes culture, body fluids "affront a subject's aspiration toward autonomy and self-identity." They threaten subjectivity because they testify to the fraudulence or impossibility of the clean and proper. The physical properties of body fluids attest to their indeterminacy. They are without shape or form of their own; they flow, seep and leak from, engulf and infiltrate the body (Grosz, 194). The disgust and horror that these fluids evoke reflects the fear of being engulfed or submerged into something that has no boundaries of its own, something that refuses "to conform to the laws governing the clean and proper, the solid and the self-identical," Grosz suggests (194–95). In this respect the fear evoked by body fluids resembles culturally formed fears about female sexuality. Grosz emphasizes that female sexuality does not actually resemble viscosity. Rather, it is the result of the way the (patriarchal) social order renders female sexuality/corporeality marginal, indeterminate and viscous, and also attributes disgusting, horrifying connotations to the viscous and sticky, that produces the perception of a link between female sexuality and horrifying viscosity (Grosz, 195).

It is my contention that in the same way that viscous substances which seep and flow from the body horrify and evoke the maternal, so can those which we must contemplate taking into our bodies. Undoubtedly some foods, although they are culturally acceptable, cause personal revulsion, and others, in excess, produce disgust. While "comfort" foods are desired, for example, a surfeit of sweet, soft, sticky foods can prove to be sickening. Some sticky foods, like honey, suggests Mary Douglas, can have properties which evoke fears of being engulfed. She quotes Sartre: "An infant, plunging its hands into a jar of honey, is instantly involved in contemplating . . . [its] formal properties of solids and liquids and the essential relation between the subjective experiencing self and the experienced world."[36] She then goes on to explain, following Sartre's essay, that the viscous

> is unstable, but it does not flow. It is soft, yielding and compressible. There is no gliding on its surface. Its stickiness is a trap, it clings like a leech; it attacks the boundary between myself and it. Long columns falling off my fingers suggest my own substance flowing into the pool of stickiness . . . to touch stickiness is to risk diluting myself into viscosity. Stickiness is clinging, like a too possessive dog or mistress.[37]

It seems to me unlikely that many people would feel this way about honey in particular. But foods with viscous qualities can undoubtedly be very off-putting: consider how disgusting a slightly undercooked fried egg seems when you have a queasy stomach, for example. For a child, whose goal is subjectivity, or perhaps for someone whose notions of self are precarious, the clinging, possessive mother poses a similar threat to that described by Douglas and Sartre in relation to slimy, sticky food. Failure to separate from the mother, to pull away from her and to resist the draw of the oneness she represents, means being incorporated into her intermediate state. If, as I have argued, food can metaphorically represent/replace the mother, then it follows that its properties can be aligned with hers in the same way that Grosz suggests the viscosity of body fluids is aligned with female sexuality. Thus, while comfort food evokes the loving mother, viscous food evokes the smothering mother.

Kristeva links the smothering qualities of the mother/parent with oral disgust, which is she claims, the most archaic form of abjection. She illustrates this by using an example of another food that can be disgusting, the skin of the milk. This, she suggests, is repulsive and induces the subject to retch and choke (3). Grosz explains that the desire to expel or to refuse to take food in is the child's refusal of "the very stuff signifying parental/maternal love. In expelling it, the parents' demands are also refused"

(Grosz 1989, 74). Kristeva suggests that in the symbolic act of choking on the skin of the milk the child rejects not only the idea of taking in the mother/food but also feels revulsion toward and rejects the notion that its own body/self has limits or boundaries which disrupt the constitution of subjectivity (Kristeva, 3). In this way she implicitly confirms that indeterminate, sticky, or cloying foods can evoke the smothering mother and be perceived as a threat to subjectivity.

Kristeva's (and Grosz's) alignment of the viscous and cloying with the maternal and the engulfing qualities of the *vagina dentata* is clearly illustrated in Jacqueline Wilson's *The Illustrated Mum*. Marigold is a difficult mum to live with. She has bipolar disorder, also known as manic depression, and refuses medication. Her daughters, Star and Dolphin, have had a precarious upbringing to say the least; Marigold's mothering veers between abandoning them all night while she goes out drinking, to obsessively trying to prove she's a good mother by, significantly, providing them with a surfeit of sweet food, as Dolphin recalls:

> "Remember that time last summer when it was hot and Marigold told us to open the fridge and there it was simply stuffed with ice cream. Wasn't it wonderful?"
>
> "We ate Cornettos and Mars and Soleros and Magnums, one after another, and then when they all started to melt Star mixed them all up in the washing-up bowl and said it was ice cream soup."
>
> "We lived on stale bread and carrots all the rest of that week because she'd spent all the Giro," said Star.[38]

On another occasion Marigold bakes cakes, so many that they cannot eat them all and they go stale. Dolphin and Marigold go to the park intending to feed the cakes to the ducks. Discovering that there are no ducks in the park that day, they decide to build a gingerbread house out of cake, like the one in "Hansel and Gretel," decorating it with buttercups and daisies. They pretend that two dormouse sisters will come and live in the house. To protect the dormice from stoats and foxes Marigold pretends to put a hex around the house. Dolphin particularly enjoys having her mother to herself: "It felt wonderful. Marigold wasn't sad or scary at all, she was the best fun ever" (*Illustrated Mum*, 59). However, Marigold's intensity is overwhelming and her need to prove herself to be a good mother is suffocating. That night Dolphin dreams she is in the cake cottage with her mouse sister:

> We sat at our fairy cake table and nibbled the thick icing with our sharp teeth but it tasted sickly sweet. We washed our paws and whiskers at the cupcake kitchen sink but golden syrup poured out

of the taps and we were coated in sweet yellow slime. We crawled stickily up the sponge stairs and curled up in our jam roll beds but the fruit cake walls all around us started crumbling and the marzipan ceiling suddenly caved in. A huge red vixen was up above us, eyes glinting. She opened her jaws wide and I screamed and screamed. (63)

This is an extraordinary evocation of what I have been arguing. The sweet foods in this passage evoke the mother and the rapport and the fulfillment of the child's primal relationship with her. However, too much rich sweet food is overwhelming, smothering, and produces disgust and abjection. Dolphin and her sister are so engulfed in sweet, slimy, and sticky golden syrup that their movements are restricted and they must crawl up to bed. The fox with the wide-open jaws in Dolphin's dream is clearly red-haired Marigold. Wilson's narrative links sweet viscous food with the smothering engulfing qualities of the maternal and it also evokes the *vagina dentata*. It is perhaps also significant that Wilson has Marigold and Dolphin build a house, which, in Dolphin's dream, proves not to be a place of safety as is generally the case, but collapses upon the sisters leaving them vulnerable to the fox's wide jaws. David Sibley argues that the house is culturally viewed as a haven and is "a locus of sentiment." He cites Gaston Bachelard's view of the house/home as a womb, a place recalled in dreams, "giving access to the initial shell which shelters the being."[39]

Psychologically, Marigold's excessive behavior and neediness is threatening because it hinders Dolphin's separation from her. Marigold's mental health deteriorates to the extent that she is hospitalized, at which point Dolphin is propelled into action and sets off in search of her father. As her relationship with him progresses, she becomes more understanding of and able to deal objectively with her mother's condition. Thus, Wilson's narrative appears to confirm (in a way similar to Ende's and Burnett's) the psychological need to separate from the mother and turn to the father for the proper development of subjectivity.

Additionally, Wilson's narrative confirms Irigaray's proposition that the mother has no other valued social role. Marigold's unhappiness appears to stem from her inability to find and keep a man. She was clearly in love with her eldest daughter's father but he left her before she knew she was pregnant. She tries to be a good mother but fails miserably. This failure is symbolized in the narrative by the imperfect cakes and cookies she produces. Her realization that she will never win Star's father back and that Star has left her to go and live with him, results in her mental breakdown. There are no roles other than motherhood for women in Wilson's narrative. The mother of one of Dolphin's school friends is obviously emotionally distressed, socially withdrawn, and unable to function because her husband has left her and the foster mother Dolphin lives with admits that all she's good at is looking after children. Implicit in Wilson's discourse is the notion that being a wife and mother is a woman's only role/function. Failure to perform this role satisfactorily results in depression and exclusion from society. It is interesting and ironic to note that Ende's discourse about the perfect mother figure, Dame Eyola, also confirms the exclusivity of her function. When Bastian has "had his fill of her care and tenderness" and "his craving [for her fruit] had been stilled" (*Neverending Story*, 348) all her leaves, flowers, and fruits fall off, her eyes close and "she looked like a black, dead tree." Outside the House of Change "[w]inter had come overnight. The snow lay knee-deep and nothing remained of the flowering rose garden but bare, black thornbushes. Not a breeze stirred. It was bitter cold and very still" (350). Bastian's desire formed the maternal domain of which Dame Eyola was part; with his desire fulfilled the maternal aesthetic/domain/function becomes redundant; Dame Eyola has no other reason for existence and so she shrivels up and dies! Here the child is also framed as a vampire, sucking the life out of his substitute mother.

It is significant I think that the difference between the images of the women/mother figures I have so far discussed seems to involve their use of food as a means of power exchange. The good mother provides the eater with beneficial sustenance/energy/power; in exchange she seems content with the emotional satisfaction she receives. The smothering mother, however, provides food that inevitably poisons the eater in some way, draining them of vitality/power/subjectivity, which she absorbs, so that instead of feeding, it is she who consumes. These vampiric figures embody what Klein claims happens in the unconscious/imagination of the infant during the oral stage, whereby the parsimonious unloving "bad breast" is cast as the object of dread, "so that the hated breast becomes the hateful and hating breast"[40] and the child fears that the mother will turn and consume the one who desires to consume her.

GENDER ROLES

Psychological ambivalence for the mother figure does not solely result from the infant's initial concerns with gratification and lack. These feelings are strengthened as the child begins to form notions of gender. Chodorow focuses on the ongoing interpersonal relationships that shape a child's behavior and personality, and suggests that the child's relationship with her or his mother is crucially important in forming both girls' and boys' expectations of gender.[41] Chodorow suggests that from the start mothers treat infants differently according to gender. Girl babies are likely to evoke

a stronger identification with the mother, who, in nursing her own female infant, is re-experiencing herself as a cared-for baby. Identification
with a boy baby may be less strong, and mothers tend to push their sons
toward assuming an oppositional "sexually toned male-role relation to
her" (Chodorow, 48). At around two or three years old children become
more aware of gender. The father and men in general, become more important. A boy's masculine gender identification must replace his former
identification with his mother. Importantly, Chodorow points out that
because most male activities take place outside the domestic sphere in
which he has spent his time,[42] the boy's gender identification becomes a
"positional" one, one that is oppositional to most of his daily experiences.
Thus, his identification often becomes negative. He defines masculinity as
that which is not female. This includes the perceived sociocultural role, as
well as biology. As he differentiates himself from his mother, he comes to
deny his relationship with her and to devalue the female both psychologically and culturally (Chodorow, 49). Thus, the boy's ambivalence for the
mother, which was initiated during his early feeding relationship with
her, is legitimated and strengthened. Her position, as the object of both
love/desire and hatred/rejection, is reinforced. The powerlessness and
subordinated status of her socially assigned domestic role is acknowledged
and accepted as a natural aspect of her gender.

A girl, on the other hand, possesses no obvious or logical way of dis-
identifying from her mother (Benjamin 1988, 78). Her independence
is underplayed; compliance and self-denial (perceived as facets of her
mother's identity) sustain the girl's tie to her mother. According to Benjamin, "the girl's sense of self is shaped by the realization that her mother's
source of power resides in her self-sacrifice" (79). There are potential
dangers in the girl's position. Sceats warns: there may be a danger of
extended attachment and insufficient separateness; too close a bond may
result in mother-daughter hostility, overcontrol, guilt feelings, loss of a
sense of self for the mother, and/or a lack of self-identity for the daughter
(Sceats, 17). In contemporary Western culture identifying with the mother
means, as Chodorow points out, identifying with what is perceived to be
a "devalued passive" position. The girl has difficulty consciously rejecting
identification with the female sociocultural role because of "continuing
oedipal maternal identification and boundary confusion with the mother"
(Chodorow, 65). In other words, although she recognizes and might wish
to reject the subordinated sociocultural position of the female, Chodorow's theory implies that she has little choice but to accept it as her gender
role. Thus, as Grosz points out, Chodorow suggests that while the body
remains naturalistic and pre-cultural, it is but the base for the individual's
interpellation into ideology. In order, for example, for the girl to avoid the

passive subordinated status of her mother, a transformation at the level of ideology has to take place, so that different meanings and values are assigned to maternity (Grosz 1994, 17).[43] Sceats, referring to Chodorow's work, labels the repeating pattern of mothering, whereby mothers inevitably produce daughters with mothering capacities and evident desire to mother, as a "self-perpetuating … vicious circle" (Sceats, 17). Girls, as well as boys, continue to have ambivalent feelings about the body and role of the mother. For girls in particular the maternal figure may symbolize their own inevitable entrapment, passivity, and degradation.

FEEDING WORK

Kaplan speculates about the changes in the conception of women in relation to family and gender roles in recent decades, which, she asserts, has been a time of "intense transition." She shows that considerable anxiety is present in discourses about motherhood, and that this results from the notion that childbirth and childcare are "no longer being viewed as an automatic, natural part of a woman's life-cycle" (Kaplan, 181). Whereas in earlier periods woman was synonymous with mother (the only other possibilities being virgin or whore), definitions are now more complex. "That child-bearing is no longer automatic has spawned a whole series of discourses and representations that figure forth contradictory ideologies and unconscious fantasies" (182). Women's roles appear on the surface to have changed. They now include "career woman," although considerable anxiety exists about this, as reflected in the popular media. Having a career means "trying to be like a man" (182) and rejecting motherhood, or becoming what is popularly and problematically termed "a supermum,"[44] trying to juggle career and family. Concurrently, the domestic mother position is no longer deemed to be an acceptable role, being derogatorily referred to as "*just* a housewife."

While some current (public) female role/image alternatives appear to exclude the domestic, in popular media representations and in reality, the domestic and, in particular, food provisioning, are still very much linked to the feminine. Kate Kane argues that although the media now accepts a range of ways of conceiving women's role and image, some kind of female specificity is demanded. In food commercials "that specificity is an 'eternal' feminine that defines women as primarily maternal and underpins an 'entire edifice' of female stereotypes." Kane argues that the corporate sector, the state, and the mass media have the most to gain from the maintenance of this status quo and the inference of the naturalness of woman's place in the home. Domestic labor is still regarded as "women's work." Through the perpetuation of the ideal of the good mother, huge profits are generated for corporations and stability for the state. Concomitantly, a mode of consciousness is legitimated, based on sexism. Constructions of the feminine as maternal in the popular media, such as television advertisements, sell more than just laundry products; they also sell cultural values.[45]

Although, arguably, social roles are changing and in more and more households domestic work, including food provisioning, is being shared, cultural change is slow. Vincent Duindam, citing the work of D. Morgan, confirms that most of the evidence shows that there are "very slow changes in the direction of men's participation" in domestic duties and child care[46] and this is supported by the lack of male figures performing these roles in children's books. In the conservative world of children's literature it is the female, rather than the male, in general, who is still linked to the domestic. Gillian Tunstall's survey of the images of mothers in contemporary children's picture books published in the previous two decades found that they had changed little in terms of the role and activities undertaken by the women portrayed. Women were still, generally, cast as traditional homemakers and nurturers whose primary concerns were the care of the family and routine domestic chores, and who invariably wore an apron. Tunstall found that women were still largely characterized as passive, caring, and supportive. Rarely were they shown to have intelligence, initiative, independence, creativity, or even humor. A mere 10 percent were portrayed as working outside the home.[47] The family, generally, still depends upon woman's subordination, her acquiescence to the notion and realities of relegating her individual interests in favor of the needs of her family. Sarah Blaffer Hrdy believes that maternity is synonymous with self-sacrifice.[48] Those who are mothers may sympathize with her view. Revealingly, she refers to her personal experience of motherhood, when she gave her precious time and "bodily resources" to her children and subordinated her own aspirations to their desires, as being "consumed" by them (Hrdy, 540).

Given that the images of the mother and food and the notion of maternal love metaphorically stand in for each other in culture, the related sociocultural imperatives involving feeding work are significant. DeVault's American study found that in the overwhelming majority of families it was women who performed the "feeding work" although fifty percent of them also worked outside the home.[49] This work included the provision of a proper meal and arranging for the family to sit down and eat it. DeVault argues that what is perceived to be women's work of feeding the family, of creating and staging the family-meal-as-event, can be seen as counteracting the centrifugal forces which push the family apart as each individual member pursues his or her own schedules, commitments, interests, and priorities. Thus, DeVault maintains, feeding literally *produces* family (cited by Beardsworth and Keil, 82). In writing up their 1997 study of the sociological significance of food Alan Beardsworth and Teresa Keil find Anne Murcott's 1982 research into the importance of the "cooked dinner" in South Wales remains "influential" (83). Murcott found that the provision of a 'proper' cooked meal on a regular basis was deemed to be vital to the health and welfare of family members, and therefore as one of a woman's most crucial obligations. Murcott argues that the cooked dinner has important social functions; it demonstrates that a wife "has been spending her time in an activity appropriate to her status and gender." Notably, "The extended time commitment and the protracted labor involved can be seen as devices for tying the wife into the domestic setting, enforcing and expressing...her domesticity" (quoted by Beardsworth and Keil, 83–84). Both DeVault and Murcott emphasize the way a woman's perceived feeding role, her obligation to provide a proper cooked dinner (and thus her compliance with the good mother paradigm), is viewed as vital to the health, welfare, and production of family. In other words, the performance of the meal ritual is seen to somehow magically bind the family together, for the social good, but at the woman's expense.[50]

In Gillian Rubinstein's *Beyond the Labyrinth*, stay-at-home-mother, Chris Trethewan, fulfills her domestic role in an exaggerated way; her home-making skills are honed to a degree that suggests a desperate attempt to invoke the ideal family:

> The lasagne looks artistic, Victoria thinks, but then everything in Chris Trethewan's house does. The table, set for Sunday evening tea, looks like a magazine photograph—the peasant-like earthenware dish that holds the perfectly-browned lasagne, the sea-green chunky tumblers, the home-made plaited bread.[51]

While Sunday dinner is often a special meal within the structure of weekly meals, Chris's offering seems, as Heather Scutter suggests, "constrained."[52] Scutter argues that there is something about the way this meal has been served that is too perfect, which would be likely to put "eaters on their guard, which hinders the hedonism associated with the appetite and the pleasure doled out by the boundless love of the mother figure." Scutter suggests that Chris's meal is modeled on an idealized image, one of conformity to social expectations (71–72). Chris's creation and staging of the family-meal-as-event is, as DeVault suggests, meant to literally produce "family." It is as though Chris reasons that by performing her role perfectly, she will magically invoke a perfect, functional loving family. Unfortunately for her, the work she does is largely invisible and not particularly appreciated. It is significantly only Victoria (a guest) who notices her efforts, but she only "thinks" and does not speak about it. Chris's husband Geoff tears a piece off her homemade plaited bread "just as though it is ordinary bread and not a work of art" (*Labyrinth*, 45). Elspeth Probyn has suggested that there are "power-plays that structure familial eating and the ideology of the family that eats together has been largely undertheorized."[53] Within the discourse set up by Rubinstein in this narrative, Chris's position appears to be one of total powerlessness. Her attempt to wield power through feeding is denied because her work is considered to be valueless in the eyes of the state, society, and of her own family. She is significantly not part of the intellectual discussion within the narrative but implicitly appears to have retreated into the domestic realm in what Scutter suggests seems like "an act of passive resistance to being directed by the economic demands of patriarchy or the political tenets of feminism" (71). Although she professionalizes what she produces in accordance with idealized images presented in magazine photographs, its inherent value is framed as merely aesthetic, and even this is negated by her husband's careless dismissal. Thus, the position of the traditional feminine has implicitly been drained of most of its use-value and all of its power in this narrative.

In children's literature, as in popular culture, it is often the case that food is used to make implicit judgments about a woman. Her mothering skills, including her capacity to love and nurture, and her willingness to sacrifice herself for her family, are thus put on trial. There is a surprisingly narrow range of what constitutes good feeding and thus good mothering. In Rubinstein's *Answers to Brut*, Caspian and his sisters, Spirit and Skye, are fed a vegetarian diet by their mother. All three children are thin and fair with a "slightly unearthly look about them, which people thought was angelic."[54] Caspian, however, thinks that this look comes from a lack of protein. Although she is softly spoken and looks very gentle, their mother has "a will of iron" (*Answers*, 10). She feeds them on raw vegetables and yoghurt dip, brown rice and mushrooms, soy-milk flavored with carob, lentil burgers, and bean sprouts. They are forbidden ice blocks, lollies, sugar, and meat. Caspian longs for a "good diet of hamburgers," which would make them look like everyone else (9). Interestingly, it is Caspian's masculinity that appears to be particularly problematized by his mother's values; he "suffers most from his family's eccentric ways" (12). While his younger sisters appear to accept readily the food their mother provides, Caspian approaches his meal hesitantly and resorts to swallowing his mouthful of mushrooms "bravely" (10). Implicit in the text is the notion that Caspian's mother is at fault for alienating him from the real world, from the rigors of life, and even from "real" masculinity, with her middle-class, new-age pacifism and vegetarianism. He is initially weak and ineffectual in confronting situations because he has been poorly prepared. He must turn his back on the values she represents in order to find his true self. Caspian has "a moment's vision of himself grown up, able to choose for himself what he would eat and drink and what he would watch on television. [This vision] made him feel strong and powerful" (43). Caspian's desire to eat what he chooses, in other words, to cease to take in his mother, articulates his desire to separate from her, to leave her maternal influence. This is echoed in his wish "to belong to himself" (44). Thus, in contrast to Chris Trethewan, Caspian's mother *is* able to wield power through feeding, but her feminine power is perceived to be a direct threat to masculine power and must be overcome. Rubinstein's discourse effectively denies the mother figure any real power even when the domestic role has been professionalized as in both these narratives.

Neither of Rubinstein's mothers are framed as explicitly bad women. Enid Blyton, on the other hand, had no compunctions about emphatically representing poorly feeding mother figures as villainous women and explicitly blaming them for social problems. In *Five Run Away Together* the picnic provided by Mrs. Stick consists of "sandwiches [which] were not very nice. The bread was too stale; there was not enough butter inside, and they were far too thick."[55] As Keith Barker remarks, it is not at all surprising that Mrs. Stick and her family turn out to be crooks.[56] Blyton uses bad or poor food again in *The Six Bad Boys,* this time to signal deficient mothering. She contrasts three families, two of which produce delinquent sons. The good boy is the product of good mothering and good food. The father of one of the bad boys is dead. His mother goes out to work and he cannot go home from school for lunch. Instead he suffers "strange, lonely lunches" of sandwiches.[57] After school he returns home to find that his mother has left him some cake on a shelf in the garden shed. But "he never touched it. 'Leaving out food for me as if I was the cat next door!' he grumbled to himself. 'I'll wait till she comes home, and have supper—proper supper, even if she has to cook it when she's tired'" (*Bad Boys,* 88). The other bad boy comes from a broken home. His mother drove the father away with her "nagging...bickering and quarrelling" (77). Whereas the mother of the good boy makes a "lovely" birthday cake, the "best I've ever seen! And I bet it tastes good too," this boy's mother never makes birthday cakes—such things were always "such a burden" to her (68). Blyton implies that only good mothering can produce good children and that a good mother must provide good food and 'be there' for her children. Her fiction supports her personal view of the role of the mother:

[In our family w]e all have a sense of humour. We are all (thank goodness!) good-tempered. Nobody sulks, nobody complains, nobody is unkind. But that, of course, is largely a matter of upbringing. Spoilt children are selfish, complaining and often conceited. But whose fault is that? It is the mother, always the mother, that makes the home. The father does his share, he holds the reins too —but it is the mother who makes a happy, contented home. She is the centre of it. She should always be there to welcome the children home, to see to them and listen to them. I was lucky to have a gift that could be used at home. I could not have left my husband or my children and gone out into the world to make my career. All true mothers will know what I mean when I say that...[58]

Blyton's comments seem ironic given her daughter Imogen's description of her mother as "arrogant, insecure, pretentious...and without a trace of maternal instinct."[59] But, the ideological stance she advocates still pervades contemporary popular discourses as Murcott's and DeVault's studies confirm and as the packaging from a recently purchased pack of Arnott's Farmbake Chocolate Chip Fudge Cookies shows. Arnott's narrative extols the virtues of "convenience" foods but, the sub-text reveals, home-made is still best. The advertising text is headed by the trademark "The Taste of Home," followed by the words "the fresh Farmbake taste that everyone loves...a cookie that tastes just like you would make at home."[60] Clearly notions of nostalgia are deliberately evoked by the combination of the words "home" and "Farmbake" ("farm" evoking the rural, coupled with "bake" evoking cozy kitchens and notions of home as haven). The text continues, "A love of sharing is what Farmbake is all about...Hand them round at home or on trips, and enjoy the fresh Farmbake taste that everyone loves" ("fresh" despite the "best before" date being six months after they were purchased.). The conflation of love and the sharing of food is here used to remind purchasers of the traditional "role that food provisioning, and the orchestration of food events plays in the construction and reproduction of families" (Warde, 151). DeVault's study recognizes the way in which "the feeding work traditionally undertaken by women is both produced by and produces 'family' as we have known it—the work itself 'feeds' not only household members but also 'the family' as ideological construct."[61] DeVault emphasizes not only the technical but also the emotional and social aspects of food provisioning. The Arnott's narrative calls upon women's inherent awareness of the emotional obligations of food provisioning and offers its product as a substitute for the real thing. The fact that it is a substitute for the real thing thus also evokes a sense of guilt.

Interestingly, shop-bought biscuits are used by Robin Klein in *The Listmaker* as a device to support her characterization of Piriel as unfit in the role of substitute mother for Sarah. For a long time Sarah has lived with her elderly aunts because her father is frequently away on business but he is about to be married to Piriel and Sarah is excited about living as a family in the new apartment with them. Before the wedding, Sarah and her friend visit Piriel at the new apartment. Piriel has not been expecting them but, after showing off her designer kitchen, offers them a cold drink and biscuits before sending them home.[62]

> I've got some absolutely delicious almond biscuits as well, though I'm afraid you'll have to content yourself with just two each. I'm expecting visitors later this afternoon.
>
> The biscuits were so thin you could almost see light filtering through each one, and they had come from a specialist bakery just down the street. (*Listmaker*, 174)

Sarah daydreams about having friends to visit when she is living at the apartment. She decides she will, "stop at that same shop and buy yummy things for afternoon tea, too." But, she can't quite see her friends "appreciating delicate little almond wafers from a gourmet bakery. Jammy cream buns were more their style" (174—75). Klein's discourse frames the insubstantial biscuits, the designer kitchen, and Piriel, who is cast as the epitome of the assertive and dedicated career woman, as non-nurturing and unhomely. Piriel's food provisioning certainly does not produce family. Indeed, Klein's narrative culminates in Sarah deciding not to go and live permanently with her father and stepmother but to stay instead with her aunts who, importantly, provide her with food and love in generous helpings. Sarah, having come to the realization that her father and Piriel don't even really want her to attend their registry office wedding, is upset:

> I stared blurrily down at the plate [Aunty Nat] set on the kitchen table. It held two baked potatoes stuffed with salmon in cheese sauce, and there was a salad to go with it. Aunty Nat had made me a special one, a kind of joke between us which dated back to preschool days. To coax me to eat salad then, she'd make a little person from a pear half, with punk carrot hair, lettuce-leaf skirt, and shoes cut from tomato quarters. Looking at it now somehow made me want to blub. I ate a celery sock and the beetroot hand-bag, then had to stop rather quickly and fumble for the tissues... (*Listmaker*, 215)

In direct contrast to Piriel's purchased designer biscuits, Aunty Nat's food is homemade, wholesome, and has literally been shaped by love. The time and thought necessary to produce the "special" salad specifically for Sarah is juxtaposed with the fact that Piriel had spent no time or effort nurturing her. The almond biscuits are intended for Piriel's guests. The guests' perceived needs take precedence over Sarah's and her friend's. Piriel is thus characterized as totally nonnurturing and unwilling to accommodate the maternal food/love provisioning imperative that is intrinsically part of the production of family. Piriel's characterization shows her to be a self-centered, career-driven, and therefore powerful and masculinized woman, but it is her inability to nurture through food provisioning that is ultimately significant in this narrative and leads to Sarah's realization that she, her father and Piriel will never be a family in the traditional sense.

It is rare to find instances of males providing food in children's literature. One such is Will in Philip Pullman's *The Subtle Knife*. Will nurtures Lyra through food, cooking an omelet for her. He has knowledge of relevant food rules and domestic hygiene practices[63] It could be argued, however, that Will is feminized by the role he performs, especially given that he is also earlier seen to be caring for his sick mother. Pullman's framing of the boy as having murdered a man (8) may serve the purpose of counteracting the feminizing effect of his implicit domestication.

Harry Potter is explicitly subordinated by having to perform domestic duties in *Harry Potter and the Philosopher's Stone*. His aunt raps on the door of the cupboard under the stairs, where he sleeps, and tells him "get a move on, I want you to look after the bacon. And don't you dare let it burn, I want everything to be perfect on Duddy's birthday" (*Philosopher*, 19–20). Harry not only cooks the bacon but also fries eggs and serves breakfast (20–21). Within the context of this introductory chapter Harry is obliquely cast in the role of servant and unequivocally excluded from the Dursley family unit. He is thus constructed as a poorly treated orphan and as a character worthy of the reader's sympathy. However, this discourse also serves to reinforce the powerlessness and subordination of his Aunt Petunia's domestic role and that performed by all other feeding figures both within and outside Rowling's narrative. Notably the other domesticated feeding figures in Rowling's stories are Hagrid the gamekeeper, Hermione, Mrs. Weasley and, later in the series, the House Elves. Feasts are produced magically at Hogwart's School of Witchcraft and Wizardry in *Philosopher's Stone*. But in *Goblet of Fire* we discover that there are house elves in the kitchens at Hogwarts who work as unpaid servants. Presumably, as the kitchens exist at all, this is where the domestic work is carried out which produces meals for the school community.

Harry's initial positioning as downtrodden performer of domestic work has specific implications for Hermione, in particular. It is always Hermione, rather than Harry or Ron, who performs a feeding role, bustling around making tea (*Prisoner,* 241; *Goblet,* 131) or "doling beef casserole onto each of their plates" (*Goblet,* 183). While Hermione's acts of feeding place her, in feminist terms, in an explicitly subjected position in a text that clearly reflects the mores of an outdated patriarchal social order, this is implicitly confirmed by these acts being aligned with Harry's enforced performance of a feeding role. It is interesting to note that in a later installment in the series, *Harry Potter and the Order of the Phoenix* (2003) Rowling has Ron and Harry perform some domestic, food-oriented tasks and I have wondered whether this explicit change is due to the feminist criticism her previous work had received.

It is unusual to find a feeding father figure in children's literature. Robin Klein features one in *Dresses of Red and Gold*, a book of semi-autobiographical stories. Mum has been summonsed by telegram to go and look after her sick brother and Dad is left to look after their three daughters. The girls are dubious about his ability to do so: "Don't take this the wrong way, but you don't really know much about housekeeping and cooking, Dad."[64]

> "Nothing to know," Dad said. "It's all commonsense and planning ahead, like making porridge the night before and not wasting time on fancy stuff. Take what I'm making for tea now…spuds baked in the ashes, then scoop out the guts, plonk in bacon and a dollop of chutney, can of peaches to follow—and Bob's your uncle." (*Dresses,* 31)

Arguably, the abject is evoked by the notion of scooping "guts" out of something and certainly food poisoning is suggested by plonking bacon into the potatoes, unless Dad remembers to cook it properly beforehand. There are obviously working-class inflections in the type of food being described as well as in the language being used to describe its preparation. Despite the suggestion of slapdash incompetence, the meal as an event turns out "to be delightfully like an indoors picnic, and afterwards he played Five Hundred with them all evening, using the contents of Mum's button jar as betting money" (32). But Dad's oatmeal porridge which he "had made the previous evening and left simmering lumpily at the side of the stove all night" turns out to be "revolting" and "had to be thrown out to the ungrateful chooks" (33). Dad is not a competent feeding father. He is no substitute for Mum and has been used to being fed, organized, and mothered by his wife. Instead of acting *in loco parentis* he acts as a child, sitting on the floor to eat and playing cards, and letting his daughters "wag school" so that they can go fishing with him (45). Within the context of Klein's narrative the mother's role as the only possible ideal feeder is reinforced.

An extraordinarily tender, nurturing example of a competent feeding male is to be found in David Almond's *Skellig*.[65] Michael discovers the frail figure of what he presumes to be an old tramp in the rickety garage of the house he and his family have recently moved into. He keeps the old man a secret from his parents and feeds and cares for him bringing, at the stranger's request, Chinese takeaway food, aspirins for his arthritis, and bottles of brown ale. Michael goes to some considerable effort to obtain these items. Michael must hold the food tray up to Skellig's chin so that he can dip his fingers into the food and slurp up the contents (*Skellig*, 26–27) and he pours the beer into Skellig's mouth from the bottle (72). This is a complex story with many layers of meaning. Michael discovers that Skellig is not a man but a being with wings—part angel and part bird. Skellig's frailty mirrors that of Michael's baby sister, born prematurely with a serious heart problem. Michael is desperate for his sister to get better but, like his parents, he must rely on doctors and their uninspiring medical expertise to make her well. Skellig refuses medical or adult help but, under Michael's nurturance, he begins to grow stronger. Michael's spiritual belief in Skellig grows and he asks the angel-like being to "think about the baby...Will you think about her in hospital? Will you think about her getting better?" (54). In one of several spiritual and moving sequences in Almond's text, Skellig is instrumental in the baby's recovery. Both her survival and the strength she gains are seen to parallel Skellig's and his, notably, results from Michael's nurturing.

AS HER MILK IS CONSUMED SO IS SHE...

The land of milk and honey has been colonized, plundered, and consumed by patriarchal culture. Like the petulant infant that Melanie Klein describes, phallocentric logic wants to attack the mother's breast and eat it up. Women, mothers or not, are as Grosz argues, "submerged in" and eclipsed by maternity and part of the good mother paradigm is food provisioning. This suits patriarchal culture, it suits the state and capitalism, it suits authors of children's stories who need a shortcut to representing the mother, but it doesn't necessarily suit women.

5

THE WICKED WITCH

A Pathological Image of Mother

Scale of dragon, tooth of wolf,
Witches' mummy, maw and gulf
Of the ravined salt-sea shark,
Root of hemlock digged i'th'dark,
Liver of a blaspheming Jew,
Gall of goat, and slips of yew
Slivered in the moon's eclipse,
Nose of Turk, and Tartar's lips,
Finger of birth-strangled babe,
Ditch-delivered by a drab,
Make the gruel thick and slab.
…Double, double, toil and trouble,
Fire burn, and cauldron bubble.
—William Shakespeare, *Macbeth*, Act 3, Scene 5

IN HIS STUDY OF STEREOTYPES, Sander Gilman uses object-relations theory to explain how the infant's sense of difference (inside/outside, self/other, good/bad) is formed by the denial of its demands for food, warmth, and comfort. "As the child comes to distinguish more and more between the world and self, anxiety arises from a perceived loss of control over the world."[1] The "world" he refers to provides food, warmth, and comfort and, significantly, it revolves around the mother.

Gilman goes on to confirm that "very soon" the child begins to combat the anxieties it feels by "adjusting his mental picture" of people, objects and self so that they can appear "good" or "bad." The good self mirrors the preseparation state where the infant was "in control" and indivisible from the world/mother and thus free from anxiety, the bad self perceives separation and outsideness, is unable to control the environment and thus becomes anxious. With the split of both the self and the world into good and bad, the bad self is distanced and identified with the mental representation of the bad object. This act of projection saves the self from confronting the contradictions present in the necessary integration of bad and good aspects of the self.

Such a split, Gilman contends, is the basis of structural oppositions that divide the world not only into good and bad but also into us and them and self and other. Gilman emphasizes that because there is no real line or division between self and other, an imaginary line must be drawn and, so that the illusion of the difference between self and other is never troubled, this line must be dynamic and shift in accordance with stresses occurring in the psyche. Thus, we can move from fearing to glorifying, or between hating and loving the other (17). Importantly, according to Gilman, stereotypes arise when subjectivity is threatened; they help us to deal with instabilities in the way we perceive the world. "This is not to say they are good," Gilman remarks, "only that they are necessary" (18). There is an important distinction to be made, however, between "normal" stereotyping which helps us to preserve an illusion of control over the self and the world, and what Gilman refers to as "pathological stereotyping." He claims that for the pathological personality every confrontation with an other sets up an echo of the anxiety triggered by the initial division of the world into good or bad. While we may refer to the stereotype as a "momentary coping mechanism," we should retain the ability to distinguish the individual from the stereotyped class into which the object might automatically be placed. The pathological personality, however, does not develop this ability, and instead sees the entire world in terms of a rigid line of difference (18). The previous chapter examined paradigms of the good mother and the smothering mother. This chapter looks at a stereotypical image of the third paradigm (the bad mother), an image that is a favorite in fairy tales, classic, and contemporary stories for children—the wicked witch.

The witch is a traditionally monstrous female character featured both in contemporary (adult) horror stories and in children's fairy tales. Joseph Campbell argues that women were first attributed with magical powers because of their mysterious abilities to create life.[2] Historically and mythologically, according to Barbara Creed, woman was perceived as the source of a particularly powerful form of magic during pregnancy.[3] A woman's curse was thought to be far more dangerous than a man's, and a "mother's curse" meant certain death.[4] When, in the fourteenth century, the Catholic church deemed witchcraft heresy, the services performed by witches, including midwifery, were labeled as crimes. Many of the witches' alleged crimes were sexual in nature. They were accused, among other things, of copulating with the devil, causing male impotence, and stealing men's penises (Creed, 75). Creed refers to *The Malleus Maleficarum* (1484), an inquisitor's manual for witch prosecution, commissioned by the Catholic church and shows that the persecution of witches was founded upon a "morbid interest in the witch as 'other' and a fear of the witch/woman as an agent of castration" (74). The major reason given for woman's otherness was her carnal nature. Women were "less intelligent, less spiritual, more like children... *The Malleus Maleficarum* is permeated by an extreme hatred of women and fear of their imaginary powers of castration" (75).

In psychoanalytic theory, the woman as witch is positioned as a phallic woman and as an oral sadistic mother (Campbell, 5). In terms of patriarchal discourses, she is defined as abject by being antithetical to the symbolic order. She unsettles the boundaries between the rational and the irrational, symbolic and imaginary, nature and culture (Creed, 76). In children's literature the witch is still a popular figure. Where she is constructed as evil, she is frequently fetishized and associated with abjection, cannibalism, and castration.[5] The witch is often cast as the embodiment of the bad breast—the devouring mother figure.

Many writers reiterate Melanie Klein's object-relations theory in their explanations of the development of ambivalence toward the mother figure. Sheldon Cashdan, for example, comments that "the realities of infant life force the child to face the unsettling realisation that the person responsible for its survival is both consistent and inconsistent, both gratifying and frustrating—both good and bad."[6] Alan Dundes searches for a more literal explanation for the fear of being eaten by the mother:

> Infants who breast-feed eventually learn that when their teeth are in place, [the first tooth appearing at around six months old] they possess their first real weapon. Any mother or wet nurse can testify to the pain that such little teeth can inflict when a nursing baby becomes satiated or unhappy during nursing. Through the principle of *lex talionis*, a guilty act is punished by the same means as those employed in the commission of the original crime. Hence biting or eating the mother's breast would be punishable by the mother's (or father's) biting or eating the naughty infant.[7]

Susanne Skubal asserts that the infant psyche copes with the crucial opposing concepts of "love and hate, nutritive feeding and destructive devouring, by splitting the mother figure into good and bad," until such time as it can tolerate and understand its ambivalent feelings toward her.[8] E. Ann Kaplan also addresses the internal unconscious (imaginary) splitting of the mother, which arises from the child's experience at the breast, suggesting that this is later literalized in the notions of the "idealized" nurturing mother and the dominating "phallic" one.[9] Creed, too, suggests that the primal feeding relationship has crucial cultural repercussions: the "relationship of the child as suckling to the nursing mother provides the model for all other relationships during this period; it is characterized by the concepts of eating and being eaten." Creed argues that the incorporative threat issuing from the maternal body is most likely to be focused upon the mother's facial and genital mouths (113). Manifest in all these versions, or interpretations, of Klein's theory is the notion that the first feeding relationship between infant and mother is vitally significant in the development of the infant's psyche and results in ambivalent cultural attitudes toward women.

As Creed shows whenever woman is represented as monstrous it is almost always in relation to her mothering and reproductive functions (7). The threat she exudes is usually related to consumption. Thus the wicked witch, as an expression of the dyadic, devouring mother of the oral phase, threatens to devour her victims, to consume or destroy their bodies or body parts, and to annihilate their psyches—forms of literal and metaphorical castration. In terms of infant development the first threat the mother/witch poses is cannibalism.

THE CANNIBALISTIC MOTHER

In "Hansel and Gretel," the mother figure is split along the lines Klein proposed and clearly has cannibalistic desires. The Grimm brothers' rewrote and refined their version of the tale before it was published in 1857. It bears little resemblance to the original oral tale told to Wilhelm in 1810.[10] While the mother figure is clearly demonized in this story, the father's involvement in abandoning his children is carefully downplayed.

The tale begins with the stepmother plotting to abandon the children in the woods because the family does not have sufficient food to feed them. At dawn she wakes them: "Get up, you lazybones! We're going into the forest to fetch some wood."[11] She and their father take them into the forest and leave them there, but Hansel leaves a trail of white pebbles and the children follow it back to their home. Their stepmother pretends to be pleased to see them, but when "the entire country was once again ravaged by famine" (*Grimm Tales,* 60) she scolds and reproaches their father until he agrees to abandon them a second time. This time Hansel leaves a trail of breadcrumbs but birds devour them and the children are lost. They venture deeper and deeper into the forest, walking all night and day with nothing to eat except some berries. They come upon "a little house made of bread. Moreover, it had cake for a roof and pure sugar for windows" (61). The children set to and break off pieces of the house and begin to eat. "Suddenly the door opened, and a very old woman leaning on a crutch came slinking out of the house. Hansel and Gretel were so tremendously frightened that they dropped what they had in their hands" (61–62). However, the old woman coaxes them with welcoming words, takes "them both by the hand," and leads them into her house where she serves them "a good meal of milk and pancakes with sugar and apple and nuts. Afterward she makes up two little beds with white sheets, whereupon Hansel and Gretel lay down in them and thought they were in heaven" (62). The old woman's behavior belies her initially frightening appearance: the food she gives them, which is notably sweet and rich, together with the comfort, warmth, and safety symbolized by the beds with white sheets, represent the good mother and the primal dyadic relationship ("heaven").

> The old woman, however, had only pretended to be friendly. She was really a wicked witch on the lookout for children, and she had built the house made of bread only to lure them to her. As soon as she had any children in her power, she would kill, cook and eat them. It would be like a feast day for her. (62)

The witch locks Hansel up in a cage and wakes Gretel up by yelling: "Get up, you lazybones! I want you to fetch some water and cook your brother something nice. He's sitting outside in a pen, and we've got to fatten him up. Then, when he's fat enough, I'm going to eat him" (62).

This is a portrait of a powerful cannibalistic woman, the bad mother, who is directly juxtaposed with the good mother figure. Two facets of the mother figure are represented in this fairy tale: the evil, threatening, cannibalistic one embodied by the witch/stepmother and the comforting, feeding persona initially presented by the old woman to lure the children. The link between the stepmother and the witch is made explicit—they both wake the children with the phrase "Get up, you lazybones" and they are both dead by the end of the story: the stepmother is the facet of the bad mother/breast who denies the children nourishment and abandons them; the witch is the mother/breast who threatens to retaliate. The duplicitousness of the bad mother is also emphasized: in her manifestation as the stepmother she pretends to be pleased when the children find their way home; as the witch she pretends to be a kind, generous good mother in order to lure the children into her house. Bruno Bettelheim considers "Hansel and Gretel" to be a tale about a child's inappropriate oral aggression, that "gives body to the anxieties and learning tasks of the young child who must overcome and sublimate his primitive incorporative and thus destructive desires."[12] But it is noteworthy that in this tale the children are orally nonaggressive. They do break off pieces of the house and "nibble" them but then they are about to "perish of hunger and exhaustion" (*Grimm Tales*, 61). It is the witch who is aggressive and cannibalistic, but Bettelheim does not discuss this.

It is interesting to consider the ending of the tale in terms of psychoanalytic notions of child development. The children's task is to escape the clutches of the devouring mother and to proceed from the oral phase to the oedipal stage and a meaningful relationship with their father. The realm of the mother in this tale is symbolized by the witch's house. They live in her house for a month while she feeds Hansel on "the very best food" and waits for him to get fatter. Hansel, then, partakes of the good breast while Gretel, who "got nothing but crab shells" (62) to eat, is denied it. They are clearly in the oral, pre-oedipal phase. By threatening to eat Hansel, the witch/bad mother clearly intends to incorporate and psychically obliterate him. Gretel kills the witch/bad mother by pushing her into the oven so that she is "miserably burned to death." The threat of incorporation she poses is thus neutralized.

Since the children have now successfully separated from the witch/ mother, they are able to reenter her house/domain "since they no longer had anything to fear." There the children find "chests filled with pearls and jewels all over the place" (63) and they fill pockets and apron with this treasure before leaving the house for good. Tracy Willard contends that while the good mother is not reclaimed literally or explicitly in this tale, she is symbolically reclaimed through the treasure the children find in her house.[13] I suggest that this tale illustrates the process whereby children reconcile themselves to the duality of the mother; her presence and absence, her giving and withholding of food, and the gratification and frustration that result. The children in the tale not only kill off the bad mother but they also leave behind the oral phase. When they arrive at the house in the forest, all they are interested in is food (gratification from a maternal source), but when they leave the house/maternal domain they take treasure (economic wealth associated with the father) with them which enriches their lives, so that they can enter the paternal oedipal domain, and live with their father in "utmost joy" (*Grimm Tales*, 64).

In her analysis of "Hansel and Gretel," Willard equates the trajectory of the tale directly to Klein's theory. She sees the children's home (or mother's body) as a place that becomes hostile to them, expelling them into the forest and denying them food. They try to return but are rejected and thrust out to fend for themselves. The children find a house in the woods that appears to offer them what they desire (a return to the mother's body) but it turns out to be a trap. Thus "the dangers of returning home are clearly outlined." The children, Willard argues, must deal with the image of the split mother so that they can attain "a fully integrated image of the mother" (Willard, section 26). They do this by committing matricide, an act which Kristeva argues is the clearest path to autonomy.[14] By killing the witch/bad mother, the children are free to return to their father, but they take with them the "best parts" of the split mother figure, symbolically represented by the jewels (Willard, section 26). This tale then can be interpreted as having a neat correlation with Klein's theory and direct links to the dyadic feeding relationship. The symbolism of food and the theme of eating (including cannibalism) in the story have profound psychic resonances with infantile anxieties relating to the mother which is arguably why the story continues to be popular.

But what of the role of the father in this tale? The Grimm brothers' version celebrates the oedipal complex and reinforces patriarchal hegemony. As Zipes argues, this story twice demonizes the omnipotent mother figure but it also, significantly, was rewritten by the Grimms in order to rationalize the abandonment of the children by their father and to bolster phallocentric discourses. Hansel and Gretel must, Zipes argues, "seek solace and security in a father, who becomes their ultimate authority figure" while the mother is conveniently killed off (Zipes 1997, 58). This situation marries with Jessica Benjamin's theorization of object relations whereby the child disidentifies with the mother and maternal power and turns to the father for help in order to overcome the perceived negative aspects of the mother.[15] However, once his help/authority has been accepted the father figure remains in control, continues to dictate the child's life, and can be "benevolent or sadistic" (59). Patriarchal hegemony and phallocentric logic are thus reinforced in the Grimms' narrative and the outcome is rendered natural or rational.

One of the best-known and strangest characters (from a Western perspective) in Russian folk tales is a witch called Baba Yaga. According to Elizabeth Warner, there are two Baba Yagas, a good one and a bad one. Sometimes within a single narrative, Baba Yaga may display good and evil characteristics. She benignly feeds the hero in "Little Ivan The Clever Young Man," for example, and provides him with a "hot steam-bath,"[16] but threatens to devour Vasilisa the Beautiful.[17] Baba Yaga lives in a dense and dark forest in a cottage built on chicken's legs that revolves on command. She is an aged, ugly crone and her nose and teeth are long and sharp.

Not only is she emaciated like a skeleton, but the fence and gates of her house are built of human bones. According to Warner, "some scholars say" that Baba Yaga's house guards the frontier between the mortal and spirit worlds (Warner, 85). Baba Yaga, like Hansel and Gretel's adversary, has a penchant for human flesh and kidnaps small children. Vasilisa escapes from Baba Yaga's clutches because she has her "mother's blessing" to help her, embodied in a doll which advises her and performs the tasks set her by the witch. When Baba Yaga finds out that Vasilisa has been blessed, she sends her home to her stepmother and stepsisters unharmed and with the light they had sent her to fetch. The light given to Vasilisa by the witch is contained in a skull stuck on a pole. The blazing eyes of the skull stare straight at the stepmother and her daughters. "They tried to hide but everywhere they went the eyes followed them. By morning they were shrivelled to a cinder and only Vasilisa was left" (Warner, 89). Vasilisa subsequently takes a room with an old woman and waits for her father to return from his business trip. With the doll's help, she spins a quantity of fine linen thread, weaves a cloth "so delicate it could be drawn through the eye of a needle" and sews twelve shirts for the Tsar. The Tsar is delighted with her work and invites the seamstress to his palace, falls in love with her and asks her to marry him. When Vasilisa's father returns he is overjoyed to hear of the good fortune that has befallen his daughter. He and the old woman, with whom Vasilisa has been living, come to live in the palace (Warner, 89–92).

The trajectory of the story of "Vasilisa the Beautiful" is similar to that of "Hansel and Gretel" in a number of ways. Just as they did, Vasilisa must come to terms with the dualistic nature of the mother figure and develop a meaningful relationship with her father/the symbolic order. Her stepmother expels her from the house and sends her into the forest, just as Hansel's and Gretel's did, and her stepmother and the witch figure also epitomize the bad breast/mother figure. For Vasilisa the doll embodies the blessing or loving and nurturing aspects of the mother, while the stepmother/witch again represents the evil, cannibalistic characteristics. Vasilisa is not lured into Baba Yaga's house as Hansel and Gretel are, however. Instead, she recognizes the threat the house and the witch represent but must still approach and comply with Baba Yaga's commands, fulfilling the onerous tasks she sets. Thus, Vasilisa must face up to and deal with that which she fears just as Maggie Kilgour suggests the infant must do in relation to the breast.[18] The step/mother is again dealt with through matricide but Vasilisa retains the best parts of the mother figure in the body of the doll, which she carries "in her pocket until the day she die[s]" (Warner, 92). Arguably Vasilisa has reconciled with her ambivalent feelings toward her mother who is then reclaimed in the figure of the old woman. Again in this story, economic wealth is associated with the paternal and provides a happy ever after ending.

The emphasis on the devouring aspects of these wicked witches is significant. Baba Yaga's sharp teeth and the bones and skulls with which her house is constructed are described in oral sadistic terms as Campbell suggested (73). Vasilisa must enter the witch's domain through gates made of human legs, with human hands for bolts and a mouth with sharp teeth for a lock (Warner, 87). Freud discussed the significance of the teeth (in dreams) and proposed that they represented the female genitals, the lower part of the body being transposed to the upper so that "it is most likely that the mouth refers to the vagina and the rows of teeth which open and close to a phantasy about castrating vaginal teeth" (Creed, 118). The gateway to Baba Yaga's house suggests some transposition of the lower body to the upper and certainly emphasizes the incorporative aspects of the maternal mouths. The devouring vagina mouth with teeth—the *vagina dentata*—is a symbol for the castrating and incorporating aspects of the cannibalistic female.

THE CASTRATING MOTHER

The concepts of the *vagina dentata* and the monstrous feminine are, as Creed succinctly points out, constructed by and within a patriarchal phallocentric ideology and are invoked by castration anxiety experienced by the male spectator (Creed, 2). Freud originally posited that men viewed women with horror because they appear to be castrated and evoke in them the fear of being similarly mutilated.[19] In Freud's narrative, castration was posed as a threat coming specifically from the father in the following scenario: the boy, being passionately attached to the mother, begins to see his father as a rival and imagines that the father will castrate him, making his genitals resemble his mother's. Thus, the father is constructed as the castrator, the one who mutilates genitals, and the mother/woman is constructed as castrated. The boy's desire for the mother is eventually overwhelmed by his fear of castration and so he renounces his desire for her in preference for becoming like his father, secure in the knowledge that he will one day inherit his father's power and have a woman of his own. The mother's body and her castrated genitals inspire a fear of castration in the boy, but according to Freud, they do not threaten to castrate (Creed, 109–110). Lacan also argues that the woman's genitals lack the penis, which is the mark of human completeness, and that she is, therefore, regarded as castrated.[20] The girl, according to Freud's thesis, must accept that both she and her mother are castrated, which is the origin of penis envy.[21] While the girl desires the phallus and the social position it construes, she must recognize and align herself with her mother's subordination and apparent monstrosity.

Many theorists have since questioned the assumption that the woman is castrated. Creed argues convincingly that, "woman . . . terrifies because man endows her with imaginary powers of castration" (87). She provides an extensive rereading of Freud's analysis of the "Little Hans" case history in order to argue that the origin of Hans's phobia was fear of the mother's genitals, not as castrated but as castrating organs. Creed suggests that Hans not only feared that "his father might punish him for his desire to have his mother for himself, he also feared his mother might castrate him as a punishment for masturbation and/or because of his erotic longings for her." Therefore, Creed surmises, "Freud's theory that the father is the castrator is only part of the story" (89). She is not the only one to question Freud's insistence on the role of the father as castrator. Karen Horney suggests the "prominence given to the anxiety relating to the castrating father is . . . tendentious"[22] and Erich Fromm also argues that Freud misinterprets the case and that "the dread of castration originates with Hans's mother."[23]

Creed shows that "fear of the castrating female genitals pervades the myths and legends of many cultures . . . [and is] central to the horror film." In the myths Creed refers to, "the threatening aspect of the female genital is symbolized by the *vagina dentata* or toothed vagina" (105). In Yanomamo myth, for example, one of the first women on earth possesses a vagina that could transform into a toothed mouth that ate her lover's penis (Walker, 1034). According to Erich Neumannn, some myths represent the toothed vagina as an animal or animal-companion of the female deity;[24] one such is Scylla, the devouring whirlpool whose upper body has the form of a beautiful woman while the lower part consists of three snapping hellhounds (Creed, 106). Another classic and much-quoted example is that of Medusa. "With her head of writhing snakes, huge mouth, lolling tongue and boar's tusks, the Medusa . . . [is regarded] as a particularly nasty version of the *vagina dentata*" (111). Creed points out that

> the myth of the woman as castrator clearly points to male fears and phantasies about the female genitals as a trap, a black hole which threatens to swallow them up and cut them into pieces. The *vagina dentata* is the mouth of hell—a terrifying symbol of woman as the "devil's gateway" . . . [it] also points to the duplicitous nature of woman, who promises paradise in order to ensnare her victims. The notion of the devouring female genitals continues to exist in the modern world; it is apparent in popular derogatory terms for women such as "man-eater" and "castrating bitch." (106)

In "Hansel and Gretel," the witch "promises paradise in order to ensnare her victims" in the form of a return to the primal mother-infant relationship, symbolized by the food her house/domain is made from, by the milk and sugared pancakes she feeds to them, and the beds with white sheets she prepares for them. The children think they are in heaven/paradise. The paradise Creed specifically refers to, however, is sexual satisfaction, an exclusively (according to adult mores) adult heaven. The equivalent narrative lure for children is food, especially sweet, rich food, metonymically standing in for the primal relationship.

The White Witch in C. S. Lewis's *The Lion, the Witch and the Wardrobe* lures Edmund with a particularly sweet food—Turkish delight—and he receives sensuous satisfaction from its consumption and his relationship with her. Mervyn Nicholson claims that sweet foods and sugar, in particular, are associated with deception, compulsion, and transience. But, I might add, they are significantly also culturally associated with love and romance. Nicholson proposes that the Witch effectively seduces Edmund by feeding him sweet magic Turkish delight.[25] I suggest, however, that she seduces Edmund with a range of delights designed to evoke the sensual satisfaction of the primal relationship with the mother, including sweet food.

The wand-wielding, fur-clad White Witch is a tall and overbearing fetishized figure[26] who is initially described as being white-skinned, so pale, in fact, that her face is as white as "icing sugar, except for her very red mouth."[27] Thus, an element of intense sweetness is immediately introduced in relation to the body of the Witch, which is overlaid by the sexuality of her *very* red mouth. Notably, David Holbrook associates the Witch's red mouth with bloodiness.[28] The emphasis on her mouth evokes notions of the *vagina dentata*. Narratives that feature devouring monsters and/or feature close-ups or descriptions of gaping jaws, sharp teeth, and bloodied lips play on the spectator's or reader's fears of bloody incorporation, according to Creed: "Sometimes the lips are only slightly parted and either a trace of blood trickles over the bottom lip or both lips are smeared with blood. Often the teeth are threateningly visible." This image is central to the vampire genre and, Creed argues, is linked to the *vagina dentata* regardless of the gender of the character (107).

The Witch initially questions Edmund impatiently and looks at him sternly. Once she realizes that Edmund is human and therefore may be useful to her, however, she speaks to him in "quite a different voice." "My poor child," she says, "how cold you look! Come and sit with me here on the sledge and I will put my mantle round you and we will talk" (*Lion,* 36). Although "Edmund did not like this arrangement at all...he dared not disobey" and he steps on to the sledge and sits at the Witch's feet. She puts "a fold of her fur mantle round him and tucked it well in" (36). Thus the Witch, who is described, intriguingly as "covered in white fur up to her throat" (33) rather than specifically *wearing* fur (implying almost that the fur is part of her body) engulfs Edmund in her fur mantle.[29] The Witch initially offers Edmund something hot to drink. This magic liquid is presented in a jeweled cup: "Edmund felt much better as he began to sip the hot drink. It was something he had never tasted before, very sweet and foamy and creamy, and it warmed him right down to his toes" (36). This may be something that Edmund does not remember having tasted before but the warmth, sweetness, and creaminess of the drink she creates for him is evocative of his pre-oedipal relationship with his mother.

The White Witch then asks Edmund what he would "like best to eat" and he very politely asks for "Turkish Delight, please, your Majesty" (36). She produces a round box tied with green silk ribbon, which contains "several pounds of the best Turkish Delight. Each piece was sweet and light to the very center, and Edmund had never tasted anything more delicious. He was quite warm now, and very comfortable" (37). Margaret and Michael Rustin point out that Edmund receives sensuous pleasure from the magic food and drink he consumes. Notably, his face becomes "very red" (39) after he has consumed the Turkish delight, which could be a sign of sexual arousal. On the other hand, of course, it could just indicate that he has indigestion. I favor the former explanation because if he had bellyache he presumably wouldn't have subsequently pleaded for more (*Lion*, 41). The Rustins also link the White Witch with the mother figure by suggesting that because Edmund (an evacuee) had been "feeling hungry for his mother's love and care" he was particularly vulnerable to her seduction techniques. For the Rustins, as well as for myself, the sweet food represents "comfort at an infantile level." This is, they suggest, "reminiscent of so much of the consumption of sweet stuff by children."[30]

As Edmund is eating, the White Witch "kept asking him questions." At first Edmund tries to remember his manners: "that it is rude to speak with one's mouth full, but soon he forgot about this and thought only of trying to shovel down as much Turkish Delight as he could" (*Lion*, 37). If, as the axiom "manners maketh man" suggests, manners are indeed the veneer of civilization and thus symbolic of subjectivity then Edmund can be said to have regressed into a precivilized state. "The more he ate the more he wanted to eat, and he never asked himself why the White Witch should be so inquisitive." "She got him to tell her" everything she wanted to know (37). Edmund speaks at the Witch's behest, not of his own free will. As Nicholson points out, she feeds him magic food, and he feeds her information (29). In this respect, the Witch resembles the figure of John Keats's "La Belle Dame sans Merci," "full beautiful, a faery's child,/ Her hair was long, her foot was light,/ And her eyes were wild," who seduces men with sweet sticky food: "She found me roots of relish sweet,/ And honey wild, and manna dew;" and then metaphorically feeds on her victims.

Edmund's relationship with the White Witch is far from equitable. The food she feeds him literally intoxicates him: he loses the ability to make sound judgments, behaves badly, and speaks injudiciously. The Turkish delight is an enchanted and addictive substance: "anyone who had once tasted it would want more and more of it, and would even, if they were allowed, go on eating it till they killed themselves" (*Lion*, 38). Edmund becomes the Witch's servant, betraying his brother and sisters to her. His desire to repeat the sensuous satisfaction he experienced becomes an obsession and he "wanted to taste that Turkish Delight again more than he wanted anything else" (42).

In terms of the trajectory of Klein's thesis, Edmund's relationship with the White Witch can be seen to reflect that of the infant to the mother/breast and is similar to that between Hansel and Gretel and the wicked witch they encounter. Edmund is ejected from the maternal domain when he is sent away as an evacuee from his London home to the Professor's house in the country. The White Witch offers him a substitute primal/oral/sensual relationship with her. She seduces him with the good breast, plentiful ("several pounds") of Turkish delight and the creamy, sweet drink she produces for him. But, once he is under her spell and addicted, she refuses him food, becoming the parsimonious withholding breast. Once he has finished all the Turkish delight, Edmund looks "very hard at the empty box and wish[es] that she would ask him whether he would like some more" (*Lion*, 38). Even when he begs: "Please, please...please couldn't I have just one more piece of Turkish Delight to eat on the way home?" (41) she refuses.

The White Witch offers Edmund the paradise Creed refers to and the heaven Hansel and Gretel experience. She tells him about her maternal domain—a house, which is a "lovely place" (39), explicitly located in a feminized space "between...two hills" (40).[31] She has, she tells him, "no children of my own. [And] I want a nice boy whom I could bring up as a Prince and who would be King of Narnia when I am gone" (39). Thus she unequivocally offers to be a (substitute) mother to him; he will be Prince to her Queen. In her maternal domain, she tells him "he would wear a gold crown and eat Turkish Delight all day long" (39). The delights the Witch offers him obliterate all thoughts of danger: "When he had first got on to the sledge he had been afraid that she might drive away with him to some unknown place from which he would not be able to get back." But he forgets "about that fear" (39). He is totally seduced by her bodily presence, food and promises of heaven.

Edmund's desire for the maternal domain can be read as incestuous and therefore transgressive. In Freudian terms, Edmund's sexual development should involve turning from the mother to the father and the symbolic order. His desire for the body of the mother should have been overcome by his fear of castration (psychically the "unknown place from which he would not be able to get back"). But instead he regresses and forgets about that fear, gives in to his unruly desires and embraces the sensuous experiences (of the oral phase) offered to him.

Nicholson suggests that in literature, when a woman takes control and uses food "not as a means of supplying the male—and hence articulating her subordinate power status in relation to the male—but as a means of entrapping and...enslaving him," she enacts "a primal rebellion, a thing almost too terrible to think of for patriarchal culture, a focus of anxiety so intense that it is almost paralyzing" (48). It is pertinent to focus momentarily, with regard to Nicholson's use of the word paralyzing, on the way the White Witch paralyzes/castrates her victims. She turns them to stone in the same way that the Medusa's gaze paralyzes her victims. The White Witch's powers evoke the horror and dread of the Medusa herself, the epitome of the castrating *vagina dentata*.

Edmund "join[s]" with the White Witch, becoming as one with her; as such he loses his subjectivity and is psychically castrated. She has recreated for him the experience/environment of the primal relationship and used it to trap and enslave him. The White Witch is also a smothering mother figure, and her body is linked to notions of abjection through the surfeit of sweet food that she magically produces and feeds to him so that he becomes sticky (*Lion,* 39) and is sickened (43). It may be argued that Edmund is actually poisoned by the Turkish delight, which has made him feel sick and to which he has become addicted. By taking in the poisonous food, Edmund becomes as one with the poisoning mother. His previous "spiteful" (29) character is transformed into a truly evil one. He commits an act which is signaled by the narrator as "one of the nastiest things in this story" (44); thus it is compared to the evil things the White Witch does, such as her assimilation of the Christmas partygoers when she turns them to stone (106) or even the murder of Aslan (141). Edmund becomes a traitor and the nasty thing he does is his first act of treachery—he betrays Lucy, ostensibly for his own gain and denies that he has been to Narnia. When the others find out Peter calls him a "poisonous little beast" (55). Thus, it may be said that Edmund is poisoned, is assimilated by his poisoner and becomes poisonous.

Lewis's White Witch is a fascinating evocation of all that is culturally and psychologically fearful about the figure of the woman from a phallocentric patriarchal viewpoint. She is clearly fetishized, evokes the *vagina dentata* and notions of abjection. She seduces, poisons, assimilates, and castrates. Her powers induce horror, but she is also alluring.

THE WITCH'S POWERS

The witch's evil powers are seen to be part of her "feminine" nature and she is positioned, according to patriarchal discourses, as closer to nature and the geographic landscape than man and able to control the forces of nature such as tempests, hurricanes, and storms (Creed, 76). The White Witch, as Mr. Tumnus the faun informs Lucy, "has got all Narnia under her thumb. It's she that makes it always winter. Always winter and never Christmas" (*Lion,* 23). Narnia is covered by snow: "There was crisp, dry snow under [Edmund's] feet and more snow lying on the branches of the trees. Overhead there was pale blue sky, the sort of sky one sees on a fine winter day in the morning" (31). This beautiful landscape is also, however, a "strange, cold, quiet place" (32). The description of the Witch's body is interesting in this regard. "Her face was white—not merely pale, but white like snow or paper or icing sugar . . . It was a beautiful face . . . but proud and cold and stern" (33). The body of the White Witch is paralleled with the snowy landscape, both being beautiful but specifically cold and white with/as snow, austere and forbidding. Spring only comes to Narnia when the Witch's powers wane. The White Witch's landscape is sterile and frozen; she is positioned as antithetical to and transgressive of mythic concepts aligning the female with fertility. She is both explicitly responsible for controlling the seasons and maintaining Narnia in its wintry state and implicitly aligned, by the description of her snow-white body, with Nature and the landscape, a reiteration of the patriarchal discourses Creed discusses.

Paul Stewart's *The Weather Witch* is a story about a witch from the sixteenth century who can control the weather.[32] She can produce flashes of lightning from her fingertips, a "viciously cold wind," hail and sleet, or alternatively "searing tongues of flame" with which to assail her victims (*Weather Witch,* 145). Notably these forces are produced because the witch is angry "to the point of frenzied madness" (144). Creed confirms that the witch is often described in terms of irrationality (76). In structuralist terms, irrationality, the body and the feminine, are opposed to the masculine rational mind. As Elizabeth Grosz points out, hysteria has been designated by masculine interests "the feminine neurosis *par excellence.*"[33] The Weather Witch's powers are therefore aligned with classic notions of feminine weakness. Significantly, in another allusion to feminine attributes this time associated specifically with the body, the Weather Witch explains that, "[a] spell must live if it is to take effect." A potion consists of "all the necessary ingredients...but [they are] lifeless" until she "breathe[s] life into them."

> the old witch closed her eyes, took a long, deep breath and bent down over the cauldron. Her long, silvery-grey hair dipped down into the seething elements and as she exhaled, her whole body seemed to empty itself. (260)

The witch's potion/power is associated with her female generative capacities, the mysterious magical but abject process whereby she gives/produces life from within her body.

The witches in Pat O'Shea's remarkable story *The Hounds of the Morrigan* are also able to control the weather.[34] They can create rain by kicking the clouds with their "wicked" feet, lightning by tapping their teeth, and thunder by laughing (*Morrigan,* 7). The Great Queen, the Morrigan, is the most powerful of all the witches:

> The Morrigan sneezed. Out from the dark crimson caves of her dainty nostrils came twin jets of darkish air that turned into long billowing clouds, graphite grey. They spread out and formed a thick canopy over the whole area...and everything had become dark and dreary...The wind began to moan, a low and very lonesome sound, that gradually increased in strength to a savage howl...Up above the heavy clouds billowed and wreathed and seemed to boil. The darkness...was as a cloak between themselves and all that lay beyond a mere couple of feet or so ahead of them. Pidge started to worry that they might fall into a squashy, muddy hole, or a quaking, swallowing bog...there was the danger that they might be swallowed. His thoughts ran wild and he imagined the earth as a monstrous animal with many, many concealed mouths; and he feared it. He thought of mouths, all of them capable of opening under their feet without warning, to swallow them down a muddy gullet into a heaving prison of a stomach. (224–25)

Again, the weather spell is produced by and from the witch's body. Pidge is aware that he and his sister are being pursued by the Morrigan's hounds and that she is using her magic to try to capture them but he is often unsure whether the people and situations they come across in their quest are good/natural or evil/enchanted. Pidge's abject fear of being swallowed up by the bog is a psychological dread emanating from his fear of the

Morrigan. Significantly, however, this relates directly to the *vagina dentata* and the evil devouring abject mother-figure.

Creed confirms that the witch is often described as scheming and evil and is also associated with a range of abject things such as filth, decay, spiders, bats, cobwebs, brews and potions (Creed, 76). Hansel and Gretel's witch is "very old" (*Grimm Tales*, 61), and has "red eyes [that] cannot see very far, but [she has] a keen sense of smell, like [an] animal" and when she walks she "slinks" (62) or "waddles" (63). Baba Yaga too is an "aged, ugly crone" and associated, through her emaciated skeletal body and her use of human bones as building materials, with the world of the dead (Warner, 85) and with decrepitude and decay and, therefore, abjection. The Weather Witch is also described as a "very, very old woman indeed" (*Weather Witch*, 134) (she is in fact supposed to be around four hundred years old). She has the "expressionless stare of the dead" (53). "Joe had never seen a person with such lifeless eyes before." "Her face was so dry and lined that it looked more like elephant hide than human skin" (134). Her features are "angular" (188) "gaunt" (53), and viciously hard. Her teeth are "blackened" (227) and her "yellowed" eyes have a "morbid" gaze (134). This witch is animalistic as well as being aligned with lifelessness/death, decay and disease. As Kristeva argues, the corpse evokes the most extreme abjection: it is "the most sickening of wastes…It is death infecting life."[35] The corpse undeniably signals the body's corporeality. Decay, disease, infection and the corpse itself pose a threat "to identity that comes from without…life [is threatened] by death" (Kristeva, 71). There is near-universal horror at confronting a corpse/death (Grosz, 75).

In direct and ironic contrast, O'Shea's witch, the Morrigan, is initially presented as "tall and blonde and very beautiful" (*Morrigan*, 102); "her eyelids were smooth and oval like white sugared almonds and her mouth was a faultless rosebud" (223). But cultural paradigms of beauty are overturned and even ridiculed in this narrative. The Morrigan's appearance evokes laughter when she meets with her companions. All three witches regard "the *idea* of beauty as the height of nonsense" (103, emphasis in original) and the Morrigan thinks that she looks "disgusting" (223). The Morrigan's true appearance is also fascinating:

> she appeared as a skinny, grizzled old hag, whose face looked as if it was carved out of yellow soap. Her nose was like a walnut with long and strong black hairs that closely resembled prawn whiskers sticking out of her nostrils. Her moustache was a fringe of wiry white, stuck out in a nimbus round her mouth, like a chimney-sweep's brush. She had at least five hundred warts, some—one on

top of another, four or five times over. Her ears spiralled out of her head, looking like two pink, fleshy corkscrews and each lobe was as big as a duck egg. The eyebrows were two tufts of coarse red hair. Her eyes were purple and her eyelids hairless. Her teeth hung down over her chin; they were so long that they grew in tangles and they were as grey as Dead Men's Fingers. Her hands were as big as dinner-plates, blackish-green with grey scales and her feet were twice as big as meat-platters, fat and glistening white with wrinkled edges. Her toes moved about in a hesitant way like blind worms, seeking. (103)

On the one hand, this witch is described in traditional terms, although with parodic exaggeration: she is an old hag with warts and an overabundance of facial hair. On the other hand, her grotesque appearance is described using culinary similes: some refer to food and some to kitchen equipment. The first category includes walnuts, prawns, duck eggs, and Dead Men's Fingers.[36] The second category includes a corkscrew, a dinner-plate, and a meat-platter. The Morrigan is associated with the abject in terms of excess, disease, decay, poison and sliminess. Despite the irony involved in her description, in the context of O'Shea's story, the Morrigan is a real and terrible threat. The children meet a wise, old angler who tells them "She is the Goddess of Death and Destruction" and "would make Nero look like a bit of fried bread." Her "evil heart" is "so small it would flap about inside a midge's skin." At this Pidge is "thrilled with horror and fright" (122).

Following the tradition established in "Hansel and Gretel" and re-iterated in Edmund's encounter with the White Witch, the Morrigan's sidekicks attempt to lure Pidge and his sister Brigit to their house with food. "Do come home with us and have some tea," [Melodie Moonlight] said "silkily." But these are not traditional witches and their offerings do not evoke the good breast/mother. Instead, their food is an ironic smorgasbord of the edible and inedible, ordinary and extraordinary, railway café menu and recipe for death: "Red Cap Pasty, Peggy's Leg, Kiss Pie and Walking Stick, Hafner's Sausages and Soup of the Day." But Pidge thought that Melodie Moonlight's "voice sounded like a cat singing the death song of a mouse" (68) and the children decline her invitation. Despite the comedic elements, the reader and the characters are in no doubt that the witches are evil and will commit evil deeds. A guard-frog outside the witches' house informs the children that, "Tresspassers will be kilt stone dead!" The witches are apparently "fonda kids, mingled wit' herbs in a big black pot wit' onyins bilin in it. Thim's not fonda frogs thanksfully" (71). But the frog is mistaken about the witches' tastes because when

Pidge finally enters their house he sees on the table "the frog... cowering on a plate under a meat-cover of metal gauze, which stood horrifyingly close to a dish of stuffed olives, buttered bread and an arrangement of condiments and pickles, as if he were part of a meal" (77). These witches are undoubtedly unconventional but retain traditional cannibalistic and castrating tendencies.

Various phallic accoutrements fetishize the Morrigan's sidekicks: one of them smokes cigars and the other chews tobacco, and they speed around the Irish countryside on a Harley Davidson. As Creed remarks, soft-porn magazines often contain images of women sitting astride a motorbike (116). These witches are also castrating, and it is significantly an adult male who becomes their victim. When a police sergeant calls at their house to investigate some stolen furniture, he finds himself dressed, not in his Garda uniform, but

> as a little girl in a pale-blue frock with puffed sleeves and a tie belt ...
>
> [H]is own beefy, well-muscled, hairy legs were wearing dainty white ankle-socks and his feet were in buckled hornpipe shoes ...
>
> [I]nstead of his truncheon, there was a skipping rope with wooden handles and tinkle-bells in his great, big fist...
>
> Resting on his broad chest were the ends of two fat, flaxen plaits, tied with lavender ribbons. He touched one of the plaits, found that it was real and felt all the way up to his head, where he discovered that his Garda headgear had somehow changed into a cotton sun-bonnet.
>
> Worst of all, one of the legs of his pretty pink knickers was hanging down below his knee, exposing his frills to the world ...
>
> "The leg of your drawers is hanging down, Sergeant," Breda [Fairfoul] said vulgarly. (*Morrigan*, 96–97)

The (phallic) signifiers of the Sergeant's masculinity and his position as upholder of the laws (both patriarchal and judicial) are removed/subsumed by the witches' magic. He is feminized and symbolically castrated by this transformation. In another interesting reversal of cultural norms, the Sergeant is sexually harassed. John Stephens remarks that sexuality in children's books is "usually displaced into questions of undress."[37] Significantly, O'Shea's narrator has informed the reader that the Sergeants' "knickers" are showing, but the witch refers to them "vulgarly" as "drawers." But she is not only vulgar, she is also arguably aggressive and deliberately sexually intimidating. The Sergeant finds himself in the (feminized) position of being a sexual object. As Laura Mulvey has argued, women are usually the ones displayed as sexual objects and, within movie narratives, the image of the castrated woman gives order and meaning to phallocentric patriarchal discourses.[38] The castrated man in O'Shea's narrative, on the other hand, reinforces the phallicism of the witch who castrated him and reiterates cultural notions of the witch/woman/mother as castrating.

Lewis's White Witch is also phallicized and simultaneously castrating. Mr. Tumnus tells Lucy the likely punishment he will receive when the White Witch finds out he has disobeyed her orders:

> [S]he'll have my tail cut off, and my horns sawn off, and my beard plucked out, and she'll wave her wand over my beautiful cloven hoofs and turn them into horrid solid hoofs like a wretched horse. And if she is extra and specially angry she'll turn me into stone. (*Lion*, 24)

Mr. Tumnus is indeed charged with High Treason and petrified. His home is wrecked by the Witch's Secret Police and a picture of his father is, significantly, "slashed into shreds with a knife" (56–57). Again, it is in particular the signifiers of the phallus that are the target of the Witch's violent aggression. Later in the story Edmund is threatened with castration. Unable to perform the ritual on the Stone Table as she would have preferred because "That is where it has always been done before," the White Witch instructs the Dwarf to put "it" (Edmund) against the trunk of a tree (123).

> He saw the Witch take off her outer mantle. Her arms were bare underneath it and terribly white. Because they were so very white he could see them, but he could not see much else, it was so dark in this valley under the dark trees.
>
> "Prepare the victim," said the Witch. And the dwarf undid Edmund's collar and folded back his shirt at the neck. Then he took Edmund's hair and pulled his head back so that he had to raise his chin. After that Edmund heard a strange noise—whizz—whizz—whizz. For a moment he couldn't think what it was. Then he realised. It was the sound of a knife being sharpened. (124)

The narrative shifts from a lingering focus on the witch's white skin to the image of Edmund's involuntarily exposed throat, to the threatening sound of a blade being sharpened. Edmund is rescued, but a chance remark by one of his rescuers who trips over something is significant. The rescuer exclaims "Oh, sorry, it's only an old stump!" and Edmund "went off in a dead faint" (125). Holbrook suggests that the emphasis on certain images in this passage—the whiteness of the witch's skin, her bare arms,

Edmund's throat, the unseen knife, and the stump—reveal an underlying obsession with sexual maiming (Holbrook, 12).

The clearest evocation of the White Witch's castrating powers occurs when she orders her followers to shave off Aslan's mane. "Snip-snip-snip went the shears and masses of curling gold began to fall to the ground…the face of Aslan look[ed] all small and different without its mane." His "enemies" mock his impotence: "jeering at him, saying things like 'Puss, Puss! Poor Pussy,' and…'Would you like a saucer of milk, Pussums?'" (*Lion, 139*).

As Creed mentions, the witch traditionally has familiars, animals or birds who share her supernatural powers or who act as servants and are associated with abjection. The White Witch's associates include a "vile rabble" (142) of "[o]gres with monstrous teeth, and wolves, and bull-headed men; spirits of evil trees and poisonous plants…Cruels and Hags and Incubuses, Wraiths, Horrors, Efreets, Sprites, Orknies, Wooses, and Ettins" (138). They are described in terms of abjection: they are foul, black, vile, evil, and poisonous. This rabble spits and kicks Aslan once he is shorn and muzzled. The Weather Witch has a pack of guard-dogs and cats that move "slinkily [and] stealthily" (*Weather Witch,* 122), and have "cruel yellow eyes…like flames." "Half of them were like massive Dobermans, sleek and powerful with lolling tongues hanging almost carelessly over razor-sharp teeth. The feline half of the pack were smaller, but with their glinting fangs and claws, looked no less dangerous" (123). The cats and dogs are part of the foul weather the witch creates and rains down upon her victims. The Morrigan has a pack of hounds that follow Pidge and Brigit. The children know that if they run in sight of them the hounds will hunt to kill. The danger the children are in is made explicit when one "bold" hound breaks away from the pack and pursues a deer.

> This breach in discipline was too much for the others and baying loudly they went after the bold one…Soon the leading hound made a sort of leap forward and sank his teeth into the hind quarters of a deer. An indescribable sound came from the doomed animal's throat, and then there was the snarling and excitement as the victim fell on its side, with its delicate legs moving stiffly in the air. The deer tried to raise its head from the earth but a hound took it by the throat and sank down on it. In the finish the hounds were sprawled all over their kill, dipping their heads to its flesh and nuzzling it. The scene now looked almost affectionate, as the hounds licked the blood of the deer. (*Morrigan,* 184)

The figure of the witch embodies the fear of the bad breast/mother figure proposed by Klein.[39] This fear, which originates in a sense of loss and a desire to reinstate oneness, is pathologically transformed by patri-archal culture resulting in the production of the image of, and discourses about, the witch. The metamorphosed mother/witch is orally focused and sadistic; she has an enormous insatiable appetite, the ability to engulf subjectivity, and the desire to castrate. She is culturally associated, like/as the mother, with abjection through her body's generative capacities, and through the food/potions with which she entices and poisons. The witch's duality makes her, like the breast for the infant, paradoxically both attrac-tive and repellent. In all the stories mentioned in this chapter the witch is seen to be duplicitous and dualistic. The wicked witch in "Hansel and Gretel" and Lewis's White Witch are juxtaposed with and pretend to be good mother figures. In the Russian folktales featuring Baba Yaga she can be good or bad, and her cannibalistic tendencies in the story of Vasilisa the Beautiful are contrasted to the blessings given by the good mother, embodied by the doll. The Weather Witch tries to justify her actions by purporting a maternalistic relationship with the villagers she has impris-oned but is really just satisfying her own desires. She is also contrasted with the benevolent figure of the children's grandmother who assumes control of the weather once the evil witch is dead. The Morrigan does not pretend to be anything other than evil but the conventionally beautiful appearance she adopts is duplicitous and designed to seduce. The dispar-ity between the Morrigan and various good mother-substitute figures is also emphasized within O'Shea's narrative. These witches/women then, often appear on the surface to be attractive; they may initially provide sweet, delicious, comforting food and promise "heaven" to the stories' protagonists but, just as the infant fears the mother will, these witches desire to devour those they feed. The relentless pursuit of their victims by the witches I've described and their desire to incorporate/consume them are a reflection of the infant's nostalgic desire for the primal state, a state of total unity and oneness, where self and other, eater and eaten, inside and outside coalesce.

I must now reemphasize the cultural construction of the phallocentric image of mother as witch/monstrous feminine, which plays upon the infant's psychological fear of abandonment (the bad breast) and desire for oneness. This construction takes place within systems of order and representation that privilege masculinity, that sublimate the debt to maternity and ultimately give structure to the "entire history of western thought" (Grosz, 120). If, as Irigaray suggests, mother-daughter (and for that matter mother-son) relationship/s can be restructured then desire itself can be reorganized "so that the lost object that founds desire—the object whose loss begins the chain of substitute metonymic objects of desire—need not be given up or lost…Identity need not be seen as a definitive separation of the mother and child" (cited in Grosz, 125). It follows that without the definitive separation from the mother demanded by patriarchal culture the rigid dichotomous characterizations of the two sexes can be rejected, along with their corresponding oppositional attributes—subject/object, self/other, inside/outside and active/passive etc. (Grosz, 125). In discourses that construct the mother as witch, the pathology of phallocentric culture can be revealed and the horror they evoke deconstructed. Once this has been done, their allure and the perverse pleasures they evoke can be enjoyed.

6

HAIRY ON THE INSIDE

From Cannibals to Pedophiles

> Those slavering jaws; the lolling tongue; the rime of saliva on the grizzled chops—of all the teeming perils of the night and the forest, ghosts, hobgoblins, ogres that grill babies upon gridirons, witches that fatten their captives in cages for cannibal tables, the wolf is worst, for he cannot listen to reason...Fear and flee the wolf; for worst of all, the wolf may be more than he seems.
> —Angela Carter, "The Company of Wolves"[1]

STORIES ABOUT MONSTERS who threaten to consume, whether they are wolves, witches, sharks, or aliens, continue to be the mainstay of much grotesque-horror fiction aimed at both children and adults. Monsters such as these act outside cultural and social prohibitions and represent the antithesis of civilized humanity. Those who eat badly threaten the coherence of the social order, reveal the precariousness of humankind's place at the top of the food chain and remind us of the corporeality of our bodies—that our flesh can be classified as meat just as readily as that of any other animal. Monstrous eaters also remind us of the moral dilemma that eating evokes; even the most everyday and benign act of eating involves aggression and the sacrifice of another living organism. As Mikhail Bakhtin puts it in *Rabelais and His World*: "the body...swallows, devours, rends the world apart, is enriched and grows at the world's expense."[2]

In preceding chapters, I have examined the ways in which the first feeding relationship is of vital importance in the formation of individual subjectivity and cultural stereotypes. Initially, the infant is as one with the mother/breast; there is no distinction between self and other, eater and eaten, inside and outside. Maggie Kilgour points out that this situation contains dangerous elements of cannibalism: "In this primary stage of identification the eater *is* the eaten—or at least imagines it is."[3] The child soon discovers, however, that what it considered to be part of itself is in fact separate or outside of its self. Thus, the familiar becomes strange (Kilgour, 12). Kilgour emphasizes the way structural differences are produced and perpetuated by this situation and believes that the inside/outside opposition is the foundation of all binary oppositions. She shows how the model for the inside/outside opposition is "based on bodily experience and the sense that what is 'inside' one's own body is a coherent structure that can be defined against what lies 'outside' of it" (4). Indeed, Freud in "Negation" suggests that the inside/outside opposition is the basis for all future decisions:

> Expressed in the language of the oldest, that is, of the oral, instinctual impulses, the judgment is: "I should like to eat this," or "I should like to spit it out"; and, put more generally: "I should like to take this into myself and to keep that out." That is to say: "It shall be *inside* me" or "it shall be *outside* me" ... the original pleasure-ego wants to introject into itself everything that is good and to eject from itself everything that is bad. What is bad, what is alien to the ego and what is external are, to begin with, identical.[4]

As Kilgour comments, this crude schema defines everything inside as good while everything outside is bad. This hypothesis is presented as universally significant on an individual level. In the West, however, this system of values extends from the individual level to motivate many more sophisticated notions of individual, social, and corporate values, so that outsiders or "others" are defined as bad, evil or transgressive and are a source of fear (Kilgour, 4). In Western society and culture at least, and universally on an individual level, control can be maintained if the other is somehow subsumed or incorporated so "that there is no category of alien outsideness left to threaten the inner stability" (5). Melanie Klein theorized that the infant's fear of being devoured by the mother is a reaction to its own desire to assimilate or possess that which is external to the self.[5] In a similar way, Kilgour argues individuals/cultures/societies project the desire for assimilation onto the other, "a tactic that has been shown to be at work in psychic defenses, misogyny, racism and imperialism" (5).

The dualism inside/outside can arguably be cited as the basis of the nostalgia for (but also fear of) a state of unity or oneness found in many myths and fables. Kilgour cites the paradise of Genesis and Milton, Coleridge's dream of "Self, that no alien knows" ("Religious Musings"), and Ahab's Moby-Dick as fictions that are

> bound to a nostalgia for a state of total incorporation that underlies many of the major trends of western thought: idealism, scientific rationalism, traditional psychoanalysis, as well as imperialism, and theories in general that try to construct a transcendental system or imagine a single body that could contain all meaning. (5)

The dualism inside/outside, therefore, derived from the infant's first feeding relationship, arguably has universal significance and it provides the basis of many aspects of Western cultural belief systems. In the West, there is a ubiquitous and explicit desire in individuals, cultures, social, and corporate organizations to create order, dispel disorder, and quell transgression by eliminating the other. Kilgour remarks that recent studies of imperialism and colonial discourses have shown how a society's desire to appropriate other cultures can be disguised through the projection of that impulse onto the other (5), that is, by labeling the other "cannibal." The appropriation of other cultures by the West is achieved by a process of assimilation, inculcation or through consumption. Elspeth Probyn argues that Western anthropology and Western interests in general have had something of a preoccupation with the notion of cannibalism, which, she says, "reveals much about the colonial imagination."[6] "Eating the Other," according to bell hooks, is a metaphor for imperial violence (cited by Probyn, 70).

Even though, as Klein argues, cannibalism is a phantasy universally experienced by infants, it is a taboo so great that it is deemed to be an inhuman act performed by those outside civilized society. Indeed, the cannibal, as the epitome of monstrousness, serves to define humanity. Cannibalism is a trope that can be interpreted as a metaphor and in this chapter I will examine historical metaphors of cannibalism, used in stories for children, in an attempt to trace the changing cultural fears that evoke them. Stories about monsters with abominable appetites have multiple functions: they may reflect a desire for familial or social integrity; they may reveal cultural unease about social hierarchies; they may warn of material dangers and therapeutically rehearse the fears invoked by such threats, wearing them out through repetition; they may explore issues regarding intergenerational and familial rivalries, confirming the individual's place in society; they may reveal society's concerns about the need to discipline the appetites and behavior of children; and they may reflect social anxieties about enemy others, the identity of whom changes over time.

Cannibalism as a practice continues to be part of human history.[7] Margaret Visser reports that it has been practiced in "Africa south of the Sahara, in Oceania, America North, Central and South, in northern Europe, and in the ancient Mediterranean region."[8] In Western anthropological terms, aggressive cannibalism, or eating the enemy, is known as exophagy. William B. Seabrook apparently witnessed this practice during his travels to the French Ivory Coast in the 1930s. The Guere tribe ritually ate the flesh of men from conquered tribes killed during battle.[9] Visser reveals that endo-cannibals, who ritually consume dead family members, have been described as "cemeteries for their dead" and that they may believe, for instance, that the "life essence" of the dead relative must be ingested to ensure the good health and continuing fertility of their tribe (Visser, 11–12). Susanne Skubal refers to endophagy as "affectionate" cannibalism and suggests it was "a response to separation anxiety, a way of perpetuating presence and undoing loss."[10] Kilgour suggests cannibalism might also be seen as a form of nostalgia, recalling "a deeper, if ambivalent desire to recover a time before the emergence of modern individuated subjectivity" (247).

Interestingly, Philip Pullman includes both forms of cannibalism in the trilogy, *His Dark Materials*. In the first book, *Northern Lights*, Iorek Byrnison defeats the king of the armoured bears:

> [He] sliced open the dead king's unprotected chest, peeling the fur back to expose the narrow white and red ribs like timbers of an upturned boat. Into the ribcage Iorek reached, and he plucked out Iofur's heart, red and steaming, and ate it there in front of Iofur's subjects.
>
> Then there was acclamation, pandemonium, a crush of bears surging forward to pay homage to Iofur's conqueror.
>
> Iorek Byrnison's voice rose above the clamour.
>
> "Bears! Who is your king?"
>
> And the cry came back, in a roar like that of all the shingle in the world in an ocean-battering storm:
>
> "Iorek Byrnison!"[11]

Iorek's exophagous act may be interpreted as a consolidation of power. He consumes the heart (the metaphorical repository of courage and the soul) of the king and replaces him in the social order. He becomes king. This marries with Skubal's report: in some societies it was apparently common for the victorious cannibal to take the name of his victim, thus completing the full process of incorporation and identification, a process which, she suggests, "call[s] to mind the communicant who takes the name of Christ-ian" (Skubal, 105). In Pullman's third book, *The Amber Spyglass*, Iorek commits endophagy.

> [B]ecause the Texan aeronaut was one of the very few humans Iorek had ever esteemed, he accepted the man's last gift to him. With deft movements of his claws, he ripped aside the dead man's clothes, opened the body with one slash, and began to feast on the flesh and blood of his old friend...something...possessed his heart, something bright and hard and unshakeable: vengeance...The good man's flesh and bone would both nourish him and keep him restless until blood was spilled enough to still his heart.[12]

Again the heart is used as a metaphor for the emotions and Iorek's affection for the man and knowledge of his bravery and undeserved death stir his desire for revenge. The eater is transformed by both these acts of eating. In "Totem and Taboo," Freud suggests that by incorporating parts of a person's body through the act of eating, one at the same time acquires the qualities possessed by him.[13] In many respects, therefore, the psychological aspects of cannibalism reflect a yearning for wholeness, oneness or integrity, notions also apparent in sexual desire, communion rituals, and "back to the womb" impulses (Sceats, 5). Cannibalism is, thus, an act that not only provides the eater with physical sustenance but also has inherent metaphoric symbolism. It is interesting to note that Pullman's descriptions of Iorek's cannibalism are not framed as particularly monstrous.[14] Indeed, it is implied that his actions are appropriate, honorable, and dignified. This is an unusual stance given that, in general, cannibalism is condemned by Western society, is accepted as part of the practices of an inferior culture and is generally ascribed to an other who is uncivilized and primitive.[15]

COLONIAL DISCOURSES

The trope of the native as cannibal with an inordinate capacity to consume human flesh as an especially delectable food is, according to Gananath Obeyesekeve, a white cultural construction and central to the construction of the nonEuropean as "Other".[16] Clare Bradford has shown how the trope was used in early Australian literature to produce and reinforce the discourse of Aboriginal as Other. As she remarks, cannibalism is the "ultimate in colonial projections of fear of the Other, constituting the most extreme manifestation of savagery and the absolute proof of white superiority."[17] In Richard Rowe's adventure novel *The Boy in the Bush* (1869) for example, Aborigines are generally treated as savages, cannibals and,

Bradford adds, "convenient moving targets during episodes of warfare" (6). Rowe's narrative contains the following passage: "[I]n a fight with another tribe, several of his captors were slain. The corpses were brought back and roasted, peeled like potatoes, and eaten by their own comrades."[18] Bradford comments that the phrase "eaten by their own comrades" implies "a special kind of decadence" and it suggests that eating one's enemies might perhaps be preferable (38). Rowe's description of the cooked flesh being "peeled like potatoes" introduces a notion of culinary familiarity and ordinariness to the proceedings. The attention to detail and deliberation of the cooking method described reads almost like a recipe. The everyday quality of the simile used, juxtaposed with the fact that human flesh is being consumed, is likely to produce shudders of disgust.

An exophagous episode occurs in R. M. Ballantyne's *The Coral Island* (1858). Ralph, who narrates the story, describes a battle between two groups of "savages." The victorious tribesmen kindle a fire and bring forward one of their bound enemies:

> Next moment one of the savages raised his club, and fractured the wretched creature's skull. He must have died instantly; and strange though it may seem, I confess to a feeling of relief when the deed was done, because I now knew that the poor savage could not be burned alive. Scarcely had his limbs ceased to quiver when the monsters cut slices of flesh from his body, and, after roasting them slightly over the fire, devoured them.[19]

The "civilized" white narrator is distanced from the horrific act committed by the monstrous savages because he makes his sensibilities and sympathies clear. It is interesting, though macabre, to note the contrast between the cooking methods used in Ballantyne's and Rowe's texts. In Rowe's story, the description of the eaters peeling the roasted corpse before eating produces notions of a peculiarly restrained and considered ritual. In Ballantyne's, however, disgust and abjection are evoked by the image of slices of flesh being cut from the victim's body when he had "scarcely" stopped moving. Significantly, the flesh of the victim is only roasted "slightly" suggesting rawness; Ballantyne thus makes use of the raw/cooked dualism, which Claude Lévi-Strauss theorized, and which equates structurally to the nature/culture, primitive/civilized oppositions.[20] In both narratives, cannibalism symbolizes the brutish, immoral, uncivilised state in which the natives exist. This, of course, serves to highlight the civilized, moral superiority of the white Westerners and to justify racist discourses. With reference to Australian literature, Bradford emphasizes that "colonial and Aboriginalist discourses survive in contemporary texts that promote the central tenet of these discourses—the inherent superiority of western culture." The doctrine is, however naturalized through narrative strategies that normalize and often make it difficult to identify (Bradford, 47).

Kilgour succinctly remarks that, while the act of cannibalism has traditionally been used to establish difference and construct racial boundaries dividing the civilized from the savage, it also paradoxically dissolves the differences between eater and eaten, desire and dread, love and aggression, human-as-subject and meat-as-object. In this way it unsettles discrete categories and confuses opposites and this is why it ultimately evokes horror (Kilgour, 240).

PARENTAL CANNIBALISM IN FAIRY TALES

As I remarked earlier, acts of monstrous eating are usually confined to the page or screen of the gothic horror narrative, but they also, somewhat ironically, occur in fairy tales traditionally deemed to be appropriate bedtime reading for young children. Jack Zipes argues that fairy tales featuring wolves, witches, and ogres had a more literal meaning in their original form and he suggests that as such they performed a didactic role with a more material and less psychological function. Citing the work of Marianne Rumpf, he writes:

> one of the most common European warning tales…in the Middle Ages involved hostile forces threatening children who were without protection. Either an ogre, ogress, man-eater, wild person, werewolf, or wolf was portrayed as attacking a child in the forest or home. The social function of the story was to show how dangerous it could be for children to talk to strangers in the woods or to let strangers enter the house.[21]

Rumpf argues that werewolves in particular were often the subjects of such cautionary tales and that in France, during the sixteenth and seventeenth centuries:

> There was a virtual epidemic of trials against men accused of being werewolves…similar to the trials against women as witches…[they were] generally charged with having devoured children…There were literally thousands if not hundreds of thousands of such cases. (Zipes, 19)

Oral tales of werewolves, including early versions of the story of "Red Riding Hood," Rumpf argues, existed in the nineteenth and twentieth centuries in areas where werewolf trials were most common in the fifteenth, sixteenth, and seventeenth centuries (Zipes, 20). Zipes confirms that the original storytellers of Perrault's and the Grimm brothers' literary tales were influenced first and foremost by the material conditions of their existence. "Little children were attacked and killed by animals and grown-ups in the woods and fields. Hunger often drove people to commit atrocious acts" (23).

George Devereaux, citing "Multatuli (1868)," pseudonym of novelist Edward Douwes Dekker, reports that during medieval famines and "even during the great postrevolutionary famine in Russia" the "actual eating of one's children or the marketing of their flesh" occurred. He concludes that "the eating of children in times of food shortage is far from rare."[22] During a later period, Jonathan Swift notoriously satirized British policy toward the famine in Ireland in "A Modest Proposal" (1729), when he suggested with impassive rationalism that the starving Irish "raise their children as delicacies to be consumed at table."[23] Hunger, as Zipes has noted, can drive people to think about and even commit atrocities.

In premodern Europe, famine "plays a prominent role in fairy tales [which] comes as no surprise when we consider the chronic food shortages and periods of scarcity that afflicted those who shaped these stories."[24] While cannibalism does not appear to have been particularly commonplace in Europe, child abandonment was. According to Maria Tatar, it "took place with astonishing regularity in pre-modern Europe, where rates of child abandonment in urban areas probably ranged from 15 to 20 percent of registered births" (Tatar, xxi). In the light of such statistics, the fate of Hansel and Gretel (being abandoned in the woods by parents because the family was starving) was a real possibility for urban children. Marina Warner has also suggested that tales of bogeymen and ogresses who steal babies and children—a probable euphemism for child abandonment—were also used as "a justification for neglecting babies with birth defects or other problems. A changeling could be discreetly made to disappear, as an evil gift of the fairies, or even of the devil" (Warner, 28). Thus, fairy tales not only warned against but also echoed the awful truth of child abandonment (and consumption) in times of famine and were also a supernatural explanation for the disappearance of unwanted children.

"Hansel and Gretel" is perhaps the best known tale that starts with a time of famine, but so do "Tom Thumb," "The Knapsack, the Hat, and the Horn," "God's Food," "The Sweet Porridge," and "The Children of Famine."[25] This last tale, "The Children of Famine," exemplifies the plight of families unable to feed their children. When the mother in this story runs out of food, she becomes "unhinged and desperate" and tells her two daughters that she will have to kill them so that she will have something to eat. The children desperately attempt to pacify their mother by begging for crusts of bread, but this only gives them a temporary reprieve. Finally and inconclusively they offer to "lie down and sleep...until the Judgement Day arrives" and their mother departs "and nobody knows where she went" (*Grimm Tales,* 704–5). Tatar reports that according to historical evidence cases of real-life maternal cannibalism were not unknown but were invariably linked to mental derangement caused by malnutrition. Documented cases of maternal cannibalism are extremely rare, but when recorded in medical or legal documents, they always occur in connection with a baby, not a grown child (Tatar, 193).

Warner differentiates between the meanings of metaphors of maternal and paternal cannibalism in classical myth. Significantly, she associates maternal cannibalism with motives that are "merely practical [and] callous," being an act that "nullifies the meaning of maternity, rather than attempting to supplant the mother's role" as, she argues, does paternal cannibalism. She believes that paternal cannibalism represented an "inverted birthing: biological ownership through incorporation" (Warner, 56). Paternal cannibalism is exemplified in "The Juniper Tree" (171), a story that, according to Tatar, has "long been recognized as one of the most powerful of all fairy tales" (Tatar, 212). In this tale, which purports to record events which took place "some two thousand years ago" (*Grimm Tales,* 171), a boy child is born to a woman who had prayed day and night for a child. However, she dies shortly after giving birth. As she had requested, her husband buries her under the juniper tree. He later marries a woman who has a daughter of her own whom she loves, but she hates her stepson. There follows "what is probably the most savage scene of revenge staged in any fairy tale" (Tatar, 212). The stepmother encourages the boy to look for an apple in a chest that has "a large heavy lid with a big, sharp iron lock" (*Grimm Tales,* 172). Prompted by the devil, she kills the boy by slamming the lid of the chest "so hard that his head flew off and fell among the apples" (173). Then she cuts up the boy's body and makes it into a stew that she serves to his father when he returns home. He eats with relish,

> "Oh, wife, the food tastes great! Give me some more!" The more he ate, the more he wanted. "Give me some more," he said. "I'm not going to share this with you. Somehow I feel as if it were all mine." (173–74)

This story is resolved by the death of the stepmother and the restoration of the boy to life through the magical, maternal influence of the juniper tree. The boy takes his father and stepsister by the hand "and all three were very happy. Then they went into the house, sat down at the table, and ate" (179). It is significant that it is the boy who takes control of his family and takes them into the house. The meal they eat together signals a normalization of family relations and an end to the cataclysmic events of the past (Tatar, 226).

Warner points out that in this tale, as in the myth of Kronos, the Greek myth of divine origin, incorporation into the father does not mean absolute death. "Paternity, in this fairy tale . . . can bring forth the whole child again" (Warner, 63). Significant to Warner's understanding of this tale is the sequence of the act of consumption and metaphorical rebirth that serves to consolidate paternal power. Biology is negated; the threatening physical presence of the step/mother is eradicated, although she continues to affect the course of the story through the juniper tree. Warner sees this fairy tale and the Greek myth as

> a lesson in the resignation of the passage of time, the overtaking of age by youth, and the necessarily stepped character of the genealogical ladder through life . . . Terrible tales of aberration and abomination constantly invoke, by inversion and trespass, an ideal of normal practice and expected categories. (Warner, 65–67)

Fairy stories that feature paternal cannibalism seem to have significantly different emphases to those where a mother figure threatens to consume a child. In the previous chapter, I showed that the monstrous mother or wicked witch figure in many stories symbolizes the bad breast of infantile phantasy theorized by Melanie Klein. Defeating the witch arguably signifies separation from the mother, a necessary stage in psychic development. Significantly, although gullible and apparently hungry, the father figure in "The Juniper Tree" is not a malevolent figure. Indeed, it is the mother figure who is again split into good and evil, who is duplicitous and must be overcome. Being consumed by the father does not mean psychic obliteration or death as it does when the mother devours. Instead, this tale explores issues such as personal identity, procreation, intergenerational, familial and patriarchal power relations and authority and confirms the male child's privileged role in society.

THERAPEUTIC OUTCOMES

Contemporary stories of eaters with cannibalistic appetites frequently contain lurid detail intended to sicken and horrify the reader/viewer. It is pertinent to consider why such gut-churning detail, such as features in Thomas Harris's Hannibal Lecter series, for example, appears to be so compelling. Oral folktales, too, were originally far more gruesome than the sanitized versions generally in current circulation. Their censorship was a deliberate maneuver designed to comply with Christian ethics.[26] Tatar cites Italo Calvino, who was so shocked by the cannibalistic elements of the oral version of "Little Red Riding Hood," that he rewrote it. In Calvino's source, the wolf kills the heroine's grand/mother, uses her tendons to latch the door, chops up her flesh to make a meat pie, and pours her blood into a wine bottle. The heroine, with obvious pleasure, consumes both the meat pie and the blood (Tatar, 209). Yvonne Verdier argues that by consuming the flesh and blood of her grandmother the young girl symbolically replaces her; the grandmother's death in this folk tale thus signifies the continuity and reinvigoration of custom that was important for the preservation of society (cited by Zipes, 24). This cannibalistic consumption is symbolic in the same way as that described in Pullman's narrative when Iorek Byrnison becomes king. The folk tale thus explores notions of intergenerational and familial relations in terms of the female child's role in society. Tatar points out the interesting way in which this version of the tale effaces the line dividing the agent from the victim of oral aggression (Tatar, 209–10). In this way the tale, in its original version (gruesome details intact), may prove to be therapeutic. The listener may identify with the active role of the heroine and is not forced into identification with the girl as victim.

In many children's playground games the line between agent and victim is similarly effaced. In Philip Pullman's *Northern Lights*, children are being systematically "stolen" and supposedly eaten by a group of "invisible kidnappers" who are referred to as the "Gobblers." The threat of being "took" by the Gobblers is used by parents to encourage their children to behave, "Don't stay out late, or the Gobblers'll get you!" The children playing on the street invent a game called "kids and Gobblers" based on the game of Hide and Seek. "You hide and I'll find you and slice you open, right" (*Northern Lights*, 46). Similarly, one of the playground games I best remember from my childhood in Wales in the late 1960s was "What's the time Mr. Wolf?" Once the "wolf" had caught his "dinner," the victim became the new wolf and the game continued. Turner, Factor, and Lowenstein devote a whole chapter to this and similar games in their collection, *Cinderella Dressed in Yella*, and date the "Mr. Wolf" game to the period "c. 1935–1970" in Australia.[27] Scherf maintains that these types of games and their repetitions help children to "master anxiety and the shudders of horror, and finally to wear them out" (cited by Tatar, 210). On a similar note, but referring to games adults play with young children, anthropologist Gregory Bateson devised a theory of play that proposed that "testing the limits of safety and entertaining the terror of murder and torment help to confirm the child's sense of security with the parent or caregiver." One of his girl child patients told him, "When we play monsters, and mummy catches me, she never kills me, she only tickles me" (cited by Warner, 144). Warner believes, however, that these games and fairy tales such as "Little Red Riding Hood" are primarily didactic:

> This kind of terror-play can comfort and thrill at the same time only when there is deep, familiar trust between the players—one of the latent messages of lullabies, nursery rhymes and fairy tales is not to trust the stranger, especially the big stranger of the male kind, but to remain at home, at rest in the familiar small world close to hand.
>
> Games of thrills and spills, stirring phantoms of bogeymen, snatchers, and watchers, then become part of the process of learning the norms of social languages, and of differentiating oneself within them. (144–45)

Warner recognizes the duality of these narratives and games: they "comfort and thrill." She also confirms what Zipes and Rumpf suggest: games and stories that evoke terror are cautionary tales, warn of material dangers, and didactically reinforce the notion of the child's rightful place in the social hierarchy. They also, through repetition, therapeutically wear out the immediacy and intensity of the fear and horror they produce, a process that may be described as desensitization.

In her insightful chapter on lullabies, "Sing Now Mother… What Me Shall Befall," Warner asserts that lullabies have a similar therapeutic function. While the principal function of lullabies was, by implication, to lull the baby to sleep, the songs also calm the caregiver and make their daily struggle bearable. Significantly, they also "carry female voices and concerns across time on their words and in their tunes." But lullabies not only induce comfort and sleep, they also often include blessings for the well-being of the child and attempt to ward off danger by anticipating and invoking figures of death and punishment. The repetitive nature of the lullaby is "a form of incantation. A lullaby is weak domestic magic, alert to its own inadequacy" (Warner, 192–94). Traditional myths and fairy tales and even, arguably, contemporary horror genre narratives also have this sort of restorative effect, tempering fear by facing what generates it in fictional form. In a similar way, Warner argues that the extremes of participatory performances such as rock concerts, orgiastic jubilation such as experienced at raves, and spectator entertainments such as horror films can be viewed as rites of passage, testing endurance. They "defin[e]…the living, impervious, sovereign self" as well as providing the ecstatic "high" of surviving (Warner, 125). The adrenalin high Warner refers to may account for the addictive quality of these activities and narratives.

Narratives in the horror genre have always inspired both dread and delight although the monster's physiognomy has tended to change over time reflecting social unease about enemy others. Warner argues that throughout history the characters invoked in warning stories are "frequently drawn on enemy Others in their own time and place. Gypsies, Jews, Turks, [and] blacks have all been used to scare the young into obedience" (Warner, 161). In the world Pullman creates the Gobblers serve the same purpose. The following British lullaby features Napoleon Bonaparte as the enemy other.

Giant Bonaparte
Baby, baby, naughty baby,
Hush, you squalling thing, I say!
Peace this moment, peace, or maybe
Bonaparte will pass this way.

Baby, baby, he's a giant,
Tall and black as Rouen steeple,
And he breakfasts, dines, rely on't,
Every day on naughty people.

Baby, baby, if he hears you,
As he gallops past the house,
Limb from limb at once he'll tear you,
Just as pussy tears a mouse.

And he'll beat you, beat you, beat you
And he'll beat you all to pap,
And he'll eat you, eat you, eat you,
Every morsel, snap, snap, snap![28]

The threat of Bonaparte as cannibalistic monster is used to caution the infant and has a clearly didactic function, as well as voicing fears about the enemy whose identity is historically relevant. Similar melodies have been used to lull French and Spanish babies, with Wellington and Bismarck, or El Coco, the Bull, or the Moorish Queen standing in for Bonaparte (Tatar, 32). The oral threat remains constant.

RED RIDING HOOD'S JOURNEY

As my aim in this chapter is to examine the way cultural fears have historically evoked changing emphases in metaphors of cannibalism, it is both productive and interesting to trace the evolution of one particular tale and, given its continuing popularity and relevance, "Little Red Riding Hood" seems a good choice. As I have already hinted, older oral versions of the story appear in retrospect to be particularly bloodthirsty, but Tatar points out that adult audiences had relied for centuries on the telling of such tales "to shorten the hours devoted to repetitive household chores or harvesting tasks." Is it any wonder, she asks, "that they demanded fast-paced adventure stories filled with bawdy episodes, violent scenes, and scatological humour?" (37).

In his *The Trials and Tribulations of Little Red Riding Hood*, Jack Zipes includes an early oral variant of the tale, "The Story of Grandmother" (21–23), which was supposedly the source material for Perrault's (1695) tale. The little girl in this story has no red hood (Perrault introduced this element in his later version). She is asked by her mother to carry a "hot loaf and bottle of milk" to her granny. "At the crossway she met *bzou*, the werewolf,"[29] who asked her whether she was going to take the "path of needles or the path of pins?" (Zipes, 21). On hearing that the little girl is to take the path of needles, the werewolf takes the path of pins to the grandmother's house. Meanwhile the little girl gathers needles.[30] The werewolf kills the grandmother "and put some of her meat in the cupboard and a bottle of her blood on the shelf." When the little girl arrives the wolf tells her to put the bread and milk in the cupboard and to help herself to the meat and "the bottle of wine on the shelf." "After she had eaten, there was a little cat which said: 'Phooey!...A slut is she who eats the flesh and drinks the blood of her granny.'" The werewolf instructs the little girl to undress "And come and lie down beside me" (21). As she removes each item of clothing she asks, "Where should I put my apron [and, in turn, bodice, dress, petticoat, long stockings]?" and the wolf responds, "throw [them] into the fire my child, you won't be needing [them] anymore" (21–22). When the little girl has "laid herself down in the bed" the familiar dialogue begins: "Oh granny, how hairy you are!" "The better to keep myself warm, my child." The wolf makes excuses for possessing various masculine characteristics until the little girl finally exclaims, "Oh granny, what a big mouth you have!" and receives the reply, "The better to eat you with, my child!" At this the little girl says, "Oh granny, I have to go badly. Let me go outside." The wolf tries to persuade her to "Do it in the bed, my child!" but she protests, "Oh no, granny, I want to go outside" (22). The werewolf attaches a rope to the little girl's foot and lets her go outside where she promptly ties the end of the rope to a plum tree and escapes. The werewolf becomes impatient calling out "Are you making a load out there? Are you making a load?" but there is no reply. Although he follows her, he arrives "at her house just at the moment she entered" (23).

In the first written version of the tale by Perrault, "*Petit Chaperon Rouge*"—Little Red Riding Hood" (Zipes, 91–93), the protagonist must take biscuits and butter to her grandmother who is ill. In Perrault's story, Little Red Riding Hood makes a number of fatal errors: first, she stops to talk to the wolf, then she gives him directions to grandmother's house, and finally she amuses herself "by gathering nuts, chasing butterflies, and making nosegays while the wolf zooms off, taking a shortcut to the house" (Tatar, 37). The wolf eats the grandmother and puts on her clothes and, when the little girl enters the house, he tells her to leave her clothes and come to bed. The "celebrated dialogue"[31] sequence follows but the child's urgent request "to go" and her subsequent escape are missing from this story. Instead, the wicked wolf eats her (Zipes, 93). Tatar suggests that while oral folk versions of the story were more concerned with "entertaining an audience by rehearsing a sequence of racy episodes and sensational events," later versions such as Perrault's and the Grimms' were more about "presenting lessons" (37). There are several major changes in Perrault's version that alter not only the outcome but also, importantly, the characterization of the little girl. Significantly, the little girl's overt cannibalism and the "ritualistic striptease" (Dundes, 21) are left out.

Tracey Willard points out that in its oral variants "this is one of the few (if not the only) . . . European tales (featuring female cannibalism) in which cannibalism is perpetrated by a child and by a 'good' character." She argues that this act, although committed in ignorance on the part of the child and affected by trickery, makes the little girl powerful and, therefore, potentially dangerous. Perrault's omission of this element disempowers the character.[32] Zipes also argues that Perrault's tale disempowers the girl but his reasoning differs: he explains that in the oral folk tale version/s the little girl is clever and self-reliant whereas in Perrault's version she is "totally helpless" and neither shrewd nor assertive enough to outwit the wolf (Zipes, 25). With regard to the endophagy in the oral tale, as I mentioned above, Zipes sees this as a ritualistic act symbolizing the young girl's replacement of her grandmother. The oral version is thus a tale celebrating the girl's coming of age (24). In this respect, the folk version of this tale reflects the sentiments present in "The Juniper Tree" and in the Greek myth of Kronos, confirming the natural progress of time and youth overtaking age.

Zipes argues that although Perrault's "upper-class version" of "Little Red Riding Hood" disempowers the protagonist, this attitude reflected contemporaneous ways of thinking about the child. Referring to Philippe

Aries' *Centuries of Childhood*, Zipes explains that during the period "an independent children's literature and culture were being developed to civilize children according to stringent codes of class behaviour" (25). Whereas the peasant girl of the oral version had been "forthright, brave and shrewd," Perrault's Red Riding Hood is "pretty, spoiled, gullible and helpless" (26). Perrault's version talks about "vanity, power, and seduction, and it introduced *a new child*, the helpless girl, who subconsciously contributed to her own rape" (27, emphasis in original). The threat presented by the were/wolf remains the same—consumption/rape. The change occurs in the girl's ability to counter the threat. She is not the worldly-wise, resourceful, and powerful girl in the folk tale, but instead becomes a disobedient child requiring punishment. The story becomes a didactic tool, implicitly warning of young girls' and women's propensities for transgressive behavior as much as, if not more than, the wolf's desire to take advantage of what such girls ostensibly offer. This changing emphasis reflects, primarily, a shift in attitudes toward children, as Zipes suggests and Tatar confirms when she explains that textual indicators in the tale "consistently construct a sybaritic heroine rather than a rapacious wolf" (38).

The Grimms' collection of fairy stories, which included "Little Red Riding Hood," was originally published in two volumes (1812 and 1815). Within a few decades their versions of the stories became known throughout Europe and beyond.[33] The Grimm brothers' adaptation of "Little Red Riding Hood," which they called "*Rotkappchen*"—"Little Red Cap," further sanitized the tale. In their story, there was a "sweet little maiden. Whoever laid eyes upon her could not help but love her" (in Zipes, 101). She is sent by her mother to visit her sick grandmother with cake and wine. In contrast to the oral folk tale where no prohibitions are put upon the child, so that the heroine cannot be perceived to be disobedient or transgressive, the Grimms' story includes an extensive list of dos and don'ts. She is specifically told to get an early start on her journey before it becomes hot and to "be nice and good and don't stray from the path, otherwise you'll fall and break the glass, and your grandmother will get nothing. And when you enter her room, don't forget to say good morning, and don't go peeping in corners" (101–102). Although Little Red Cap promises to "do just as you say," when she meets the wolf in the forest she stops to talk to him. Because she "did not know what a wicked sort of an animal he was" she is not afraid of him (102). Even though illustrations show her carrying a basket (though the text does not mention it), the wolf asks Little Red Cap what she is carrying under her apron (102). This question, Willard suggests, alludes to the food she is carrying but is also sexually suggestive (Willard, section 19). When the wolf asks her where her grandmother lives, she gives him explicit directions: "Another quarter of an hour from here in the forest. Her house is under the three big oak trees. You can tell it by the hazel bushes" (Zipes, 103). When the wolf suggests that she pick some of the beautiful flowers that are growing all around her and listen to the birds' lovely singing instead of "march[ing] along as if [she] were going straight to school," Little Red Cap concurs and runs off the path, "plung[ing] into the woods to look for flowers. And each time she plucked one, she thought she saw another even prettier flower and ran after it, going deeper and deeper into the forest." Indeed, she forgot all about her grandmother until "she had [collected] as many [flowers] as she could carry" (103). Much emphasis is therefore placed on the seductive suggestions of the wolf and the hedonistic active pleasures Little Red Cap opts for rather than obeying her mother's instructions, which advocate passivity.

In this version of the story, the wolf gobbles up granny, puts on her clothes and nightcap, gets into her bed, and draws the curtains. When Little Red Cap enters the traditional dialogue begins. "No sooner did the wolf say ['The better to eat you with'] than he jumped out of bed and gobbled up poor Little Red Cap" (103–104). Significantly, "After the wolf had satisfied his desires, he lay down in the bed again, fell asleep, and began to snore very loudly" (104). The wolf's desires are implicitly carnal as well as explicitly gastronomic; his after-dinner nap is akin to post-coital slumber.

A passing huntsman rescues both females—he cuts open the wolf with a pair of scissors and Little Red Cap and her grandmother emerge, a process of paternal rebirth similar to that in the Kronos myth. Male agency is thus twice valorized in this Grimm version. The wolf is killed by having his open belly filled with stones, again a clear connection to the myth in which Kronos swallows his children to prevent being usurped by them and is tricked into eating a rock instead of his youngest child. The moral to the story is summed up in Little Red Cap's last thought addressed to herself: "Never again will you stray from the path by yourself and go into the forest when your mother has forbidden it" (104). However, the Grimms hammer home the moral of the story by illustrating how well Little Red Cap has learned her lesson. They repeat the early events of the tale, but this time the girl is good, doesn't stray from the path and proceeds straight to Grandmother's. Grandmother astutely guesses the wolf's plan but outwits him, placing a trough of sausage-smelling water on the hearth. On the roof "Grayhead," enticed by the smell, leans down until he falls into the trough and drowns (104–105).

An examination of the sanitized variants of "Little Red Riding Hood" in relation to the structural oppositions inside/outside, good/evil discussed at the beginning of this chapter is revealing. The little girl is cautioned by her mother to stay upon the path, to remain inside the boundaries of the social order and not to stray into the forest, representing outside, disorder, and chaos. The wolf is also coded as outside: he is deviant, a transgressor, outside social control. Little Red Riding Hood strays outside and is assimilated by the wolf assuming a state of unity with him. Notably, being eaten by the wolf does not result in digestion. Instead, she becomes as one with the wolf and his wild evil nature. As was the case with her granny in the oral folk tale, and with Iorek Byrnison in Pullman's story, Little Red Riding Hood becomes part of the wolf and, significantly, he becomes part of her. The wolf is an enemy other, rapacious, wild, and inhuman, threatening the cohesiveness of the social order, but so is the little girl according to this discourse. Her transgressive act (leaving the inside path) places her on the outside. She becomes the wolf.

It is significant that the versions of "Little Red Riding Hood" that continue to be most widely circulated stick to versions of Perrault's or the Grimms' adaptations, continuing "the stereotyping of little girls as innocent creatures who must be protected by strong male guardians... preaching obedience and the regulation of a little girl's sexuality" (Zipes, 66). Furthermore, Zipes argues that "all [the] traditional heroines of 'Little Red Riding Hood' stories... [are] responsible for... [their] own downfall and for the rapaciousness of wolflike creatures... a self-induced rape and murder" (49). Thus, while the tale warns of the physical dangers posed by a wolf/stranger, it also emphasizes the need to regulate the (female) appetite for pleasure, and, most significantly, it blames the victim for her fate.

"Little Red Riding Hood" is probably one of the best-known traditional fairy tales and it continues to be influential and to spawn new translations. While the trouble caused by the transgressive behavior of young girls is implicit in "Little Red Riding Hood," it is still the cannibalistic wolf/stranger who is the explicit enemy in the story. In Angela Carter's translation of Perrault's version, the moral of the story is made absolutely clear:

> Children, especially pretty, nicely brought-up young ladies, ought never to talk to strangers; if they are foolish enough to do so, they should not be surprised if some greedy wolf consumes them, elegant red riding hoods and all.
>
> Now there are real wolves, with hairy pelts and enormous teeth; but also wolves who seem perfectly charming, sweet-natured and obliging, who pursue young girls in the street and pay them the most flattering attentions.
>
> Unfortunately, these smooth-tongued, smooth-pelted wolves are the most dangerous of all.[34]

Thus, while real wolves were an actual danger in medieval times, they have since become a metaphor for those who are, as Carter puts it, "hairy on the inside" (290). The threat of consumption/cannibalism they now exude is a metaphor for rape. The wolf has become a pedophile.

CONTEMPORARY WOLF TALES

C. S. Lewis's faun, Mr. Tumnus, half-man, half-goat, has suspect intentions when he invites Lucy to his house for tea in *The Lion, the Witch and the Wardrobe*.[35] As a faun he can be identified with Pan, the goat-god in Greek mythology who was the god of pastures and wild places. He was extremely lustful and renowned for pursuing virginal nymphs.[36] Lucy's response to Mr. Tumnus's invitation is polite but initially expresses reservations: "Thank you very much, Mr. Tumnus ... But I was wondering whether I ought to be getting back." The faun is persuasive, however, swaying her with promises of food: "It's only just round the corner ... and there'll be a roaring fire—and toast—and sardines—and cake."[37] Lucy is won over and soon "found herself walking through the wood arm in arm with this strange creature" (*Lion*, 17–19). Mervyn Nicholson claims that metaphorically, in inviting Lucy to tea, Mr. Tumnus is attempting to seduce her. He points out that the appearance of food and drink is a natural appetizer to seduction.[38]

Mr. Tumnus's book collection reveals his interests: "They had titles like *The Life and Letters of Silenus* or *Nymphs and Their Ways*' (*Lion*, 19). In Greek mythology, Silenus was a drunken satyr, constant companion and tutor to Dionysus (Bacchus), and leader of his revelers. Satyrs were spirits with goat-like characteristics not least of which was their uninhibited lust (Philip, 41, 58). While nymphs were in mythology spirits of nature represented as beautiful young women, the word is also the root of nymphet, a girl who is sexually precocious and desirable, and of nymphomaniac. Some of the titles in Mr. Tumnus's library clearly have sexual overtones.

Mr. Tumnus is "in the pay of the White Witch" (*Lion*, 23) and has been commissioned to capture for her any "Son of Adam or ... Daughter of Eve" he might meet in the woods. He confesses that he has "pretended to be [Lucy's] friend and asked [her] to tea, and all the time [he's] been meaning to wait till [she was] asleep and then go and tell *Her*" (24, original emphasis). But, as I argued in chapter 2, the tea Mr. Tumnus provides for Lucy is coded as unequivocally wholesome and he cannot go through with the betrayal.

Margaret Mahy's book, *The Changeover*, captures the menace of the child-targeting sexual predator.[39] This is a modern fairy tale containing many traditional elements: witches, a stepmother, a budding romance, and a monster that consumes innocent children. Carmody Braque is an ancient supernatural spirit who survives by absorbing the vitality of humans. Laura is looking after her three-year-old brother Jacko. The little boy entrances Braque:

> "Oh…" he cried when he saw Jacko, "a baby!" He put a very heavy, bleating emphasis on the first half of the word. "A baaaab-y!" he exclaimed again in a high-pitched voice, breathing out as he bleated…breathing in at the very end so that the word was finally sucked away to nothing. (*Changeover*, 20)

Braque is like a wolf in sheep's clothing. His teeth are "too big for his thin, rubbery lips to cover them…his whole face was somehow shrunken back around his smile…He was almost completely bald…and there were dark blotches on his cheeks and neck, almost, but not quite like bruises" (20). The man has "another discoloured blotch" on his hand "as if he were starting to go bad" (21). Notions of disease and decay are conjured up by Braque's description and this is reiterated by the "dreadful smell" that emanates from him and strikes Laura "like a blow—a smell that brought to mind mildew, wet mattresses, unopened rooms, stale sweat, dreary books full of damp pages and pathetic misinformation, the very smell…of rotting time" (20–21).

Braque thinks Jacko is "absolutely scrumptious," and, even though Laura hasn't bought anything in his shop, he offers to give Jacko a little ink stamp on his hand to match the Mickey Mouse one he received previously from the librarian. With "fearsome generosity" Braque cries,

> "I'll make it up to the little brother, poor, wee lambie. Do I see a stamp on the right paw? How about another on the left? Hold it out, you little tiger, tiger burning bright, and you shall enter the forests of the night." (21–22)

Braque pounces like "an elderly mantis on an innocent fly," pressing the stamp onto the back of Jacko's hand. The stamp "was the very face of Carmody Braque himself" and "seemed to be *under* his skin, not on top of it" (23, emphasis in original). There is no mistaking the animalistic consuming nature of this particular monster. Laura tries to wash the "mark" off when they get home "but the stamp was part of him now, more than a tattoo—a sort of parasite picture tunnelling its way deeper and deeper, feeding itself as it went" (31). Braque is a "lemure," "a wicked spirit that has managed to win a body for itself." He parasitically absorbs the life energy of his victims in order to sustain his human form. The stamp is Braque's "mark," a conduit connecting him to Jacko, which enables him to consume the child's "essence" (82). The implicit sexuality of Braque's appetite becomes clear when he confesses to Laura that he's "something of a gourmet":

> "I've fed on so many by now I'm very very choosy. Girls like you, with rather more vitality perhaps, or sleeker, or those younger still—eight is an attractive age I think, ten is almost too old...I enjoy an innocent, sucking baby...Oh, the delectable banquet of possibility all you people offer me!" (162–63)

Mahy's story concerns not only Laura's changeover from child to adult but also her supernatural initiation into witchcraft. Becoming a witch and placing her own mark on Braque is the only way she can save Jacko. She and Sorensen, known as Sorry, a young male witch, work out a plan. She must persuade Braque to accept her as a victim in exchange for relinquishing his hold on Jacko. Sorry and Laura discuss the way she should present herself to Braque in order to tempt him:

> "We'll tempt him with variety," Sorry said, "with the prospect of a willing sacrifice. Can you manage to look alluring and yet act as if you were constantly shrinking away from the thought of him?"
> "Shall I try to look slinky?" Laura asked. (158)

Sorry tells Laura she's "too young for slinky." She's "Young and knobbly—you know, like a foal! But you're a bit of a mixture, for all that, and that's what just might get him." Laura asks him what he means by "a mixture." "You know!" he said. "At first you look skinny, but you're quite voluptuous in your way. If anyone thinks about you, that is!" (158–59). While there is clearly sexual tension between Sorry and Laura, her appeal to Braque must be sexualized because he is recognized as a sexual predator attracted to children. Braque's desire focuses on the young, innocent, and vulnerable,[40] his mark penetrates the body and he parasitically feeds on his victims. The insidious consuming nature of this monster is clearly pederastic.

In a similar way, Maurice Gee's *The Fat Man* features an adult who implicitly exudes sexual menace.[41] Colin Potter is a hungry child—skinny, and greedy (*Fat Man*, 9). He steals a bar of chocolate belonging to the fat man, Herbert Muskie. Significantly, immediately prior to this theft Colin had spied upon Muskie taking a bath in a creek. Much emphasis is placed upon the description of Muskie's body.

> [He is] white with soapsuds. They were pasted down his arms and across his shoulders. Froth blossomed in his armpits and stood like whipped cream on top of his head. He soaped his belly and

tried to reach his back...He soaped all the creases in his fat and scraped the suds out with his fingernails.

Colin lay under the ferns and watched. He saw the man's behind gleaming like an eel's belly in the water. He saw him roll and submerge and come up with his head as smooth as an egg and the black hair on his chest pasted down like slime. He squirted creek water from his mouth like a draughthorse peeing and washed around his ears and dug in them, wiggling his finger...[He] swam on his back to the deep part of the pool, where he rolled over like a whale. He was good in the water...he smeared [handfuls of creek mud] on his belly and laughed. He could float so well, Colin thought, because he was so fat. (11–12)

Muskie, wearing only his underpants, discovers Colin eating his chocolate and grabs him "with the strength of a possum trap" and threatens to "belt him" (14). He stands over the boy with "his bare sole on Colin's ankle" (15). Colin has "never seen anyone as terrifying" as Muskie. He was "round and fat...pink and white and quivering." His chest is "folded" and he has "creased sides and [a] blown-up belly...His eyes were angry. They were small and deep and blacker than sheep pellets." "Muskie was like something that had rushed into the daylight from the back of a cave and was looking at what it had caught. For a moment Colin believed he was going to be killed" (14).

The alignment of Muskie with the bestial evokes disgust because disgust results from "a psychic need to avoid reminders of our animal origins."[42] Furthermore, there is something revolting about the contorted fleshiness of his obesity. Probyn speculates that it is the idea of all the food that went into the making of an obese body that makes it disgusting; the rolls of fat show "the visible evidence of...contamination by what they have ingested" (Probyn, 130). She cites Claude Fischler who argues that the obese make society queasy because they remind us of the finitude of food; "the consequence is clear: whoever consumes more than their fair share, deprives others of theirs" (in Probyn, 130). If this is the case, then the comparison of Muskie, who's had more than his fair share, with Colin, who has been deprived, is unavoidable.

Both Colin and the reader view the man bathing, a ritual normally performed in private and, indeed, Muskie presumes he is alone. Protagonist and reader are consequently cast in the role of voyeurs. Muskie's obvious sensuous enjoyment of both the water and the process of cleaning his body together with the implicit "peeping Tom" position assigned to the viewing children (Colin and reader) introduces a sexual imperative into the narrative. While it evokes horror and disgust, the description of Muskie's body also, therefore, holds a level of fascination. Disgust, as William Miller points out, "can attract as well as repel; the film and entertainment industries, among which we might include news coverage, literally bank on its allure" (Miller, x). Julia Kristeva, too, argues that disgusting things involve us in "a vortex of summons and repulsion" and similarly that the related abject "beseeches and pulverizes the subject" simultaneously.[43] The description of Muskie's body is both disgusting and curiously alluring. Part of the fascination for the hungry, skinny child must lie in the fact that, inherent in the obese body, is the reality of the vast quantities of rich food required to produce it—food that the child must inevitably covet. Arguably, the sense in which Muskie's bulk literally embodies the rich, fattening foods which have produced it is emphasized by the way his body is garnished by froth which "stood like whipped cream on top of his head" (*Fat Man*, 11).

Muskie drops "a gob of spit" onto the chocolate bar and, quoting the old adage "waste not, want not," he forces Colin to "open up" and eat it (14–15). He threatens the boy with a razor until he complies. Muskie's near nakedness and his size and strength relative to the skinny powerless child coupled with their relative proximity (Colin's head is presumably level with Muskie's groin) make this scene particularly horrific. The ingestion of the gob of spit violates deeply held norms about the polluting, contaminating nature of body fluids, which have already been called to mind by the description of the man's body. The forced penetration of the child's mouth/body by the spit-covered chocolate leads me to interpret this event as akin to oral rape.

Mahy's and Gee's narratives in particular warn of but also invoke stranger danger. The monster looks human (specifically like a man). As with most monsters, he has an uncontrolled appetite for the wrong thing. He desires to consume children, to use his adult power to corrupt the innocence of childhood, and to violently annihilate. He is the child abuser, the pedophile.

As I commented at the beginning of this chapter, it is the inhumanity of the monster that we fear. Probyn argues, in particular, that, "the cannibal reminds us of that which cannot be included in the polis, the social life of man. Yet its very exclusion serves to define humanity." The cannibal "is to be understood as the ground zero of humanity, the very limits of being human" (Probyn, 88). Contemporary fears about pedophiles make them representative of the ground zero of humanity and child abuse, one of the defining moments when man becomes inhuman. As Warner argues, "child-snatchers, child-killers, sexual violators of the young horrify us at some deeper, personal level than even the atrocities of recent civil wars" (Warner, 385). Fictional monsters embody cultural fears of such inhumanity toward those we value and most fear to lose. Warner in fact believes that "pedophiles are our late millennial ogres" (386). Pederasts such as Mahy's Carmody Braque and Gee's Herbert Muskie represent, for contemporary culture, the epitome of monstrousness. They have human faces but they are, to reiterate Angela Carter's phrase, "hairy on the inside."

As I have shown, cannibalism evokes horror because it unsettles discrete categories and blurs oppositions. It dissolves the difference between the eater and the eaten, between the human as subject and the human as object, between inside and outside, desire and dread, love and aggression (in the case of endophagy), allure and horror. It is a topic that both comforts and thrills. It comforts because it feasibly fulfills the subconscious desire for oneness, which is theoretically part of everyone's psychological background. And yet it is the ultimate in abjection. To eat human flesh requires the abandonment of one's own subjectivity as it is subsumed into and with an/other body. The corporeality of the bodies, the eater's and the eaten, is privileged over individual subjectivity, which is effectively abandoned. To do this, in terms of Western philosophy, means to literally dehumanize one's self. The fact that someone (even in this day and age) might choose to do so is horrific. Cannibalism, however, turns out to be an act that can be deconstructed and analyzed to reveal the precariousness of the definitive binary categories that are the basis of dominant structuralist discourses.

7

THE AGE OF DISGUST

Rude Books for Rude Boys

Mary had a little lamb,	Mary had a little lamb -	Mary had a little chook,
Her father shot it dead,	The doctor was surprised,	She kept it in a bucket,
And now it goes to	But when Old MacDonald	'Cause every time she
school with her	had a farm	let it out
Between two chunks	He couldn't believe his	The rooster used to
of bread.	eyes.	fuck it.

JUNE FACTOR COLLECTED these children's play rhymes from Australian school playgrounds.[1] They reveal children's interest in those aspects of human existence usually absent from polite conversation. "[V]ulgar play rhymes of amusement" such as these, Ian Turner argues, come from "those childhood years when the children are making their first break from their parents, and consequently from their parents' standards, when they are seeking their independent identity in the society of their peers." Turner understands such "childish vulgarity [to be] an unsophisticated act of rebellion."[2] Certainly the language used may be deemed to be low within the prevailing hierarchy of adult aesthetics. However, the psychological fears and taboos children are tapping into and exploring in their play rhymes are not merely unsophisticated childish concerns, but culturally based unconscious fears also shared by adults. In the first rhyme, notions of who eats whom and the food chain are perhaps being explored, while the second and third rhymes explore themes of reproduction and sexuality. The third rhyme also breaches and therefore tests taboo language rules.

These children's rhymes and the stories written *for* children that I examine in this chapter, reveal underlying anxieties about the incorporative and generative functions of the human body and their taboo cultural status.

These play rhymes fit into the category of carnivalesque children's texts as defined by John Stephens because "they function to interrogate official culture in ways comparable to the traits of carnival identified in the work of Mikhail Bakhtin."[3] Bakhtin describes the medieval world of carnival as being suffused with laughter, bodily pleasures, hierarchical inversions, and bad taste. Aspects of carnival humor were found in ritual spectacles such as feasts, pageants, and marketplace festivals, in comic verbal compositions (oral and written parodies) and in billingsgate (curses, oaths, slang, and profanities). The laughter evoked by carnival humor was bawdy, crude, and irreverent. Rank and privilege were overturned; kings were portrayed as fools and peasants as royalty. Carnival depicted the official world seen from below.[4]

While the children's play rhymes cited above include overt references to sexuality, carnivalesque-grotesque and grotesque-horror style texts written *for* children frequently feature the human body, but usually only refer obliquely to sexuality. In these stories, sexuality is displaced onto other "gross" body functions such as eating and drinking, especially eating taboo foods or excessively, and expelling body wastes and fluids.[5] According to Bakhtin,

> Eating and drinking are one of the most significant manifestations of the grotesque body. The distinctive character of this body is its open unfinished nature, its interaction with the world. These traits are most fully and concretely revealed in the act of eating; the body transgresses here its own limits: it swallows, devours, rends the world apart, is enriched and grows at the world's expense. The encounter of man with the world, which takes place inside the open, biting, rending, chewing mouth, is one of the most ancient, and most important objects of human thought and imagery. Here man tastes the world, introduces it into his body, makes it part of himself.[6]

Bakhtin emphasizes two particular aspects of the eating body that produce psychological anxiety. First, his choice of words accentuates the brutality of the process. Everything about eating connotes violence and destruction; other living organisms must be destroyed so that our bodies are sustained. Inherent in every mouthful we take is the image of the food chain and humankind's precarious position at its apex. The anxiety this knowledge causes is explored in the first "Mary had a little lamb" parody. Second, the notion of the "open unfinished nature" of the body is important, as Julia Kristeva has also shown. She argues that our personal disgust and the various social taboos that are associated with the body's functions and its waste products "attest to a psycho-social horror at what transgresses borders and boundaries. Bodily fluids, waste, refuse—feces, spit, blood, sperm etc. are examples of corporeal by-products provoking horror at the subject's mortality."[7] This is because, in structuralist terms, these fluids flow from what is considered to be their proper place on the inside of the body, to the outside; they assert and privilege the body's materiality over and above the individual's subjectivity, inducing feelings of disorder and impurity.

Our personal sense of being or having a body with a definitive boundary, that contains or houses our self or subjectivity, is a fiction. In reality the body is, as Bakhtin argues, an "open unfinished" structure. Our bodies are permeable organisms vulnerable to invasion (by poison or virus, for example) and constantly under re-creation. This reality jeopardizes finite notions of subjectivity. Food and bodily wastes frequently, even constantly, transgress the body's boundaries. It is this messy reality that produces psychological anxiety. We like to think of our bodies as intact, of our subjectivity as defined, but the borders between the body and the rest of the world are transgressed every time we eat and breathe, defecate, vomit, sneeze, and sweat.

Carnivalesque-grotesque narratives directly address the personal and sociocultural anxieties induced by knowledge of the vulnerability of both the individual and the social bodies. Vulgar, obscene, and taboo-breaking forms of comedy in popular culture are neither a modern nor a culturally specific phenomenon. The presence of grotesque humour has been noted in youth culture, in particular, for at least the last few hundred years.[8] Bakhtin's work revealed the use-value of grotesque texts for medieval and Renaissance popular culture, and Maria Tatar confirms their appeal, suggesting that audiences relied on oral tales containing bawdy humor, violence, and scatology to relieve the tedium of repetitive household chores or harvesting tasks.[9] In a late eighteenth-century chapbook[10] for example, Jack the Giant-Killer tricks the ogre Blunderbore by swaddling his own belly, stuffing the swaddling with animal lights (lungs) and other gross foodstuffs, and then splitting it open, proclaiming loudly that in this way he can feast on his dinner over and over again. Blunderbore, delighted with this economy, greedily emulates Jack, slitting open his belly from which "dropt his Tripes and Trolly-bubs."[11] The continuing appeal of this type of narrative attests to the problematic cultural construction of body functions and fluids as abject and disgusting, the importance of the inside/outside dualism in both individual and social psyches, and the psychological and social need to overcome abjection in order that society can function normally.

SUBVERSION, INVERSION, DIVERSION, PERVERSION

The carnivalesque is characterized by "subversion, inversion, diversion, and perversion" of official order but simultaneously, because of its impermanency, it also represents "ordered disorder, regulated deregulation, organized chaos, authorized antiauthorizationism, controlled decontrol of the emotions, and ultimately reinforcement rather than subversion of the status quo."[12]

Can the grotesque images in carnivalesque texts contain any subversive potential at all? According to Kristeva they can: such narratives are able to "lay bare, under the cunning, orderly surface of civilizations, the nurturing horror that [socio-cultural systems] attend to pushing aside by purifying, systematizing, and thinking."[13] In other words, for children, carnivalesque-grotesque material can reveal what adults are trying to suppress and it makes a move toward deconstructing sociocultural systems and laying bare their values. However, what these narratives do not reveal is the underlying misogynistic discourses that form the basis for such systems and values and, in fact, I think they may work (perhaps through the *jouissance* they evoke) to normalize such discourses.

The picture storybook *Fungus the Bogeyman* by Raymond Briggs is a brilliant example of what Warner calls "Rabelaisian unbuttonedness" and of the grotesque body of carnival writ large (Warner, 157). Fungus, who, as a bogey, naturally picks his nose,[14] lives in the slimy, reeking puddle-strewn tunnels of bogeydom, far, far below the world of drycleaners (humans). Bogeys are quite different from clean and proper human beings. Fungus and his family like to sleep in slimy, damp, dirty beds and they encourage slugs and snails to live between the sheets (*Fungus*, 3). They work hard to keep their skin filthy and slimy and they cultivate their body odor until they stink. The family's bathroom cabinet contains bottles of Bogegas underarm oderant, Old Mice, and, of course, toilet water (4). On their breakfast table are boxes of "flaked corns," "gripe nits," and "golden waxy bits," which they eat with sour milk (6). Fungus's job is to venture into the world of drycleaners at night to scare them, by banging on doors, appearing at windows, and poking sleeping babies until they wake up crying. The ultimate achievement in the art of the bogeyman is to engender a boil on the neck of his victim (21). The book amusingly features a culturally-transgressive "perverse cult" of "Young Bogeys" known as "drop-ins" who "profess to like bright colours and noise" and who have smuggled "ancient gramophone recordings and equipment . . . from surface rubbish dumps" and use them with "a total disregard for tradition, custom and even law. Worse still, some of the more extreme members of the cult have begun to keep themselves clean, scraping off their protective layers of dirt and slime and taking baths in warm, clean water." The illustration shows them jiving to rock and roll ("See you later, Bogie baiter") in blue suede shoes surrounded by packages of Omo, Vim, and Ajax (25).

Unlike many other carnivalesque-grotesque narratives produced for children, this story does not appear to directly privilege adult mores and control because Briggs does not reestablish the status quo at the end of his story. However, his book only works to produce laughter because it sets up the world of bogeys in direct opposition to adult (human) mores. The book is very clever and the word play is amusing, but the laughter it evokes stems from the way bogeydom opposes adult human cultural norms. In order for the opposition to be funny, those norms must be known. By highlighting deviance within the text, the norm outside the book is reiterated and given authority. As Heather Scutter comments with regard to jokes in children's fiction, "apparent subversion may prove, on deconstruction, to mask a form of socialization which actually reinforces existing cultural values and beliefs, and encourages the child [reader] to accept the status quo."[15]

According to Bakhtin, the "essential principle of grotesque realism" is "degradation, that is, the lowering of all that [official culture regards as] high, spiritual, ideal, abstract; it is a transfer to the material level, to the sphere of earth and body" (Bakhtin, 19). Grotesque humor, then, literally debases or brings down to earth high cultural aesthetic concerns using laughter. Laughter itself, however, arguably stems from a culturally derived sense of humor and grotesque humor is, therefore, a licensed affair. William Miller points out that there are norms that define what is funny, that determine the "domain of the laughable and ridiculous." These norms, he argues, demand that "mockery take such a form that it reveals its limits and thereby pays homage to that which is mocked."[16] Certainly, Briggs' text appears to do this. Stephens, taking up Bakhtin's notion of the grotesque carnival text "bringing down" authority, believes that one of the most important functions of the carnivalesque children's text is its didacticism, confirming through a dialectic of high and low aesthetics what is considered eternal and transcendent and what is temporal and material. Children's carnivalesque texts are, he says, "transgressive of such things as social authority, [and] received paradigms of behaviour and morality" (147) but by transgressing them they also confirm them. "Carnivalesque texts, by breaching boundaries, explore where they properly lie" (135–36). Stephens argues that through carnivalesque explorations and transgressions of adult concerns children are able to determine the "world's knowability and stability" (131). They are also, he suggests, coming to terms with the "potential wildness of ... [their] own inner being," exploring the notion of the corporeality of their bodies so that such notions can be recognized and resigned to the category of abject and/or taboo (136). If this is the case, then, grotesque narratives written for children, and even their own play rhymes, while appearing to question and transgress adult social mores, actually serve an extraordinarily conformist and, with regard to the reiteration of the cultural association of the abject with femininity, a misogynist purpose.

It is vital to clarify that sociocultural taboos exist because of social and psychological fears concerning the abject/grotesque functions of the body. The fears exist because of misogynist individualistic cultural discourses that define the abject. These discourses define the abject as an intrinsically maternal/feminized concept. The ability to recognize the abject is, as Elizabeth Grosz (following Kristeva) explains, "a condition of symbolic subjectivity" (71). In order to achieve stable subjectivity, every individual needs to recognize the abject and to suppress it, to achieve "mastery" over it, to separate or "distinguish [her or him]self from its repressed or unspeakable condition" (72). However, while the abject can be recognized and suppressed, it cannot ever be fully obliterated, but always "hovers at the borders of our existence, threatening the apparently settled unity of the subject with disruption and possible dissolution" (71). Grotesque narratives thus function to keep the abject at a safe distance while therapeutically assisting individuals to identify and master it and thus to achieve 'proper' subjectivity. Kristeva has argued that "madness, holiness and poetry" can similarly "breach yet also confirm symbolic conventions" (Grosz, 77). Again though, it is important to reiterate that subjectivity is achieved by suppressing that which is culturally associated with the maternal/feminine body. Grotesque narratives also, therefore, work conservatively to justify the taboo status of the abject and to confirm the otherness of the maternal/female body. They are not, therefore, radically transgressive/subversive but, rather, serve patriarchal hegemonic interests.

PERVERSE PLEASURES

Children undoubtedly enjoy reading transgressive grotesque books not only because they break adult rules and taboos, but also because they provide visceral, that is embodied pleasure. The pleasure produced by grotesque narratives can be akin to jouissance (Barthes, 1976). Grace and Tobin suggest that jouissance is a "diffuse" pleasure: "it is pleasure without separation—bliss, ecstasy, pure affect. Jouissance is an intense, heightened form of pleasure, involving a momentary loss of subjectivity. It knows no bounds." In this respect it surpasses *plaisir*, which "is more conservative, accommodating, and conformist than jouissance" (177).

Fiske sees the roots of plaisir in the dominant ideology: "It produces the pleasures of relating to the social order: jouissance produces the pleasures of evading it."[17] Grace and Tobin argue that plaisir is an everyday pleasure that represents "conscious enjoyment" capable of being expressed in language. Jouissance, on the other hand, is the pleasure of special moments (177). In relation to these definitions, Kenway and Bullen suggest that adult and child pleasures tend to be "polarized along the axes of plaisir and jouissance respectively" (83) so that, for example, whereas adults generally purchase goods, including food, toys, videos, and books for their utilitarian values rather than specifically for pleasure, child consumers tend to purchase for pure enjoyment, and adults and children are, once more, set up in opposition to each other.

Significantly, Kristeva associates jouissance with the primal, prelinguistic and borderless union between infant and mother that precedes subjectivity. She uses the term "semiotic" to describe this state. The semiotic is associated with the body, its drives and the abject and is specifically opposed to language, the father, and the social order, which it both precedes and exceeds. In this respect the semiotic itself can be said to be transgressive (Kenway and Bullen, 70). As I have previously mentioned, the semiotic is the psychological equivalent of, and loosely based on, Bakhtin's concept of the carnivalesque. The semiotic, the abject and carnivalesque all contain elements which are "irrational, improper . . . unclean, profane, taboo, hybrid." While carnival is socially sanctioned (and controlled), the abject is forbidden, unspeakable and repressed (Kenway and Bullen, 70). Notably, as I've shown, the semiotic and the abject/grotesque are clearly placed by patriarchal discourses on the side of the feminine and maternal. They directly oppose the patriarchal social order, the symbolic and, therefore, proper notions of subjectivity (Grosz, 78). Ultimately, they threaten individual and social order. It is no wonder then that what adults regard as the junk food of children's literature becomes the focus of a power struggle between parent and child.

Not only do most adults find carnivalesque-grotesque books antithetical to their priorities with regard to children's reading, but they also tend to disapprove of children's enjoyment of gross topics. Kenway and Bullen argue that this sense of disapproval, disgust, or abjection is intensified by the "quasi-erotic and transgressive connotations of jouissance" (70). Furthermore, and importantly in relation to my argument in this chapter, they argue that the jouissance which children derive from consumer culture (and I include all types of popular fiction series books under this heading) is "designed to ensure that they unreflexively consume rather than interpret such texts. Jouissance is about producing a surge of affect, not the reflexive pleasure of knowing about what is happening as it happens" (Kenway and Bullen, 75). This implies that child readers tend to passively accept the discourses presented to them in popular narratives, their quest for enjoyment overriding any broader concerns.

CONSUMING CHILDREN

Bazalgette and Buckingham, writing about recent television programming for children, argue that it is designed "precisely to exclude adults" and their values.[18] This also applies to books in the carnivalesque-grotesque genre. The content and format of these books and the marketing strategies used to promote sales serve to exclude adults and emphasize oppositional perspectives. Additionally, as Lee puts it, children have been constructed as a separate and lucrative market by the deliberate cultivation of "a critical social distance from, and negation of, the values that were espoused by their parent culture."[19]

While adults and children may differ in their opinions of scatological humor there is no doubt that it sells. According to Michael Bradley, writing in the *Sydney Morning Herald*, booksellers and librarians agree that, "anything in the children's comedy genre that mentions bums is an instant winner...bodily functions are big business."[20] In the last twenty years or so, children have acquired a significant increase in spending power. They also have a burgeoning desire for independence and a psychological need to overcome abjection and come to terms with taboo topics. It is children, rather than bodily functions per se, that represent the opportunity for "big business." In a cyclic maneuver children's supposedly rebellious interest in gross humor is being exploited. Marketing strategists are addressing children as a separate market that *ought* to find the grotesque funny. Rather than being truly transgressive then, their interest is constructed as normative. Children, especially the boys to whom these stories are generally addressed, are framed as naturally rude and the rude books themselves are seen to be answering their particular need or demand. Perversely, these books are also sometimes constructed as being worthy of adult esteem because they get boys to read. Books in this genre are generally formulaic, with largely stereotypical characters, predictable plots and safe banal endings. They frequently contain misogynistic discourses. They represent, according to Jack Zipes, "a dumbing down of children"[21] and children's literature.

GENDERED PLEASURE, GENDERED POWER

The language used in grotesque narratives for children is generally not coarse and abusive (unlike their own texts) because it is written and licensed by adults. Stories written for them in these genres often contain language that might be categorized as within the realms of mild taboo, designed to titillate, rather than shock. The language itself reinforces adult authority—children all know plenty of abusive language (as their play-rhymes clearly show) but its very absence from their literature didactically reinforces the taboo. Roald Dahl directly refers to this in his version of "Goldilocks" in which the little girl, he suggests, is a less than pleasant character. She has just sat upon and broken baby bear's chair:

> A nice girl would at once exclaim,
> "Oh dear! Oh heavens! What a shame!"
> Not Goldie. She begins to swear.
> She bellows, "What a lousy chair!"
> And uses one disgusting word
> That luckily you've never heard.
> (I dare not write it, even hint it.
> Nobody would ever print it.)[22]

It is interesting to note Dahl's judgment upon what "nice girls" say and to see how he frames his protagonist by implying that her abusive language is so foul that it is unprintable. She is therefore definitely not a nice girl and is deemed to be abject. The readers are nice, however, because Dahl tells them that they have "never heard" the offending word. As the word is not mentioned this is a pretty safe bet. The text explicitly and implicitly signals suitable language for children's use. Carnivalesque texts for children often include playful intrusion by the narrator as Dahl's does. This draws attention to the social forces which, Stephens argues, determine the relationship between signs and things, reinforcing what is socially desirable with regard to cultural and linguistic mores (156). Furthermore, the reader is thus suddenly and deliberately situated outside the text, by the narrator's intrusion, and so is discouraged from empathizing with the protagonist. Indeed, the reader is encouraged to disapprove of Goldie's language, to take the culturally legitimate stance, to be mildly amused but also shocked, to be ultimately disapproving and condemning. Dahl uses the technique again to condemn Goldilocks, once more reinforcing the condemnation with mention of the abject. Goldilocks has climbed into baby bear's bed with her shoes on:

> Most educated people choose
> To rid themselves of socks and shoes
> Before they clamber into bed.
> But Goldie didn't give a shred.
> Her filthy shoes were thick with grime,

> And mud and mush and slush and slime.
> Worse still, upon the heel of one
> Was something that a dog had done.
> I say once more, what *would* you think
> If all this horrid dirt and stink
> Was smeared upon your eiderdown
> By this revolting little clown?
>
> (*Revolting Rhymes,* 33, emphasis in original)

Here the narrator directly addresses readers and seeks their opinion ("what would you think?"). In employing this tactic, Dahl further distances readers from Goldilocks, refusing to allow identification with and implicitly condemning her activity and power. Dahl's work is openly didactic, reinforcing his personal notions of appropriate behavior for girls. This is cleverly achieved through his undoubted wit, word play, and by stretching the limits of the taboos he is ultimately reinforcing.

Other writers' work may not be so blatantly didactic but nevertheless may contain underlying themes that contribute to misogynist discourses. The apparently oppositional world of *Fungus the Bogeyman*, for example, is premised upon a very conventional social structure and therefore works to reinforce stereotypes. Briggs shows Fungus's wife, Mildew, serving breakfast to her husband and son while Fungus reads the paper. Bogey "ladies" apparently feel compelled to grow their hair to cover their horns, which are seen to be a particularly masculine characteristic and not attractive for females (*Fungus,* 4). Mildew's role is traditionally and conventionally domestic and involves shopping, housework and childcare. Young bogey ladies work in stereotypically feminine jobs such as cinema usherette (12), barmaid (26) and librarian (28). After work bogeymen go to the pub and play pool (27). They enjoy "stick-ups" (which don't require pins because the paper is slimy and sticks by itself) featuring pictures of "fat, ugly, heavily-clothed, old Bogey women." A picture and description of "Sully Sloven (88-93-99)" is featured. "Grey-haired Sully is 84. Her favorite color is bile green and her favorite pets are her twenty-seven sewer-rats" (7). The ideal bogey woman is blatantly derived from and implicitly refers to the stereotypical exploitative pin-up—thin, beautiful, scantily clad, and young—and confirms the legitimacy of the lascivious male gaze. I would argue that while the author has transparently played with the grotesque aspects of real life to comedic effect, the fact that he has not also turned traditional roles upside-down implies that they are immovable. I further suggest that the active work his readers must perform in order to decipher Briggs's engaging text and to realize its inherent humor serves to reinforce the narrative's integral misogynistic subtextual discourses.

An examination of a variety of grotesque series books for children reveals that they are not only frequently gender-biased in terms of language and content but also in terms of their implicit authorization of "rude" behavior for boys. Paul Jennings constantly writes narratives that involve an improper transgression of the body's boundaries (often by food/non-food) or abject bodily fluids. For example, in *The Cabbage Patch Fib,* he writes about a boy who puts a strand of spaghetti up his nose and then snorts it into his mouth;[23] in "One Finger Salute," a boy eats a live lizard's tail;[24] in "Piddler on the Roof" another boy pees into a domestic water tank,[25] and in "Snookle" a genie-like being picks the male protagonist's nose for him.[26] Significantly, the majority of Jennings' protagonists are male and are actively involved in whatever grotesque taboo-transgressing endeavor takes place within the narrative. Jennings has written several books of short stories and while a definitive survey of all his texts is beyond the scope of this study, female central characters appear to be rare. At random, I have perused three of his short story collections: *Unbelievable, Unreal* and *Unseen.*[27] Only one out of twenty-five stories features females as main characters. They are the twin girls in "Birdscrap" who get shat upon by a flock of seagulls. "Bird droppings rained down like weighted snow... there was no escape from the guano blizzard which engulfed them... The girls sat there panting and sobbing."[28] The beach shack to which they retreat is buried beneath an "oozing pile" of bird droppings (95). The girls are framed as the innocent and largely passive victims of an attack organized by the ghost of a gull shot by their late father. This framing differs from the other twenty-four stories in the three collections where, in contrast, the significant male hero takes an active part in the proceedings.[29] This is not to say that Jennings does not feature females in his stories at all.

In *The Gizmo Again,* for example, Jack decides to join a gang of bullies at his school as an alternative to being bullied.[30] He bullies another boy as part of his initiation into the gang by shoving an ice-cream cone into his face. The ice-cream man, who witnesses Jack's behavior, gives him a magic gizmo that sticks to his hand so that he cannot remove it. The ice-cream man may be seen as a socializing agent and the gizmo as the instrument of Jack's punishment, which contains many grotesque/abject elements. Jack shrinks with each step he takes until he is "as small as a baby" (*Gizmo,* 32). He encounters a dog and gets "showered in yellow dog pee" (33). The dog "puts his huge face right up to [Jack's] little one. His breath is hot and wet and foul... he grabs [Jack] by the back of [his] t-shirt... [and shakes Jack] about like a loose bag of bones" (34). Dribble from the dog's mouth runs down all over Jack and mixes with the pee (35). The reader is thus prepared for Jack's next disgusting encounter, which happens to be with a "giant" little girl who mistakes him for a doll and picks him up:

> She is licking my face. Next she sucks my eye. So hard that it feels as if my eyeball is going to plop out. Then she sucks my nose. Her tongue is huge and spongy and dribbly. The tip of it goes up one nostril. She is putting her tongue up my nose. Oh, foul, foul, foul. Help me. Please, someone help me. The brat is sucking my face with her giant mouth. I can't breathe. I can't talk. I can't stand it. Everything goes black. (39)

Jack's eye does not actually plop out but the thought of what should be properly secured 'inside' coming out, is horrific and disgusting. Tongues too should remain, according to social etiquette, inside the mouth. Poking one's tongue out is generally considered to be rude or threatening. Licking is associated not only with eating/tasting but also with sexual practices. This little girl sucks Jack's face. This episode is clearly sexualized: the image of the girl's "giant mouth" is framed as a monstrous *vagina dentata* and her active violating tongue as phallic. The girl is cast as abject by her actions and by her direct contact with the inside of Jack's nose and indirectly by the fact that he is already covered in dog pee and dribble.

But Jack's punishment is not over. The giant girl takes him home and "shoves" him into a toy high-chair. She has a toy tea-set "all set out for a tea party" (40). However, what occurs next is not a social event but a domestic scenario reminiscent of a mother-infant feeding interaction. "Be a good boy," the girl tells Jack as she prepares to spoon-feed him (40). She mixes up flour, salt, pepper and mustard and to moisten the mixture "she spits into [it] about six times and stirs it all up. It is a horrible, spitty, smelly mess" (41).

> "Open up," she says. Oh no. She is going to feed me. I grit my teeth but it is no good. I am too small. She pushes the mixture into my mouth and holds my jaw closed with her fingers. The taste is terrible. I want to vomit but I can't because my mouth is held closed.
>
> "Naughty boy. Eat your din dins," she says.
>
> I am choking. There is only one thing to do. I swallow the revolting mix.
>
> "Good boy," says the horrible little girl. She starts putting more on the spoon. (42–43)

The giant mother figure force-feeds the baby, violating his body's boundaries and compelling him to swallow/incorporate her abject body fluid.

By the end of the story, Jack has figured out how the gizmo works. He walks backwards until he becomes "as big as a house" and then confronts the gang of bullies. He picks them up and, holding them "very close" to his face (58), he lets out a burp. "It is like a thousand thunderstorms together. It is the loudest, smelliest burp in the history of the world. It just about blows their heads off" (60). The gizmo transfers itself to the gang leader, Gutsit. He shrinks to the size of a doll and is found by the same little girl, now referred to as "the little brat." She picks up Gutsit:

> Then she does something terrible. Awful. I try not to smile when I see what she does to Gutsit.
>
> She looks down the back of his pants. "Naughty boy," she says. "You've done a poo." Quick as a flash she pulls down Gutsit's pants. Then she grabs his ankles in one hand and lifts up his legs. She takes out a handkerchief and starts to wipe his bottom. Gutsit yells and screams and howls as the little girl wipes away like crazy. It must be quite a while since he has had his bottom wiped and he does not like it one bit.
>
> Finally the little girl stops wiping. "Come on," she says to Gutsit. "It's dinner time." (*Gizmo*, 62)

Jack is framed within the context of the narrative as deserving of punishment and he is shamed and (literally) belittled by the form his punishment takes. But the instrument of his punishment, the gizmo, is also instrumental in his revenge. Jack's burp is an abject act but is justified and even lauded for its magnitude. The unnamed girl in this story, however, is constructed as an overly powerful monstrous and abject figure. She performs as a kind of overenthusiastic smothering mother figure, taking a "crazy" delight in wiping poo from Gutsit's bottom. The laughter the narrative evokes stems from what befalls the main male character but, during the giant little girl episodes, it is at her expense.

R. L. Stine's *The Haunted Mask* is one of the Goosebumps series.[31] While it probably doesn't evoke laughter, the text may well produce a thrill of a different kind. The story, which again contains many abject elements, features eleven-year-old Carly Beth who is a "scaredy-cat," and the victim of the pranks and jokes played by her classmates. Steve and Chuck "loved to scare Carly Beth. They loved to startle her, to make her jump and shriek. They spent hours dreaming up new ways to frighten her" (*Haunted Mask*, 5–6). There comes a point, however, when Carly Beth decides to get her revenge and she purchases a "really scary" mask for Halloween from a party store. Although the storeowner warns her against it, she chooses a "hideous" mask that looks so real that the "skin appeared to be made of flesh, not rubber or plastic" (33). It has "a bulging, bald head. Its skin was a putrid yellow-green. Its enormous, sunken eyes were an eerie orange and seemed to glow. It ha[s] a broad, flat nose, smashed in like a skeleton's nose. The dark-lipped mouth gape[s] wide, revealing jagged animal fangs" (33–34).

Carly Beth's mother has made her a cute yellow duck costume for Halloween and presumes she is going to wear it, but Carly Beth deceives her and sets out wearing the mask. She also carries a painted plaster model of her own head, which her mother has created, stuck on a pole. Carly Beth is very excited about how scary she looks and determines to be "the terror of Maple Avenue" that night (49). The mask is very tight and seems to change the timbre of her voice so that it sounds "deep, raspy [and] evil" (43). Carly Beth's intention is to give Steve and Chuck a big fright, but she tries out her costume on a couple of other kids first. "A ferocious roar escaped her throat. A deep, rumbling howl that frightened even her" (57). Their Mom accompanies the two children and she is annoyed and tells Carly Beth to "pick on someone [her] own age" (58). Normally Carly Beth would have apologized but "hidden behind the ugly mask...she didn't feel like apologizing. She felt...anger" (58). She snarls at the woman and tells her to go away. "Carly Beth was breathing hard, her breath escaping the mask in low, noisy grunts. I sound like an animal, she thought, puzzled. What is happening to me?" (59). Furious thoughts rage through Carly Beth's mind. She feels as though she wants "to tear [the] woman apart," to "chew her to bits," to "tear her skin off her bones" (60–61). "*I'm crazy. Crazy, crazy, CRAZY,*" Carly Beth thinks to herself as the mask becomes hotter and tighter (61, emphases in original). Carly Beth's behavior becomes more and more violent and her temper out-of-control. She steals candy from two boys dressed as mummies and attacks her best friend, "scar[ing her] to death" (66). When Carly Beth finally encounters Steve and Chuck, she pretends that the plaster model on the pole is "all that's left of" Carly Beth. The boys are well and truly frightened and they flee in terror. Carly Beth enjoys the feeling of triumph, "[t]he thrilling sweetness of revenge" (81). Stine has built considerable tension into his narrative, tension which is released when Carly Beth achieves her goal. While the protagonist experiences the thrill of revenge, therefore, the child reader may experience the "surge of affect" that is the thrill of jouissance.

But Carly Beth is punished for being a powerful and active girl and for deceiving her mother by her inappropriate consumption of material goods (the mask). She finds that she cannot remove the mask; there is no longer a line between the mask and her skin: "the mask had become her face" (91). She returns to the store where she purchased it and the storeowner tells her that the mask is, in fact, a "real face," the result of a failed experiment (101). Carly Beth has literally become "a monster." Only "a symbol of love" will enable her to return to normality (104). The plaster of paris head, which is an explicit symbol of her mother's love, is Carly Beth's salvation (12). She puts the head on over her own masked head and a gap appears between the mask and the skin of her neck. She is, at last, able to remove the monstrous mask and to return home. In the mirror, her own face "stared back at her … [it] was normal again. All normal" (119). The return to normality, to home, to her mother's authority and the status quo is signaled by Carly Beth's mother "instruct[ing]" her to come into the kitchen, and to drink the "nice hot cider" she has prepared for her. Carly Beth "obediently" does as she is told (120), thus accepting parental authority and implicitly her own role in the social order.

By becoming monstrous in appearance and behavior, Carly Beth has transgressed social rules that determine proper female behavior and consumption. While Steve and Chuck's behavior is licensed within the narrative (and within sociocultural expectations), Carly Beth's powerful, assertive behavior and language, and her desire for revenge are seen as deviant and she must be punished. In terms of the tone and timbre of her voice and the language she uses, Carly Beth-as-monster is an illegitimately speaking subject just like Mary in *The Secret Garden*. Like Mary's, Carly Beth's voice is inappropriately powerful and her assumed subjectivity noncredible. Carly Beth epitomizes the patriarchal stereotype of the female as abject and loathsome. Only her mother's love/maternal influence and her retreat into passivity enable her to regain her proper place in the social order, as obedient girl child.

It is my contention that child readers may well experience different reactions to these texts depending on their gender. If, as Grace and Tobin suggest, jouissance is a form of pleasure produced by transgressing the social order and plaisir, which is a lesser pleasure, is produced by consciously relating to it, then the positioning of the characters in these two narratives is likely to evoke different levels of reading pleasure according to the gender of the reader. Both Jack and Carly Beth are punished in these stories. But Jack's punishment is finite and he is valorized for being gross and rude, whereas the giant little girl is condemned, within the subtext, for being naturally abject and maternal. The boy reader, identifying with Jack, can enjoy the character's transgressive behavior and relate to the way he can't help but smile as he watches Gutsit's humiliation (*Gizmo*, 62). The boy reader perhaps experiences jouissance as Jack is rewarded (by an adult) with "an ice-cream as big as a car" (63). Jouissance is evoked for the boy reader by confirmation of his ability (as a male) to share Jack's transgressive stance and by the text's implicit endorsement of his position of superiority in relation to the degraded female. The girl reader also sees the way the characters are implicitly framed, but she must recognize the degraded female position as her own.

Carly Beth is punished because she acts outside the social order, and reveals, like the giant little girl, the confluence of the abject and the female. The girl reader must again recognize that compliance is the only position available to the female in this narrative. Throughout this narrative, the boy reader, on the other hand, receives confirmation that while the female character's (temporary) power is scary, it is illegitimate and short-lived. It is my belief that the reading pleasures of girls and boys are often polarized along the axes of plaisir and jouissance respectively, just as Kenway and Bullen suggest adult and child pleasures differ (83). The girl reader thus takes up an ostensibly "adult" and accommodating stance in relation to the social order, while the boy is positioned as the "real" child. As the status quo is confirmed in Stine's narrative, so too is the boy reader's privileged position in the patriarchal hierarchy. That these texts' inherent pleasures are differential probably accounts for their particular popularity with boys. Anecdotally, prepubescent boys seem to prefer rude books, while girls appear to prefer series books with problem-solving helpful heroines like Ann Martin's *Baby-Sitters Club* series and Bonnie Bryant's *Saddle Club* series.

As I've argued, grotesque narratives fascinate because they oppose adult culture. In structuralist terms, the grotesque/abject opposes official (patriarchal) order; the corporeal body is opposed to transcendence (as Stephens points out), to reason and to civilized society. The carnivalesque celebrates the corporeal body and is alluring not only because it is transgressive but also perhaps because it allows for a metonymic closeness to the presymbolic maternal aesthetic. This may be more attractive to boys because they must, according to the demands of the symbolic order, definitively separate themselves from the maternal/female body/aesthetic. Boys recognize themselves as opposite to and separate from the position of abjection and its cultural subordination and take pleasure in their privileged status. But, this means that they are able to indulge and revel in the undoubtedly viscerally thrilling aspects of corporeality, knowing, all the while, that this is a temporary indulgence and normality/order awaits. It is perhaps like playing with warm mud or clay and smearing it all over your hands and face. You can particularly enjoy the transgressive aspect of the experience as well as appreciate the texture and sensuousness of it—because you know it will wash off easily. Again this points to differential levels of pleasure being available to girls and boys. In indulging in the semiotic/corporeal, boys temporarily suspend or momentarily lose subjectivity (as Grace and Tobin suggest) and experience jouissance. Girls, on the other hand, are assigned by phallocentricism, to the female/abject/ corporeal position. Their experience of the carnivalesque-grotesque texts I have analyzed involves the milder pleasure of "relating to the social order," that is, of plaisir. For girls then, their pleasure is tempered by the fact that they cannot wash off patriarchal culture's construction of the female body and its material functions as abject. Of course, there are also the rules of polite society to contend with, rules that insist that girls' bodies be more modest and controlled than boys. The differential pleasures produced by stories like those written by Jennings and Stine thus tend to reinforce the obviousness of stereotypical gendered behavioral expectations.

In her discussion of Stine's work, Vicki Coppell argues that the Goosebumps series is particularly "scary" from the academic's perspective because it "represents a commercial and intellectual exploitation of the young and inexperienced reader who [has] little agency to resist."[32] Coppell's argument may be applied to all similarly formulaic popular fictions written for children. Goosebumps books, she claims, are aimed at the child "as a consumer rather than a reader." She points out that the intellect of the child is controlled in two ways: first, by marketing a series that appeals and delivers an "irresistible thrill," and second, by controlling the reader's intellect by the presentation of stereotypical images which engender a false and inadequate perception of individuality premised upon a patriarchal outlook that images male over female as normative (Coppell, 14).

SEXUAL ANXIETIES

Here's a scary story for your birthday . . . Someday you'll probably grow up and marry a girl!
—Hallmark (greeting card sent to my son when he was nine years old).

Through myth and legend, historical cultural misogyny, and contemporary patriarchal culture, women have been constructed as dangerous and uncontrollable. Psychological ambivalence toward the mother figure, with its origins in the first feeding relationship, is fed by culturally determined bias. Consequently, the mother/woman/female is a frightening figure and the prospect of a heterosexual relationship with a "girl" is a "scary" prospect for the prepubescent boy.

Nancy Veglahn argues that dreams and fantasies tell us much about our attitudes toward "the opposite sex."[33] Citing Ravenna Helson, she suggests that literary "fantasy lends itself to the depiction of unconscious forces" (Veglahn, 107–108). Referring specifically to authors who create monstrous other-sex characters, she further argues that "[w]hen a writer creates a figure of incarnate evil, some of the writer's deepest loathings are likely to appear, not consciously or intentionally, but with the force of inner truth" (108).

> In most fantasies and fairy tales it is the destruction of the other-sex monster that carries the emotional charge of the story, relieving the anxieties of reader and writer. The monsters are ultimately vanquished, and thus young readers may be relieved of some of their anxieties about gender identification and about their relationships with persons of the opposite sex. (109)

In my opinion sociocultural discourses exploit infantile anxieties to the extent that prepubescent boys may experience fear and loathing at the thought of sexual activities with a female other. As Veglahn suggests, vanquishing this monstrous other may relieve some of that fear.

Stine has created a female character who personifies the monstrous feminine in *Creature Teacher*, another Goosebumps book.[34] It is worth considering this narrative in some detail because it addresses the range of fears and anxieties also present in the trio of "Mary had a little lamb" parodies quoted at the beginning of this chapter. These involve the realities of the food chain and the fear of being eaten, as well as those related to heterosexual activity. Twelve-year-old Paul Perez is sent to a remote boarding school by his parents because he doesn't take his schoolwork seriously. Paul's new teacher is Mrs. Maaargh. She is massive, has "the biggest head [Paul's] ever seen on a human" and has "wet brown… [c]ow's eyes… [and] pale yellow skin, like the skin on chickens in the supermarket. Her cheeks were so flabby, they bounced on her neck as she grinned. Her whole face sagged over her shoulders like dough" (*Creature Teacher*, 24–25). She is wearing "a shiny red dress" (22) that bounces up and down as she moves (26) but no shoes. "Her [bare] feet were huge! As big and puffy as pillows! They made disgusting, wet smacking noises against the wooden floor." She has no toes. "Instead, thick, shiny black claws curled out from the tops" [of her feet] (26). When she first meets Paul in the classroom, she tells him in a "gravelly voice" (22) to "Come here… Let me have a taste." She grabs his arm and "with a low grunt, she lowered her head. Stuck out a fat pink tongue, glistening wet and as wide as a cow's tongue. And she licked my arm all the way from the wrist to the shoulder" (23). Paul's arm "tingled. It felt sticky and wet. Mrs. Maaargh let go of [him]. She grinned. Thick gobs of saliva clung to her teeth" (24).

Mrs. Maaargh's name sounds like a scream of terror but, perversely, is also the familiar name of Mother. Significantly, the creature teacher is likened to a cow (a lactating mammal just like "Ma"). The indeterminate, seeping body of the creature teacher is horrifying and abject according to misogynist culture, but is also, because of its irreducible difference from the male, typically female. In *Volatile Bodies,* Grosz suggests that

> in the West, in our time, the female body has been constructed not only as a lack or absence [of the phallus] but with more complexity, as a leaking, uncontrollable, seeping liquid; as formless flow; as viscosity, entrapping, secreting; as lacking not so much or simply the phallus but self-containment—not a cracked or porous vessel, like a leaking ship, but a formlessness that engulfs all form, a disorder that threatens all order.[35]

Grosz emphasizes that this is not how women are, but how women are culturally constructed. Their corporeality is "inscribed as a mode of seepage" (203), their bodies coded in opposition to the apparent "solid" status of male bodies, as "a body that leaks" and is fluid (204). Grosz quotes Iris Young who has written a study of the experience of being/having breasts and who suggests that from the male standpoint the breasted body of woman becomes "blurry, mushy, indefinite, multiple and without clear identity" (204–205). Stine describes Mrs. Maaargh's body in terms of puffy, saggy, flabby bounciness invoking notions of an excess of squashy, malleable, seeping flesh.

The creature teacher is an indeterminate being: she is a monster masquerading as human. Her students must obey her because she has power and authority over them within their social order, even though they know her true identity. As Kristeva has argued, it is not lack of cleanliness or health that necessarily causes abjection but what "disturbs identity, system, order" (4). Mrs. Maaargh epitomizes the misogynist view of the female; she is a borderline creature, disrupting order, refusing control, and specifically seen as other to the male. She is, as Kristeva suggests of the feminine, "synonymous with a radical evil that is to be suppressed" (70).

Interestingly, it is not just sexual anxieties related to congress with the female body that are expressed in Stine's narrative, but also a fundamental anxiety relating to the food chain. Ironically, Mrs. Maaargh keeps a hierarchical list of everyone in Paul's class. It is more than just an achievement chart; it is literally a food chain. Everyone in her class works really hard to stay on top because Mrs. Maaargh is going to *eat* whoever is on the bottom of her chart at the end of term. In order to create tension within the narrative, the author has the monster eat a series of non-foods before she approaches the hero: she eats one of her own black foot claws; she devours the class's pet white bunny leaving only its fluffy white tail behind; and, she drinks a bottle of skunk scent.

Inevitably, Paul ends up at the bottom of the food chain and is dragged down to a dungeon-like furnace room by Mrs. Maaargh. The creature teacher is out of control, outside the proper social and moral order. She claims that because she is a monster she won't feel sorry about eating Paul and doesn't know right from wrong (*Creature Teacher*, 112). But, she clarifies, as she prepares to push Paul into the furnace, she's not an animal and doesn't eat her meat raw; she prefers to cook it first (114). Thus, her position is again blurred because, according to Claude Lévi-Strauss's argument cooking food signifies civilized human behavior.[36] The creature teacher is somewhere on the borderline, sometimes outside and sometimes inside the social order.

> Mrs. Maaargh prepares to devour Paul:
> Holding [him] tightly, she opened her mouth wide. Her gums began to swell. Four rows of crooked teeth curled out from them. Thick gobs of white saliva rolled down her ugly teeth.
> She began grunting loudly. Her chest heaved up and down. Her fat tongue rolled over the rows of teeth.
> She lifted [Paul] off the floor with both hands ...
> She snapped her jaws hungrily. (114)

This is a rather extraordinary evocation of the *vagina dentata*. The text works to create and confirm the male fear of woman as a castrating, incorporating entity. The sexual nature of the anxiety is revealed when Paul manages to escape from the monster. He has discovered that if he can make her laugh "she will fall asleep and sleep for six months" (120). Paul drops to his knees in front of the monster and after overcoming his revulsion, begins to tickle her feet:

> Could I do it? Could I *touch* those disgusting, wet, pillow feet? ...
> My stomach churned. I felt sick!...
> I had no choice I had to do it ...
> So soft. So mushy. So moist.
> I began to tickle...
> I tickled the foot some more.
> Moved my fingertips up and down the mushy, soft skin...
> I heard her gasp. (122–123)

Mrs. Maaargh begins to laugh and Paul tickles harder.

> Her laughter rang out through the long basement tunnels. Harsh, hoarse laughter that sounded more like a dog barking than laughter.
> I ran my fingers up and down the disgusting foot.
> She laughed and laughed. Hiccuped and laughed.
> And then she slumped heavily to the floor. (123)

Once the monster has fallen (asleep) Paul climbs quickly to his feet, his stomach churning. "My fingers tingled. My whole body itched and tingled" (123). "I stared down at her. I still felt too sick to speak. I could feel the wet touch of her foot on my fingers" (124). Ma—embodiment of the monstrous feminine complete with *vagina dentata* and presumably the personification of the writer's deepest loathings (if Veglahn is correct)—is thus overcome. The sexual connotations of this narrative are unmistakable.

Miller suggests that disgust is "a key component of our [Western] social control and psychic order" (5). For him sexual and nonsexual love involve "a notable and non-trivial suspension of some, if not all, rules of disgust" (xi). "As a prelude to normal sexual behaviour," he claims, "we must learn to overcome at least some of the initial horror and disgust" (14) provoked by knowledge of sexual relationships. Furthermore, he suggests that overcoming the disgust that prevents desire is part of the thrill of the carnivalesque Rabelaisian delight in the grotesque (112–113). James Twitchell concurs when he argues in *Dreadful Pleasures* that horror films are similar to "formulaic rituals," which provide adolescents with social information. "Modern horror myths prepare the teenager for the anxieties of reproduction...they are fables of sexual identity."[37] Thus, the voyeuristic overcoming or transgressing of a taboo or prohibition is arguably psychologically therapeutic and produces pleasure. The thrill readers experience depends upon their knowledge of disgust norms and their desire to transgress/overcome them.

There is nothing positive or affirming in the framing of the feminine by either Stine or Jennings. This is in direct contrast to the way bodily elements were treated in medieval grotesque humor. Bakhtin has shown that its inherent exaggeration had a "positive, assertive character" (19), explaining that the lower stratum of the body was regarded ambivalently by the folk, being not only the site of excretory function but also "the area of the genital organs, the fertilizing and generating stratum" (148). While "modern indecent abuse and cursing have retained dead and purely negative remnants of the grotesque concept of the body" (28), the medieval viewpoint, he claims, preserved positive connotations of birth, fertility, and renewal. Contemporary narratives for children appear to promote only the negative aspects of the grotesque body.

Young children in the age group at which much carnivalesque-grotesque and grotesque-horror genre series books are aimed, are at their most vulnerable stage of social and intellectual development (Coppell, 9). Appleyard has argued that the "specific developmental task of children of this age [around six to twelve years old] is to gather and organize information about the new world they have been launched into."[38] Similarly, Bronwyn Davies claims that children use stories to constitute themselves as male or female with appropriate patterns of power and desire.[39] The contemporary popular fictions described in this chapter offer children only the hegemonic patterns of a patriarchal social order with its ideological biases firmly in place. There isn't even a hint of an alternative in these stories: the female is unequivocally aligned with the body, with abjection and with viscous monstrosity, while the male is clearly distanced from them. Again and again the tired old structuralist constructions are dragged out and dusted down. "Rude" books like these merely serve to reiterate the way boys are licensed to displace their own abjection (assigned to them in their role as "feminized" children in a powerful adult order) onto girls and women, who are naturally constructed as abject in a patriarchal order. The humor in these stories rewards boy readers, but for girls it is tainted and often even cruel.

8

DISORDERLY EATING

A Taste for Control

If Desdemona was fat who would care whether or not Othello
strangled her?

—Margaret Atwood, *Lady Oracle*[1]

Aurora's mother used to tell her to not worry about the monsters
under her bed, because imaginary things can't hurt you. But they
can. They can kill you.

—Helen Barnes, *Killing Aurora*[2]

I want to fly far away, to never-never land, where I'm not ashamed,
where it's ok to eat all sorts of things, not a humiliating, dirty thing
to do. I'd be beautiful and free, and there'd be no scales, no mirrors.
Never-be-hungry land, never-be-judged land, never-be-Mom land,
always-be-me land. Second star to the right, and straight on till
morning—is that how you get there?

—Deborah Hautzig, *Second Star to the Right*[3]

IN PREVIOUS CHAPTERS I HAVE ESTABLISHED that eating in an orderly
fashion, according to social and cultural precepts, is a prerequisite for
being human. An individual who eats badly and breaks cultural taboos
undermines the integrity of the social structure. Focusing on the body of
the child as an overeating or noneating organism, as I do in this chapter,
highlights notions of subjectivity and agency, and reveals the social forces

acting upon individuals, controlling their consumption so that they literally embody culture.

In common with other human practices that are constructed as normal, obvious, and legitimate, eating behaviors can often be based on historically and culturally specific ideologies. Cultural discourses control eating behaviors, shape bodies and confer subjectivity. Western anxieties about fat, consuming a "healthy" diet, and female slenderness, for example, produce some of the "most powerful normalising discursive strategies of our time."[4] Eating, and specifically the cultural imperative to eat correctly, is a means by which society controls individual identity.

Fictional narratives written for children that reflect cultural discourses are instrumental in teaching not only socially acceptable eating behaviors, but also gendered notions of appropriate body image. A child's appetite, as I have previously argued, must, according to adult culture, be restrained until the child attains self-control. Control and restraint are key words in healthy eating discourses. However, in direct contrast, Western capitalist society promotes consumption as a primary value of life. Marketing messages promise that beauty (including an ideal body shape) can be obtained through the purchase of products or services that will transform the body, part by part.[5] The idea of undergoing some sort of physical transformation or cosmetic makeover is, in prevailing discourses, associated not only with attaining "beauty" as it is culturally defined, but also with achieving subjectivity and agency, especially for females. Underlying these discourses is the notion that beauty is *not* just skin deep but that physical appearance is a manifestation of identity. Aurora, in Helen Barnes's novel *Killing Aurora*, discussed in detail later, believes that her cartoon hero Electra, who is so thin her neck and waist are the same width, "*is* what she looks like" (*Aurora*, 87, original emphasis). Furthermore, Aurora equates beauty/being thin with agency: "you can do anything you like and say anything you want, if you're thin" (48).

Both the anorexic and the obese transgress healthy eating rules although the cultural meanings associated with each are very different. Both have noncompliant bodies that defy cultural paradigms of beauty and represent abject forms of being within dominant cultural ideologies; they lack agency, are denied subjectivity and connoted as inhuman and monstrous. Recalcitrant bodies, as physical evidence of transgressive eating, may, however, work to question ideologies and, to a certain extent, subvert hegemonic discourses. But transgressive behavior (whether enacted by disorderly eaters or others), as Robyn McCallum points out, does not necessarily constitute agency because the very act of resistance implies subjection to that which is resisted. McCallum proposes that a sense of self, of personal identity, or subjectivity, is constructed through the interplay of subjection and agency. An individual is subject to the forces of prevailing dominant ideologies and discourses while, at the same time, being able to resist their pressures, to a certain extent, through deliberate and conscious thoughts and actions.[6] An individual may, through productive transgression and transformation, be empowered and achieve agency, or alternatively, through self-damaging transformation or counter-productive transgression, be constrained and even consigned to abjection (de Villiers, 6). It is only when the bodies of the obese and the anorexic are transformed by properly controlled eating so as to conform to, and literally embody, social and cultural health and beauty paradigms, that they can achieve proper subjectivity.

The trope of the obese child is used in children's literature to relay adult culture's rules about keeping children's appetites under control. There is a clear indication, particularly in classic texts, that a child's naturally hedonistic appetite must be restrained. If parents prove to be inadequate for this task then an alternative socializing agent or authority must be introduced so that the body of the child is suitably transformed. The transformation or makeover is seen to be a necessary part of a movement toward subjectivity and agency, which would otherwise be denied.

Michel Foucault not only argues that experience and identity are shaped by ideologies, but also that individuals consume discourse, which can result in "voluntary" self-oppression.[7] The anorexic is sated and sickened by the discourses that surround her and she refuses the food her body craves. As her body wastes away it is as though she herself is being consumed by discourse. In an attempt to comply with, or perhaps to escape, dominant cultural paradigms and achieve agency, the self-oppressed and starving girl attempts a self-transformation. But her skeletal frame does not embody culture. Her excessive control is seen to be as transgressive as the obese child's lack of control. Both are consigned to abjection and considered to be monstrous.

THE OBESE CHILD

Maurice Gee's description of Muskie's obese body in *The Fat Man* evokes disgust and abjection.[8] His gross rolls of fat seem to provide evidence of contamination by the (unhealthy, fat-laden) foods he has eaten. He embodies excess; his body shows that he has consumed more than his fair share, suggesting that somewhere, someone has gone without. Obesity is, in Western culture, indicative of excessive appetite, of a lack of self-control, of laziness, and of an unwillingness to conform to accepted paradigms of beauty. Arguably it also signifies a lack of morality. Susan Bordo argues that the firm, developed body has become a symbol of "correct attitude;"

that one "cares" about oneself and how one appears to others. While muscles express sexuality, it is a controlled, managed sexuality that is "not about to erupt in unwanted and embarrassing display."[9] In contrast, the obese body signifies the wrong attitude and a lack of care about body image. It connotes voracious and uncontrolled (sexual) appetite.

Roald Dahl believed that adults have a relentless need to civilize "this thing that when it is born is an animal with no manners, no moral sense at all."[10] His story, *Charlie and the Chocolate Factory*, drives home his views.[11] Charlie is a polite, passive child. He respects his elders, is hard working, unselfish, thoughtful, and he knows how to control his appetite. Every year on his birthday, Charlie receives from his poverty-stricken family "one small chocolate bar to eat all by himself" (*Charlie,* 16).

> He would place it carefully in a small wooden box that he owned, and treasure it as though it were a bar of solid gold; and for the next few days, he would allow himself only to look at it, but never to touch it. Then at last, when he could stand it no longer, he would peel back a tiny bit of the paper wrapping at one corner to expose a tiny bit of chocolate, and then he would take a tiny nibble—just enough to allow the lovely sweet taste to spread out slowly over his tongue. The next day, he would take another tiny nibble, and so on, and so on. And in this way, Charlie would make his sixpenny bar of birthday chocolate last him for more than a month. (17)

This passage exemplifies the qualities Dahl apparently appreciates in a child: civilized manners, frugality, and, most importantly, restraint and control. It is interesting to note, however, that Charlie finds his golden ticket to the Chocolate Factory through an act which is ostensibly transgressive. When Charlie's father loses his job the food situation at home becomes "desperate. Breakfast was a single slice of bread for each person now, and lunch was maybe half a boiled potato. Slowly but surely, everyone in the house began to starve" (56). "[E]very day Charlie Bucket grew thinner and thinner ... The skin was drawn so tightly over the cheeks that you could see the shapes of the bones underneath. It seemed doubtful whether he could go on much longer like this without becoming dangerously ill" (56). Charlie finds a fifty pence coin in the snow and, instead of taking it to his parents so that they can buy food for whole family, he goes straight to the nearest shop and buys a bar of chocolate. (Incidentally, the shopkeeper strikes Charlie as being particularly "fat and well-fed" [62].) Charlie "cram[s] large pieces" of the chocolate bar into his mouth. Significantly, he is described as "wolfing" it down. "[I]n less than half a minute, the whole thing had disappeared down his throat" (63). Charlie buys a second bar, reinforcing his transgression, and it is under the wrapper of this Whipple-Scrumptious Fudgemallow Delight that he discovers the Golden ticket (64). Roni Natov points out that questing heroes often have to "break some taboo" and "revolt" against the familial/social structure in order to create change. Tradition must be subverted so that evolution can occur. This, she reveals, is at the heart of the hero's quest.[12] It is significant that Dahl carefully constructs Charlie as being *in extremis* before his transgressive act takes place.

In contrast, all the other children in the story who find golden tickets, have excessive appetites and desires, and show the deleterious influences of consumer-media culture. Veruca Salt is an acquisitive, impulsive and selfish consumer of material goods. She screams at her father, lying on the floor for hours, "kicking and yelling in the most disturbing way" (40) until she gets what she wants, producing the ultimate display of "pester power."[13] Nine-year-old Mike Teavee, on the other hand, is described by Dahl as a "television fiend" (78). He is an avid consumer of gangster films, the more violent the better. He wears "no less than eighteen toy pistols of various sizes hanging from belts around his body" (49) and indignantly resists being deprived of the TV even for a short time. He thinks that gangster movies are "terrific...especially when they start pumping each other full of lead, or flashing the old stilettos, or giving each other the one-two-three with their knuckledusters! Gosh, what wouldn't I give to be doing that myself! It's the *life*, I tell you! It's terrific!" (50, emphasis in original). The Oompa-Loompas' song provides the vehicle for Dahl's critique: television is a "monster" (172); children should be kept away from "the idiotic thing." It hypnotizes them (171), making them lethargic and mindless to the point of being "absolutely drunk" (172).

IT ROTS THE SENSES IN THE HEAD!
IT KILLS IMAGINATION DEAD!
IT CLOGS AND CLUTTERS UP THE MIND!
IT MAKES A CHILD SO DULL AND BLIND
HE CAN NO LONGER UNDERSTAND
A FANTASY, A FAIRYLAND!
HIS BRAIN BECOMES AS SOFT AS CHEESE!
HIS POWERS OF THINKING RUST AND FREEZE!
HE CANNOT THINK—HE ONLY SEES! (172, capitals in original)

It is interesting that Dahl was so early (1964) in advancing this verdict about the corrupting influence of television, which has since become the popular view and which Neil Postman's much-cited thesis, some eighteen years later, mirrors.[14]

While it might be argued that Dahl's characters Salt and Teavee are metaphorical consumers of goods and the media respectively, Dahl's

Augustus Gloop is uncontrollably consuming in the literal sense. He is obese and his consuming desire is for chocolate. Augustus is

> so enormously fat he looked as though he had been blown up with a powerful pump. Great flabby folds of fat bulged out from every part of his body, and his face was like a monstrous ball of dough with two small greedy currant eyes peering out. (36)

In common with Gee's description of the obese body of Muskie, Gloop's body, and his face in particular, seem to embody the food which produced it. His head is a currant bun! Furthermore, reference to Claude Lévi-Strauss's raw/cooked dualism, which he aligns with nature/culture, suggests that Augustus's doughy face evokes notions of precultural primitivism and irrational mindlessness.[15]

Augustus's mother reveals that all he's interested in is food (36). It is his greed, his lack of control that leads to his downfall and is implicitly condemned in Dahl's narrative. During the tour of the chocolate factory, "as you might have guessed," interjects the narrator, Augustus quietly sneaks down to the edge of the chocolate river and is discovered "scooping hot melted chocolate into his mouth as fast as he could" (96). It is the narrator's coercive comment, addressed to child readers, that implicitly invites them to condemn Augustus, but also to see his action as an inevitable consequence of his being fat, greedy and lacking in self-control.

Mr. Wonka tells Augustus that he "*must* come away. You are dirtying my chocolate!" (97, emphasis in original) and both his parents remonstrate with him.

> But Augustus was deaf to everything except the call of his enormous stomach. He was now lying full length on the ground with his head far out over the river, lapping up the chocolate like a dog.
>
> "Augustus!" shouted Mrs. Gloop. "You'll be giving that nasty cold of yours to about a million people all over the country!" (97)

Emphasis is placed upon the child as a source of contamination. He is all body and no mind: his body's appetite overwhelms him. In psychoanalytic terms, it could be argued that Augustus has failed to properly separate from his mother, signified by his insatiable and transgressive desire for food. He is stuck in the oral phase, the phase of maternal influence. Food is the wrong object for his desire; he ought to have turned to the father/phallus in order to achieve proper masculine subjectivity. Augustus is connoted as monstrous and denied agency by his inappropriately directed and excessive desire.

Inevitably, Augustus falls into the river and is sucked up a pipe into the chocolate factory's machinery. His animalistic, uninhibited greed and his obese body are modified by Wonka's machinery, which may be read as a sort of corrective socializing agent. After being processed by the factory, he is as "thin as straw" (182) and presumably cured of his excessive appetite/chocolate addiction. Rendered acceptable to (adult) society, he is sent home. Similarly, Violet Beauregarde is cured of her addiction to chewing gum, Veruca Salt gets her comeuppance by being covered with rubbish, having passed through the factory's garbage system (an authorial comment on the value of the material consumer goods she desired perhaps), and Mike Teavee has been punished for his excessive consumption of television by being, in a sense, consumed by it.[16]

It is interesting and important to note, with regard to Dahl's construction of these characters, that notions of class and race are also implicated. Although Charlie has middle-class manners and mores, he is an idealistic representation of the British working class. Veruca Salt belongs decidedly within the despised nouveau riche category and is presumably American, since her father is "in the peanut business" (40). Violet Beauregarde and Mike Teavee are also affiliated with America; Violet by her incessant gum-chewing and Mike by his penchant for American Westerns and gangster movies. Augustus's last name suggests he might be German.[17] The class and race issues implied here are significant in relation to the nuances of excessive and vulgar appetite and childish monstrousness. There are marked differences between historical notions of childrearing in Britain and America. The austere diet of British children was deemed to have character building properties[18] while, in contrast, American childrearing methods were seen to be vulgar and overindulgent and associated with the nouveau riche. Dahl's cultural conservatism marries with Dick Hebdige's claims that populist discourses about culture and taste in Britain in the 1930s–60s tended to focus on the "leveling down" of moral and aesthetic standards and the erosion of fundamentally British values and attitudes. This perceived decline in standards was believed to stem from "Americanization" (an influx of American mass culture encompassing goods, production techniques, music, etc.), and reflected fears of the homogenization of British society.[19]

The song sung by the Oompa-Loompas reveals that, as Augustus journeys through the fudge machine, "He will be altered quite a bit/ He'll be changed from what he's been" (105). Augustus's body undergoes a transformation or makeover, achieved with surgical precision:)

> Slowly, the wheels go round and round,
> The cogs begin to grind and pound;
> A hundred knives go slice, slice, slice (105)

The cogs that "grind and pound" and especially the "hundred knives" that cut Augustus down to size, bear a ghastly resemblance to the "knives that 'sculpt' our bodies to make us beautiful forever" critiqued by Kathryn Pauly Morgan in her article "Women and the Knife: Cosmetic Surgery and the Colonization of Women's Bodies."[20] It is surely not unreasonable to align the transformation of Augustus's body, through a process of mechanical sucking (through the pipes), grinding, and slicing, with socially-legitimized forms of cosmetic surgery such as those detailed by Morgan: liposuction (a process which involves sucking fat cells out from underneath the skin with a vacuum device) and "nips and tucks" (surgical reduction involving cutting out wedges of skin and fat) (Morgan, 25–53). It is pertinent to suggest that, in Augustus's case, the physical surgery or makeover he undergoes is a parable of moral surgery. It is intended to change not only his outward appearance but also his attitude, and to signal his movement toward a more mature subjectivity.

Eric Linklater's *The Wind on the Moon*, published in 1944, which is extraordinarily concerned with food, perhaps has a different emphasis.[21] Dinah and her sister Dorinda are framed as naughty girls, deliberately transgressive of adult rules. Their rule breaking, however, is constructed as enormously enjoyable. Dinah believes that food is more important than knowledge and she and her sister are "very fond" of eating. Dinah "suddenly perceived that one of the best ways of being naughty was to be utterly and shamelessly greedy. At the same time she felt marvellously hungry, so that to be greedy seemed the most natural thing in the world" (*Wind on the Moon*, 14). In one day the girls supposedly consume the following:

> For breakfast they ate porridge and cream, fish and bacon and eggs and sausages and tomatoes, toast and marmalade, and rolls and honey. For dinner they ate roast beef and cold lamb, boiled mutton with caper sauce, Scotch broth and clear soup, hare soup and lentil soup, roast chicken with thyme and parsley stuffing, boiled fowl with oatmeal and onion stuffing, roast duck with apple sauce, apple-tart and cherry pie, Yorkshire pudding and plum pudding, trifle and jelly, potatoes and brussel sprouts and cauliflower and French beans and green peas, and all sorts of cheese. For tea they had scones and pancakes, crumpets and pikelets, muffins and cream buns, plum cake and seed cake and cream cake and chocolate cake, and often some bread and butter as well. And for supper they had stewed fruit and fresh fruit, oranges and bananas and baked apples, and half a gallon of milk at the very least. (20–21)

This menu is quintessentially English and very upper class. Most significantly, Linklater wrote this story during a period of post-war government-enforced food rationing when the food items he describes would have generally been unavailable even to the most privileged adult or child. This passage is written, not only for the author's own pleasure, but also to provide hedonistic pleasure to his readers, children and adults alike.

The girls' indulgence is deliciously unrestrained but, understandably, they became

> fatter and fatter. They got so fat, and quickly got fatter still, that every three or four days they burst their frocks and split their vests, and were quite unable to pull their stockings over their fat round legs. (21)

I should emphasize, however, that their indulgence is constructed as premeditated and entirely self-indulgent and is framed within the narrative as transgressive in a defiant and deliberately naughty way, rather than being revolting, vile, and foul as Dahl describes Augustus's greed (*Charlie*, 104). Although the girls "knew it was wicked to be so greedy," having started they find it difficult to stop (*Wind on the Moon*, 21). Between meals the girls eat:

> biscuits and strawberry jam and Devonshire cream with raspberry jam, and sponge cake with damson jam. Between dinner and teatime they usually ate a pound of chocolates and some candied fruit and a few caramels. And about midnight they often woke and went downstairs to the kitchen, where they ate whatever they could find, such as cold chicken, and hard-boiled eggs and custard and plum tart and a slice or two of cake. (22)

The girls transgress a number of food rules about the sequence and timing of meals—they eat between approved mealtimes and eat excessively. Their behavior is clearly deviant but also undoubtedly pleasurable. Their mother, worried by her daughters' weight gain, tries to appeal to their vanity by telling them that their appearance is "truly disgusting." She is "ashamed to be the mother of two little girls who look more like balloons than human beings. Not long ago I thought you were the prettiest children I had ever seen...But now I can hardly bear to look at you, you are both so ugly" (22). Notably, Linklater has an adult and, more specifically, a mother, speak these words of condemnation. Dinah and Dorinda express no regrets about their size.

Like Augustus, Dinah and Dorinda are eventually punished for being obese. Their mother and their governess "roll and bounce" the girls into the village to see the doctor. In the village square "fifty or sixty boys and girls" prick the "big balloons" with pins until they begin to cry (27). The girls cry and cry for "days and days. They lost their appetites, and wanted nothing to eat." They cried, "all through the Christmas holidays, and every day they got thinner and thinner. They got as thin as a lamp-post, and then as thin as a walking-stick, and thinner than that" until they were "as thin as matchsticks" (30). This slimming-down process has uncomfortable resonances in contemporary culture where anorexia nervosa is a serious and growing phenomenon, although it was unlikely to have been an issue during Linklater's time.

Unlike Augustus Gloop who is ruled by his appetite and oblivious to everything else, Dinah and Dorinda's greed is thoughtful. Although he punishes his characters and the girls are forced to admit "they had enjoyed eating too much" (31), Linklater's narrative does not, in my opinion, condemn his obese characters with the virulent force that Dahl's does. Maria Nikolajeva is more critical of Linklater, suggesting that the girls' interest in food is "sickly" and "a natural sign of immaturity."[22]

More recent children's novels that feature fat children are intended to be rather more therapeutic. Margaret Clark's *No Fat Chicks*, for example, glances over the beauty versus brains debate.[23] The book's title refers to a bumper sticker being used by a group of boys at Mandy's high school to intimidate, humiliate, and ostensibly to deny agency to girls who do not comply with dominant discursive notions of femininity. According to Nita Mary McKinley, the bumper sticker reflects cultural hostility toward fat women and illustrates the connection between ideal weight and ideal women. A "chick," that is an appropriately feminine woman, must be both attractive and nonthreatening (that is, immature) and small. A "fat chick," McKinley points out, would be an oxymoron.[24]

In Clark's story, the sticker implicitly symbolizes the cultural pressure and objectification many young women experience on a daily basis. Mandy is a very clever young woman, but for her being brainy is a "problem" because it's not "considered cool" (*Fat Chicks*, 8). Her body does not comply with notions of ideal femininity. She is not obese and does not eat badly; she is a strong and fit person and represents her school at netball. But, because she is "large with big bones" she believes she is unattractive and could "double for a lump of cheddar cheese" (4). Mandy starts a new sticker campaign, "Clever is Cool," but this does not counter the discourses and misogyny that produced the "No Fat Chicks" stickers. Clark's story reveals that the ideological discourses that produce "sexist fad[s]" (158) cannot be overcome. Rather, it implies that people should make the most of whatever talent they have and that brainy girls may be lucky enough to find a guy who appreciates them. Clark's story concludes with Mandy finding romance with a "gorgeous" (197) "tall, blond suntanned guy" (196) she met on the Internet. Before they go out together, however, she too must submit to a transformation, a makeover by her stepmother "wielding the hair dryer like a magic wand" (198). Just like Cinderella's fairy godmother, Mandy's stepmother transforms her appearance so that she complies with socially acceptable paradigms of beauty. With her hair "sleek and smart" and make-up hiding her sunburnt nose and cheeks and making her eyes look "huge and mysterious," Mandy has to admit that although "big," she is "in [her] own way...beautiful" (199).

It is interesting and significant that the narratives in this section have featured the transformation or makeover of children's bodies so that they comply with accepted paradigms of beauty or, in the case of the younger children, properly controlled childhood. John Stephens has shown that, semiotically, the trope of the makeover, so often used in contemporary teen fiction, is frequently framed as a central metonym of growth and a movement toward subjectivity and maturation. It supposedly demonstrates to the character concerned that "she can transform her life and thus realize her full potential."[25] On the one hand, such discourses reiterate the notion that bodies, especially female bodies, are transformable, and on the other, they act to endorse cultural beauty paradigms and the imperative that female bodies *should* be transformed. While Mandy is neither obese nor a child, her enforced makeover (her stepmother grabs her arm and hauls her away, ignoring her protests and ordering her to "Be quiet and sit still" [*Fat Chicks,* 198]) is similar to the transformations that Augustus and Dinah and Dorinda go through. In each case the changes produce, or aim to produce, a body that conforms to social norms. The changes also, as Stephens suggests, reflect the individual's movement toward a more mature self. Thus "what appears inscribed on the body's surface [is seen to] function[] as a pointer to the depths within" (Stephens, 7).[26] In countless movies, magazines, and teen (or young adult) novels, aimed at girls, the makeover is shown to be the way to transform the self and notably, to achieve agency and happiness through social acceptance. Most significantly, even when a range of body morphologies is confirmed as "natural," it is always the *slimmest* body types that are valorized (Stephens, 7).

Peter Howell argues that the ideal body type portrayed in the media is unrealistically thin and represents a body weight that, for the majority of women, would be unhealthy. The ideal is so thin, he claims, that an individual would have to strive very hard and engage in extreme behaviors in order to achieve and maintain the ideal body type.[27] Young women at the cusp of adulthood, especially those who are more than usually insecure about their body image, are particularly vulnerable to these images and discourses.

THE STARVING CHILD

Hilde Bruch was one of the first to write about the modern phenomenon of excessive dieting caused by a fear of becoming fat. She defines anorexia nervosa as "the relentless pursuit of thinness through self-starvation, even unto death."[28] Anorexia has since been widely theorized with a number of often opposing causes being suggested. Certainly, there is a huge amount of information available on the subject, not only in academic libraries but also on the Internet where pro-anorexia Web sites flourish. In this section, I analyze two young adult (YA) novels concerned with anorexia. My analysis directly relates to the theory that has been written about the phenomenon. One of the books I will focus on is *Killing Aurora* by Helen Barnes, which won the Victorian Writer's Festival YA Fiction Award in 1999 and was also entered in The Children's Book Council (CBC) Awards. When books are listed for CBC awards, they immediately become favorites for inclusion in the English teaching syllabuses. The second book is *Second Star to the Right* written nearly two decades earlier by American author Deborah Hautzig in 1981. This book was brought to my attention via the favorable reviews it received online. One reader describes the book as "heartfelt, touching, and inspirational."[29] The reviews indicate that anorexia sufferers are keen to read novels about the disease and that schools encourage students to do research projects about it.

Given the accuracy of their depictions of the disease, both the Barnes and Hautzig narratives are undoubtedly derived from the plethora of theoretical writings on the topic and/or from the author's personal experience.[30] It is my contention that realist texts such as these that depict the progress of a spreading disease may have a range of functions: they undoubtedly act as an indictment and critique of the collusion of capitalism and contemporary (patriarchal) culture's view of femininity, with its aggressive objectification of the female body and framing of female heterosexuality as meek and submissive; they may serve therapeutic purposes for sufferers and provide a sense of community;[31] they may also, however, function as how-to manuals that valorize their protagonist's actions.

It is estimated that eight million Americans have an eating disorder. Of the population, one in two hundred suffers from anorexia and 10–15 percent of these are male. In Australia approximately one in one hundred adolescent girls develop anorexia and it is the third most common chronic illness for adolescent girls (after obesity and asthma). Within six months of treatment 25 percent of sufferers remain chronically ill or die.[32] There is no definitive cause of anorexia: it is multidetermined and each case is different. However, when any individual starts to diet they generally do so to change their self-perceived body image. Noelle Caskey confirms that "the anorexic [in common with every other young woman] grows up viewing her body as a reflected image of the desires of others."[33] Anorexics initially desire to be thin, because this, they determine, will lead to social acceptance within their peer group, agency, and thus happiness. Both novels describe their fourteen-year-old female protagonists negative body images, perceived lack of social acceptance within their peer groups, and lack or loss of autonomy in the family home. Both girls progress from dieting to self-starvation.

Caskey, following Bruch (*The Golden Cage,* 1978), confirms that for many girls, growing up in families where parents, especially mothers, rule and direct their lives, the boundary between self and m/other may not be clear cut. Anorexics are often peculiarly oversensitive to the desires of others (Caskey, 179). Hautzig's character, Leslie, is a very good girl and "always does the right thing." Her mother "never had to be ashamed of me—that's why she loved me, I guess. I was just like her." Leslie is very concerned with other people's feelings, and even thinking "rotten things" about other people made her "feel as guilty as if I'd really hurt someone" (*Second Star,* 15). Leslie "feel[s] for people, and with people, and [her Mom] especially, more acutely and understandingly than people four times [her] age" (74). She has real problems separating herself and her needs from her mother's. She complains that her mother "pretends to be selfless, yet manages to suck me dry till I don't even feel like a person. Till I can't tell us apart" (120). For a girl there is a danger of a lingering overattachment to the mother in the process of acquiring gender identification; she need not reject the mother and her role, as a boy child must. As Sarah Sceats has suggested, too close a bond between mother and daughter may result in either or both experiencing a lack of autonomy and sense of self.[34] Leslie's notions of self are obviously weak and her identity is still tied to her mother's. Toward the end of Hautzig's story, Leslie, weighing only 76 pounds (around 34 kilos) and in a delirious state, is clearly confused: "Mother, me, we, are, one, none, good-bye" (98).

Bruch argues that anorexics "grow up confused in their concepts about the body and its functions and deficient in their sense of identity, autonomy and control. In many ways they feel and behave as if they had no independent rights, that neither their body nor their actions are self-directed, or not even their own."[35] Caskey suggests that this is why such girls are so vulnerable to the messages of popular culture concerning both their achievements and their beauty (179). Barnes seems to suggest that her character, Aurora, is more susceptible to the media's messages than some of the other girls she rides home from school with, because she has a negative body image. Even though the other girls agree that the images of models in magazines are touched up, that "they use a fish-eye lens to make their heads look bigger than their waists," for example, "Aurora is not deceived . . . [she believes] the flat tummy, the clear skin and the thin thighs [are achievable] . . . You have to believe your eyes. The impossible is mandatory. Everyone knows it" (*Aurora*, 41). Aurora appears to be particularly vulnerable to the pressures, codes, and regulatory forces that confine women. According to her school principal, young women's choices are limitless, but for Aurora there is no choice: in a parody of the school motto *Potens sui,* Self control (10), Aurora elects to consume the insidious discourses that surround her and not to consume food.

The notion that the anorexic is docile and lacks autonomy has, however, been criticized by feminists such as Bordo who argues that thinness connotes willpower and independence in our culture and that the anorexic may be starving herself to underline her self-control and strength.[36] Indeed, Lilian Furst argues that an eating disorder can be "a vehicle for self-assertion." Whether the condition leads to triumph or destruction is immaterial; eating disorders represent the last protest left to the socially disempowered but, also, paradoxically, a means for sufferers to attain a kind of domination.[37]

Susan Rubin Suleiman argues that the female body is "not only (not even first and foremost) that of a flesh-and-blood entity, but that of a symbolic construct."[38] Thus it is never unmediated but always carries meaning. Malson discusses the way physical appearance is culturally considered to be an essential part of femininity. Ideal femininity in contemporary Western culture is signified by thinness, which in turn connotes properly controlled desire and a moral character. This image is reinforced in the popular media, and self-care discourses.[39] Thinness is a heterosexually based definition of female attractiveness and the patriarchal order defines popular tastes and standards and therefore, influences and even controls the dieting behaviors of women.[40] Aurora checks her weight daily (1). At 51 kg (112 lbs.) she recognizes that she's "the fattest she's ever been" (4). She assumes the messages on magazine covers advocating "*Thin thighs in thirty days, drop a dress size by Saturday, get rid of your cellulite forever*" are addressed to her. "She feels remaindered and discount-binned . . . *I've let myself go*, she moans to herself" (5, italics in original). Leslie is similarly concerned with the way her body looks and believes that her new sweater makes her look fat. She is unhappy because her body does not comply with cultural paradigms of ideal femininity: "I wouldn't be half bad-looking if I were thin . . . If I were thin, my life would be perfect"

(*Second Star*, 12). She resolves to diet in order to increase her feelings of self-worth: "I'm going to be thin," Leslie determines, "And happy" (42). But while she starts off presuming she will achieve happiness by becoming thin, her goal becomes critically distorted. Basing her quest for happiness upon the ephemeral goal of being sufficiently thin leads her to starvation. She thinks she'll "know when I'm thin because I'll be happy" (61), but happiness eludes her and so the dieting goes on and on.

As I have shown previously, for women, a small appetite is synonymous with self-control. Malson confirms that in her conversations with anorexic women dietary restraint was seen to be a signifier of self-control (125). Children quickly learn that self-control is an important cultural precept. Research among children in grades four to six in South Australia, for example, has found that they consistently rated larger or fatter people as lazier, less attractive, less confident, less hard-working and more unhappy, based on photographs. They also believed that if an individual's weight was under control they were more likely to be a disciplined person.[41] Leslie feels proud of herself when she achieves control over her body. "For the first time in my life, I felt in control. And I knew I wouldn't break. It was like something in me had finally erupted... I can do it this time; I *will* do it" (*Second Star*, 42, emphasis in original). Leslie reveals, "You can learn to love anything, I think, if you need to badly enough. I trained myself to enjoy feeling hungry... [if I feel hunger pangs] it means I'm getting thinner. So it feels good. I feel strong, on top of myself. In control" (44). There are two major issues here: first and paradoxically, there can be a certain level of pleasure gained from self-starvation. Anorexia offers sufferers what Susanne Skubal refers to as a "phantasy of omnipotence." The anorexic regains control over her weight and body shape, her (a)sexuality, her reproductive system (through amenorrhoea), her excretory function, and temporarily, her whole sense of identity. In addition, she exerts tremendous pressure on her family and against cultural demands for order and conformity.[42] Second, this passage echoes the notion that the body and mind are separate and in conflict which complies with Smith's suggestion that the discourses of Cartesian dualism and Christian asceticism in Western culture combine to produce the ideal of a bodiless subject (Smith, 83). The physical body can seem to be a burden for some girls, a fleshy shell of womanliness complete with breasts and hips, within which they are trapped. Their physique evokes an objectifying gaze and demeaning misogynist treatment, which can make them feel helpless and victimized.

Martha McCaughey shows that anorexia is often manifested following an objectifying comment or after a girl begins to grow into a womanly shape.[43] This is illustrated in both of these narratives. Leslie is out with a girlfriend when "two men leaning languidly against a mailbox on the corner" begin to hiss and make loud kissing noises at them. "Hey sweetheart, come home with me" one of them calls. "Look at those pretty little tits." But Leslie blames herself for the men's lasciviousness: "Why did I wear such a clingy sweater? A sweater that shows off my pretty little embarrassing tits" (*Second Star*, 17). She is desperate to get away and "almost wanting to cry" although her friend remains calm and advises her to ignore the men. Aurora must walk past a building site on her way to school. The workmen habitually "down tools and goggle at" the schoolgirls, sharing "verbal notes and ratings as if it were a bloodstock auction" (*Aurora*, 78–79): "Here's a blondie for you, Kevin. Hey, lovie, look over here. Hey, you, girlie, cheer up and show us your tits" (79). Aurora's stepfather's attitude doesn't help. He laughs, "You should take it as a compliment... They're only showing their appreciation. You've got a snotty attitude, young lady" (80). McCaughey points out that (patriarchal) culture, like Aurora's stepfather, assumes that women like feeling objectified by men; indeed, that this defines femininity. But, she rightly points out, "harassment is disparaging for an entitled young woman who discovers that men often experience sexual interest in women to the exclusion of intellectual, collegial, respectful interest" (McCaughey, 140). Thus, dieting may start not just because anorexics hate the way their bodies look, but because they hate the way others look at their bodies (148). They may thus be paradoxically resisting patriarchal culture while they appear to be emulating its ideals.

Anorexics characteristically do not want to follow in their mother's footsteps, to become self-sacrificing and socially limited, or a "supermum."[44] Using the premise "we are what we eat," the anorexic refuses to become a woman by refusing to eat. Aurora wishes she could halt her body's changes. She is "sure that she could have stopped her breasts and hips from appearing if only she'd been conscientious enough" (*Aurora*, 5). Bordo points out that cultural fears of "The Female" with all its more fearful archetypal connotations, voracious hungers and sexual insatiability, add to the anorexic's rejection of womanhood (41).

Aurora is uncomfortably aware of the corporeality of bodies. To her the train carriage is "full of noses stuffed with snot, and blackheads, greasy hair, piggy eyes and huge festering spots at breaking point. If the train braked suddenly they could all drown in pus" (*Aurora*, 33–34). Aurora's own body revolts her. In the shower, she cannot escape how round her belly is. "She thought it was flat, but it's not. It's not flat at all. When she touches it, it gives like foam rubber. It disgusts her" (71). For some anorexics the processes of the body are so horrific that they diet so as to eliminate everything regarded as impure. In Jane Rogers's short story "Grateful,"[45] written in the first person, the significantly nameless and suicidal schoolgirl narrator is horrified by the corporeality of her body. "Under skin and blood and flesh and all the other muck, bones are white. To know that gives me hope. When the crap is peeled away, when the flesh has rotted back to mulch, the bones are white. *Underneath*, it's clean" ("Grateful," 95, emphasis in original). The thought of introducing food into her body is repellent:

> The thing about food is, it decays...In that warm stomach. All those chewed bits. Disgusting, filthy mixed-up stinking muck. Where does it go? It turns into crap...I am not interested in inserting lumps of dead animal and vegetable matter into myself. I am not interested in being made of living crap. I do not have to be a tube for food, and last for eighty years. (97–98)

Julia Kristeva has argued that, when the subject "finds the impossible within; when it finds that the impossible constitutes its very *being*, that it *is* none other than the abject, horror and disgust result."[46] "Grateful" is a pathological expression of the psychological fear we all feel about having to eat to live, but must overcome in order to survive. In order to achieve subjectivity and to be accepted as properly human, every individual must learn the clean and proper rules. These rules are culturally specific and relate to, among other things, what may be eaten and what must be avoided. The human body is permeable and therefore vulnerable to dangerous substances. Thus, we must guard against pollution. Credible human subjectivity relies on constantly monitoring the boundaries of the individual and social body. But the anorexic monitors her intake pathologically so that almost nothing passes from the outside to the inside or vice versa. The reality of the body's constant flux with the outside and the thought of taking in foods, which she considers to be bad, become abhorrent.

In a desperate attempt to get Aurora to eat, her mother prepares a special lunch for her with asparagus, rice crackers, and Evian water. "I bought all the food you like. The stuff you're always talking about."

> "There's butter on the crackers," Aurora says, sullenly.
> "It's that no-fat margarine. See? Look on the lid." Her mother's eyes are wide and already showing signs of desperation.
> "I can't eat margarine!" Aurora yells. "It makes me vomit. I can't eat it! I can't eat any of this. How could you? I can't eat anything now." (*Aurora*, 140)

Aurora's mother frantically scrapes the margarine off the crackers and places the food before her daughter, who stares at it:

> The shiny residue on the rice crackers catches the light. Disgusting. Fat shines, fat is glossy and slippery and velvety on the tongue. Of course she can't eat it.
>
> Her lips are slick with spit as she contemplates it. Her stomach heaves. Aurora panics...
>
> With two fingers she breaks a corner off one of the crackers, a tiny, tiny corner, shakes the crumbs off vigorously, tries to scrape the shine of the margarine off with a fingernail. The minuscule scrap of food sits on her tongue, her mouth fills with saliva, but even as she tries to swallow, there is an invisible barricade in her throat, and it comes back up again. She spits it out. "It's covered in grease!" she squeals, wiping her slick lips with her sleeve. "It's filthy!" (141)

The anorexic takes the clean and proper rules to extremes. Fat is, according to Western healthy eating discourse, bad for us, but to Aurora it is "filthy," and abject. It is prevented from entering her body by a barricade, her mind's method of defense against her body's appetite. Leslie, too, articulates the duality of her thinking about her body when she explains that she no longer wants "the food in me even for a few minutes. I can't any more" (*Second Star*, 63). It is as if the anorexic wants to transcend the body altogether. The original intention may have been to diet, to get thin, and to achieve social acceptance, but their denial of appetite eventually leads to a denial of the material needs of the body, to disembodiment. Thus, the anorexic appears to take the structuralist view, making meaning from discourses related to Cartesian dualism and Christian asceticism, (as Smith suggested), and Puritanism. She pits the integrity and the coherence of the inside against what is outside, and valorizes mind in preference to body. This system, as Maggie Kilgour points out, in which order is maintained by conferring authority and control of a "superior term" over an "inferior" may lead to annihilation of one of the terms.[47] In the case of the anorexic, according the mind authority over the body and denying the latter's needs leads to starvation unto death and the annihilation of both. Attaining human subjectivity involves accepting the body's corporeality, but consigning it to abjection. Undoubtedly, this in itself is a dualistic and psychologically unsettling position.

Bruch reports that many anorexics talk about having "a dictator who dominates me" or, "a little man who objects when I eat." Bruch claims that the little ghost, the dictator, the "other self" is always male (58). Leslie has a dictator inside her, who is, however, of unspecified gender:

The dictator. He/she/it—I've never been sure which—was responsible for my sticking to my regimen...it was as though this person, this dictator, had taken up residence inside me to keep me in line. It wasn't simply that I chose not to eat; I was forbidden to. Even thinking about eating forbidden foods brought punishment..."How dare you," this voice inside me would say. "You greedy pig!" (*Second Star*, 44)

Aurora also has a genderless dictator referred to as the "Dirty Creature" or tapeworm. She "calls up her terrifying powers of self-punishment, unaware that this time she has invoked the big one, the Dirty Creature, the horror head, and it stretches and yawns as it awakens inside her" (*Aurora*, 108). "The tapeworm in [Aurora's] head starts its business again: your knees are fat, your upper arms are soft, you're a beast" (115).

Both authors evoke notions of cannibalism: Aurora "doesn't know it, but she's shrinking on the inside as well. When there's no fat left to burn, the Dirty Creature will start to select from her hidden organs. So secretly, silently, she begins to consume herself, to disappear into herself, into nothing" (*Aurora*, 180). Leslie, too, feels her stomach "eating itself, chewing at itself, burning itself" (*Second Star*, 77). The anorexic's cannibalism connotes her alienation from society, her position as non-subject. She reduces her physical presence, makes herself smaller until she begins to disappear into no-thing, no-body.

In many respects, the anorexic seems to be pathologically aware of her body but also, paradoxically, alienated from it. Although Aurora checks herself "at least two hundred times a day" (65) she "has no idea what she looks like any more...her weight on the scales is the only reflection she can understand" (66). "Although [she] knows she is thin, she only knows it in some parts of her head. When strangers look at her it is always because she is fat" (185). Leslie, too, loses all perspective in relation to her body image: "All the thin people I used to wish I looked like weigh at least twenty-five pounds more than I do—and still they're thinner. I don't understand" (*Second Star*, 82).

The sense of alienation from the body, or disembodiment, is apparent in these narratives, which reinforces the notion of the separation and dualism of the mind and body. Both characters' sense of being a body, some-body, seems weak. They feel a need to reduce and transcend the physical self, to do away with or deny the body's material needs, to exist in terms of mind-as-self, without taking in nourishment to feed the body-as-self.

The anorexic's desire to be thin is an exaggerated expression of Western culture's morbid fear of being fat. This in turn stems from a lack of tolerance toward a naturally diverse range of body shapes and sizes. The media constantly presents a barrage of idealized images of slim glamorous women. That women *should* take care of themselves, watch what they eat, dress fashionably, tone, tan, bleach, wax, pluck, paint, exfoliate, moisturize, curl, and straighten (among other things) in a relentless quest to transform their bodies' surfaces, becomes not only culturally (and commercially) acceptable but expected. Even elective cosmetic surgery is moving out of the domain of the "secretively deviant" and "becoming the norm" (Morgan, 28). McKinley reports that weight dissatisfaction is so common among women (in the West) that it is called "normative" (106). Dieting behavior is thus normalized. Confronted by an advertisement with "a headless bikini girl" (who looks about the same age as her) holding a bottle of "Superslim," Aurora notes that "Everyone's on a diet . . . It's a social thing, really. Everybody does it" (*Aurora*, 5). Limiting the range of foods consumed so that fatty foods are avoided, and reducing the amount of food eaten, are culturally considered to be healthy strategies. Taking care of oneself explicitly involves controlling one's appetite. The anorexic takes these precepts to dangerous extremes, transgressively refusing to consume normally, refusing to maintain a proper body, and defiantly rejecting the imperative to embody culture.

HOW-TO-STARVE MANUALS

The big question that immediately arises, is, what effects do narratives such as Hautzig's and Barnes's have on their readers? I suspect that a novel focusing on anorexia may not affect girls who have positive body images in quite the same way as it might affect those girls who exhibit body dissatisfaction, or who have existing eating disorders. The latter groups may use books like these as how-to-starve manuals.[48] Bruch reports that a number of her anorexic patients claimed to have discovered "how to purge or starve from the innumerable books and television programs on bulimia and anorexia" (Bruch, 24). Hautzig's novel, for example, gives explicit details of Leslie's diet and exercise regime (which also reveals the obsessive nature of her mind-set): She starts off doing 45 sit-ups a day, and "gradually upped the numbers by nines, till I was doing 675 . . . nine was my magic number" (*Second Star*, 42). Leslie becomes bulimic when, following a moment of weakness, she consumes a forbidden marzipan strawberry and becomes "panic-stricken" (45) until she realizes that she can get rid of it by making herself vomit. "At first I pulled [my finger out of my mouth] as soon as I began gagging, but the dictator hammered at me: 'This simply won't do, Hiller. Leave it in, jerk, how do you expect it to work otherwise?' And out came the marzipan, not tasting a whole lot different from the way it had on the way in" (46). Leslie felt as though she'd "stumbled upon a miracle…this is the answer. This is like magic! I've undone it—removed the stain, erased the marzipan mistake…Double your pleasure, double your fun…Now I can be a good girl again…Have my cake and eat it, too" (47).

In my opinion girls who are highly dissatisfied with their bodies may interpret the image of a committed strong-willed heroine and her determination to refuse food, tolerate punishing exercise routines, and overcome physical discomfort and even pain, as something worth emulating. The protagonists in both novels are seen to achieve success and to receive the accolade of their peers for their successful dieting behavior. The irony of the "hushed tones of respect" used by Aurora's peers to comment upon what a "nice figure" she has (*Aurora,* 100) and their looks of "stunned admiration" (101), when she has in fact been starving herself for weeks, may be lost on girls who desire social acceptance from their own peers. Arguably then, this literature may contribute to the prevalence of eating disorders among young women and girls.

A series of *Gossip Girl* novels by Cecily von Ziegesar has recently appeared in stores. These stories feature a group of girls from New York City who live a pampered lifestyle and whose concerns revolve around fashion, friendships, and boys. Bulimia is framed as just part of the lifestyle:

> Fudge-frosted brownies on little white plates sat temptingly on a shelf at eye-level. [Blair] picked one up, examined it for any defects, and then put it on her tray. Even if she actually decided to eat it, she could always throw it up later.
>
> It wasn't much, but at least she had *that* much control over her life.[49]

For girls who are unhappy about their body image, this normalization of a symptom of a psychiatric illness is surely dangerous. This narrative privileges disordered eating as an expression of control and offers bulimia as a sort of twisted recompense for disappointment. This strategy involves taking comfort or refuge in sweet food but without the guilt. This novel contains repeated references to being thin, not just as an ideal but as an imperative: "[t]he way to any girl's heart is to tell her she looks tiny. Girls kill to be tiny" (*Gossip Girl,* 114). The problem is that some girls kill themselves in the quest to be tiny.

In her review on Amazon.com "Rosan" refers to the novels as "highly addictive high-society fluff," while "E. Northrop" claims that the book in the series that she read was "the equivalent of eating McDonald's—tasty but really bad for you, including the guilt of having indulged."[50] These remarks are revealing. Like many other series books for children, the

Gossip Girl novels have little real substance; they are, like *Goosebumps* books and many carnivalesque-grotesque series books, considered by adults to be the junk food of children's literature. They are appealing to readers because they are in one way or another transgressive. This (licensed) transgression, as I suggested with reference to grotesque style books, can produce jouissance. The blurb on the back of the second novel in the *Gossip Girl* series refers to the book as "a nasty, guilty pleasure" and to the series as "addictive." In line with Kenway and Bullen's comments about consumer culture quoted previously, I suggest that the *Gossip Girl* books produce a surge of affect but that their very triviality encourages passive and unreflexive consumption rather than interpretative thinking. Thus, the style and format of these books works to increase their appeal to the age group who are most vulnerable to discourses that privilege thinness as a Western cultural ideal. That they also promote bulimia as a normalized strategy to achieve this ideal must be harmful.

COUNTERING DISCOURSE

As previously mentioned, Clark's *No Fat Chicks* proffers little in the way of tactics to counter misogynist cultural discourses. Barnes's *Killing Aurora* is unusual in that it features two protagonists who triumph over patriarchal culture in their own idiosyncratic and politicized way. While Aurora internalizes the ideological forces that confine her and consumes herself with transgressive extremes of self-control, her friend Web attempts to expunge their pressures through transgressive (and illegal) behavior, which involves, among other things, neutralizing offensive graffiti (*Aurora*, 191). She considers the image of "a three-metre cock with testicles the size of basketballs" spray-painted across a warehouse wall. "From the tip sprays enough cum to drown all the good people of Richmond." It's an image she's seen before, "It's everywhere" (189). This image is significantly "like wallpaper." In other words, as part of an ideological discourse, it is so prevalent, so everyday, so natural that nobody sees it anymore, nobody thinks about it. Web does think about it, however, and decides to "inform herself, to make an effort to look at this scientifically, like a semiotician. What does it mean?" (189). She decides that, "It's not friendly. It's not welcoming. It's not erotic. It's not playful" (189). She agrees with Aurora that the image is "vulgar" but adds that it's also "stupid and misinformed." Web "draws a huge vagina" "at the end of the painted cock" complete with "a prominent clitoris," "squiggly, goatish pubic hair" and "a row of pointed [teeth] around the outside, some pointing in, some pointing out" (190). She "rationalizes" what she's done, the difference she's made to the image. The "big hairy penis, with the bigger, *dentate* vulva either laying in wait for it, or chasing it, depending on how you looked at it" (190, italics in original) is no less of an "affront" but it is now "definitely more outrageous." The difference is, she concludes, that even the people who drew the graffiti cock "would loathe it now. Even they would be appalled. Especially they, she likes to think" (191). Web rewrites the world, not through censorship but by creating a proliferation of images and it is thus that she wrests power from her oppressors with her oppressive counter-graffiti. She has agency, having taken control from those who would deny her. Web drags Aurora around with her, starving, weak, lethargic, and "placid as a milking cow" (191), as she subverts the controlling discursive narratives represented by the intimidating graffiti cock and the headless bikini girl.

By spending time with Web instead of being confined to a solipsistic state, Aurora breaks one of her most fundamental self-imposed rules and it feels "just the tiniest bit good" (191). She begins to realize that "maybe she is not the most crucial thing in the world" (216–17) after all. Aurora's subsequent development of agency and a confident subjectivity involves the destruction by fire of the house she has been forced to share with her mother and sleazy stepfather, a domestic space that has never been home. Aurora now has the power to ignore the voice of the "tapeworm." Hospitalized and fed through a tube, she begins to gain weight, to feel more substantial, and, as she does so, her world expands. "If she keeps eating" she believes, "she won't blow away" (219). Her pathological thinking is reversed. Now she believes her body's mass will make her some-body. Aurora refuses to return to live with her mother and stepfather and instead goes to live with an aunt. She becomes a cigarette smoking, chocolate-scoffing, "plump Goth girl" with dirty fingernails (220). She is a new person, a real person, "not merely a healthy, augmented version of the sick Aurora" but "someone else, sprung fully formed from sick Aurora's bones" (221). This Aurora has breasts that squeeze out above her low-cut top, "while her midriff rolls out below" (222). Neither her "brand-new buxom body" (224), nor her revisioning as a Goth, fits closely with the cultural ideal. But Aurora's thoughts and actions, including her consumption of cigarettes and chocolate, are deliberate and conscious. Although her new image is culturally transgressive (though nowhere near as transgressive as her previously skeletal appearance), her transgression is productive and produces agency. Aurora is aware that she cannot escape from the context of ideological inscription, but because she is informed she can resist it, and "laugh" (204) at the way her new body defies its instruction.

It is notable that the number of male anorexics is still relatively small. In children's stories, boys who refuse food are rare. One example is "The Slow-Eater-Tiny-Bite-Taker," a short story from Betty MacDonald's *Mrs*

Piggy-Wiggle, published in 1947. According to J. Ellen Gainor, Mac-Donald's story blends details from her personal observations of children with her knowledge of a child whose parents were divorcing, who stayed with her sister for a time.[51] Briefly, following Gainor, this story concerns a child who is infantilized by his mother while his father plays a harsh disciplinary role. With no control over his own life or identity Allen starts to control his food intake. Mrs. Piggy-Wiggle, MacDonald's wise woman figure, instructs Allen's mother to feed him using increasingly diminutive dishes. The smaller the place setting, the smaller the individual seems psychologically and emotionally, Gainor suggests. At the same time, Allen's physical size in relation to the tiny dishes makes him appear gigantic. This forces his mother to realize how she has infantilized him and she begins to treat him as someone more mature and responsible. Allen is also given the responsibility of feeding and caring for a pony. He is so physically weak, though, that he is unable to do so without asking for help. Thus, he realizes the repercussions of refusing to eat properly. Allen's recovery and maturation are symbolized by a reversal of the order of the dishes. Gainor points out that this story has an easy resolution but it does recognize familial difficulties and tensions experienced by the maturing child. She equates the story with "mild cases [of anorexia] with spontaneous recovery" (Gainor, 40).

Anorexia seems to be considered an acceptable topic for young readers. Obese children, on the other hand, are rarely featured in contemporary children's literature and are unlikely to be explicitly condemned as they often are in the classics. J. K. Rowling's Dudley Dursley, cousin to Harry Potter, proves to be an unusual exception. It is significant, however, that Dahl's *Charlie and the Chocolate Factory* continues to be very popular, in book and movie format. Dahl's virulence toward the obese child reflects cultural discourses that condemn the obese child's out-of-control appetite. Popular wisdom reflects Dahl's view that the effects of consumer-media culture are deleterious, and that parents, especially mothers, should limit their children's consumption. Obesity in children, especially, is seen to be primarily a problem of lack of restraint, and a failure to achieve proper subjectivity. The solution is to reinstate and strengthen (patriarchal) control.[52]

Neither the obese nor the anorexic is properly controlled and both defy proper cultural embodiment. As I have mentioned, "control" is a key word in Western cultural discourses about healthy eating and appropriate embodiment, and these ideals are related ultimately to Puritanical notions of morality. While the anorexic's disembodiment reflects, perhaps, her desire to transcend the flesh and escape the prerogatives of cultural discourses, it is seen to be transgressively overzealous. Her refusal of food may be read as a rejection of ideological femininity and its subjected social role. She rejects the phallus (the implicit symbol of her subjugation) as her proper object of desire, by refusing to embody the feminine ideal.[53] Her behavior and her skeletal body are culturally regarded as deviant.

What is particularly evident in narratives about the anorexic body, and the body in structuralist discourses in general, is the tendency to emphasize the disconnection between the mind and the material body. In Western culture, the individual's material body is, in a way, displaced in consciousness by the notion of a body image, that is formed in homage to media representations. The material body and its appetites continue to be thought of as antithetical to the quest to achieve idealized beauty. Eating disorders, then, cannot be explained in terms of individual pathology but must be attributed, at least in part, to phallocentric logic.

For young readers, who are "highly susceptible to ideologies"[54] and who are trying to find a "lived narrative" in which they can imagine themselves,[55] novels such as *Killing Aurora,* which manages to articulate at least some of the issues surrounding anorexia and to critique at least some aspects of phallocentric logic, are important and worthy of further study. Hopefully this novel, read thoughtfully, will encourage readers to follow Web's example—to question the obviousness of cultural ideologies and to compete, rather than try to disappear as Aurora initially does. Barnes's novel provides readers with a way of countering the forces that confine young women without self-oppression and starvation. It shows that agency and subjectivity can be achieved by being informed, so that oppressive images and discourses can be rationalized and subverted.

AFTERWORD

CULTURAL RULES ABOUT FOOD AND EATING PRODUCE and perpetuate the basic structural oppositions inside/outside, self/other, good/bad and, significantly, adult/child, and male/female. We are what we eat and those that don't eat like us, including children, are therefore designated "other" to varying degrees. We make choices about food, not only, not even primarily, for reasons of health, but as markers of identity—if we do make an ostensibly "healthy" choice, that also signifies who we are and is emblematic of the values we hold true.

While the Victorian nursery regime restricted children to a meager and bland diet bereft of anything sweet or fat-laden, contemporary corporations market foods for children which, although still bland, are often *high* in sugar, fat and salt, over-processed, and suffused with artificial additives. They design, manufacture, and market "junk" foods (and other consumer-media goods) to children, regardless of the health of the child's body and/or mind, knowing that to many adults such foods are anathema. Concern about the fatty foods causing the obesity "epidemic" is perhaps equivalent to the food scares caused by salmonella and BSE (Bovine Spongiform Encephalopathy) in the United Kingdom in the 1980s: fast or junk foods are seen as over-processed, unnatural, and literally poisonous. Individualist political discourses and the quest for profit have produced the current crop of neophobic, obese, and largely sedentary children (and adults).

With their minds and bodies shaped by commercial interests, children have also become commodities. Middle-class Western children (at least) are being churned out on a global production line so that they

211

are all constituted in the same way, with the same food, the same books, the same toys, the same clothes, the same movies and video games, the same music, the same sports, the same after-school activities, the same political policies governing the same educational philosophies in their schools. Desperate parents are striving to structure their children's every waking moment, to direct every aspect of their lives, and to purchase all the goods and services supposedly required to produce multi-skilled children fully-equipped to become successful adults. Successful adults, of course, are defined by their ability to consume, their identities signaled by the material goods they own.

I have said that the cultural imperative to eat correctly is a means by which society controls individual identity. In recent decades the imperative to consume, not just the right food, but also the right (quantity and brand of) goods and services, has come to signify identity. It is commercially advantageous for society to encourage a homogenized culture with the same aspirations and desires. To fulfill this goal the middle class must grow, the other must be marginalized, and unreflexive acceptance of consumer-media culture must be encouraged.

This is indeed a bleak outlook. It is important for their good health that we feed all our children a diet that includes a wide variety of foods and that we encourage them to accept and enjoy a range of flavors. Individual health and the health of society depend upon acceptance of the notion that neither are autonomous entities but rather rely upon the incorporation of various and diverse elements from outside in order to survive. Defining everything outside as "bad," as the anorexic perhaps does, can lead to starvation. A poor diet produces a limited intellect.

Despite cultural rules, when we actually think carefully about the physical process of eating we can see that it breaks down monolithic structuralisms—what was outside and other becomes inside and self—and we literally become what we eat. The process of writing similarly involves the consumption of material, ideas and words from outside, digesting and re-constructing them. By paying special attention to all sorts of food narratives we can see that, for example, food choices are ruled by culture and are largely arbitrary. Similarly, the inside/outside dualism applied to the body is impossible, and the boundary between self and other is revealed to be of our own making. Children's literature also proves to be "impossible" as Rose (1984) has argued. Children's literature consumes aspects of culture, but does not reflect life; that is, it is not true to life. It regurgitates culture and serves it up to children in a heavily mediated form.

Food events within children's literature seduce child readers and add flavor and spice to the narrative. They lend aspects of materiality to the text so that mediation is unsuspected. Ultimately, however, as far as their intended audience is concerned, tales about eating or being eaten usually legitimate and bolster cultural rules and misogyny. It is noticeable that lavish fantasy feasts tend not to appear in the most recent fiction for children. High tea and picnics belong perhaps with the cluster of values that romanticize childhood. Food in the West is plentiful and child readers' desires are no longer shaped by deprivation. They don't long for anything because they have everything in abundance.

When food events are featured in contemporary stories for children they are often problematic and, significantly, not intended to produce pleasure for protagonist or reader. Food has become an abject object in contemporary culture. On the one hand what we might term "prestige" food, prepared by celebrity chefs or featured in glossy magazines, is fetishized. On the other hand, everyday food is the enemy and its intake is pathologically monitored. Living standards in the West are generally high. There is plenty of food available to sustain us, but we are never satisfied. When we tell our children stories, which are ultimately about ourselves, these are the values that we feed to them.

NOTES

Introduction

1. C. S. Lewis, *The Lion, the Witch and the Wardrobe* (1950, rpt., London: Collins, 1990), 41–42; hereafter cited in text as *Lion*.
2. Lynne Vallone, "'What is the Meaning of all this Gluttony?': Edgeworth, The Victorians, C. S. Lewis and a Taste for Fantasy," in *Papers: Explorations into Children's Literature* 12, no. 1 (2002): 47.
3. Barbara Creed, *The Monstrous-Feminine: Film, Feminism, Psychoanalysis* (London: Routledge, 1993), 107.
4. Mervyn Nicholson, "Food and Power: Homer, Carroll, Atwood and Others," in *Mosaic* 20, no. 3 (1987): 38.
5. Louis Althusser, "Ideology and Ideological State Apparatuses," trans. Ben Brewster, 1965, rpt., *Critical Theory Since 1965*, eds. Hazard Adams and Leroy Searle (Tallahassee: University Presses of Florida and Florida State, 1986), 245.
6. Peter Hunt, *Understanding Children's Literature* (London: Routledge, 1999), 1; hereafter cited in text.
7. Jacqueline Rose, *The Case of Peter Pan or The Impossibility of Children's Fiction* (1984, rpt., London: Macmillan, 1992), 2.
8. Norman Lindsay, *The Magic Pudding* (1918, rpt., Sydney: HarperCollins, 2000), 18; hereafter cited in text as *Magic Pudding*.
9. Sigmund Freud, "Negation," 1925, rpt., *The Freud Reader*, ed. Peter Gay (New York: Norton & Co., 1989), 668.
10. Maggie Kilgour, *From Communion to Cannibalism: An Anatomy of Metaphors of Incorporation* (Princeton. NJ: Princeton University Press, 1990), 4.
11. Susan Bordo, "Anorexia Nervosa: Psychopathology as the Crystalization of Culture," *Cooking, Eating, Thinking: Transformative Philosophies of Food*, eds. Deane W. Curtin and Lisa M. Heldke (Bloomington: Indiana University Press, 1992), 34–35.
12. See John L. Smith, *The Psychology of Food and Eating: A Fresh Approach to Theory and Method* (Basingstoke: Palgrave, 2002), 83.

13. Elizabeth Grosz, *Volatile Bodies: Toward a Corporeal Feminism* (Sydney: Allen & Unwin, 1994), 21.

14. Elspeth Probyn, *Carnal Appetites: FoodSexIdentities* (London: Routledge, 2000), 3.

15. See Wendy R. Katz, "Some Uses of Food in Children's Literature," in *Children's Literature in Education*, 11, no. 4 (1980): 192; Perry Nodelman, *The Pleasures of Children's Literature* (New York: Longman, 1996), 196; and Maria Nikolajeva, *From Mythic to Linear: Time in Children's Literature* (Lanham, MD: Scarecrow Press, 2000), 11.

16. Mem Fox, *Possum Magic* (1983, rpt., Adelaide: Omnibus, 1987), 12; hereafter cited in text as *Possum Magic*.

17. Michel Foucault, *Power/Knowledge: Selected Interviews and Other Writings (1972–1977)*, trans. Colin Gordon, Leo Marshall, John Mepham, and Kate Soper, ed. Colin Gordon (Brighton: The Harvester Press, 1980), 98.

18. Judith Butler, *Gender Trouble: Feminism and the Subversion of Identity* (1990, rpt., New York: Routledge, 1999), 71.

19. Michel Foucault, *Discipline and Punish: The Birth of the Prison*, trans. Alan Sheridan (New York: Vintage, 1979), 30.

20. See Nick Mansfield, *Subjectivity: Theories of Self from Freud to Haraway* (St Leonards, Australia: Allen & Unwin, 2000), 39 and 43.

21. E. B. White, *Charlotte's Web* (1952, rpt., London: Macmillan, 1983).

22. See Nancy Chodorow, *The Reproduction of Mothering* (Berkeley: University of California Press, 1978), 57; Janice Doane and Devon Hodges, *From Klein to Kristeva: Psychoanalytic Feminism and the Search for the "Good Enough" Mother* (Ann Arbor: University of Michigan, 1992), 12; and Sarah Sceats, *Food, Consumption and the Body in Contemporary Women's Fiction* (Cambridge: Cambridge University Press, 2000), 5.

23. Peter Hunt, "'Coldtonguecoldhamcoldbeefpickledgherkinssaladfrenchrollscresssandwidgespottedmeatgingerbeerlemonadesodawater....' Fantastic Food in the books of Kenneth Grahame, Jerome K. Jerome, H. E. Bates and Other Bakers of the Fantasy England," in *Journal of the Fantastic in the Arts* 7, no. 1 (1996): 25, 9.

24. Mikhail Bakhtin, *Rabelais and His World*, trans. Helene Iswolsky, (1965, rpt., Bloomington: Indiana University Press, 1984); hereafter cited in text.

25. John Stephens, *Language and Ideology in Children's Fiction*, (London: Longman, 1992); hereafter cited in text.

26. Cited by Elizabeth Grosz, *Sexual Subversions: Three French Feminists*, (Sydney: Allen & Unwin, 1989), 71; hereafter cited in text.

27. See Margaret Visser, *Much Depends on Dinner: The Extraordinary History and Mythology, Allure and Obsessions, Perils and Taboos of an Ordinary Meal*, (New York: Macmillan, 1986), 121 and William Miller, *The Anatomy of Disgust*, (Cambridge, MA: Harvard University Press, 1997), 117.

Chapter 1

1. Jean Anthelme Brillat-Savarin, *The Physiology of Taste, or Meditations on Transcendental Gastronomy* (1825, rpt., New York: Dover Publications, 1960), 3.

2. Lewis Carroll, *Alice's Adventures in Wonderland and Through the Looking Glass* (1865, rpt., London: Oxford University Press, 1971), 79; hereafter cited in text as *Alice*.

3. Joyce Carol Oates, "Afterword: Reflections on the Grotesque," in *Haunted: Tales of the Grotesque* (New York: Dutton, 1994), 307.

4. Peter Farb and George Armelagos, *Consuming Passions: The Anthropology of Eating* (Boston: Houghton Mifflin, 1980), 3–4, hereafter cited in text.

5. Elizabeth Grosz, *Sexual Subversions: Three French Feminists* (Sydney: Allen & Unwin, 1989), 74–75; hereafter cited in text.

6. Paul Rozin, "Sociocultural Influences on Human Food Selection," in *Why We Eat What We*

Eat: The Psychology of Eating, ed. Elizabeth D. Capaldi (Washington, DC: The American Psychological Association, 1996), 247; hereafter cited in text.

7. Julia Kristeva, *Powers of Horror: An Essay on Abjection*, trans. Leon S. Roudiez (New York: Columbia University Press, 1989); hereafter cited in text.

8. Sidney Mintz, "Eating and Being: What Food Means," in *Food: Multidisciplinary Perspectives*, eds. Barbara Harriss-White and Sir Raymond Hoffenberg (Oxford: Blackwell, 1994), 104.

9. Anthony Horowitz, *Stormbreaker* (London: Walker Books, 2000), 123; hereafter cited in text as *Stormbreaker*.

10. Orientalized/orientalism refers to Edward Said's notion of the way the oriental is constructed as exotic and other, through hegemonic Western discourses of knowledge which represent, translate, contain, and manage the intransigence and incomprehensibility of the racial other. (L. Gandhi, *Postcolonial Theory: A Critical Introduction* (St. Leonards, Australia: Allen & Unwin, 1998), 142–43.)

11. Philip Pullman, *The Subtle Knife* (London: Scholastic, 1998), 8; hereafter cited in text as *Subtle Knife*.

12. Elspeth Probyn, *Carnal Appetites: FoodSexIdentities* (London: Routledge, 2000), 2; hereafter cited in text.

13. J. K. Rowling, *Harry Potter and the Goblet of Fire* (London: Bloomsbury, 2000), 221, original emphasis.

14. Carolyn Daniel, *All That Glitters is Not Gold* (unpublished Honors dissertation, Melbourne: Victoria University of Technology, 2000).

15. C. S. Lewis, *The Horse and His Boy* (1954, rpt., London: Collins, 1990); hereafter cited in text as *Horse and His Boy*.

16. Lynne Vallone, "What is the Meaning of all this Gluttony?": Edgeworth, The Victorians, C. S. Lewis and a Taste for Fantasy," in *Papers: Explorations into Children's Literature* 12, no.1(2002): 51.

17. E. B. White, *Charlotte's Web* (1952, rpt., London: Macmillan, 1983); hereafter cited in text as *Charlotte's Web*.

18. Margaret Visser, *The Rituals of Dinner: The Origins, Evolution, Eccentricities, and Meaning of Table Manners* (London: Penguin, 1993), 299; hereafter cited in text.

19. William Miller, *The Anatomy of Disgust* (Cambridge, MA: Harvard University Press, 1997), 2.

20. Margaret Visser, *Much Depends on Dinner: The Extraordinary History and Mythology, Allure and Obsessions, Perils and Taboos of an Ordinary Meal* (New York: Macmillan, 1986), 121.

21. Note also the Darwinian resonances. Carroll's work was published six years after Darwin's *Origin of the Species* (1859). The classification of little girls as serpents has a well-documented theological history. (Juliet Dusinberre, *Alice to the Lighthouse: Children's Books and Radical Experiments in Art* (Basingstoke: Macmillan, 1987), 8.)

22. The third book in Horowitz's series about Alex Rider involves an encounter between Alex and a mad Russian general who intends to wipe out most of Northern Europe and north Russia with a nuclear explosion. Curiously, this man prefers to eat his food raw, including eggs. He is therefore clearly placed outside culture in terms of Lévi-Strauss's theory. Ironically he echoes Lévi-Strauss's premise: "Man is the only creature on the planet that needs to have his meat and vegetables burned or broiled [grilled] before he can consume them." The general thus separates *himself* from the majority of humankind, and aligns himself with the primitive/animal/object as opposed to human culture. (Anthony Horowitz, *Skeleton Key* (London: Walker Books, 2002), 221–22.)

23. Peter Hunt, *An Introduction to Children's Literature* (Oxford: Opus/Oxford University Press, 1994), 167.

24. Using this premise and an exemplary insight into that which horrifies, Alfred Hitchcock evokes the disgust reaction in the movie *To Catch a Thief* when Mrs. Stevens deliberately

contaminates edible food by stubbing out her cigarette in a fried egg (cited by Visser 1993, 306). Again this premise is used in an article in *Vogue* (1999), which refers to a "new" diet that entails "spoiling food." The idea is to "douse whatever you like to eat in massive amounts of Tabasco, thus ensuring you won't be tempted. Another clever trick is to put your cigarette out in your half-eaten dessert, putting an end to picking" (cited by Probyn, 24). In relation to the *Vogue* article, such practices surely solicit the question just who is in control, the eater or the eaten?

25. Madhur Jaffrey explains that as a child growing up in Delhi, sharing food was taboo. "Even in my family," she reports, "where we were quite liberal, I never took a sip from my sister's glass or a bite from her apple. At least not without my mother's disapproval. Any food eaten by someone else was considered 'unclean' or *jhoota*." (Madhur Jaffrey, *A Taste of India* (1985, rpt., London: Pavilion Books, 2001), 12.)

26. Lucy Rollin points out that young children may not think Templeton so unattractive as adults do. Speaking psychoanalytically, Rollin claims that Wilbur remains generally in the oral stage, while Templeton with his hoarding and gorging is a much more anal character. Young children are chronologically and psychologically much closer to their own anality than most adults, and are therefore, Rollin reasons, less likely to find Templeton's behavior unattractive. (Lucy Rollin, "The Reproduction of Mothering in *Charlotte's Web*," in *Children's Literature*, 18, 1990, 52 n. 4; hereafter cited in text.)

27. He carries Charlotte's egg sac using his mouth like a surrogate womb (*Charlotte's Web*, 163).

28. Frances Hodgson Burnett, *The Secret Garden* (1911, rpt., London: Heinemann, 1975); hereafter cited in text as *Secret Garden*.

29. Julia Briggs, "Transitions: 1890–1914," in *Children's Literature: An Illustrated History*, ed. Peter Hunt (Oxford: Oxford University Press, 1995), 167.

30. It is significant that the narrator earlier refers to Mary as a "little pig" (*Secret Garden*, 1).

31. Phyllis Bixler, *Frances Hodgson Burnett* (Boston, MA: Twayne, 1984), 17, 75.

32. Gillian Avery points out that the food items described in *The Secret Garden* betray Burnett's American background. In reality English children would have been fed on nursery fare such as bread and milk. "Ham and eggs being thought indigestible, butter and cream too rich, [and] raspberry jam debilitating to the character." (Gillian Avery, *Behold the Child: American Children and Their Books (1621–1922)* (London: Bodley Head, 1994), 158; hereafter cited in text.)

33. It might be supposed that the natural foods the children eat disrupt the nature/culture raw/cooked opposition referred to earlier. However, it is interesting to note that prior to the late nineteenth century nature was equated with purity and culture was seen to be essentially corrupting. The more elaborate, luxurious, and less natural the food, the more it was seen to be unsuitable for children. As the century progressed and man was increasingly seen to control and subjugate nature, attitudes shifted. (Valerie Mars, "Parsimony Amid Plenty: Views from Victorian Didactic Works on Food for Nursery Children," in *Food, Culture and History, Vol. 1*, eds. G. Mars and V. Mars (London: The London Food Seminar, 1993), 152.)

34. Roderick McGillis argues that the "Magic" in *The Secret Garden* signifies the spiritual power of the Christian God. (Roderick McGillis, *A Little Princess: Gender and Empire* (New York: Twayne, 1996), 22.)

35. Maggie Kilgour, *From Communion to Cannibalism: An Anatomy of Metaphors of Incorporation* (Princeton, NJ: Princeton University Press, 1990), 8.

36. Sigmund Freud, 'Three Essays on the Theory of Sexuality,' 1924, rpt. in *The Freud Reader*, ed. Peter Gay (New York: Norton & Co., 1989).

37. Ann Rosalind Jones, "Writing the Body: Toward an Understanding of L'Ecriture Feminine," in *The New Feminist Criticism: Essays on Women, Literature and Theory*, ed. Elaine Showalter (London: Virago Press, 1986), 375.

38. Peter Singer, *Animal Liberation* (1976, rpt., London: Cape, 1990).

39. Rollin points out that the only adult who does allow the possibility of animal speech is Dr. Dorian and he does so from the perspective of the power of the imagination (Rollin, 47). In other words, he sees talking animals only as part of Fern's fantasy; a fantasy that she must soon, in terms of the narrative discourse, leave behind.

40. C. S. Lewis, *The Silver Chair* (1953, rpt., London: Collins, 1990), 104–105.

41. Marina Warner, *No Go the Bogeyman: Scaring, Lulling and Making Mock* (London: Vintage, 2000), 142, 154; hereafter cited in text.

42. Note the pun on adult manners. To cut may also mean to hurt the feelings of a person or to pretend not to recognize someone.

43. In Carroll's fantasy the food items, including the pudding, refuse to be eaten. Carroll's pudding is quite different to Lindsay's Puddin', discussed in the Introduction, who is perhaps more pragmatic about his function and appears to enjoy being consumed.

44. Douglas Adams, *The Restaurant at the End of the Universe* (London: Pan, 1980), 89; hereafter cited in text as *Restaurant*.

45. In Fay Weldon's novel for adults, a married couple on a diet lie in bed, hungry, talking about their favorite food. Alan suggests hare soup "with fresh rolls and lots of butter. And then roast duck with roast potatoes and green peas. Followed by apple pie and cheese and biscuits. A Brie, I think, just at the right point of squishiness, with that slight and marvelous taste of something on the verge of going bad. Something you can suspect of being rotten, but you know you're allowed to eat." (Fay Weldon, *The Fat Woman's Joke* (1984, rpt., Chicago, Ill: Academy, 1995), 93.)

46. In a similar fashion, (in an episode of their cooking program) the *Two Fat Ladies*, Clarissa Dickson Wright and the late Jennifer Patterson, "drooled over the young boys from King's College, Cambridge, remarking on the fact that the white ruffles around the singers' necks make them 'look like deliciously edible little lamb chops'" (Probyn, 69). Sarah Blaffer Hrdy suggests that the sheer deliciousness and erotic appeal of a baby's soft, plump flesh may have evolved to help reluctant mothers positively discriminate and choose to nurture rather than abandon an infant. This in itself, she suggests, proves that caring for an infant is *not* instinctual. (Sarah Blaffer Hrdy, *Mother Nature: A History of Mothers, Infants, and Natural Selection* [New York: Pantheon, 1999], 483.) Thus, it may be said that small babies are *naturally* scrumptious.

47. Rosalind Coward, *Female Desire: Women's Sexuality Today* (London: Paladin, 1984), 87; hereafter cited in text.

48. Otto Fenichel argues that the idea of being eaten is not only a source of fear, but under certain circumstances may also be a source of oral pleasure. (Otto Fenichel, *The Psychoanalytic Theory of Neurosis* (1946, rpt., London: Routledge & Kegan Paul, 1966), 64.) Sarah Sceats claims that "benign or idealistic cannibalism" is evident in passionate lovers' fantasies and in visceral responses to babies. (Sarah Sceats, *Food, Consumption and the Body in Contemporary Women's Fiction* (Cambridge: Cambridge University Press, 2000), 35.) Ironically, and somewhat perversely, there are Web sites devoted to adult 'cannibal' fantasies—both those who want to eat and those that want to be eaten. These sites primarily provide information and images of consensual role-play for sexual gratification. One site, referred to as "Muki's Kitchen" apparently features photographs of female models trussed up in pans, with various orifices stuffed with fruit or vegetables. Katherine Gates, writer of deviantdesires.com argues that such fantasies may have their origins in the fetishist's exposure to children's literature or in the child's older female relatives' habit of saying things like "Oh, you're so cute, I could just gobble you up!" (http://www.deviantdesires.com/kink/cannibal/cannibal.html)

49. P. L. Travers, *Mary Poppins* (1934, rpt., London: Collins, 1978), 151.

Chapter Two

1. A. A. Milne, *Now We Are Six* (1927, rpt., London: Methuen, 1980), 66–68, original emphases.

2. Lewis Carroll, *Alice's Adventures in Wonderland* and *Through the Looking-Glass and What Alice Found There* (1865, rpt., London: Oxford University Press, 1971), 80; hereafter cited in text as *Alice*.

3. Wendy Katz, "Some Uses of Food in Children's Literature," in *Children's Literature in Education*, 11, no. 4, 1980: 3.

4. See Jack Zipes, *Fairy Tales and the Art of Subversion: The Classical Genre for Children and the Process of Civilization* (1983, rpt., New York: Routledge, 1991); hereafter cited in text.

5. Norbert Elias, *The Civilizing Process: The History of Manners*, trans. Edmund Jephcott (1939, rpt. Oxford: Basil Blackwell, 1978).

6. Maria Tatar, *Off With Their Heads! Fairy Tales and the Culture of Childhood* (Princeton, NJ: Princeton University Press, 1992), xvi; hereafter cited in text.

7. Judith Rowbotham, *Good Girls make Good Wives: Guidance for Girls in Victorian Fiction* (Oxford: Basil Blackwell, 1989), 3; hereafter cited in text.

8. Lynne Vallone, *Disciplines of Virtue: Girls' Culture in the Eighteenth and Nineteenth Centuries* (New Haven, CT: Yale University Press, 1995), 5; hereafter cited in text.

9. Anna Krugovoy Silver, *Victorian Literature and the Anorexic Body* (Cambridge: Cambridge University Press, 2002), 3; hereafter cited in text.

10. Popular nursery rhymes like this one promote girls' goodness and condemn misbehavior: "There was a little girl/who wore a little hood,/ And a curl down the middle/ of her forehead:/ When she was good,/ she was very, very good,/ But when she was bad,/ she was horrid." (*Mother Goose Nursery Rhymes*, 1922, rpt., no editor/compiler (London: Chancellor Press, 1986), 118; hereafter cited in text.)

11. Margaret Visser, *Rituals of Dinner*, 1–2; hereafter cited in text.

12. Cited by John L. Smith, *The Psychology of Food and Eating: A Fresh Approach to Theory and Method* (Basingstoke: Palgrave, 2002), 6–7; hereafter cited in text.

13. Maria Edgeworth, "Preface," in *The Parent's Assistant*, vol. 1 (1800, rpt., New York: Garland, 1976), xi.

14. John Locke, "Some Thoughts Concerning Education," 1690, rpt., in *Child-Rearing Concepts, 1628–1861: Historical Sources*, ed. Philip J. Greven Jr. (Itasca, IL: Peacock, 1973), 39.

15. Both cited by Robert Crawford, "A Cultural Account of 'Health': Control, Release and the Social Body," in *Issues in the Political Economy of Health Care*, ed. John B. Kinley (New York: Tavistock, 1984), 77.

16. Valerie Mars, "Parsimony Amid Plenty: Views from Victorian Didactic Works on Food for Nursery Children," in *Food, Culture and History*. Vol. 1., eds. G. Mars and V. Mars (London: The London Food Seminar, 1993), 152; hereafter cited in text.

17. Cited by J. C. Drummond and Anne Wilbraham, *The Englishman's Food: Five Centuries of English Diet* (1939, rpt., London: Pimlico, 1991), 340; hereafter cited in text.

18. Maria Edgeworth, "The Birthday Present," in *The Parent's Assistant*, vol. 2, (1800, rpt., New York: Garland, 1976), 4–7.

19. Christina Rossetti, "Speaking Likenesses," 1874, rpt., in *Forbidden Journeys: Fairy Tales and Fantasies by Victorian Women Writers*, eds. Nina Auerbach and U. C. Knoepflmacher (Chicago: University of Chicago Press, 1992), 328; hereafter cited in text as "Speaking Likenesses."

20. The slimy and sticky girls are related to notions of abjection and disgust.

21. As I explained in the last chapter in relation to the gorging habits of Templeton the rat, young children may not think excessive eating so unattractive as adults do.

22. Barbara Creed, *The Monstrous-Feminine: Film, Feminism, Psychoanalysis* (London: Routledge, 1993).

23. Margaret Hallissy, *Venomous Women: Fear of the Female in Literature* (New York: Greenwood, 1987), 15.

24. Jacqueline Rose, *The Case of Peter Pan or The Impossibility of Children's Fiction* (1984, rpt., London: Macmillan, 1992), 2, original emphasis.

25. Nina Auerbach and U. C. Knoepflmacher, *Forbidden Journeys: Fairy Tales and Fantasies by Victorian Women Writers* (Chicago: University of Chicago Press, 1992), 321; hereafter cited in text.

26. Gillian Avery, *Behold the Child: American Children and their Books (1621–1922)* (London: Bodley Head, 1994), 156; hereafter cited in text.

27. Judith Butler, *Gender Trouble: Feminism and the Subversion of Identity* (1990, rpt., New York: Routledge, 1999); hereafter cited in text.

28. Carolyn Sigler, ed., *Alternative Alices: Visions and Revisions of Lewis Carroll's Alice Books: An Anthology* (Lexington: The University Press of Kentucky, 1997), 50.

29. With regard to Alice getting angry and making a space for herself: Marianne Hirsch argues that anger is an expression of subjectivity, "To be angry is to claim a place, to assert a right to expression and discourse." (Marianne Hirsch, "Maternal Anger: Silent Themes and 'Meaningful Digressions' in Psychoanalytic Feminism," in *Minnesota Review* 29, Fall 1987: 82.)

30. The March Hare tells Alice that "It wasn't very civil of [her] to sit down [at the table] without being invited" (*Alice,* 67) and the Hatter rebukes her for making personal remarks (73).

31. Anna Krugovoy Silver points out that treacle, "with its secondary meaning of excessive sentimentality," is a vehicle for Carroll's critique of "the idealized conception of girls as sweet and gentle darlings of the home." Carroll, through Alice's comment and the Dormouse's confirmation, implies that women are restricted by this ideology and that, at least metaphorically, it makes them "*very* ill" (Silver, 72).

32. Edith Lazaros Honig describes Carroll's satirization of the Victorian processes of instruction as a "revolution" in children's literature. (Edith Lazaros Honig, *Breaking the Angelic Image: Woman Power in Victorian Children's Fiction* (New York: Greenwood Press, 1988), 76; hereafter cited in text.)

33. John Stephens, *Language and Ideology in Children's Fiction* (London: Longman, 1992), 121; hereafter cited in text.

34. The caterpillar is, it should be noted, an expert at metamorphosis.

35. Carroll signals the "reality" of this particular cake. Although Alice expects to grow or shrink after eating a little bit of it she is surprised to find that she does neither. "To be sure," the narrator interjects, "this is what generally happens when one eats cake; but Alice had got so much into the way of expecting nothing but out-of-the-way things to happen, that it seemed quite dull and stupid for life to go on in the common way. So she set to work, and very soon finished off the cake" (*Alice* 15). This is therefore not a magic cake but a "common" real cake.

36. It is also very interesting to consider that Carroll/Dodgson was "very abstemious always" and "took nothing in the middle of the day except a glass of wine and a biscuit." He apparently found "his little friends'...healthy appetites" alarming. "When he took a certain one of them out with him to a friend's house to dinner, he used to give the host or hostess a gentle warning, to the mixed amazement and indignation of the child, 'Please be careful, because she eats a good deal too much.'" (Stuart Dodgson Collingwood, "An Old Bachelor," 1971, rpt., *Alice in Wonderland: Lewis Carroll,* ed. Donald J. Gray (New York: Norton, 1992), 316.)

37. Juliet Dusinberre, *Alice to the Lighthouse: Children's Books and Radical Experiments in Art* (1987, rpt., Basingstoke: Macmillan, 1999), 89.

38. Beatrix Potter, *The Complete Tales of Beatrix Potter* (1902–1930, rpt., London: Penguin, 1989), 12; hereafter cited as *Peter Rabbit*.

39. Perry Nodelman, "Making Boys Appear: The Masculinity of Children's Fiction," in *Ways of Being Male: Representing Masculinities in Children's Literature and Film*, ed. John Stephens (New York: Routledge, 2002), 4; hereafter cited in text.

40. Enid Blyton, *The Faraway Tree Stories* (1939–1946, rpt., London: Mammoth, 1994), 544.

41. Dorothy Wall, *The Complete Adventures of Blinky Bill* (1939, rpt., Pymble, NSW: Harper Collins, 1992), 127–132; hereafter cited as *Blinky Bill*.

42. I suggest an alternative reading of Lucy's tea with Mr. Tumnus in chapter 6.

43. C. S. Lewis, *The Lion, the Witch and the Wardrobe* (1950, rpt., London: Collins, 1990), 17–20; hereafter cited in text as *Lion*.

44. Gwen Raverat (1885–1957), a friend and contemporary of Virginia Woolf, remembers that, although obviously from a wealthy family, she was only allowed porridge for breakfast as a child with salt, not sugar. Twice a week she was also allowed: "one piece of toast, spread with that dangerous luxury, Jam. But, of course, not butter too. Butter and Jam on the same bit of bread would have been an unheard-of-indulgence—a disgraceful orgy … there was only bread-and-butter and milk for tea, as Jam might have weakened our moral fibre … sugar was thought to be unwholesome; and fruit, though a pleasant treat, rather dangerous." Raverat is quoted in the body of chapter 3 and reproduced here for convenience. (Gwen Raverat, "Porridge with Salt – No Sugar," 1954, rpt., *The Faber Book of Food*, eds. Claire Clifton and Colin Spencer (London: Faber & Faber, 1993), 20–21.)

45. Mary Douglas, *Implicit Meanings: Selected Essays in Anthropology* (1975, rpt., London: Routledge, 1999), 255.

46. Turkish delight is extremely sweet and not really a "food" at all, being made of sugar, water, gelatin, and flavorings. It is also, as the Rustins point out, a reference to the suspect sensibilities of the East. (Margaret and Michael Rustin, *Narratives of Love and Loss: Studies in Modern Children's Fiction* (London: Verso, 1987), 57.)

47. The Beaver's comments reflect the notion that food is transformative, as I argued in chapter 1. They also echo Charles Kingsley's belief that the body was an image of the soul. Hence, in *The Water Babies* (1863), when Tom transgresses by eating forbidden sweets, he grows prickles all over his body.

48. Donald E. Glover, *C. S. Lewis: The Art of Enchantment* (Athens: Ohio University Press, 1981), 138.

49. Maurice Sendak, *Where the Wild Things Are* (New York: Harper & Row, 1968).

50. Maria Tatar, *Off With Their Heads! Fairy Tales and the Culture of Childhood* (Princeton, NJ: Princeton University Press, 1992), xvi–xvii.

51. Louis Sachar, *There's a Boy in the Girls' Bathroom* (London: Bloomsbury, 2001), 3; hereafter cited in text as *Boy*.

52. The tone in which the moral of Sachar's story is delivered is far more gentle than the "repellent intensity" of the way the moral is thrust home in Christina Rossetti's "Speaking Likenesses." (Gillian Avery, "Fairy Tales with a Purpose," in *Alice in Wonderland: Lewis Carroll*, ed. Donald J. Gray (New York: Norton, 1992), 323.)

53. Elizabeth Parsons, "Construction Sites of Sexual Identity: A reading of Emily Rodda's *Bob the Builder and the Elves*," in *Papers: Explorations into Children's Literature*, 11, no.3 (2001): 32–33; hereafter cited in text.

54. Emily Rodda, *Bob the Builder and the Elves* (Sydney: ABC Books, 1998), 56; hereafter cited in text as *Bob*.

55. In "Making Boys Appear: The Masculinity of Children's Fiction" (2002) Perry Nodelman cites William Pollack who argues that rage/anger is the only emotion that boys are legitimately able to express. Pollack points out that this "boy code" is of course, a cultural construct (in Nodelman, 10). Furthermore, Nodelman suggests that in order to appear desirable males must suggest aggression, strength and danger, but not necessarily behave

accordingly. Paradoxically they must be "domesticated" but look strong and powerful (rather like a pet dog, he adds) (Nodelman, 7–8). Thus, for boys and girls, gender identity is a performance, as Judith Butler suggests, which "produce[s] the effect of an internal core or substance...*on the surface* of the body" (Butler, 136, emphasis in original).

56. Valerie Walkerdine, *Schoolgirl Fictions* (London: Verso, 1990), 127.

57. From the nursery rhyme "What Are Little Boys Made Of?" The version published in *Mother Goose's Nursery Rhymes* in 1922 has "snaps and snails, and puppy-dogs' tails." Girls, of course, are made of "sugar and spice, and all that's nice" (*Mother Goose's Nursery Rhymes*, 206).

58. Significantly, the provision of a hot meal by Max's unseen mother implies all these qualities.

Chapter Three

1. Kenneth Grahame, *The Wind in the Willows* (1908, rpt., London: Methuen, 1989), 13–14.

2. Frank Richards, "The Artful Dodger," in *The Magnet* 1,142: xxxvii, January 4, 1930, p. 15.

3. John Ronald Reuel Tolkein, *The Hobbit* (1937, rpt., London: Harper Collins, 1993), 21–22.

4. Enid Blyton, *The Mountain of Adventure* (1949, rpt., London: Macmillan, 1983), 11.

5. J. K. Rowling, *Harry Potter and the Philosopher's Stone* (London: Bloomsbury, 1997), 92–93; hereafter cited in text as *Philosopher's Stone*.

6. Dirks claims that in Britain, France and Germany famine was experienced in one region or another approximately every couple of years up until the later half of the nineteenth century. (Cited by John L. Smith, *The Psychology of Food and Eating: A Fresh Approach to Theory and Method* (Basingstoke: Palgrave, 2002), 17.)

7. Jack Zipes, *The Complete Fairy Tales of the Brothers Grimm* (1987, rpt., New York: Bantam Books, 1992), 376; hereafter cited in text as *Grimm Tales*.

8. J. C. Drummond and Anne Wilbraham, *The Englishman's Food: Five Centuries of English Diet* (1939, rpt., London: Pimlico, 1991), 87; hereafter cited in text.

9. It is not until later versions that the house is made of gingerbread. *The Oxford English Dictionary* gives the fifteenth century as the earliest common use of the word "gingerbread." Sugar was originally brought to Europe as part of the spice trade. In medieval Europe the crystallized sap of sugar cane was known as "Indian salt." Sugar was a precious commodity, highly valued and very expensive. It was reportedly worth its weight in silver. (Alan Beardsworth and Teresa Keil, *Sociology on the Menu: An Invitation to the Study of Food and Society* (London: Routledge, 1997), 244.) It is interesting to note that, historically, versions of the "Hansel and Gretel" story have become sweeter and sweeter. This ties in with research done by Sidney Mintz, which showed that the consumption of sugar per capita in Britain increased twenty-five times between 1700 and 1809, and five times more in the nineteenth century. This led him to the conclusion that, for all the evidence of humans' innate liking for sweet foods, this huge increase in consumption could only be explained in terms of the interaction, through time, of economic interests, political power, nutritional needs, and cultural meanings. (Sidney Mintz, *Sweetness and Power: The Place of Sugar in Modern History* (New York: Viking, 1985), 18.)

10. I discuss "Hansel and Gretel" again in chapter 5 in relation to phallocentric discourses and the stepmother/witch figure.

11. Flora Thompson, *Lark Rise to Candleford* (1939, rpt., London: Penguin, 1973), 331; hereafter cited in text as *Lark Rise*.

12. Julia Briggs and Dennis Butts, "The Emergence of Form: 1850–1890," in *Children's Literature: An Illustrated History*, ed. Peter Hunt (Oxford: Oxford University Press, 1995), 130–31.

13. Jonathan Gathorne-Hardy, *The Rise and Fall of the British Nanny* (London: Hodder & Stoughton, 1972), 58; hereafter cited in text; Anne Murcott, "Family Meals — A Thing of the Past?" in *Food, Health and Identity*, ed. Pat Caplan (London: Routledge, 1997), 43; hereafter cited in text.

14. Jane Austen was born in 1775 and was one of eight children.

15. Valerie Mars, "Parsimony Amid Plenty: Views from Victorian Didactic Works on Food for Nursery Children," in *Food, Culture and History*, Vol. 1, eds. G. Mars and V. Mars (London: The London Food Seminar, 1993), 152–53; hereafter cited in text.

16. Ethel Turner, *Seven Little Australians* (1894, rpt., Pymble, Australia: Harper Collins, 1992), 11; hereafter cited in text as *Seven Little Australians*.

17. Valerie Mars confirms that as the nineteenth century progressed and man was increasingly seen to control and subjugate nature attitudes shifted so that culture was valorized over primitive nature (Mars, 152). This is not necessarily a new movement however; it also perhaps echoes Puritan ideals which were later inflected with Darwinian notions of the primitive.

18. P. L. Travers, *Mary Poppins* (1934, rpt., London: Collins, 1978), 11–12.

19. Molly Keane, "Hunger," 1985, rpt., in *The Faber Book of Food*, eds. Claire Clifton and Colin Spencer (London: Faber & Faber, 1993), 2.

20. Gwen Raverat, "Porridge with Salt – No Sugar," 1954, rpt., in *The Faber Book of Food*, eds. Claire Clifton and Colin Spencer (London: Faber & Faber, 1993), 20–21.

21. Peter Stearns, "Children and Weight Control: Priorities in the United States and France," in *Weighty Issues: Fatness and Thinness as Social Problems*, eds. Jeffrey Sobal and Donna Maurer (New York: Aldine de Gruyter, 1999), 13; hereafter cited in text.

22. These views appear to have been widespread but not pervasive. Puritan fundamentalism still remained influential in some areas of the United States.

23. Gillian Avery, *Behold the Child: American Children and their Books (1621–1922)* (London: Bodley Head, 1994), 158; hereafter cited in text.

24. Dorothy Wall, *The Complete Adventures of Blinky Bill* (1939, rpt., Pymble, Australia: Harper Collins, 1992), hereafter cited in text as *Blinky Bill*. Blinky Bill is an Australian story originally published in the English market. While it pandered to British food fantasies it was also shaped by the Great Depression of the 1930s, suffered in Australia as in the rest of the Western world.

25. Keith Barker, "The Use of Food in Enid Blyton's Fiction," in *Children's Literature in Education*, 13.1, 1982: 4; hereafter cited in text.

26. Barbara Stoney, *Enid Blyton: A Biography* (London: Hodder & Staughton, 1974), 27.

27. 1s. 6d. in 1940 is equivalent to roughly £2.50, A$6, or US$4.50 in today's terms.

28. Nicholas Tucker, "The Rise and Rise of Harry Potter," in *Children's Literature in Education*, 30.4, 1999: 224; hereafter cited in text.

29. Enid Blyton, "Five On a Hike Together," 1951, rpt., in *Fabulous Famous Five* (London: Hodder & Staughton, 1974), 69; hereafter cited in text as *Five on a Hike*.

30. Enid Blyton, *Five Get into a Fix* (1958, rpt., Leicester : Brockhampton Press, 1974), 58; hereafter cited in text as *Five in a Fix*.

31. Lynne Vallone, "'What is the Meaning of all this Gluttony?': Edgeworth, The Victorians, C. S. Lewis and a Taste for Fantasy,'" in *Papers: Explorations into Children's Literature* 12, no. 1 (2002): 47.

32. Strictly speaking synaesthesia is a condition whereby ordinary stimuli elicit extraordinary conscious experiences. For example, standard black digits may elicit highly specific color experiences and specific tastes may produce unusual tactile sensations. Smilek and Dixon "suspect" that synaesthesia is "somehow related to the hypothetical mechanism of binding, whereby all the disparate qualities of an object . . . are tied or bound together in the evocation of that object . . . [Thus] A silver candlestick signifies value, a certain color, metallic properties, a particular function (holding candles), romantic dinners and so on;

the thalamus, deep within the brain, may briefly label the neural correlates of all these precepts or concepts ... so that they are transiently brought together, as it were, to represent a silver candlestick!" (D. Smilek and Mike J. Dixon, "Towards a Synergistic Understanding of Synaesthesia: Combining Current Experimental Findings with Synaesthetes' Subjective Descriptions," in *Psyche: An Interdisciplinary Journal of Research on Consciousness* 8, no. 1, http://psyche.cs.monash.edu.au/v8/psyche-8-01-smilek.html; accessed 3/31/2004, 1–4.) I would like to suggest that the written words 'raspberry jam, scones and clotted cream,' for example, can bring together such notions as their color, texture, smell and taste as well as suggestions linked to nostalgia—of summertime, holidays, childhood, the mother-figure, etc. For the reader deeply involved in the text I believe the sensations of smell and taste can be evoked.

33. Elizabeth Grosz, *Volatile Bodies: Toward a Corporeal Feminism* (Sydney: Allen & Unwin, 1994), 99; hereafter cited in text.

34. Comedy author Monica McInerney reports that Blyton's *The Magic Faraway Tree* had particular resonance for her when she was a child. She recalls, "I loved all her books. I can still remember picturing lands at the top of trees, chairs that grew wings and biscuits that went 'pop' when you bit into them. I could see, hear and taste everything that she described." (Monica McInerney, "All in the Mind: Books that Changed Me," ed. Rosemarie Milsom, in *Sunday Life: The Sunday Age Magazine*, May 2, 2004, 12.)

35. Sigmund Freud, "Three Essays on the Theory of Sexuality," 1924, rpt., in *The Freud Reader*, ed. Peter Gay (New York: Norton & Co., 1989), 263; hereafter cited in text.

36. Margaret and Michael Rustin, *Narratives of Love and Loss: Studies in Modern Children's Fiction* (London: Verso, 1987), 45–46; hereafter cited in text.

37. C. S. Lewis, *The Lion, the Witch and the Wardrobe* (1950, rpt., London: Collins, 1990), 37, emphasis added; hereafter cited in text as *Lion*.

38. Kim Chernin, *The Hungry Self: Women, Eating and Identity* (1985, rpt., New York: HarperCollins, 1994), 98.

39. Stephanie Theobald, "Queen of Tarts," in *The Sunday Age: Good Weekend*, September 9, 2000, 62.

40. Roland Barthes, *The Pleasure of the Text*, trans. Richard Miller (London: Jonathan Cape, 1976), 21; hereafter cited in text.

41. Elizabeth Grosz, *Sexual Subversions: Three French Feminists* (Sydney: Allen & Unwin, 1989), 52, 70.

42. Raymond Williams, *Marxism and Literature* (Oxford: Oxford University Press, 1977), 128–135.

43. John Stephens, *Language and Ideology in Children's Fiction* (London: Longman, 1992), 59; hereafter cited in text.

44. Hugh Crago, "Can Stories Heal?" in *Understanding Children's Literature*, ed. Peter Hunt (London: Routledge, 1999), 168; hereafter cited in text.

45. Wendy Katz, "Some Uses of Food in Children's Literature," in *Children's Literature in Education*, 11.4, 1980: 192.

46. Perry Nodelman, *The Pleasures of Children's Literature* (New York: Longman, 1996), 196.

47. Maria Nikolajeva, *From Mythic to Linear: Time in Children's Literature* (Lanham, MD: Scarecrow Press, 2000), 129.

48. Mary Douglas refers to food as a "blinding fetish" in our culture, in as much as "we cannot control our own uses of food" (Mary Douglas, "Food as a System of Communication," in *In the Active Voice* ed. Mary Douglas (London: Routledge, 1982), 123.) Elspeth Probyn, on the other hand, refers to food as "a deeply fetishised commodity." (Elspeth Probyn, *Carnal Appetites: FoodSexIdentities* (London: Routledge, 2000), 88.) Douglas is referring to Freud's notion of sexual fetishism while Probyn invokes Marx's concept of commodity fetishism (Freud, 1962; Marx, 1967, cited by Carole M. Counihan, *The Anthropology of Food and Body: Gender, Meaning, and Power* (London: Routledge, 1999), 200.)

49. Sarah Sceats, *Food, Consumption and the Body in Contemporary Women's Fiction* (Cambridge: Cambridge University Press, 2000), 22; hereafter cited in text.

50. C. S. Lewis, "On Three Ways of Writing for Children," in *Only Connect*, ed. Sheila Egoff (Toronto: Oxford University Press, 1980), 207.

51. It should be noted that, strictly speaking, food cannot act as a direct substitute for sex given that they operate in different networks of power. (Michel Foucault, *Discipline and Punish: The Birth of the Prison*, trans. Alan Sheridan (New York: Vintage, 1979).) However, in narratives they can be seen to function in parallelism.

52. Linda Jaivin, *Eat Me* (Melbourne: Text Publishing Company, 1995).

53. I am including Rowling's work in my discussion because I believe many elements of her work are derived from the British classics, particularly her use of food. (See Carolyn Daniel, *All that Glitters is not Gold*, unpublished Honors diss., Melbourne: Victoria University of Technology, 2000.)

54. Enid Blyton, *Faraway Tree Stories* (omnibus edition), (1939–1946, rpt., London: Mammoth, 1994), 298–300, emphasis added.

55. Allison James, "Confections, Concoctions and Conceptions," in *Popular Culture: Past and Present*, eds. Bernard Waites, Tony Bennett and Graham Martin (London: Routledge, 1989), 295; hereafter cited in text. See also Ellen Seiter, *Sold Separately: Children and Parents in Consumer Culture* (New Brunswick, NJ: Rutgers University Press, 1995), 116.

56. In terms of children's fiction thought of as unappetizing by some contemporary adults, I am referring to series books such as Goosebumps and Babysitters Club, and to Blyton's books which have been heavily criticized. All of these remain immensely popular with children.

57. Nicholas Tucker, *The Child and the Book: A Psychological and Literary Exploration* (Cambridge: Cambridge University Press, 1981), 111; hereafter cited in text.

58. Julia Kristeva, *Powers of Horror: An Essay on Abjection*, trans. Leon S. Roudiez (New York: Columbia University Press, 1982).

59. P. Fuery, *Theories of Desire* (Melbourne: Melbourne University Press, 1995), 63.

60. Jane Kenway and Elizabeth Bullen, *Consuming Children: Education — Entertainment — Advertising* (Buckingham: Open University Press, 2001), 70.

Chapter Four

1. Elias Canetti, *Crowds and Power*, trans. Carol Stewart (1960, rpt., Middlesex: Penguin, 1981), 258–59.

2. Thomas Fox Averill, *Secrets of the Tsil Café* (Ringwood, Australia: Penguin, 2001), 6. I am reminded that the yolk of an egg is also "just a food" but it is, I suppose, more akin to the placenta of a mammal in as much as it provides the fetus with sustenance.

3. Julia Kristeva, "Stabat Mater," trans. Leon S. Roudiez, 1977, rpt., in *A Kristeva Reader*, ed. Toril Moi (New York: Blackwell, 1993), 180.

4. Quoted by Roni Natov, *The Poetics of Childhood* (New York: Routledge, 2003), 64, hereafter cited in text. It is this presymbolic moment or psychological space that Julia Kristeva refers to as the semiotic.

5. Christopher Bollas, "The Aesthetic Moment and the Search for Transformation," in *Transitional Objects and Potential Spaces: Literary Uses of S. W. Winnicott*, ed. Peter L. Rudnytsky (New York: Columbia University Press, 1993), 41; hereafter cited in text.

6. Winifred Gallagher, *The Power of Place: How Our Surroundings Shape Our Thoughts, Emotions, and Actions* (New York: HarperCollins, 1993), 123; hereafter cited in text. It is interesting that Kristeva refers to her earliest memories of her mother as "spatial."

7. Jessica Benjamin, *The Bonds of Love: Psychoanalysis, Feminism, And the Problem of Domination* (New York: Pantheon, 1988), 12; hereafter cited in text.

8. Sarah Sceats, *Food, Consumption and the Body in Contemporary Women's Fiction* (Cambridge: Cambridge University Press, 2000), 5; hereafter cited in text.

9. Janice Doane and Devon Hodges, *From Klein to Kristeva: Psychoanalytic Feminism and the Search for the "Good Enough" Mother* (Ann Arbor: University of Michigan, 1992), 12; hereafter cited in text.

10. Nancy Chodorow, *The Reproduction of Mothering* (Berkeley: University of California Press, 1978), 57; hereafter cited in text.

11. The desire or yearning for the restoration of the maternal aesthetic can be labeled transgressive. For Kristeva the presymbolic semiotic is a source of jouissance but it is a phase that, in terms of psychological development, should be left behind as the individual becomes part of the symbolic order. The semiotic is an intermediate indeterminate state associated with the maternal body and abjection and is thus abhorrent, uncontrolled and dangerous, from the patriarchal perspective. Desire for it is therefore transgressive.

12. Sigmund Freud, "Three Essays on the Theory of Sexuality," 1924, rpt., in *The Freud Reader*, ed. Peter Gay (New York: Norton & Co., 1989), 263–64; hereafter cited in text.

13. Rosalind Coward, *Female Desire: Womens' Sexuality Today* (London: Paladin, 1984), 88. Coward may also be referring to the sensuous satisfaction experienced by some mothers during breast-feeding. Alternatively she may be suggesting, like Mervyn Nicholson, that while the mother feeds the child physically, the child feeds the mother emotionally. Either way, both Coward and Nicholson suggest that this is a mutually dependent relationship. (Mervyn Nicholson, "Magic Food, Compulsive Eating, and Power Poetics," in *Disorderly Eaters: Texts in Self-Empowerment*, eds. Lilian R. Furst and Peter W. Graham (University Park: Pennsylvania State University Press, 1992), 49.)

14. Birch and Fisher suggest a universal preference for sweetness which, they claim, is "strong, unlearned, and well-established at birth." (Leann L. Birch and Jennifer A. Fisher, "The Role of Experience in the Development of Children's Eating Behavior," in *Why We Eat What We Eat: The Psychology of Eating*, ed., Elizabeth D. Capaldi (Washington, DC: American Psychological Association, 1996), 128–29.) Beardsworth and Keil go so far as to state that the "preference for sweetness is innate." (Alan Beardsworth and Teresa Keil, *Sociology on the Menu: An Invitation to the Study of Food and Society* (London: Routledge, 1997), 243; hereafter cited in text.)

15. Benjamin clarifies the multiplicity of meanings evoked by the breast metaphor: it can be understood "quite variously in terms of oral sexual pleasure, reduction of tension, the sense of efficacy resulting from the caregiver's responsiveness, an intense merging or oneness, [and] the 'creative illusion' that one has made the breast appear... Within a few weeks of birth, the infant has sufficient control over physiological tension that hunger may be less pressing than his interest in his mother's face. Thus nursing, as a primary metaphor of infancy, encompasses all three kinds of relationships to the other that... appear in psychoanalytic thinking: being transformed by another (as in tension relief), complementarity (as in being held), and mental sharing (as in mutual gaze) (1988: f.n. pp. 45–46).

16. Michael Ende, *The Neverending Story*, trans. Ralph Manheim (1979, rpt., Ringwood, Australia: Penguin, 1990), 358; hereafter cited in text as *Neverending*.

17. C. S. Lewis, *The Last Battle* (1956, rpt., London: Collins, 1990), 129; hereafter cited as *Last Battle*.

18. David Holbrook, "The Problem of C. S. Lewis," in *Children's Literature in Education*, 10, (1973): 22.

19. Nina Bawden, *Carrie's War* (London: Penguin, 1973), 46; hereafter cited in text as *Carrie's War*.

20. Charles Kingsley, *The Water Babies* (1863, rpt., London: Hamlyn, 1989), 118; hereafter cited as *Water Babies*.

21. Frances Hodgson Burnett, *The Secret Garden* (1911, rpt., London: Heinemann, 1975), 204, 210.

22. Maurice Sendak, *Where the Wild Things Are* (1963, rpt., New York: Harper & Row, 1992).

23. Philip Pullman, *Northern Lights* (London: Scholastic, 1995), 106, hereafter cited in text as *Northern Lights*.

24. Melanie Klein, *Love, Guilt and Reparation: And Other Works 1921–1945* (London: Hogarth Press, 1981), 291; hereafter cited in text.

25. Maria Tatar, *Off With Their Heads! Fairy Tales and the Culture of Childhood* (Princeton, NJ: Princeton University Press, 1992), 204.

26. E. Ann Kaplan, *Motherhood and Representation: The Mother in Popular Culture and Melodrama* (London: Routledge, 1992), 48; hereafter cited in text.

27. Barbara Creed, *The Monstrous-Feminine: Film, Feminism, Psychoanalysis* (London: Routledge, 1993), hereafter cited in text.

28. Elizabeth Grosz, *Sexual Subversions: Three French Feminists* (Sydney: Allen & Unwin, 1989), 121; hereafter cited in text.

29. Conversely, of course, women/wives may be resented for *not* doing so (Sceats, 21).

30. Roald Dahl, *Charlie and the Chocolate Factory* (1964, rpt., Ringwood, Australia: Penguin, 1995), 36; hereafter cited as *Charlie*.

31. J. K. Rowling, *Harry Potter and the Chamber of Secrets* (London: Bloomsbury, 1998), 7; hereafter cited as *Chamber*.

32. J. K. Rowling, *Harry Potter and the Philosopher's Stone* (London: Bloomsbury, 1997), 20; hereafter cited in text as *Philosopher*.

33. I will later show how Augustus Gloop involuntarily undergoes a form of extreme makeover. As far as Dudley Dursley is concerned, Hagrid punishes him for being "so much like a pig" by magically endowing him with a curly pig's tail which he later has to have surgically removed (*Philosopher*, 48) and, he suffers for his greedy consumption of "Ton tongue toffee" when his tongue swells until it is four foot long. (J. K. Rowling, *Harry Potter and the Goblet of Fire* (London: Bloomsbury, 2000), 47–50; hereafter cited in text as *Goblet*.)

34. Elizabeth Grosz, *Volatile Bodies: Toward a Corporeal Feminism* (Sydney: Allen & Unwin, 1994), 193; hereafter cited in text.

35. Julia Kristeva, *Powers of Horror: An Essay on Abjection*, trans. Leon S. Roudiez (New York: Columbia University Press, 1982), 5; hereafter cited in text.

36. Jean-Paul Sartre, *Being and Nothingness: An Essay in Phenomenological Ontology*, trans. Hazel E. Barnes (1943, rpt., London: Methuen, 1957), 696.

37. Mary Douglas, *Purity and Danger: An Analysis of Concepts of Pollution and Taboo* (1966, rpt., London: Routledge and Kegan Paul, 1980), 38. Echoing Douglas's linking of women with both animals and the slimy qualities of honey, Margaret Atwood's Dr. Simon in *Alias Grace* is described as "coming to hate the gratitude of women. It is like being fawned on by rabbits, or like being covered with syrup: you can't get it off." (Margaret Atwood, *Alias Grace* (London: Virago, 1997), 363.)

38. Jacqueline Wilson, *The Illustrated Mum* (London: Corgi Books, 2000), 39; hereafter cited in text as *Illustrated Mum*.

39. David Sibley, "Families and Domestic Routines: Constructing the Boundaries of Childhood," in *Mapping the Subject: Geographies of Cultural Transformation*, eds. Steve Pile and Nigel Thrift (London: Routledge, 1995), 129–30.

40. Juliet Mitchell, *The Selected Melanie Klein*, (New York: The Free Press, 1986), 20.

41. Nancy Chodorow, "Family Structure and Feminine Personality," 1974, rpt., in *Women, Culture, and Society*, eds. Michelle Zimbalist Rosaldo and Louise Lamphere (Stanford, CA: Stanford University Press, 1980), 45; hereafter cited in text. Doane and Hodges critique Chodorow's argument because, although she is critical of the mother's position of powerlessness in a patriarchal social order, she places the responsibility of gender formation solely upon the mother, taking little account of the role of culture (Doane and Hodges, 38).

42. Although Chodorow was writing in 1974 and parenting roles have changed in some families, a boy's early years are still often dominated by interactions with women. Child-care workers and kindergarten and primary school teachers are predominantly female; television, advertising, movie and storybook narratives most often feature traditional family set-ups.

43. Benjamin argues that women contribute to their own domination in patriarchal Western culture by accepting and even embracing the subordinated position in a subject/object master/slave dyad. The persistence of gender polarity relates to disidentification with or rejection of maternal power/omnipotence. She contends that it is psychological anxiety about maternal power that gives meaning to the penis as a symbol of revolt and separation, rather than maternal lack (1988: 94).

44. Susan Maushart, "Mother Load," in *The Sunday Age: Good Weekend*, August 2, 1997, 14.

45. Kate Kane, "Who Deserves a Break Today? Fast Food, Cultural Rituals, and Women's Place," in *Cooking by the Book: Food in Literature and Culture*, ed. Mary Anne Schofield (Bowling Green, OH: Bowling Green State University Popular Press, 1989), 139.

46. Vincent Duindam, "Men in the Household: Caring Fathers," in *Gender, Power and the Household*, eds., Linda McKie, Sophia Bowlby, and Susan Gregory (Basingstoke: Macmillan, 1999), 43.

47. Gillian Tunstall, *The Images of Women in Contemporary Children's Picture Books* (Sydney: University of Sydney School of Teacher Education, 1992), 33.

48. Sarah Blaffer Hrdy, *Mother Nature: A History of Mothers, Infants, and Natural Selection* (New York: Pantheon, 1999), 10; hereafter cited in text.

49. M. L. DeVault cited by Alan Beardsworth and Teresa Keil, *Sociology on the Menu: An Invitation to the Study of Food and Society* (London: Routledge, 1997), 82; hereafter cited in text.

50. Most recently, rates of childhood and adult obesity are causing increased concern. To what extent, I can't help but wonder, will the "working mother" carry the blame for children's unhealthy eating habits in the popular imagination? Having the time to prepare proper cooked meals is a luxury many families seem unable to afford.

51. Gillian Rubinstein, *Beyond the Labyrinth* (Melbourne: Hyland House, 1988), 45; hereafter cited as *Labyrinth*.

52. Heather Scutter, *Displaced Fictions: Contemporary Australian Fiction for Teenagers and Young Adults* (Melbourne: Melbourne University Press, 1999), 71; hereafter cited in text.

53. Elspeth Probyn, *Carnal Appetites: FoodSexIdentities* (Routledge: London, 2000), 38.

54. Gillian Rubinstein, *Answers to Brut* (1988, rpt., Norwood, Australia: Omnibus Books, 1992), 9; hereafter cited in text as *Answers*.

55. Enid Blyton, *Five Run Away Together* (1944, rpt., London: Hodder Children's Books, 1996), 22. There are of course (working) class inflections in the description of the thickly-cut slices of bread and scant butter.

56. Keith Barker, "The Uses of Food in Enid Blyton's Fiction," in *Children's Literature in Education*, 13.1 (1982): 8; hereafter cited in text.

57. Enid Blyton, *The Six Bad Boys* (1951, rpt., London: Arrow, 1987), 47; hereafter cited as *Bad Boys*.

58. Quoted by Barbara Stoney, *Enid Blyton: A Biography* (London: Hodder & Stoughton, 1974), 147. Blyton's views reflect the prevailing discourse about the role of women. Julia Cream confirms that during the 1950s (the decade when Blyton did much of her writing), for example, childlessness was considered deviant, selfish, and pitiable. Being a woman was synonymous with being a wife and mother. Women were not fulfilled and considered unnatural if they did not have children. (Julia Cream, "Women on Trial: A Private Pillory?" in *Mapping the Subject: Geographies of Cultural Transformation*, eds. Steve Pile and Nigel Thrift (London: Routledge, 1995), 162.)

59. Imogen Smallwood, "A Childhood at Green Hedges" cited by Gyles Brandreth, "Unhappy Families." In *The Age*, 3/31/02. http://www.theage.com.au/articles/2002/03/30/1017206160031.html; accessed 7/2/04.

60. The phrase "just like you would make at home" is particularly loaded. First, it implies that "you" (explicitly a female "you") would make cookies like these if you had the time but, because "you" don't, store-bought cookies are the perfect substitute. Second, it implicitly confirms that home-baking is the proper way to care for a family. Home-made cookies are best, store-bought cookies are second-best; they provide the same taste but lack the authenticity that comes from the added value of love that supposedly goes into home baking. This short phrase thus affirms an association between traditional home-baking and a mother's love. (For an interesting discussion about an advertisement for frozen pastry products see Alan Warde, *Consumption, Food and Taste* (London: Sage, 1997), 131–33; hereafter cited in text.)

61. M. L. DeVault, Feeding the Family: *The Social Organization of Caring as Gendered Work* (Chicago: University of Chicago Press, 1991), 236; hereafter cited in text.

62. Robin Klein, *The Listmaker*, (Ringwood, Australia: Penguin, 1997), 171; hereafter cited in text as *Listmaker*.

63. Philip Pullman, *The Subtle Knife* (London: Scholastic, 1998), 22–28; hereafter cited in text as *Subtle Knife*.

64. Robin Klein, *Dresses of Red and Gold* (Ringwood, Australia: Penguin, 1992), 31; hereafter cited in text as *Dresses*.

65. David Almond, *Skellig* (London: Hodder, 1998); hereafter cited in text as *Skellig*.

Chapter Five

1. Sander Gilman, *Difference and Pathology: Stereotypes of Sexuality, Race, and Madness* (Ithaca, NY: Cornell University Press, 1985), 17; hereafter cited in text.

2. Joseph Campbell, *The Masks of God: Primitive Mythology* (Harmondsworth: Penguin, 1976); hereafter cited in text.

3. Barbara Creed, *The Monstrous-Feminine: Film, Feminism, Psychoanalysis* (London: Routledge, 1993), 74; hereafter cited in text.

4. Barbara Walker shows that "all the world's people in the prehistoric period knew nothing of man's part in the process of reproduction" and believed that women held the divine power to give life. Similarly, she claims that the "most primitive hunting cultures have legends of still earlier ages, when women possessed all magical arts and men had none" (see Walker's comprehensive entry under "Motherhood" in *The Woman's Encyclopedia of Myths and Secrets*, (New York: HarperCollins, 1983), 680–695).

5. In some contemporary stories the witch is a rather more benign figure. She may be a wise woman expert in herbal remedies, for example.

6. Sheldon Cashdan, *The Witch Must Die: How Fairy Tales Shape Our Lives* (New York: Basic Books, 1999), 27.

7. Alan Dundes, "Interpreting Little Red Riding Hood Psychoanalytically," in *The Brothers Grimm and Folktale*, ed. James M. McGlathery (Urbana and Chicago: University of Illinois Press, 1988), 34.

8. Susanne Skubal, *Word of Mouth: Food and Fiction after Freud* (New York: Routledge, 2002), 14.

9. E. Ann Kaplan, *Motherhood and Representation: The Mother in Popular Culture and Melodrama* (London: Routledge, 1992), 107.

10. See chapter 2 in Jack Zipes, *Happily Ever After: Fairy Tales, Children, and the Culture Industry*, (New York: Routledge, 1997), 39–60; hereafter cited in text.

11. Jack Zipes, *The Complete Fairy Tales of the Brothers Grimm* (1987, rpt., New York: Bantam Books, 1992), 59; hereafter cited in text as *Grimm Tales*.

12. Bruno Bettelheim, *The Uses of Enchantment: The Meaning and Importance of Fairy Tales* (New York: Knopf, 1976), 160.

13. Tracy Willard, "Hansel and Gretel: Enter the Witch," in *Tales at the Borders: Fairy Tales and Maternal Cannibalism*, http://www.reconstruction.ws/022/cannibal/hanselandgretel. html; accessed 10/9/02, section 26; hereafter cited in text.

14. Julia Kristeva, *Black Sun: Depression and Melancholia*, trans. Leon S. Roudiez (New York: Columbia University Press, 1989), 27.

15. Jessica Benjamin, *The Bonds of Love: Psychoanalysis, Feminism, And the Problem of Domination*, (New York: Pantheon, 1988).

16. *Russian Folk Tales*, no author/editor, trans. Dorian Rottenburg (Moscow: Foreign Language Publishing House, n.d.), 181.

17. Elizabeth Warner, *Heroes, Monsters and Other Worlds from Russian Mythology* (Sydney: Hodder & Stoughton, 1985), 88; hereafter cited in text.

18. Maggie Kilgour, *From Communion to Cannibalism: An Anatomy of Metaphors of Incorporation* (Princeton, NJ: Princeton University Press, 1990), 12.

19. Luce Irigaray argues that phallocentric discourses and images of the female body repress the reality of female sexuality which is, she argues, multiple, ambiguous, fluid, excessive, and unrepresentable in terms of a phallic libidinal economy (in Grosz 1989, 115). The indefinability and excessiveness of female sexuality create considerable anxiety. The castration narrative is an attempt to control and contain it.

20. Elizabeth Grosz, *Jacques Lacan: A Feminist Introduction* (Sydney: Allen & Unwin, 1990), 116.

21. Sigmund Freud, "Three Essays on the Theory of Sexuality," 1924, rpt., in *The Freud Reader*, ed. Peter Gay (New York: Norton & Co., 1989).

22. Karen Horney, *Feminine Psychology* (New York: W.W. Norton, 1967), 138.

23. Erich Fromm, *The Crisis of Psychoanalysis* (London: Jonathan Cape, 1970), 92.

24. Erich Neumann, *The Great Mother: An Analysis of the Archetype*, trans. Ralph Manheim (Princeton, NJ: Princeton University Press, 1972), 174.

25. Mervyn Nicholson, "Magic Food, Compulsive Eating, and Power Poetics," in *Disorderly Eaters: Texts in Self-Empowerment*, eds. Lilian R. Furst and Peter W. Graham (University Park: Pennsylvania State University Press, 1992), 46; hereafter cited in text.

26. As Creed argues, the phallicized image of an aggressive, powerful woman is fetishistic in that it denies the existence of the woman as castrated. "[T]he fetish stands in for the *vagina dentata*—the castrating female organ that the male wishes to disavow. It is possible that he might hold opposing beliefs about women [as castrated and castrator] alternately or even together" (Creed, 116). The White Witch is thus simultaneously fetishized and evokes the *vagina dentata*. Creed also points out that soft-porn magazines often portray women draped in a fur coat. The image of the White Witch is clearly sexualized.

27. C. S. Lewis, *The Lion, the Witch and the Wardrobe* (1950, rpt., London: Collins, 1990), 33; hereafter cited in text as *Lion*.

28. David Holbrook, "The Problem of C. S. Lewis," in *Children's Literature in Education*, 10 (1973): 7; hereafter cited in text.

29. In addition to a mantle referring to a cloak or cape, the verb to mantle means to cover (as in snow for example), to disguise, mask, shroud,or veil. Additionally Holbrook suggests that the fur coats hanging up in the wardrobe are symbolic of the mother's body (Holbrook, 7): "There was nothing Lucy liked so much as the smell and feel of fur. She immediately stepped into the wardrobe and got in among the coats and rubbed her face against them...." (*Lion*, 12). Again, the sensuous feel of Aslan's fur is emphasized by Lewis to such an extent that Holbrook describes the relationship between the Lion and the girls as taking on "a sexual undercurrent" (12). Being engulfed in the Witch's fur mantle is a sensuous experience for Edmund, related to the maternal. But he is also clearly in danger.

30. Margaret and Michael Rustin, *Narratives of Love and Loss: Studies in Modern Children's Fiction* (London: Verso, 1987), 45–46. See also Margery Hourihan, *Deconstructing the Hero: Literary Theory and Children's Literature* (London: Routledge, 1997), 182–83.

31. Landscape (Mother Earth) is often mapped out in feminized sexual terms. In H. Rider Haggard's *King Solomon's Mines* (1885), for example, the protagonists must scale pinnacles that are in fact a pair of "smooth and rounded" (134) "extinct volcanoes" (86) known as "Sheba's Breasts." Significantly the narrator confesses: "I am impotent even before its memory. There straight before us, were two enormous mountains…shaped exactly like a woman's breasts" (85). H. Rider Haggard, *King Solomon's Mines* (London: Cassell & Co., 1885). Thus, as Nancy Armstrong points out, Haggard aligns the enticing secrets/treasures contained within the "body" of Africa, with the sexualized and exoticized female body. (Nancy Armstrong, "The Occidental Alice," in *differences: A Journal of Feminist Cultural Studies* 2, no. 2 (1990): 30–31.)

32. Paul Stewart, *The Weather Witch* (London: Random House, 1989); hereafter cited as *Weather Witch*.

33. Elizabeth Grosz, *Sexual Subversions: Three French Feminists* (Sydney: Allen & Unwin, 1989), 134; hereafter cited in text.

34. Pat O'Shea, *The Hounds of the Morrigan*, (Oxford: Oxford University Press, 1985); hereafter cited in text as *Morrigan*.

35. Julia Kristeva, *Powers of Horror: An Essay on Abjection*, trans. Leon S. Roudiez (New York: Columbia University Press, 1982), 3–4; hereafter cited in text.

36. "Dead man's fingers" are the feathery-looking gills found in crabs and lobsters. They must be removed and discarded because they are poisonous. (See Rick Stein, *Rick Stein's Seafood Odyssey* (London: BBC Worldwide, 2000), 27.)

37. John Stephens, *Language and Ideology in Children's Fiction* (London: Longman, 1992), 122.

38. Laura Mulvey, "Visual Pleasure and the Narrative Cinema," 1978, rpt., in *Issues in Feminist Film Critisicm*, ed. P. Erens, (Bloomington: Indiana University Press, 1990), 57.

39. It is worth adding that the figure of the wicked witch is largely unrepresentable in realist fiction although phallicized good/bad mother figures do appear, such as Marigold in Wilson's *The Illustrated Mum* featured in the previous chapter.

Chapter Six

1. Angela Carter, "The Company of Wolves," 1979, rpt. in *The Trials and Tribulations of Little Red Riding Hood*, ed. Jack Zipes (1983, rpt., New York: Routledge, 1993), 283; hereafter cited in text.

2. Mikhail Bakhtin, *Rabelais and His World*, trans. Helene Iswolsky (1965, rpt., Bloomington: Indiana University Press, 1984), 281.

3. Maggie Kilgour, *From Communion to Cannibalism: An Anatomy of Metaphors of Incorporation* (Princeton, NJ: Princeton University Press, 1990), 12, emphasis in original; hereafter cited in text.

4. Sigmund Freud, "Negation," 1925, rpt., in *The Freud Reader*, ed. Peter Gay (New York: Norton & Co., 1989), 668, emphasis added.

5. Melanie Klein, *Love, Guilt and Reparation: And Other Works 1921–1945* (London: Hogarth Press, 1981).

6. Elspeth Probyn, *Carnal Appetites: FoodSexIdentities* (London: Routledge, 2000), 70; hereafter cited in text.

7. In 2001 the German "cannibal," Armin Meiwes, advertised on the Internet for a "young, well-built" man to slaughter. He apparently carved up and froze portions of his victim's flesh and later ate some of it. http://news.bbc.co.uk/2/hi/europe/3075897.stm; accessed 12/9/03.

8. Margaret Visser, *The Rituals of Dinner: The Origins, Evolution, Eccentricities, and Meaning of Table Manners* (London: Penguin, 1993), 7; hereafter cited in text.

9. William Seabrook, "Cannibals," *The Faber Book of Food*, eds. Colin Spencer and Clare Clifton (London: Faber & Faber, 1993), 536–40.

10. Susanne Skubal, *Word of Mouth: Food and Fiction after Freud* (New York: Routledge, 2002), 106; hereafter cited in text.

   According to "a psychological expert," Meiwes was apparently "subconsciously trying to consume a human being to fill the void caused by the departure of his father and brother, which left him to care for his domineering mother until her death." His obsession with cannibalism led him to make life-size models of human bodies from marzipan. His Internet advertisements read: "If you are 18–25 you are my boy…Come to me, I'll eat your delicious flesh." As his victim clearly volunteered, Meiwes was convicted of manslaughter, not murder. (*Stuff: World News*, http://stuff.co.nz/stuff/0,2106,2800936a12,00.html; accessed 3/17/04).

11. Philip Pullman, *Northern Lights* (London: Scholastic, 1995), 354; hereafter cited in text as *Northern Lights*.

12. Philip Pullman, *The Amber Spyglass* (London: Scholastic, 2001), 44–45; hereafter cited in text as *Amber Spyglass*.

13. Sigmund Freud, "Totem and Taboo," 1913, rpt., in *The Freud Reader*, ed. Peter Gay (New York: Norton & Co., 1989), 496–99.

14. The fact that Iorek is a *bear* and not human obviously makes a difference, but within the context of Pullman's narrative he is framed as *more* noble than many of the human characters.

15. The Meiwes case obviously upsets all these dualisms.

16. Gananath Obeyesekeve, "Cannibal Feasts in Nineteenth-Century Fiji: Seaman's Yarns and the Ethnographic Imagination," in *Cannibalism and the Colonial World*, eds., F. Barker, P. Hulme and M. Iverson (Cambridge: Cambridge University Press, 1998), 63.

17. Clare Bradford, *Reading Race: Aboriginality in Australian Children's Literature* (Melbourne: Melbourne University Press, 2001), 38; hereafter cited in text.

18. Richard Rowe, *The Boy in the Bush* (London: Bell & Daldy, 1869), 205.

19. R. M. Ballantyne, *The Coral Island* (London: Thames, 1858), 134.

20. Claude Lévi-Strauss, "The Culinary Triangle," in *Partisan Review* (1966): 33.

21. Jack Zipes, *The Trials and Tribulations of Little Red Riding Hood: Versions of the Tale in Sociocultural Context* (1983, rpt., South Hadley, Mass: Bergin & Garvey, 1993), 18–19; hereafter cited in text.

22. Georges Devereaux, "The Cannibalistic Impulses of Parents," in *Basic Problems of Ethnopsychiatry* (1966, rpt., Chicago: University of Chicago Press, 1980), 127–29.

23. Marina Warner, *No Go the Bogeyman: Scaring, Lulling and Making Mock* (London: Vintage, 2000), 7. See also Visser 1993, 65. In her novel (for adults) *Alias Grace* (London: Virago, 1996), Margaret Atwood uses the same notion to good effect. The novel is set initially in mid-nineteenth century Ireland. Grace's family is poor, her father is an alcoholic and there are already seven children in the family. While they are not starving, food is scarce. Grace recalls that when yet another baby arrives,

   our father said we should just knock the new baby on the head and shove it into a hole in the cabbage patch, as it would be a good deal happier under the sod than above it. And then he said it made him just hungry to look at it, it would look very nice on a platter with roast potatoes all round and an apple in its mouth. And then he said why were we all staring at him. (110)

24. Maria Tatar, *Off With Their Heads! Fairy Tales and the Culture of Childhood*, (Princeton, NJ: Princeton University Press, 1992), 192; hereafter cited in text.

25. All these tales appear in Jack Zipes's collection: *The Complete Fairy Tales of the Brothers*

Grimm (1987, rpt., New York: Bantam Books, 1992); hereafter cited in text as *Grimm Tales*.

26. See Tatar, 1992 and Zipes, 1993.

27. Ian Turner, June Factor and Wendy Lowenstein, eds, *Cinderella Dressed in Yella* (Richmond, Vic: Heinemann Educational, 1978), 59.

28. Edel Wignell, *A Bogy Will Get You!* (Marrickville, Australia: Harcourt, Brace, Jovanovich, 1990), 1. (See also Tatar, 32.)

29. The wolf was crucial in archaic thinking as a symbol of the wild side of humankind and of the wilderness (Zipes, 33). Catherine Orenstein reveals that, in the parlance of the day, "when a girl lost her virginity it was said that *elle avoit vu le loup*—she'd seen the wolf." The term was used by Perrault himself in the preface to a scholarly work published in 1688. (Catherine Orenstein, *Little Red Riding Hood Uncloaked: Sex, Morality and the Evolution of a Fairy Tale* (New York: Basic Books, 2002), 26, 248).

30. The little girl's choice of the path of needles was significant for listeners. It indicated that she was to undertake a needlework apprenticeship under the direction of her mother or grandmother as part of her initiation into adulthood and society (Zipes, 24).

31. Alan Dundes, "Interpreting Little Red Riding Hood Psychoanalytically," in *The Brothers Grimm and Folktale*, ed., James M. McGlathery (Urbana and Chicago: University of Illinois Press, 1988), 21; hereafter cited in text.

32. Tracey Willard, "Little Red Riding Hood: Cannibal Mothers," in *Tales at the Borders: Fairy Tales and Maternal Cannibalism*. http://www.reconstruction.ws/022/cannibal/littlered.html; accessed 10/25/2002, sections 12–13.

33. James McGlathery, ed., *The Brothers Grimm and Folktale* (Chicago: University of Illinois Press, 1988), vii.

34. Angela Carter, *The Fairy Tales of Charles Perrault* (London: Gollancz, 1977), 28.

35. C. S. Lewis, *The Lion, the Witch and the Wardrobe* (1950, rpt., London: Collins, 1990); hereafter cited in text as *Lion*.

36. Neil Philip, *Myths & Legends* (London: Dorling Kingsley, 1999), 42–43; hereafter cited in text.

37. Lewis's book was published during a period of rationing when the majority of people in England were eating less than they had throughout the whole of the twentieth century. Food rationing began in January 1940 and continued until 1954 (Keith Barker, "The Use of Food in Enid Blyton's Fiction," in *Children's Literature in Education* 13.1 (1982): 9). In this context Mr. Tumnus's offer of cake in particular must be read as very tempting.

38. Mervyn Nicholson, "Magic Food, Compulsive Eating, and Power Poetics," in *Disorderly Eaters: Texts in Self-Empowerment*, eds. Lilian R. Furst and Peter W. Graham (University Park: Pennsylvania State University Press, 1992), 55; hereafter cited in text.

39. Margaret Mahy, *The Changeover* (1984, rpt., Ringwood, Australia: Penguin, 1995); hereafter cited in text as *Changeover*.

40. The following excerpt from an article in *Marie Claire* magazine reveals the unmistakable similarities between Braque's desires and those of "Steve, 51," a "situational child abuser" (men on holiday who experiment sexually with children). Steve prefers "Young ones … They're soft, they'll do anything and they don't complain. I like ones with no hair. They're like babies, little dolls." He says, "I'd be damned if I'd take even a fifteen year old girl now." Significantly he adds, "If you like young *meat*, you've got to go to Cambodia" (John Frederick, "Australian Sex Tourists: What Australian Men Don't Tell Their Wives," in *Marie Claire*, May 1999: 54, emphasis added). The semantic links between pedophilia and cannibalism are clear.

41. Maurice Gee, *The Fat Man* (Ringwood, Australia: Penguin, 1994); hereafter cited in text as *Fat Man*.

42. William Miller, *The Anatomy of Disgust* (Cambridge, MA: Harvard University Press, 1997), 6; hereafter cited in text.

43. Julia Kristeva, *Powers of Horror: An Essay on Abjection*, trans. Leon S. Roudiez (New York: Columbia University Press, 1982), 1, 5.

Chapter Seven

1. June Factor, *Captain Cook Chased a Chook: Children's Folklore in Australia*, (Ringwood, Australia: Penguin, 1989), 10.

2. Ian Turner, "The Play Rhymes of Australian Children: An Interpretative Essay," in *Cinderella Dressed in Yella*, eds, Ian Turner, June Factor, and Wendy Lowenstein, (Richmond, Australia: Heinemann Educational, 1978), 158.

3. John Stephens, *Language and Ideology in Children's Fiction* (London: Longman, 1992), 120–21; hereafter cited in text.

4. D. J. Grace and J. Tobin, "Carnival in the Classroom: Elementary Students Making Videos," in *Making a Place for Pleasure in Early Childhood Education*, ed. J. Tobin, (New Haven, CT: Yale University Press, 1997), 168; hereafter cited in text.

5. Heather Scutter claims that the "funniest books for children are aimed, usually at the excremental age, which comes soon after the age of innocence and predates the awkward age" (Heather Scutter, *Displaced Fictions, Contemporary Australian Books for Teenagers and Young Adults* (Melbourne: Melbourne University Press, 1999), 82. With regard to the title of this chapter, it was George Orwell who declared boyhood to be "the age of disgust" (George Orwell, "Such, Such Were the Joys," 1947. In *The Collected Essays, Journalism and Letters of George Orwell, Volume 4, In Front of Your Nose, 1945–1950*, Eds. Sonia Orwell and Ian Angus, (Harmondsworth: Penguin, 1968), 399.)

6. Mikhail Bakhtin, *Rabelais and His World*, trans. Helene Iswolsky (1965, rpt., Bloomington: Indiana University Press, 1984), 281; hereafter cited in text.

7. Elizabeth Grosz, *Sexual Subversions: Three French Feminists* (Sydney: Allen & Unwin, 1989), 75; hereafter cited in text.

8. Kathryn James, "Crossing the Boundaries: Scatology, Taboo and the Carnivalesque in the Picture Book," in *Papers: Explorations into Children's Literature* 12, no. 3 (2002): 19–20.

9. Maria Tatar, *Off With Their Heads! Fairy Tales and the Culture of Childhood* (Princeton, NJ: Princeton University Press, 1992), 37.

10. A chapbook is a small cheaply-produced book sold by a chapman or peddler, containing a story or ballad.

11. Marina Warner, *No Go the Bogeyman: Scaring, Lulling and Making Mock* (London: Vintage, 2000), 317; hereafter cited in text.

12. Brown et al., cited by Jane Kenway and Elizabeth Bullen, *Consuming Children: Education – Entertainment – Advertising*, (Buckingham: Open University Press, 2001) 72; hereafter Kenway and Bullen cited in text.

13. Julia Kristeva, *Powers of Horror: An Essay on Abjection*, trans. Leon S. Roudiez (New York: Columbia University Press, 1982), 210; hereafter cited in text.

14. Raymond Briggs, *Fungus the Bogeyman* (London: Hamilton, 1977), 32; hereafter cited in text as *Fungus*.

15. Heather Scutter, *Displaced Fictions: Contemporary Australian Fiction for Teenagers and Young Adults* (Melbourne: Melbourne University Press, 1999), 82.

16. William Miller, *The Anatomy of Disgust* (Cambridge, MA: Harvard University Press, 1997), 117; hereafter cited in text.

17. J. Fiske, *Understanding Popular Culture* (London: Routledge, 1989), 54.

18. C. Bazalgette and D. Buckingham, *In Front of the Children: Screen Entertainment and Young Audiences* (London: British Film Institute, 1995), 7.

19. M. J. Lee, *Consumer Culture Reborn: the Cultural Politics of Consumption* (London: Routledge, 1993), 106.

20. Michael Bradley, "Forget Wizards — Harry Plopper's the New King of the Bookshelf," *Sydney Morning Herald Weekend*, 8-9 June, 2002, 7.

21. Jack Zipes, *Sticks and Stones: The Troublesome Success of Children's Literature from Slovenly Peter to Harry Potter* (New York: Routledge, 2001), 9.

22. Roald Dahl, *Revolting Rhymes*, (Ringwood, Australia: Penguin, 1984), 33; hereafter cited in text as *Revolting Rhymes*.

23. Paul Jennings, *The Cabbage Patch Fib*, (Ringwood, Australia: Penguin, 1996).

24. Paul Jennings, "One Finger Salute," in *Unseen*, (Ringwood, Australia: Penguin, 1996).

25. Paul Jennings, "Piddler on the Roof," in *Unseen*, (Ringwood, Australia: Penguin, 1996).

26. Paul Jennings, "Snookle," in *Unbelievable*, (Ringwood, Australia: Penguin, 1986).

27. Paul Jennings, *Unreal*, (1985, rpt., Ringwood, Australia: Penguin, 1994).

28. Paul Jennings, "Birdscrap," in *Unbelievable*, (Ringwood, Australia Penguin, 1986), 91–92; hereafter cited in text as "Birdscrap."

29. In "Guts" (in *Unseen*), a sister and brother function as joint protagonists.

30. Paul Jennings, *The Gizmo Again* (Ringwood, Australia: Penguin, 1995); hereafter cited in text as *Gizmo.*

31. R. L. Stine, *The Haunted Mask* (New York: Scholastic, 1993); hereafter cited as *Haunted Mask.*

32. Vicki Coppell, "The Goosebumps" in Goosebumps: Impositions and R. L. Stine, in *Papers: Explorations into Children's Literature* 8, no. 2 (1998): 14; hereafter cited in text.

33. Nancy Veglahn, "Images of Evil: Male and Female Monsters in Heroic Fantasy," in *Children's Literature* 15 (1987): 109; hereafter cited in text.

34. R. L. Stine, *Creature Teacher: Goosebumps Series 2000* (London: Scholastic, 1998); hereafter cited in text as *Creature Teacher.*

35. Elizabeth Grosz, *Volatile Bodies: Toward a Corporeal Feminism*, (Sydney: Allen & Unwin, 1994), 203; hereafter cited in text.

36. Claude Lévi-Strauss, "The Culinary Triangle," in *Partisan Review* 33 (1966), 586–95.

37. James Twitchell, *Dreadful Pleasures: An Anatomy of Modern Horror* (New York: Oxford University Press, 1985), 7.

38. J. A. Appleyard, *Becoming a Reader* (Cambridge: Cambridge University Press, 1991), 62.

39. Bronwyn Davies, *Frogs and Snails and Feminist Tales: Preschool Children and Gender* (Sydney: Allen & Unwin, 1989), 47.

Chapter Eight

1. Margaret Atwood, *Lady Oracle* (London: Virago, 1991), 52.

2. Helen Barnes, *Killing Aurora* (Ringwood, Australia: Penguin, 1999), 107; hereafter cited in text as *Aurora.*

3. Deborah Hautzig, *Second Star to the Right* (New York: Greenwillow Books, 1981), 144; hereafter cited in text as *Second Star.*

4. Michelle de Villiers, 'Perpetrators and Princesses: Transgression and Subject Formation in "*Killing Aurora* and *Queen Kat, Carmel and St. Jude Get a Life*," in *Papers: Explorations into Children's Literature* 10, no. 3 (2000): 6; hereafter cited in text.

5. Mimi Nichter, *Fat Talk: What Girls and their Parents Say about Dieting* (Cambridge, MA: Harvard University Press, 2000), 7.

6. Robyn McCallum, *Ideologies of Identity in Adolescent Fiction* (New York: Garland, 1999), 4; hereafter cited in text.

7. In Jonathan Dollimore, *Sexual Dissidence: Augustine to Wilde, Freud to Foucault* (Oxford: Clarendon Press, 1991), 181.

8. Maurice Gee, *The Fat Man* (Ringwood, Australia: Penguin, 1994).

9. Susan Bordo, *Unbearable Weight: Feminism, Western Culture and the Body* (Berkeley: University of California Press, 1993), 195; hereafter cited in text.

10. Cited by Maria Tatar, *Off With Their Heads! Fairy Tales and the Culture of Childhood* (Princeton, NJ: Princeton University Press, 1992), xvi.

11. Roald Dahl, *Charlie and the Chocolate Factory* (1964, rpt., Ringwood, Australia: Penguin, 1995); hereafter cited in text as *Charlie*.

12. Roni Natov, *The Poetics of Childhood* (New York: Routledge, 2003), 252.

13. Jacobson and Mazur cited by Jane Kenway and Elizabeth Bullen, *Consuming Children: Education – Entertainment – Advertising* (Buckingham: Open University Press, 2001), 95.

14. Neil Postman proposed that contemporary children's absorption in and by the media has in fact resulted in the "disappearance" of childhood. Television, unlike print media, is, according to Postman, a total disclosure medium that reveals adults' "secrets" to children, corrupting their innocence and resulting in a blurring of the boundaries between adult and child so that the categories are no longer clearly circumscribed. This implicitly results in the end of adults' power and authority over children. (Neil Postman, *The Disappearance of Childhood* (1982), rpt., New York: Vintage Books, 1994).

15. Claude Lévi-Strauss, "The Culinary Triangle," in *Partisan Review* (1966): 33.

16. Willy Wonka explains to Mike Teavee how he can "send" a bar of chocolate from one end of the room to the other "by television." The chocolate bar has to be a big one because "it always comes out much smaller than it was when it went in," just like the pictures on ordinary television." Mike Teavee is determined to be "the first person in the world to be sent by television" and he leaps through the camera lens. The boy eventually appears on the TV screen but he's shrunk so that he's "not more than an inch tall." Wonka offers to stretch the boy back to his former size (if possible) in "a special machine" (*Charlie*, 157–68).

17. James Kincaid also believes the children in Dahl's story (apart from Charlie) are American and German and he cites this as one of the reasons why they "fail" Willy Wonka's "test." (James Kincaid, *Erotic Innocence: The Culture of Child Molesting*, (London: Duke University Press, 2000), 134.)

18. Gillian Avery, *Behold the Child: American Children and their Books (1621–1922)* (London: Bodley Head, 1994), 158.

19. Dick Hebdige, "Towards a Cartography of Taste: 1935–1962," in *Popular Culture: Past and Present*, eds. Bernard Waites, Tony Bennett, and Graham Martin (London: Routledge, 1989), 195.

20. Kathryn Pauly Morgan, "Woman and the Knife: Cosmetic Surgery and the Colonization of Women's Bodies," in *Hypatia* 6, no. 3 (1991) "Feminism and the Body; hereafter cited in text.

21. Eric Linklater, *The Wind on the Moon* (1944, rpt., Ringwood, Australia: Puffin, 1972); hereafter cited in text as *Wind on the Moon*.

22. Maria Nikolajeva, *From Mythic to Linear: Time in Children's Literature* (Lanham, MD: Scarecrow Press, 2000), 57.

23. Margaret Clark, *No Fat Chicks* (Milsons Point, Australia: Random House, 1998); hereafter cited in text as *Fat Chicks*.

24. Nita Mary McKinley, "Ideal Weight/Ideal Woman: Society Constructs the Female," in *Weighty Issues: Fatness and Thinness as Social Problems*, eds. Jeffrey Sobal and Donna Maurer (New York: Aldine de Gruyter, 1999), 110; hereafter cited in text.

25. John Stephens, "Construction of Females Selves in Adolescent Fiction: Makeovers as Metonym," in *Papers: Explorations into Children's Literature* 9, no. 1 (1999): 6; hereafter cited in text.

26. Stephens' point reflects one I made earlier about the body being an image of the soul with reference to Edmund's moral corruption which is "visible" to the Beaver, and Tom the water-baby's prickles.

27. Peter Howell, "'Relationship between Body Image and Eating Behavior," in *Body Image & Health Inc. (1999) Research Summaries*. http://www.internationalnodietday.com/Documents/RS%20body%20image&eat%20behav-ed.doc; accessed 10/3/2003.

28. In A. W. Logue, *The Psychology of Eating and Drinking: An Introduction* (New York: W. H. Freeman, 1991), 177.

29. Review may be seen at http://www.amazon.com/exec/obidos/tg/detail/-/0141305800/103-6001694-1287052?v; accessed11/3/2003.

30. For example, Hautzig uses the term "dictator" to describe the "inner voice" driving her protagonist to refuse food, a term used by one of Bruch's anorexic patients as reported in *The Golden Cage* (1978). In the Afterword to a later edition of her novel, Hautzig discusses her own struggle with anorexia.

31. Hugh Crago suggests that "the intense interest shown by many adolescent girls in accounts of anorexia, drug addiction and sexual abuse even when they themselves do not have such problems, suggests that these stories provide a way of articulating their own sense of alienation, aggression or low self esteem." He agrees that the reading of related books can provide a sense of community for sufferers, adding that, "reading can provide vicarious insights into one's problems, and even a measure of integration of previously disowned feelings." Sometimes reading can metaphorically or literally provide suggestions for resolving readers' problems. (Hugh Crago, "Can Stories Heal?" in *Understanding Children's Literature*, ed. Peter Hunt (London: Routledge, 1999), 171.)

32. See www.state.sc.us/dmh/anorexia/index.html; accessed 8/26/05, and www.eatingdisorders.org.au/fact_sheets/ResearchStatistics.pdf; accessed 8/26/05.

33. Noelle Caskey, "Interpreting Anorexia Nervosa," in *The Female Body in Western Culture: Contemporary Perspectives*, ed. Susan Rubin Suleiman (Cambridge, MA: Harvard University Press, 1985), 179; hereafter cited in text.

34. Sarah Sceats, *Food, Consumption and the Body in Contemporary Women's Fiction*, (Cambridge: Cambridge University Press, 2000), 17; hereafter cited in text.

35. Hilde Bruch, *The Golden Cage: The Enigma of Anorexia Nervosa*, (New York: Vintage, 1978), 39; hereafter cited in text.

36. In Paula Saukko, "Fat Boys and Goody Girls: Hilde Bruch's Work on Eating Disorders and the American Anxiety about Democracy, 1930–1960," in *Weighty Issues: Fatness and Thinness as Social Problems*, eds., Jeffrey Sobal and Donna Maurer (New York: Aldine de Gruyter, 1999), 43.

37. Lilian R. Furst and Peter W. Graham, eds., *Disorderly Eating: Texts in Self-Empowerment*, (University Park: Pennsylvania State University Press, 1992), 5–6. The domination sufferers ostensibly achieve is (temporarily) over oppressive media/cultural discourses and their own body's material needs, as well as over their own family members who are inevitably detrimentally affected by the anorexic's actions.

38. Susan Rubin Suleiman, ed., *The Female Body in Western Culture: Contemporary Perspectives* (Cambridge, MA: Harvard University Press, 1985), 2; hereafter cited in text.

39. In John L. Smith, *The Psychology of Food and Eating: A Fresh Approach to Theory and Method*, (Basingstoke: Palgrave, 2002), 82; hereafter Smith cited in text.

40. Asher and Asher cited by Smith, 85. See also McKinley, 107.

41. O'Connor quoted by Charisse Ede, "Size doesn't matter? Fat chance!" in *The Sunday Age* (2001), April 22.

42. Susanne Skubal, *Word of Mouth: Food and Fiction after Freud* (New York: Routledge, 2002), 72; hereafter cited in text.

43. Martha McCaughey, "Fleshing Out the Discomforts of Femininity: The Parallel Cases of Female Anorexia and Male Compulsive Bodybuilding," in *Weighty Issues: Fatness and Thinness as Social Problems*, ed. Jeffrey Sobal and Donna Maurer, (New York: Aldine de Gruyter, 1999), 140; hereafter cited in text.

44. See Kim Chernin, *The Hungry Self: Women, Eating and Identity*, (1985, rpt., New York: HarperCollins, 1994); Susan Bordo, "Anorexia Nervosa: Psychopathology as the Crystalization of Culture," in *Cooking, Eating, Thinking: Transformative Philosophies of Food*, eds., Deane W. Curtin and Lisa M. Heldke, (Bloomington: Indiana University Press, 1992); hereafter cited in text; and McCaughey, 1999.

45. Jane Rogers, "Grateful," in *Granta* 52, "Food: The Vital Stuff," 1995; hereafter cited in text as "Grateful."

46. Julia Kristeva, *Powers of Horror: An Essay on Abjection*, trans. Leon S. Roudiez (New York: Columbia University Press, 1982) 5; emphasis in original.

47. Maggie Kilgour, *From Communion to Cannibalism: An Anatomy of Metaphors of Incorporation* (Princeton, NJ: Princeton University Press, 1990), 3.

48. Anna Krugovoy Silver reveals that studies have "strongly indicated" that eating disorders are "catching:" "girls learn the behaviors from other girls and are reinforced in their food refusal or bingeing and purging by each other." (Anna Krugovoy Silver, *Victorian Literature and the Anorexic Body*, (Cambridge: Cambridge University Press, 2002), 177.) I think that it is probable that fictional stories about anorexia function in the same way.

49. Cecily von Ziegesar, *You Know You Love Me: A Gossip Girl Novel*, (London: Bloomsbury, 2003), 86; emphasis in original; hereafter cited in text as *Gossip Girl*.

50. See http://www.amazon.com/exec/obidos/tg/cm/member-glance/-/A2AD4T5-FXJWNMU/1/ref=cm_cr_auth/102-4855009-7911306?%5encoding=UTF8, and http://www.amazon.com/exec/obidos/tg/cm/member-glance/-/A3JOJTAMLWEWCS/1/ref=cm_cr_auth/102-4855009-7911306?%5Fencoding=UTF8; both accessed 8/26/05.

51. J. Ellen Gainor, "'The Slow-Eater-Tiny-Bite-Taker:' An Eating Disorder in Betty Mac-Donald's *Mrs Piggy-Wiggle*," in *Disorderly Eating: Texts in Self-Empowerment*, eds., Lilian R. Furst and Peter W. Graham (University Park: Pennsylvania State University Press, 1992), 29; hereafter cited in text.

52. It is interesting to speculate about whether the very recent medical concern about the "epidemic" of childhood obesity might produce a new range of popular discourses, which will in turn be reflected in forthcoming children's literature. For example, is childhood obesity an effect of the further influence of American culture where obesity is notoriously rife? Is it because children are spending hours in front of media screens rather than engaging in sports? Is it because working mothers don't have time to cook well-balanced meals and children are eating unhealthy junk food?

53. In terms of Freud's Oedipal drama, the girl must perform the divisive "feminine" task of rejecting her first object, the mother because, as castrated, it/she is woefully inadequate. The girl must advance to an attraction for a "better" object, the phallus of the father. This desire must in turn be displaced onto a desire for a baby from the father, and finally onto a baby from a father surrogate. (Sigmund Freud, "The Dissolution of the Oedipus Complex," in *The Freud Reader*, ed. Peter Gay (1924, rpt., New York: Norton & Co., 1989), 665.)

54. John Stephens, *Language and Ideology in Children's Fiction* (London: Longman, 1992), 68.

55. Bronwyn Davies quoted by Perry Nodelman, *The Pleasures of Children's Literature* (New York: Longman, 1996), 137.

BIBLIOGRAPHY

Primary Sources

Adams, Douglas. *The Restaurant at the End of the Universe*. London: Pan, 1980.

Almond, David. *Skellig*. London: Hodder, 1998.

Atwood, Margaret. *Lady Oracle*. London: Virago, 1991.

———. *Alias Grace*. London: Virago, 1996.

Averill, Thomas Fox. *Secrets of the Tsil Café*. Ringwood, Australia: Penguin, 2001.

Ballantyne, R. M. *The Coral Island*. 1858. London: Thames, no date.

Barnes, Helen. *Killing Aurora*. Ringwood, Australia: Penguin, 1999.

Bawden, Nina. *Carrie's War*. London: Penguin, 1973.

Blyton, Enid. *Five Go Off to Camp*. London: Hodder & Stoughton, 1948.

———. "Five On a Hike Together," 1951. *Fabulous Famous Five*. London: Hodder & Stoughton, 1974.

———. *Five Get into a Fix*. 1958. Leicester: Brockhampton Press, 1974.

———. *The Mountain of Adventure*. 1949. London: Macmillan, 1983.

———. *The Six Bad Boys*. 1951. London: Arrow, 1987.

———. *Faraway Tree Stories*. 1939–46. London: Mammoth, (omnibus edition) 1994.

———. *Five Run Away Together*. 1944. London: Hodder Children's Books, 1996.

Briggs, Raymond. *Fungus the Bogeyman*. London: Hamilton, 1977.

Burnett, Frances Hodgson. *The Secret Garden*. 1911. London: Heinemann, 1975.

Carroll, Lewis. *Alice's Adventures in Wonderland* and *Through the Looking-Glass and What Alice Found There*. 1865. London: Oxford University Press, 1971.

Carter, Angela. *The Fairy Tales of Charles Perrault*. London: Gollancz, 1977.

———. "The Company of Wolves." 1979. In *The Trials and Tribulations of Little Red Riding Hood: Versions of the Tale in Sociocultural Context*, edited by Jack Zipes, 282–91. New York: Routledge, 1993.

Clark, Margaret. *No Fat Chicks*. Milsons Point, Australia: Random House, 1998.

Dahl, Roald. *Revolting Rhymes*. Ringwood, Australia: Penguin, 1984.

———. *Charlie and the Chocolate Factory*. 1964. Ringwood, Australia: Penguin, 1995.

Edgeworth, Maria. "Preface" and "The Birthday Present." In *The Parent's Assistant* (2 vols.) 1800. New York: Garland, 1976.

Ende, Michael. *The Neverending Story.* Translated by Ralph Manheim. 1979. Ringwood, Australia: Penguin, 1990.

Fox, Mem. *Possum Magic.* 1983. Adelaide, Australia: Omnibus, 1987.

Gee, Maurice. *The Fat Man.* Ringwood, Australia: Penguin, 1994.

Grahame, Kenneth. *The Wind in the Willows.* 1908. London: Methuen, 1989.

Haggard, H. Rider. *King Solomon's Mines.* London: Cassell & Co., 1885.

"Hansel and Gretel" (attributed to the Brothers Grimm). *My Big Book of Fairy Tales.* London: Marshall Cavendish, 1987.

Harris, Thomas. *The Silence of the Lambs.* New York: Random House, 1988.

Hautzig, Deborah. *Second Star to the Right.* New York: Greenwillow Books, 1981.

Horowitz, Anthony. *Stormbreaker.* London: Walker Books, 2000.

———. *Skeleton Key.* London: Walker Books, 2002.

Jaivan, Linda. *Eat Me.* Melbourne: Text Publishing Company, 1995.

Jennings, Paul. "Birdscrap." In *Unbelievable.* Ringwood, Australia: Penguin, 1986.

———. "Snookle." In *Unbelievable.* Ringwood, Australia: Penguin, 1986.

———. *Unreal.* 1985. Ringwood, Australia: Penguin. 1994.

———. *The Gizmo Again.* Ringwood, Australia: Penguin, 1995.

———. *The Cabbage Patch Fib.* Ringwood, Australia: Penguin, 1996.

———. "Guts." In *Unseen.* Ringwood, Australia: Penguin, 1998.

———. "One Finger Salute." In *Unseen.* Ringwood, Australia: Penguin. 1998.

———. "Piddler on the Roof." In *Unseen.* Ringwood, Australia: Penguin, 1998.

Keats, John. "La Belle Dame sans Merci." In *The New Golden Treasury of English Verse,* edited by Edward Leeson, 345–46. London: Pan Books, 1980.

Kingsley, Charles. *The Water Babies.* 1863. London: Hamlyn, 1989.

Klein, Robin. *Dresses of Red and Gold.* Ringwood, Australia: Penguin, 1992.

———. *The Listmaker.* Ringwood, Australia: Penguin, 1997.

Lewis, C. S. *The Lion, the Witch and the Wardrobe.* 1950. London: Collins, 1990.

———. *The Silver Chair.* 1953. London: Collins, 1990.

———. *The Horse and His Boy.* 1954. London: Collins, 1990.

———. *The Last Battle.* 1956. London: Collins, 1990.

Lindsay, Norman. *The Magic Pudding.* 1918. Sydney: HarperCollins, 2000.

Linklater, Eric. *The Wind on the Moon.* 1944. Ringwood, Australia: Puffin, 1972.

"Little Ivan The Clever Young Man." Translated by Dorian Rottenburg. In *Russian Folk Tales.* Moscow: Foreign Language Publishing House, no date.

Mahy, Margaret. *The Changeover.* 1984. Ringwood, Australia: Penguin, 1995.

Milne, A. A. *Now We Are Six.* 1927. London: Methuen, 1980.

Mother Goose's Nursery Rhymes. No editor/compiler. 1922. London: Chancellor Press, 1986.

My Big Book of Fairy Tales. No editor/compiler. 1982. London: Marshall Cavendish, 1987.

Oates, Joyce Carol. *Haunted: Tales of the Grotesque.* New York: Dutton, 1994.

O'Shea, Pat. *The Hounds of the Morrigan.* Oxford: Oxford University Press, 1985.

Potter, Beatrix. *The Complete Tales of Beatrix Potter 1902–1930.* London: Penguin, 1989.

Pullman, Philip. *Northern Lights.* London: Scholastic, 1995.

———. *The Subtle Knife.* London: Scholastic, 1998.

———. *The Amber Spyglass.* London: Scholastic, 2001.

Richards, Frank. "The Artful Dodger." In *The Magnet* 1,142.xxxvii (January 1930): 3–28.

Rodda, Emily. *Bob the Builder and the Elves.* Sydney: ABC Books, 1998.

Rogers, Jane. "Grateful." In *Granta* 52. (Winter 1995): 94–98.

Rossetti, Christina. "Speaking Likenesses." 1874. In *Forbidden Journeys: Fairy Tales and Fantasies by Victorian Women Writers,* edited by Nina Auerbach and U. C. Knoepflmacher, 317–60. Chicago: University of Chicago Press, 1992.

Rowe, Richard. *The Boy in the Bush.* London: Bell & Daldy, 1869.

Rowling, J. K. *Harry Potter and the Philosopher's Stone*. London: Bloomsbury, 1997.
———. *Harry Potter and the Chamber of Secrets*. London: Bloomsbury, 1998.
———. *Harry Potter and the Prisoner of Azkaban*. London: Bloomsbury, 1999.
———. *Harry Potter and the Goblet of Fire*. London: Bloomsbury, 2000.
———. *Harry Potter and the Order of the Phoenix*. London: Bloomsbury, 2003.
Rubinstein, Gillian. *Beyond the Labyrinth*. Melbourne: Hyland House, 1988.
———. *Answers to Brut*. 1988. Norwood, Australia: Omnibus Books, 1992.
Russian Folk Tales, no author/editor. Translated by Dorian Rottenburg, Moscow: Foreign Language Publishing House, n.d.
Sachar, Louis. *There's a Boy in the Girls' Bathroom*. London: Bloomsbury, 2001.
Sendak, Maurice. *Where the Wild Things Are*. New York: Harper & Row, 1968.
Stewart, Paul. *The Weather Witch*. London: Random House, 1989.
Stine, R. L. *The Haunted Mask*. New York: Scholastic, 1993.
———. *Creature Teacher: Goosebumps Series 2000*. London: Scholastic, 1998.
Thompson, Flora. *Lark Rise to Candleford*. 1939. London: Penguin, 1973.
Tolkein, John Ronald Reuel. *The Hobbit*. 1937. London: Harper Collins, 1993.
Travers, P. L. *Mary Poppins*. 1934. London: Collins, 1978.
Turner, Ethel. *Seven Little Australians*. 1894. Pymble, Australia: Harper Collins, 1992.
von Ziegesar, Cecily. *You Know You Love Me: A Gossip Girl Novel*. London: Bloomsbury, 2003.
Wall, Dorothy. *The Complete Adventures of Blinky Bill*. 1939. Pymble, Australia: Harper Collins, 1992.
Weldon, Fay. *The Fat Woman's Joke*. 1984. Chicago, IL: Academy, 1995.
White, E. B. *Charlotte's Web*. 1952. London: Macmillan, 1983.
Wignell, Edel. *A Bogy Will Get You!* Marrickville, Australia: Harcourt, Brace, Jovanovich, 1990.
Wilson, Jacqueline. *The Illustrated Mum*. London: Corgi Books, 2000.
Zipes, Jack. *The Complete Fairy Tales of the Brothers Grimm*. 1987. New York: Bantam Books, 1992.

Secondary Sources

Althusser, Louis. "Ideology and Ideological State Apparatuses." Translated by Ben Brewster. 1965. In *Critical Theory Since 1965*, edited by Hazard Adams and Leroy Searle, 239–50. Tallahassee: University Presses of Florida and Florida State, 1986.
Appleyard, J. A. *Becoming a Reader*. Cambridge: Cambridge University Press, 1991.
Aries, Philippe. *Centuries of Childhood: A Social History of Family Life*. New York: Alfred Knopf, 1962.
Armstrong, Nancy. "The Occidental Alice." *Differences: A Journal of Feminist Cultural Studies* 2, 2 (1990): 3–40.
Auerbach, Nina. *Women and the Demon: The Life of a Victorian Myth*. Cambridge, MA: Harvard University Press, 1982.
———. "Alice in Wonderland: A Curious Child." In *Victorian Fiction*, edited by Harold Bloom, 403–15. New York: Chelsea House, 1989.
Auerbach, Nina and U. C. Knoepflmacher, eds. *Forbidden Journeys: Fairy Tales and Fantasies by Victorian Women Writers*. Chicago, University of Chicago Press, 1992.
Avery, Gillian. "Fairy Tales with a Purpose." In *Alice in Wonderland: Lewis Carroll*, edited by Donald J. Gray, 321–24. New York: Norton, 1992.
———. *Behold the Child: American Children and their Books (1621–1922)*. London: Bodley Head, 1994.
Bakhtin, Mikhail. *Rabelais and His World*. Translated by Helene Iswolsky. 1965. Bloomington: Indiana University Press, 1984.

Barker, Keith. "The Use of Food in Enid Blyton's Fiction." *Children's Literature in Education* 13, 1 (1982): 4–12.

Barthes, Roland. *The Pleasure of the Text*. Translated by Richard Miller. London: Jonathan Cape, 1976.

Bazalgette, C., and D. Buckingham. *In Front of the Children: Screen Entertainment and Young Audiences*. London: British Film Institute, 1995.

Beardsworth, Alan, and Teresa Keil. *Sociology on the Menu: An Invitation to the Study of Food and Society*. London: Routledge, 1997.

Benjamin, Jessica. *The Bonds of Love: Psychoanalysis, Feminism, and the Problem of Domination*. New York: Pantheon, 1988.

———. *Like Subjects, Love Objects: Essays on Recognition and Sexual Difference*. New Haven: Yale University Press, 1995.

Bettelheim, Bruno. *The Uses of Enchantment: The Meaning and Importance of Fairy Tales*. New York: Knopf, 1976.

Birch, Leann L., and Jennifer A. Fisher. "The Role of Experience in the Development of Children's Eating Behaviour." In *Why We Eat What We Eat: The Psychology of Eating*, edited by Elizabeth D. Capaldi, 113–41. Washington DC: American Psychological Association, 1996.

Bixler, Phyllis. *Frances Hodgson Burnett*. Boston, MA: Twayne, 1984.

Bollas, Christopher. "The Aesthetic Moment and the Search for Transformation." In *Transitional Objects and Potential Spaces: Literary Uses of D. W. Winnicott*, edited by Peter L. Rudnytsky, 40–49. New York: Columbia University Press, 1993.

Bordo, Susan. "Anorexia Nervosa: Psychopathology as the Crystalization of Culture." In *Cooking, Eating, Thinking: Transformative Philosophies of Food*, edited by Deane W. Curtin and Lisa M. Heldke, 28–55. Bloomington: Indiana University Press, 1992.

———. *Unbearable Weight: Feminism, Western Culture, and the Body*. Berkeley: University of California Press, 1993.

Bourdieu, Pierre. *Outline of a Theory of Practice*. Cambridge: Cambridge University Press, 1977.

Bradford, Clare. *Reading Race: Aboriginality in Australian Children's Literature*. Melbourne: Melbourne University Press, 2001.

Bradley, Michael. "Forget Wizards – Harry Plopper's the New King of the Bookshelf." In *Sydney Morning Herald Weekend* (June 8-9, 2002): 7.

Brandreth, Gyles. "Unhappy Families." *The Age* (31 March, 2002); http://www.theage.com.au/articles/2002/03/30/1017206160031.html (accessed 2/07/2004).

Briggs, Julia. "Transitions: 1890–1914." In *Children's Literature: An Illustrated History*, edited by Peter Hunt, 167–91. Oxford: Oxford University Press, 1995.

Briggs, Julia, and Dennis Butts. "The Emergence of Form: 1850-1890." In *Children's Literature: An Illustrated History*, edited by Peter Hunt, 130–65. Oxford: Oxford University Press, 1995.

Brillat-Savarin, Jean Anthelme. *The Physiology of Taste or, Meditations on Transcendental Gastronomy*. 1825. New York: Dover Publications, 1960.

Bruch, Hilde. *Eating Disorders*. New York: Basic Books, 1973.

———. *The Golden Cage: The Enigma of Anorexia Nervosa*. New York: Vintage, 1978.

Butler, Judith. *Gender Trouble: Feminism and the Subversion of Identity*. 1990. New York: Routledge, 1999.

Campbell, Joseph. *The Masks of God: Primitive Mythology*. Harmondsworth: Penguin, 1976.

Canetti, Elias. *Crowds and Power*. Translated by Carol Stewart. 1960. Middlesex: Penguin, 1981.

Caplan, Pat, ed. *Food, Health and Identity*. New York: Routledge, 1997.

Cashdan, Sheldon. *The Witch Must Die: How Fairy Tales Shape Our Lives*. New York: Basic Books, 1999.

Caskey, Noelle. "Interpreting Anorexia Nervosa." In *The Female Body in Western Culture: Contemporary Perspectives*, edited by Susan Rubin Suleiman, 175–89. Cambridge, MA: Harvard University Press, 1985.

Chernin, Kim. *The Hungry Self: Women, Eating and Identity*. 1985. New York: HarperCollins, 1994.

Chodorow, Nancy. *The Reproduction of Mothering*. Berkeley: University of California Press, 1978.

——. "Family Structure and Feminine Personality." 1974. In *Women, Culture, and Society*, edited by Michelle Zimbalist Rosaldo and Louise Lamphere, 43–66. Stanford, CA: Stanford University Press, 1980.

Collingwood, Stuart Dodgson. "An Old Bachelor." 1971. In *Alice in Wonderland: Lewis Carroll*, edited by Donald J. Gray, 313–18. New York: Norton, 1992.

Coppell, Vicki. "The 'Goosebumps' in Goosebumps: Impositions and R. L. Stine," *Papers: Explorations into Children's Literature* 8, 2, 1998: 5–15.

Counihan, Carole M. *The Anthropology of Food and Body: Gender, Meaning, and Power*. London: Routledge, 1999.

Coward, Rosalind. *Female Desire: Women's Sexuality Today*. London: Paladin, 1984.

Crago, Hugh. "Can Stories Heal?" In *Understanding Children's Literature*, edited by Peter Hunt, 163–73. London: Routledge, 1999.

Crawford, Robert. "A Cultural Account of 'Health:' Control, Release and the Social Body." In *Issues in the Political Economy of Health Care*, edited by John B. Kinley, 60–103. New York: Tavistock, 1984.

Cream, Julia. "Women on Trial: A Private Pillory?" In *Mapping the Subject: Geographies of Cultural Transformation*, edited by Steve Pile and Nigel Thrift, 158–69. London: Routledge, 1995.

Creed, Barbara. *The Monstrous-Feminine: Film, Feminism, Psychoanalysis*. London: Routledge, 1993.

Curtin, Deane W., and Lisa M. Heldke, eds *Cooking, Eating, Thinking: Transformative Philosophies of Food*. Bloomington: Indiana University Press. 1992.

Daniel, Carolyn. *All That Glitters is Not Gold*. Honors diss. Victoria University of Technology, 2000.

Davies, Bronwyn. *Frogs and Snails and Feminist Tales: Preschool Children and Gender*. Sydney: Allen & Unwin, 1989.

DeVault, M. L. *Feeding the Family: The Social Organisation of Caring as Gendered Work*. Chicago: University of Chicago Press, 1991.

Devereaux, George. *Basic Problems of Ethnopsychiatry*. 1966. Chicago: University of Chicago Press, 1980.

de Villiers, Michelle. "Perpetrators and Princesses: Transgression and Subject Formation in *Killing Aurora* and *Queen Kat, Carmel and St. Jude Get a Life*." *Papers: Explorations into Children's Literature* 10, 3 (2000): 5–11.

Dinnerstein, Dorothy. *The Mermaid and the Minotaur: Sexual Arrangements and Human Malaise*. New York: Harper & Row, 1977.

Doane, Janice and Devon Hodges. *From Klein to Kristeva: Psychoanalytic Feminism and the Search for the "Good Enough" Mother*. Ann Arbor: University of Michigan, 1992.

Dollimore, Jonathan. *Sexual Dissidence: Augustine to Wilde, Freud to Foucault*. Oxford: Clarendon Press, 1991.

Douglas, Mary. *Purity and Danger: An Analysis of Concepts of Pollution and Taboo*. 1966. London: Routledge & Kegan Paul, 1980.

——. *Natural Symbols*. New York: Pantheon, 1982.

——. *Implicit Meanings: Selected Essays in Anthropology*. 1975. London: Routledge, 1999.

——, ed. *In the Active Voice*. London: Routledge & Kegan Paul, 1982.

Drummond, J. C., and Anne Wilbraham. *The Englishman's Food: Five Centuries of English Diet*. 1939. London: Pimlico, 1991.

Duindam, Vincent. "Men in the Household: Caring Fathers." In *Gender, Power and the Household*, edited by Linda McKie, Sophia Bowlby, and Susan Gregory, 43–59. Basingstoke: MacMillan Press, 1999.

Dundes, Alan. "Interpreting Little Red Riding Hood Psychoanalytically." In *The Brothers Grimm and Folktale*, edited by James M. McGlathery, 16–51. Urbana and Chicago: University of Illinois Press, 1988.

Dusinberre, Juliet. *Alice to the Lighthouse: Children's Books and Radical Experiments in Art.* 1987. Basingstoke: Macmillan, 1999.

Ede, Charisse. "Size doesn't matter? Fat chance!" *The Sunday Age* (April 22, 2001).

Egoff, S. A. *Worlds Within: Children's Fantasy from the Middle Ages to Today.* Chicago: American Library Association, 1988.

Elias, Norbert. *The Civilizing Process: The History of Manners.* Translated by Edmund Jephcott. 1939. Oxford: Basil Blackwell, 1978.

Ellman, Maud. *The Hunger Artists: Starving, Writing and Imprisonment.* Cambridge, MA: Harvard University Press, 1993.

Factor, June. *Captain Cook Chased a Chook: Children's Folklore in Australia.* Ringwood, Australia: Penguin, 1989.

Farb, Peter, and George Armelagos. *Consuming Passions: The Anthropology of Eating.* Boston, MA: Houghton Mifflin, 1980.

Fenichel, Otto. *The Psychoanalytic Theory of Neurosis.* 1946. London: Routledge & Kegan Paul, 1966.

Fiske, J. *Understanding Popular Culture.* London: Routledge, 1989.

Foucault, Michel. *Discipline and Punish: The Birth of the Prison.* Translated by Alan Sheridan. New York: Vintage, 1979.

———. *Power/Knowledge: Selected Interviews and other Writings (1972–1977).* Translated Colin Gordon, Leo Marshall, John Mepham, and Kate Soper. Ed. Colin Gordon. Brighton: The Harvester Press, 1980.

———. *The Use of Pleasure: The History of Sexuality, Vol. 2.* Translated by R. Hurley. New York: Vintage, 1986.

Frederick, John. "Australian Sex Tourists: What Australian Men Don't Tell Their Wives." *Marie Claire* (May 1999): 50–58.

Freud, Sigmund. "Totem and Taboo" 1913. In *The Freud Reader*, edited by Peter Gay, 481–513. New York: Norton & Co., 1989.

———. "Three Essays on the Theory of Sexuality." 1924. In *The Freud Reader*, edited by Peter Gay, 240–93. New York: Norton & Co., 1989.

———. "The Dissolution of the Oedipus Complex." 1924. In *The Freud Reader*, edited by Peter Gay, 661–66. New York: Norton & Co., 1989.

———. "Negation" 1925. In *The Freud Reader*, edited by Peter Gay, 666–69. New York: Norton & Co., 1989.

Fromm, Erich. *The Crisis of Psychoanalysis.* London: Jonathan Cape, 1970.

Fuery, P. *Theories of Desire.* Melbourne: Melbourne University Press, 1995.

Furst, Lilian R., and Peter W. Graham, eds. *Disorderly Eaters: Texts in Self-Empowerment.* University Park: Pennsylvania State University Press, 1992.

Gainor, J. Ellen. " 'The Slow-Eater-Tiny-Bite-Taker:' An Eating Disorder in Betty MacDonald's *Mrs Piggy-Wiggle.*" In *Disorderly Eaters: Texts in Self-Empowerment*, edited by Lilian R. Furst and Peter W. Graham, 29–41. University Park: Pennsylvania State University Press, 1992.

Gallagher, Winifred. *The Power of Place: How Our Surroundings Shape Our Thoughts, Emotions, and Actions.* New York: HarperCollins, 1993.

Gandhi, L. *Postcolonial Theory: A Critical Introduction.* St. Leonards, Australia: Allen & Unwin, 1998.

Gates, Katherine. *Deviant Desires: Incredibly Strange Sex.* New York: Juno, 2000.

Gathorne-Hardy, Jonathan. *The Rise and Fall of the British Nanny*. London: Hodder & Stoughton, 1972.

Gilman, Sander L. *Difference and Pathology: Stereotypes of Sexuality, Race, and Madness*. Ithaca: Cornell University Press, 1985.

Glover, Donald E. *C. S. Lewis: The Art of Enchantment*. Athens, OH: Ohio University Press, 1981.

Grace, D. J., and J. Tobin. "Carnival in the Classroom: Elementary Students Making Videos." In *Making a Place for Pleasure in Early Childhood Education*, edited by J. Tobin, 159–87. New Haven, CT: Yale University Press, 1997.

Grosz, Elizabeth. *Sexual Subversions: Three French Feminists*. Sydney: Allen & Unwin, 1989.

———. *Jacques Lacan: A Feminist Introduction*. Sydney: Allen & Unwin, 1990.

———. *Volatile Bodies: Toward a Corporeal Feminism*. Sydney: Allen & Unwin, 1994.

Hallissy, Margaret. *Venomous Woman: Fear of the Female in Literature*. New York: Greenwood, 1987.

Hebdige, Dick. "Towards a Cartography of Taste: 1935–1962." In *Popular Culture: Past and Present*, edited by Bernard Waites, Tony Bennett, and Graham Martin, 194–218. London: Routledge, 1989.

Heinrich, Karen. "The Weighting Game: Body Image an Affliction." *The Sunday Age* (March 2, 2001).

Hirsch, Marianne. "Maternal Anger: Silent Themes and 'Meaningful Digressions' in Psychoanalytic Feminism." *Minnesota Review* 29 (Autumn 1987): 81–87.

Holbrook, David. "The Problem of C. S. Lewis." *Children's Literature in Education* 10 (1973): 3–25.

Honig, Edith Lazaros. *Breaking the Angelic Image: Woman Power in Victorian Children's Fiction*. New York: Greenwood Press, 1988.

Horney, Karen. *Feminine Psychology*. New York: W.W. Norton, 1967.

Hourihan, Margery. *Deconstructing the Hero: Literary Theory and Children's Literature*. London: Routledge, 1997.

Howell, Peter. "Relationship between Body Image and Eating Behaviour." In *Body Image & Health Inc. (1999) Research Summaries*; http://www.internationalnodietday.com/Documents/RS%20body%20image&eat%20behav-ed.doc (accessed 3/10/2003).

Hrdy, Sarah Blaffer. *Mother Nature: A History of Mothers, Infants, and Natural Selection*. New York: Pantheon, 1999.

Hunt, Peter, ed. *Literature for Children: Contemporary Criticism*. London: Routledge, 1992.

———. *An Introduction to Children's Literature*. Oxford: Opus/Oxford University Press, 1994.

———. "'Coldtonguecoldhamcoldbeefpickledgherkinssaladfrenchrollscresssandwidgespottedmeatgingerbeerlemonadesodawater....' Fantastic Food in the books of Kenneth Grahame, Jerome K. Jerome, H. E. Bates, and Other Bakers of the Fantasy England." *Journal of the Fantastic in the Arts* 7, 1 (1996): 5–22.

———, ed. *Understanding Children's Literature*. London: Routledge, 1999.

Jaffrey, Madhur. *A Taste of India*. 1985. London: Pavilion Books, 2001.

James, Allison. "Confections, Concoctions and Conceptions" In *Popular Culture: Past and Present*, edited by Bernard Waites, Tony Bennett, and Graham Martin, 294–307. London: Routledge, 1989.

James, Allison, and Alan Prout, eds. *Constructing and Reconstructing Childhood: Contemporary Issues in the Sociological Study of Childhood*. London: Falmer Press, 1999.

James, Kathryn. "Crossing the Boundaries: Scatology, Taboo and the Carnivalesque in the Picture Book." *Papers: Explorations into Children's Literature* 12, 3 (2002): 19–27.

Jones, Ann Rosalind. "Writing the Body: Toward an Understanding of L'Ecriture Feminine." In *The New Feminist Criticism: Essays on Women, Literature and Theory*, edited by Elaine Showalter, 361–77. London: Virago Press, 1986.

Kane, Kate. "Who Deserves a Break Today? Fast Food, Cultural Rituals, and Women's Place." In *Cooking by the Book: Food in Literature and Culture*, edited by Mary Anne Schofield, 138–46. Bowling Green, OH: Bowling Green State University Popular Press, 1989.

Kaplan, E. Ann. *Motherhood and Representation: the Mother in Popular Culture and Melodrama*. London: Routledge, 1992.

Katz, Wendy R. "Some Uses of Food in Children's Literature." *Children's Literature in Education* 11, 4 (1980): 192–9.

Keane, Molly. "Hunger." 1985. In *The Faber Book of Food*, edited by Claire Clifton and Colin Spencer, 1–2. London: Faber & Faber, 1993.

Kenway, Jane, and Elizabeth Bullen. *Consuming Children: Education – Entertainment – Advertising*. Buckingham: Open University Press, 2001.

Kilgour, Maggie. *From Communion to Cannibalism: An Anatomy of Metaphors of Incorporation*. Princeton, NJ: Princeton University Press, 1990.

———. "The Function of Cannibalism at the Present Time." In *Cannibalism and the Colonial World*, edited by F. Barker, P. Hulme and M. Iverson, 238–59. Cambridge: Cambridge University Press, 1998.

Kincaid, James. *Erotic Innocence: The Culture of Child Molesting*. London: Duke University Press, 2000.

Klein, Melanie. *Love, Guilt and Reparation: And Other Works 1921–1945*. London: Hogarth Press, 1981.

Kristeva, Julia. "Stabat Mater." Translated Leon S. Roudiez. 1977. In *A Kristeva Reader*, edited by Toril Moi, 160–86. New York: Blackwell, 1993.

———. *Powers of Horror: An Essay on Abjection*. Translated Leon S. Roudiez. New York: Columbia University Press, 1982.

———. *Black Sun: Depression and Melancholia*,.Translated by Leon S. Roudiez. New York: Columbia University Press, 1989.

Lee, M. J. *Consumer Culture Reborn: the Cultural Politics of Consumption*. London: Routledge, 1993.

Lévi-Strauss, Claude. "The Culinary Triangle." *Partisan Review* 33 (1966): 586–95.

Lewis, C. S. "On Three Ways of Writing for Children." In *Only Connect*, edited by. Sheila Egoff, 207–20. Toronto: Oxford University Press,1980.

Locke, John. "Some Thoughts Concerning Education." 1690. In *Child-Rearing Concepts, 1628–1861: Historical Sources*, edited by Philip J. Greven Jr., 18–41. Itasca, IL: Peacock, 1973.

Logue, A. W. *The Psychology of Eating and Drinking: An Introduction*. New York: W. H. Freeman, 1991.

Lowenstein, Wendy. *Shocking, Shocking, Shocking: The Improper Play-Rhymes of Australian Children*. 1986. Kuranda, Australia: Rams Skull Press, 1974.

Malson, H. *The Thin Woman: Feminism, Post-Structuralism and the Social Psychology of Anorexia Nervosa*. London: Routledge, 1998.

Mansfield, Nick. *Subjectivity: Theories of the Self from Freud to Haraway*. St Leonards, Australia: Allen & Unwin, 2000.

Mars, Valerie. "Parsimony Amid Plenty: Views from Victorian Didactic Works on Food for Nursery Children." In *Food, Culture and History Vol. 1*, edited by G. Mars and V. Mars, 152–62. London: The London Food Seminar, 1993.

Maushart, Susan. "Mother Load." In *The Sunday Age: Good Weekend* (August 2, 1997): 12–20.

McCallum, Robyn. *Ideologies of Identity in Adolescent Fiction*. New York: Garland,1999.

McCaughey, Martha. "Fleshing Out the Discomforts of Femininity: The Parallel Cases of Female Anorexia and Male Compulsive Bodybuilding." In *Weighty Issues: Fatness and Thinness as Social Problems*, edited by Jeffrey Sobal and Donna Maurer, 133–55. New York: Aldine de Gruyter, 1999.

McGillis, Roderick. *A Little Princess: Gender and Empire*. New York: Twayne, 1996.

McGlathery, James, ed. *The Brothers Grimm and Folktale*. Chicago: University of Illinois Press, 1988.

McInerney, Monica. "All in the Mind: Books that Changed Me," edited by Rosemarie Milsom. *Sunday Life: The Sunday Age Magazine* (May 2, 2004): 12.

McKinley, Nita Mary. "Ideal Weight/Ideal Women: Society Constructs the Female." *Weighty Issues: Fatness and Thinness as Social Problems*, edited by Jeffrey Sobal and Donna Maurer, 97–115. New York: Aldine de Gruyter, 1999.

Mead, Margaret. *Male and Female: A Study of the Sexes in a Changing World*. New York: Morrow, 1967.

Miller, William. *The Anatomy of Disgust*. Cambridge, MA: Harvard University Press, 1997.

Millman, Marcia. *Such a Pretty Face: Being Fat in America*. New York: Norton, 1980.

Mintz, Sidney. *Sweetness and Power: The Place of Sugar in Modern History*. New York: Viking, 1985.

———. "Eating and Being: What Food Means." In *Food: Multidisciplinary Perspectives*, edited by Barbara Harriss-White and Sir Raymond Hoffenberg, 102–15. Oxford: Blackwell, 1994.

Mitchell, Juliet. *The Selected Melanie Klein*. New York: The Free Press, 1986.

Morgan, Kathryn Pauly. "Women and the Knife: Cosmetic Surgery and the Colonization of Women's Bodies." *Hypatia* 6, 3 "Feminism and the Body" (1991): 25–53.

Mulvey, Laura. "Visual Pleasure and the Narrative Cinema." 1978. In *Issues in Feminist Film Criticism*, edited by P. Erens, 57–68. Bloomington: Indiana University Press, 1990.

Murcott, Anne. "On the Social Significance of the 'Cooked Dinner' in South Wales." *Social Science Information* 21, 4/5 (1982): 677–96.

———. "Family Meals — A Thing of the Past?" In *Food, Health and Identity*, edited by Pat Caplan, 32–49. London: Routledge, 1997.

Natov, Roni. *The Poetics of Childhood*. New York: Routledge, 2003.

Neumann, Erich. *The Great Mother: An Analysis of the Archetype*. Translated by Ralph Manheim. Princeton, NJ: Princeton University Press, 1972.

Nicholson, Mervyn. "Food and Power: Homer, Carroll, Atwood and Others." *Mosaic* 20, 3 (Summer 1987): 37–55.

———. "Magic Food, Compulsive Eating, and Power Poetics." In *Disorderly Eaters: Texts in Self-Empowerment*, edited by Lilian R. Furst and Peter W. Graham, 43–60. University Park: Pennsylvania State University Press, 1992.

Nichter, Mimi. *Fat Talk: What Girls and their Parents Say about Dieting*. Cambridge, MA: Harvard University Press, 2000.

Nikolajeva, Maria. *From Mythic to Linear: Time in Children's Literature*. Lanham, Maryland: Scarecrow Press, 2000.

Nodelman, Perry. *The Pleasures of Children's Literature*. New York: Longman, 1996.

———. "Decoding the Images: Illustration and Picture Books." In *Understanding Children's Literature*, edited by Peter Hunt, 69–80. London: Routledge, 1999.

———. "Making Boys Appear: The Masculinity of Children's Fiction." In *Ways of Being Male: Representing Masculinities in Children's Literature and Film*, edited by John Stephens, 1-14. New York: Routledge, 2002.

Orenstein, Catherine. *Little Red Riding Hood Uncloaked: Sex, Morality and the Evolution of a Fairy Tale*. New York: Basic Books, 2002.

Obeyesekeve, Gananath. "Cannibal Feasts in Nineteenth-Century Fiji: Seaman's Yarns and the Ethnographic Imagination." In *Cannibalism and the Colonial World*, Edited by F. Barker, P. Hulme, and M. Iverson, 63–86. Cambridge: Cambridge University Press, 1998.

Orwell, George. "Such, Such Were the Joys." 1947. In *The Collected Essays, Journalism and Letters of George Orwell, Volume 4, In Front of Your Nose, 1945–1950*, edited by Sonia Orwell and Ian Angus, 379–420. Harmondsworth: Penguin, 1968.

Parsons, Elizabeth. "Construction Sites of Sexual Identity: A reading of Emily Rodda's Bob the Builder and the Elves." *Papers: Explorations into Children's Literature* 11, 3 (2001): 32–38.

Philip, Neil. *Myths & Legends*. London: Dorling Kingsley, 1999.

Postman, Neil. *The Disappearance of Childhood*. 1982. New York: Vintage Books, 1994.

Probyn, Elspeth. *Carnal Appetites: FoodSexIdentities*. London: Routledge, 2000.

Raverat, Gwen. "Porridge with Salt – No Sugar." 1954. In *The Faber Book of Food*, edited by Claire Clifton and Colin Spencer, 20–21. London: Faber & Faber, 1993.

Rollin, Lucy. "The Reproduction of Mothering in *Charlotte's Web*." *Children's Literature* 18 (1990): 42–52.

———. *Cradle and All: A Cultural and Psychoanalytic Reading of Nursery Rhymes*. Jackson: University Press of Mississippi, 1992.

Rose, Jacqueline. *The Case of Peter Pan or The Impossibility of Children's Fiction*. 1984. London: Macmillan, 1992.

Rose, Nikolas. "Identity, Genealogy, History." In *Questions of Cultural Identity*, edited by S. Hall and P. du Gay, 128–150. London: Sage, 1996.

Rowbotham, Judith. *Good Girls Make Good Wives: Guidance for Girls in Victorian Fiction*. Oxford: Basil Blackwell, 1989.

Rozin, Paul. "Sociocultural Influences on Human Food Selection." In *Why We Eat What We Eat: The Psychology of Eating*, edited by. Elizabeth D. Capaldi, 233–63. Washington, DC: The American Psychological Association, 1996.

Rustin, Margaret, and Michael Rustin. *Narratives of Love and Loss: Studies in Modern Children's Fiction*. London: Verso, 1987.

Said, Edward. *Orientalism*. Harmondsworth: Penguin, 1985.

Sartre, Jean-Paul. *Being and Nothingness: An Essay in Phenomenological Ontology*. Translated by Hazel E. Barnes. 1943. London: Methuen, 1957.

Saukko, Paula. "Fat Boys and Goody Girls: Hilde Bruch's Work on Eating Disorders and the American Anxiety about Democracy, 1930–1960." In *Weighty Issues: Fatness and Thinness as Social Problems*, edited by Jeffrey Sobal and Donna Maurer, 31–52. New York: Aldine de Gruyter, 1999.

Sceats, Sarah. *Food, Consumption and the Body in Contemporary Women's Fiction*. Cambridge: Cambridge University Press, 2000.

Scutter, Heather. *Displaced Fictions: Contemporary Australian Books for Teenagers and Young Adults*. Melbourne: Melbourne University Press, 1999.

Seabrook, William. "Cannibals." In *The Faber Book of Food*, edited by Colin Spencer and Clare Clifton, 536–40. London: Faber & Faber, 1993.

Seiter, Ellen. *Sold Separately: Children and Parents in Consumer Culture*. Brunswick, NJ: Rutgers University Press, 1995.

Sibley, David. "Families and Domestic Routines: Constructing the Boundaries of Childhood." In *Mapping the Subject: Geographies of Cultural Transformation*, edited by Steve Pile and Nigel Thrift, 123–37. London: Routledge, 1995.

Sigler, Carolyn, ed. *Alternative Alices: Visions and Revisions of Lewis Carroll's Alice Books: An Anthology*. Lexington: The University Press of Kentucky, 1997.

Silver, Anna Krugovoy. *Victorian Literature and the Anorexic Body*. Cambridge: Cambridge University Press, 2002.

Singer, Peter. *Animal Liberation*. 1976. London: Cape, 1990.

Skubal, Susanne. *Word of Mouth: Food and Fiction after Freud*. New York: Routledge, 2002.

Smilek, D., and Mike J. Dixon. "Towards a Synergistic Understanding of Synaesthesia: Combining Current Experimental Findings with Synaesthetes' Subjective Descriptions." *Psyche: An Interdisciplinary Journal of Research on Consciousness* 8, (2002); http://psyche.cs.monash.edu.au/v8/psyche-8-01-smilek.html (accessed 3/31/2004).

Smith, John L. *The Psychology of Food and Eating: A Fresh Approach to Theory and Method*. Basingstoke: Palgrave, 2002.

Stallybrass, Peter and Allon White. *The Politics and Poetics of Transgression*. London: Methuen, 1986.

Stearns, Peter. "Children and Weight Control: Priorities in the United States and France." In *Weighty Issues: Fatness and Thinness as Social Problems*, eds. by Jeffrey Sobal and Donna Maurer, 11–30. New York: Aldine de Gruyter, 1999.

Stein, Rick. *Rick Stein's Seafood Odyssey*. London: BBC Worldwide, 2000.

Stephens, John. *Language and Ideology in Children's Fiction*. London: Longman, 1992.

———. "Constructions of Female Selves in Adolescent Fiction: Makeovers as Metonym." *Papers: Explorations into Children's Literature* 9, 1 (1999): 5–3.

———, ed. *Ways of Being Male: Representing Masculinities in Children's Literature and Film*. New York: Routledge, 2002.

Stoney, Barbara. *Enid Blyton: A Biography*. London: Hodder & Stoughton, 1974.

Suleiman, Susan Rubin, ed. *The Female Body in Western Culture: Contemporary Perspectives*. Cambridge, MA: Harvard University Press, 1985.

Tatar, Maria. *Off With Their Heads! Fairy Tales and the Culture of Childhood*. Princeton, NJ: Princeton University Press, 1992.

Theobald, Stephanie. "Queen of Tarts." *The Sunday Age: Good Weekend* (September 9, 2000).

Tucker, Nicholas. *The Child and the Book: A Psychological and Literary Exploration*. Cambridge: Cambridge University Press, 1981.

———. "The Rise and Rise of Harry Potter." *Children's Literature in Education* 30, 4 (1999): 221–34.

Tunstall, Gillian. *The Images of Women in Contemporary Children's Picture Books*. Sydney: University of Sydney School of Teacher Education, 1992.

Turner, Ian. "The Play Rhymes of Australian Children: An Interpretative Essay." In *Cinderella Dressed in Yella*, edited by Ian Turner, June Factor, and Wendy Lowenstein, 155–65. Richmond, Australia: Heinemann Educational, 1978.

Twitchell, James. *Dreadful Pleasures: An Anatomy of Modern Horror*. New York: Oxford University Press, 1985.

Vallone, Lynne. *Disciplines of Virtue: Girls' Culture in the Eighteenth and Nineteenth Centuries*. New Haven, CT: Yale University Press, 1995.

———. " 'What is the Meaning of all this Gluttony?': Edgeworth, The Victorians, C. S. Lewis and a Taste for Fantasy." *Papers: Explorations into Children's Literature* 12, 1 (2002): 47–54.

Veglahn, Nancy. "Images of Evil: Male and Female Monsters in Heroic Fantasy." *Children's Literature* 15 (1987): 106–119.

Visser, Margaret. *Much Depends on Dinner: The Extraordinary History and Mythology, Allure and Obsessions, Perils and Taboos of an Ordinary Meal*. New York: Macmillan, 1986.

———. *The Rituals of Dinner: The Origins, Evolution, Eccentricities, and Meaning of Table Manners*, London: Penguin, 1993.

Walker, Barbara. *The Woman's Encyclopaedia of Myths and Secrets*. San Francisco: Harper & Row, 1983.

Walkerdine, Valerie. *Schoolgirl Fictions*. London: Verso, 1990.

———. "Violent Boys and Precocious Girls: Regulating Childhood at the End of the Millennium." *Contemporary Issues in Early Childhood* 1, 1 (1999): 3–23.

Warde, Alan. *Consumption, Food and Taste*. London: Sage, 1997.

Warner Elizabeth. *Heroes, Monsters and Other Worlds from Russian Mythology*. Sydney: Hodder & Stoughton, 1985.

Warner, Marina. *From the Beast to the Blonde: On Fairy Tales and their Tellers*. New York: Chatto & Windus, 1994.

———. *No Go the Bogeyman: Scaring, Lulling and Making Mock*. London: Vintage, 2000.

Wicks, Deidre. "Humans, Food, and Other Animals: The Vegetarian Option." In *A Sociology of Food and Nutrition: The Social Appetite*, edited by John Germov and Lauren Williams, 99–115. Oxford: Oxford University Press, 1999.

Willard, Tracy. "*Hansel and Gretel*: Enter the Witch." In *Tales at the Borders: Fairy Tales and Maternal Cannibalism*; http://www.reconstruction.ws/022/cannibal/hanselandgretel.html; (accessed 10/9/2002).

——. "*Little Red Riding Hood*: Cannibal Mothers." In *Tales at the Borders: Fairy Tales and Maternal Cannibalism*; http://www.reconstruction.ws/022/cannibal/littlered.html; (accessed 10/25/2002).

——. "*Snow White, Sleeping Beauty, The Juniper Tree, The Virgin Mary's Child*: The Wicked Cannibal Queen." In *Tales at the Borders: Fairy Tales and Maternal Cannibalism*; http://www.reconstruction.ws/022/cannibal/snowwhite.html; (accessed 10/25/2002).

Willetts, Anne. " 'Bacon Sandwiches Got the Better of Me:' Meat-Eating and Vegetarianism in South-East London." In *Food, Health and Identity*, edited by Pat Caplan, 111–30. London: Routledge, 1997.

Williams, Raymond. *Marxism and Literature*. Oxford: Oxford University Press, 1977.

Zipes, Jack. *Fairy Tales and the Art of Subversion: The Classical Genre for Children and the Process of Civilization*. 1983. New York: Routledge, 1991.

——. *The Trials and Tribulations of Little Red Riding Hood: Versions of the Tale in Sociocultural Context*. New York: Routledge, 1993.

——. *Happily Ever After: Fairy Tales, Children, and the Culture Industry*. New York: Routledge, 1997.

——. *Sticks and Stones: The Troublesome Success of Children's Literature from Slovenly Peter to Harry Potter*. New York: Routledge, 2001.

Children's Literature and Culture

Jack Zipes, *Series Editor*

How Picturebooks Work
by Maria Nikolajeva and Carole Scott

Brown Gold
Milestones of African American Children's Picture Books, 1845–2002
by Michelle H. Martin

Russell Hoban/Forty Years
Essays on His Writing for Children
by Alida Allison

Apartheid and Racism in South African
Children's Literature
by Donnarae MacCann and Amadu Maddy

Empire's Children
Empire and Imperialism in Classic British Children's Books
by M. Daphne Kutzer

Constructing the Canon of Children's Literature
Beyond Library Walls and Ivory Towers
by Anne Lundin

Youth of Darkest England
Working Class Children at the Heart of Victorian Empire
by Troy Boone

Ursula K. Leguin Beyond Genre
Literature for Children and Adults
by Mike Cadden

Twice-Told Children's Tales
edited by Betty Greenway

Diana Wynne Jones
The Fantastic Tradition and Children's Literature
by Farah Mendlesohn

Childhood and Children's Books in Early Modern Europe, 1550–1800
edited by Andrea Immel and Michael Witmore

Voracious Children
Who Eats Whom in Children's Literature
by Carolyn Daniel

INDEX